Tay's Awakening: Shattered Illusions

By Tailon Dow

Edited by Khloe's Thoughts Editing

Published independently by Tailon Dow

For inquiries: <u>dow.tailon@gmail.com</u>

ISBN(paperback): 979-8-9940913-0-2

Table of Contents

Table of Contents iii

– Acknowledgement –...v

– Prologue – 1

– Chapter 1: The Breakup – 5

– Chapter 2: The Park Encounter –..14

– Chapter 3: Unwelcomed Meeting – 24

– Chapter 4: Dreams of Loss and Shadows – 39

– Chapter 5: An Unsettling Invitation –.......................................47

– Chapter 6: The Club –..57

– Chapter 7: Seeking Refuge –...69

– Chapter 8: A New Horizon – 84

– Chapter 9: Tangled Connections – 98

– Chapter 10: A Risky Intervention–...112

– Chapter 11: Past Chains Resurge – 128

– Chapter 12: Chains of Grief and Hope – 142

– Chapter 13: Homecoming Shadows –..155

– Chapter 14: Reunion of Present and Past – 165

– Chapter 15: Illusions of Normalcy –...181

– Chapter 16: Buried Truths –...198

– Chapter 17: Darkness Revelations – 211

– Chapter 18: Purpose and Determination –................................225

– Chapter 19: Shadows of the Past – 235

– Chapter 20: Training and Tribulations – 253

– Chapter 21: Rerun from the Past –..268

– Chapter 22: Betrayal and Blood – 287

– Chapter 23: A True Family – 307

– Chapter 24: To a New Normal – 328

– Epilogue – 334

About the Author 335

– Acknowledgement –

I want to dedicate this book to my wife, my dad, and my granddad. You three supported me, motivated me, and helped me more than you know throughout this whole journey.

To my dad, Jon Dow — thank you for being the first person to show me what writing really looked like. Watching you write plays and books made me want to write my own stories, dreams, and fantasies instead of just holding them in my head.

To my wife, Courtnee Dow — thank you for always being my first reader, my honest critic, and my "don't you dare quit" voice. You read this story when it barely made sense, when it was nothing but bones, and you still encouraged me to keep going even when I wanted to shelve it. I love you for that.

To my granddad, Don Ray Smith — seeing you publish your books and articles reminded me that finishing is possible. You made the dream feel real.

I also want to recognize my sister-in-law and my niece. When you both published your books, it lit a fire under me. You didn't do it to challenge me, but it pushed me anyway. I'd been sitting on stories for years and watching you two actually release yours made me realize it was time to stop talking and start finishing. Thank you for being that unexpected push.

I love all of you.

– Prologue –

It was a sunny day and the waves crashed on the beach below. On the tenth floor of the condo, a couple was just waking up. The man sat up and stretched as the woman rolled over before getting up. They looked at each other and smiled.

Her hair was ruffled, and the sheets did little to hide her naked body underneath. But the man wasn't focused on her body, but her eyes and face held his attention. He leaned in until their noses touched, pulled her face closer, then pressed his lips against hers.

She reached up and wrapped her arms around his neck, pulling him back down on the bed. He placed one hand on her waist and the other on the bed to prop himself up. They pulled away and looked at each other again.

"Well, good morning, beautiful."

"Morning, handsome."

He went in for another kiss, but she placed a finger to his lips.

"If you keep this up, we will miss breakfast. And besides, I need a shower after last night."

He chuckled. "Well, I can't help that you are so tempting that I want more of you even now."

"Hmm… Maybe later but I'm hungry now." She sat up and kissed his cheek before she turned and hopped out of the bed.

The sheets slipped off her body and he couldn't help but stare. She looked like a goddess, and just looking at her caused his stomach to slip and tighten. He even swallowed softly as he slowly slid to the edge of the bed.

She stretched once more and turned to look at him. "What?" She smiled playfully. "Like what you see?" She did a turn and winked at him.

He gripped the cover tightly and bit his lower lip as he let out a soft moan. "Why must you tempt me so, my little seductress?"

"Because I love the way you look at me like it is our first time together."

"You've got me wondering how I ever managed to land a girl like you."

She walked to the bathroom and his eyes followed her movements. The way she swished her hips, making her butt bounce, had him in a trance. Once she was in the bathroom, she turned back to face him.

"You didn't land me. I landed you."

And with that, she closed and locked the door. The man just stared at the door for a moment. He then turned his head up toward the ceiling.

"Dear God, I don't know what I did to deserve this woman but thank you. I'm going to marry her one day—soon. Just let me keep her safe until then."

He then got up and put on some basketball shorts and walked to the kitchen. He began cooking breakfast. The menu for the day was smoked salmon, grits, eggs, assorted fruits, and toast served with a mango mimosa. The woman came out just as he was finishing setting the table.

"Oh my God, Tay. I'm always amazed by your cooking skills."

"Well, I got to know how to feed my woman. Besides…" He turned to look at her. Her hair was wet, and she smelled of lavender, sandalwood, and vanilla. She wore a shirt that stopped at her hips, showing off her panties. Tay looked at her briefly before shaking his head. "Um—what was I saying?"

"That you were going to propose to me." She smiled mischievously at Tay.

"Nice try, Rin." She crossed her arms and stuck out her bottom lip.

Tay walked over to her and hugged her. "But it may be sooner than you think." Rin looked up at Tay; her smile vanished.

"Don't joke with me about this, Tay."

"I'm not joking. I plan to make you my wife very soon. I just wanted to make my proposal to you something truly special."

"Oh, Tay!!" Rin jumped onto him. She wrapped her legs around his waist and kissed him deeply. "I love you and can't wait to be your wife."

"And I promise to make you happy forever and always." They kissed again and Tay put her down. "But for now let's eat before the food gets cold."

She nodded. They took a seat and ate in silence. Once done, Rin took the plates to the sink and Tay went to take a shower. As he was undressing, his phone buzzed.

It was a text from an unknown number. He was about to ignore it but something in his heart made him change his mind.

He opened it and froze. His hand grew tense and shook. Rage welled inside him and he barely stunted the urge to cuss out loud.

The text was a picture of a girl and boy with a message saying: *if you don't want them to get hurt, meet me here alone. And don't worry about your girlfriend, she will be looked after.* It was followed by a location tag that was a five-minute walk from their condo.

Tay quickly showered and walked out. Rin was laying in bed and had changed into a robe. She left it open, showing she wasn't wearing a bra and waiting for him. Tay's jaw clenched even more than before. Seeing this, Rin sat up.

"Babe, what is wrong?"

"I need you to do something for me while I go take care of some business that just came up."

She walked up to him and hugged him. "Well, it can't be helped. You did say that you were working remotely from here and that you may have to go to a café or something to connect to work. So, it isn't like we didn't plan for this. So go take care of what you need to and come back soon."

He kissed her forehead. "I will. And while I'm gone, do you remember the drill we practiced from before?"

"How could I forget? You drilled it into me so much that I was dreaming about it."

"Well, act like this is that drill, please."

Rin looked Tay in the face. She seemed to be searching his eyes for something. But whatever she found wasn't what she wanted to see. She gave a half-hearted smile.

"Yes, I will do that. But please make this the last time. I get scared every time you make me do this drill. It feels too real."

Tay looked at her and gave his best smile in the moment and hugged her again. "I will be back in 20 minutes at most. See you then."

Tay turned and walked out the door, missing the scared look and the shiver that came over Rin as he closed the door.

As the door clicked closed, Rin wrapped the robe around her tightly. "Please come back home to me," she whispered to the empty room.

The first rays of morning light filtered through the curtains. The birds were chirping outside. But inside the room, an unease lingered in the air. Tay sat on the floor with his back against the bed.

He didn't move from his spot; his eyes glued to the floor in a daze. The words of the call he received last night replayed in his mind on an endless loop. His girlfriend of five years had told him it was over without any pretext or sign that something was wrong. Her voice, which was once beautiful and comforting to his ears, was filled with anguish and despair when she called. Now, all he could hear were her final words.

"I'm sorry. I just can't do this anymore. Please just leave me alone."

What did I do?

He couldn't think of anything he could have done to make her say something like that. They had dated consistently, and he did his best to show her loyalty, respect, and love. During their time together, she would often smile so brightly that he felt she deserved more than him.

But despite that bright smile, it had all ended with those words.

His left hand involuntarily twitched, hitting something. He slowly glanced down to see his phone. He thought of the many times that night he tried to pick it up and call her back. To ask her why she would end it. Why she never told him something was wrong. But no matter how many times he tried, his hand wouldn't obey.

Every so often, he felt slightly relieved he didn't call her back. For he feared he knew the reason why she ended their relationship. But even if he did, it was something he couldn't rectify no matter how much he wished he could. He thought back to one particular night that filled him with severe regret.

****

It was fifteen months ago. It had started like any other day and he and Rin laughed, cooked, kissed, and went through the motions of the day. Everything felt easy.

Just…Right.

But that evening, Tay received a text. Each line a reminder of the darkness that plagued his life, the past he wanted to run away from. The flame that took his family from him. His face turned into a scowl as he read the message.

Rin, who had grown used to the shift in his expression whenever something serious came through, knew immediately.

"Another drill?" she asked softly, wrapping her arms around him.

He relaxed his face and eased his breathing as he nodded. "Yeah. Just be ready."

She didn't argue. She never did. But something in her eyes that night… it wasn't just concern. Maybe something like curiosity. Or even doubt.

When he kissed her forehead and told her to hide until he gave the knock, she obeyed—at first.

Some time passed and she must have been in her head the whole time and was getting restless. So, when she heard the front door swing open, curiosity and impatience overrode caution and she came out of hiding and went to greet Tay. Maybe she just needed to know if he was being paranoid… or if there was something more.

Either way, she stepped out before the special knock sounded to signal her to come out of hiding.

Still in her slippers and smiling, she walked down the hall and turned the corner expecting to surprise Tay.

Instead, she locked eyes with a man in a mask holding a knife.

They stared at each other for a heartbeat that seemed to stretch for minutes before he charged.

She screamed and ducked; hands raised over her head.

That was when Tay burst in.

The sight of the masked intruder looming over Rin, blade raised—something in him broke.

He didn't remember all the details—just motion, impact, adrenaline. Flesh slamming into the wall, furniture, and the floor. A blur of fists and rage.

By the end of it, the man laid unconscious in a pool of his own blood.

Rin was huddled in the corner, trembling. Her eyes were wide and glassy, her breathing sharp and shallow. Tay approached slowly, touching her shoulder.

"Babe... it's okay. I'm here."

She collapsed into him, sobbing. She clung to his shirt like it was the last thing tethering her to the world.

He held her and let her cry. And in that moment, something inside her had changed. He knew it. He just didn't want to admit it.

From that day forward, whenever he asked her to do another drill, her eyes dulled. Her smile faded. She did it—but not because she felt protected. In fact, she started being fidgety even when walking around outside.

And eventually, it must have gotten to be too much.

****

Tay unclenched his fists, but the tightness in his chest stayed. He wanted to believe there was still hope. That maybe she'd come back. That maybe this was just a break, not the end.

But deep down, he knew.

Rin didn't leave because she stopped loving him.

She left because she wanted to survive.

Suddenly, his phone burst to life with sound, shocking him out of his memory.

Could it be her?

Heart racing, he snatched up the phone then he held his breath with eyes closed, sending up a silent prayer. He slowly opened his eyes and felt his heart sink to his stomach.

It wasn't her. It wasn't even a phone call. It was just his 8:45 alarm.

The urge to scream nearly overwhelmed him. He was overcome with frustration and a need to vent the building pressure inside. He stared at the phone, the thought of hurling it against the wall was a strong temptation. But with a resigned sigh, he gathered himself, stood up, and dropped the phone on the bed.

Maybe a shower is what I need?

He made his way to the bathroom while letting the phone continue to sound, adding to the weight of his already dreadful day.

Entering the bathroom, he turned on the shower. As its warmth gradually enveloped the space, he undressed mechanically, barely registering the sensation of each piece of clothing as he pulled them off.

Before stepping into the shower, he caught sight of himself in the mirror. He saw a caramel-skinned young man with a lean but toned body that showed he cared about himself, yet the moment he looked at his face he could only focus on his eyes. Eyes that were hollow and red, stinging with dark circles underneath. The thought of trying to figure out how to do right in his relationship when things didn't go right made his senses go numb. He gazed hollowly at the man in the mirror not wanting to accept the image.

"If only I was someone else…" The thought escaped from his lips before he realized it.

He shook his head weakly; he forced himself forward while vehemently refusing to think those thoughts. As he showered, each movement felt cumbersome, as if iron weights were tied to his limb. Even the water brought about a fleeting sense of warmth.

As the warmth became thicker, Tay could still feel her arms around him. His mind was so entranced; he could even smell the shampoo she used. Then reality crushed his fantasy.

She would never be a part of his life anymore.

He hung his head and closed his eyes as they ached. He felt the tears build up behind his eyelids and a few slipped out. They mixed with the water running down his locs and onto his face, giving the illusion it was just the water running down his face.

As he showered, he recited a mantra he would tell himself whenever he felt hurt: *The past won't change. The pain won't help. Keep moving.* He repeated these words to himself as he tried to fully embrace them.

Slowly, he felt his heart grow numb to the pain. Little by little, he felt like he wasn't affected by the recent lost. Stepping out of the shower, he breathed in and released, feeling the cool air in the house that competed with the warmth of the shower.

Tay smiled weakly. He knew he was not over what happened but he felt more put together—more in control than before.

He looked around his home and felt a strong sense of confinement. The walls seemed closer than before and each door was like a blockade to keep him in. *I need to get out of here*, he mused. He felt a tug at his heart that wanted to fill the space.

To feel freedom. To outrun his pain.

Tay looked in his closet for anything to wear. As he scanned the clothes, he noticed the clothes Rin had bought him a while back and he felt a pain like a knife driving into his heart.

"She is now the past and that won't change," he told himself once more.

He randomly grabbed something and threw it on. Afterwards, he noticed his phone's alarm had gone silent. He picked it up, made sure the alarm was off, then stowed it in his pocket before heading out. He grabbed his hat and keys as he made his way to the garage, barely paying attention to his surroundings. He just wanted to go outside and do something to keep his mind busy.

Once in the garage, he got in his car and started it as the garage door rolled up. He fumbled with the radio stations before pulling off. There wasn't anything on that interested him, so he loaded his playlist on Spotify and pulled out of his garage.

The sun was bright now and the sky was clear. He looked to his right and saw his neighbors were up and gone, probably already at work. He looked up and down his street. Though he wasn't in a fancy part of town, he still believed he lived in a fairly decent neighborhood.

There was the occasional party hosted at his neighbor's place and they invited him to them many times. But the neighborhood was not the ghetto, with people driving by at all times of day with music blaring trying to seem hard and tough.

It was a neighborhood he liked. Today, though, this neighborhood haunted him. It was the place he planned to bring his girl to once he made her his fiancée. Feeling even more pain cracking the mask he built around his heart, he reaffirmed his resolve with his mantra again but this time he only said it once. *The past won't change. The pain won't help. Keep moving.* He slowly breathed out the feeling and he felt his mask resettle.

As he drove around, his stomach growled, reminding him to eat. He chuckled bitterly at the irony. "Well, guess heartache can take a lot of energy," he stated to no one.

He looked around for a place to grab some food. He thought of breakfast food but nothing seemed appealing to him. As he drove around, he passed a joint that served lunch all day. And it just so happened to be one of his favorite burger joints. He turned around and pulled into the drive-thru. He ordered his favorite meal and parked to eat. After only three bites, the burger lost its flavor, and the fries tasted bland. He sighed and looked up, gazing at his surroundings. He was zoned out when he thought he heard someone say, "I like being here with you." He quickly turned to the passenger seat.

No one was there. He then looked at where he was. He realized his mistake—he was at the same spot he and his now ex had often visited.

His heart felt like it was being squeezed as he remembered all the conversations and moments they shared sitting in the parking lot eating and talking.

He shook his head. "No wonder the food felt so heavy and bland today. Guess going to a place like this was a bad move." He sighed, looking at the partially eaten food. He no longer had a desire to eat at that moment, so he wrapped the food up and placed everything back in the bag and pulled out of the parking lot.

This time, he drove aimlessly around town for thirty minutes. As he drove, he passed an arcade he frequented when he was in high school. Memories of the old games he used to play and the joy he felt from them came over him. He smiled at the memory of the excitement they held for him.

Wanting to feel something other than despair, he turned around and pulled into the parking lot. The moment he walked in, the vibrant lights of the games and the clamor of machines vying for attention made him smile like he was in high school again. The rush of wanting to place first in his favorite games, the challenge of being able to best someone at one of the fighter games— all the memories he cherished while here came flooding back to him and he momentarily felt joy. He quickly went to load credits to his card and rotated through the games.

He was enjoying himself playing a racing game he knew that Rin wouldn't want to play but were treasures to him. Once he finished that game, he got up to move to another one, when he saw something flash by in the corner of his eye. He quickly turned; his heart racing as he saw dark black hair flutter by. His hand reached out on impulse but the girl he thought he saw vanished like she was smoke. Tay looked down at his hands.

Come on man. She isn't here. This isn't like that first year of college, he reprimanded himself. Yet as he went from one game to the next, he caught fleeting glimpses of her out the edges of his vision. He occasionally felt the phantom touch of her hand on his shoulder or arm. Each glimpse or touch was another reminder of how much of a sanctuary she had been to him. As he was shooting basketballs zoned out, he realized even the arcade—once a place of joy—now felt empty.

After about fifteen minutes of trying to stay joyful, his enthusiasm had fully waned. The absence of her presence overpowered his brief happiness. He walked out with hands in his pockets, eyes downcast. He climbed back into his car and sat there, thinking.

He tried to figure out where he could go to ease his heart from the pain. With no other ideas, he decided to drive to the park and prayed that there, amidst the trees and open skies, he could find a sliver of peace.

As he drove, he occasionally glanced to his right half-expecting Rin to be there. And not seeing her there made his heart catch in his throat and his eyes burn.

"Get your shit together, man. You are acting like a total simp," he chided himself as he pushed the gas, making the car speed along the freeway. The rush of speed was a temporary balm, distracting him from his internal turmoil. And just like all things, the ride ended as he approached his exit. His grip on the wheel felt like it wanted to pull him away from the exit and keep driving. The road was fairly empty and the thought to stay on the road was more appealing. Yet his conscious whispered to him to slow down and take the exit. Following his conscious, he slowed and took the exit.

After driving another five minutes, he arrived at the park. The parking lot was about half full so he pulled in and parked toward the middle of the lot. He didn't get out immediately but just sat there as he gripped the steering wheel tightly then laid his head on his hands. His heart throbbed and it felt hollow. He still felt her touch and saw the gentle way she would look at him and smiled, as if to say everything would be alright.

"Why?! Why can't I clear my head?" he murmured softly through gritted teeth as a weariness took hold. His mask he had tried so hard to put on was cracking. Not wanting anyone to see him on the verge of tears, he waited in the car until he was able to compose himself. He sat there and breathed as he tried his best not to think of her and calm his mind. It took about five minutes for him to feel like he could hold his tears in. Once he got out the car, he turned his hat backwards, trying to give the appearance that nothing was wrong and he came to enjoy a walk. And with that, he entered the park with a simple smile.

As he walked a path that would take him around the whole park, he imagined it was a route that led to his escape—his freedom from the pain of his reality.

Just breathe and release. You can make it through this.

A few girls passed by him in the opposite direction. Their eyes lingered on him as he walked by. One waved and he gave a small smirk back out of habit. A few moments later, he ended up walking with that same group of girls— laughing and joking. He heard himself laughing at the right times, landing lines that made one or two turn away shily, and even felt one occasionally try to cozy up to him.

Yet each word he spoke seemed like another person was speaking through him. Every laugh taxed what little emotion he had left. He knew he was playing the part right.

But this conversation made his heart ache like it was stabbed with an ice pick.

The gentle flirting brought up memories of Rin and her playfulness. The sly touches that would send his heart jumping into the clouds, now dropped him deeper into the lake of misery and he was barely able to come up for air.

After a while, his face briefly turned stoic and eyes became deadpan before he quickly plastered a smile to his face. He knew then it was time to leave and he politely excused himself.

No numbers. No new connections. Not even a glance back.

Though the girls were beautiful, he could only glance over their faces. His eyes seemed to be searching—looking for Rin to appear there among them.

After walking for another fifteen minutes, he made his way to the water fountain at the center of the park and found an empty bench. He sat down and watched people walk by. The breeze was warm and gentle on his skin. A child passed, leaving a trail of bubbles as her father and mother walked behind her. Couples walked hand in hand with smiles of laughter on their faces. The day seemed to be perfect for everyone except for Tay. Seeing everyone happy intensified the stark contrast of the war raging within him.

Tay's chest tightened and the brittle mask he had built around his heart crumbled even more. He rested his elbows on his knees and looked out at the fountain in the middle of the lake. His eyes were transfixed, as if he was watching himself from outside his own body.

"Why? Why do all things that seem good to me always end in ruin?" he whispered into the wind.

Maybe… if I had just been open and honest … He swallowed hard. He clasped his hands together and held them tightly. His knee bounced up and down at a quick tempo. He shook his head to try and force his hands apart and placed them on his knees. "Yeah…" A bitter laugh escaped his lips.

"Ain't no way in hell she would have believed me." He took a deep breath and let it out as he leaned back, stretching his arms on the top of the bench. He looked at the clouds floating calmly across the sky. He envisioned himself letting go of his and drifting like the clouds.

Maybe it is easier just to end it all. To vanish without a trace.

He sat there in silence as he considered how he could go about ending his life.

I mean I can just drown in this lake. But people here will try to help.

Another moment of silence passed. *Maybe drive my car into a light pole.* A soft chuckle devoid of all emotion escaped his lips.

"Naw." He let out a sigh and looked back at the lake. "I'm too much of a coward to do any of that."

But if I could just start over… His heartbeat quickened.

That would be great. No more lies, no hiding my past. His shoulders dropped and his breath came easier. A gentle smile played on the edge of his lips. Just then, a girl jogged by and the scent of lavender and vanilla drifted to him.

His heart jumped into his throat. He lifted his head reflexively and turned his head to follow the girl but the sun reflected off a metal sign and shined into Tay's eyes. He squinted and looked back up not seeing the girl anymore but the thought of it possibly being Rin crossed his mind.

He sighed and lowered his head. "This isn't helping," he spoke softly. "I know life can be unfair, but this—" He placed a hand to his heart. "I—I don't think I can handle this."

"It feels like I'm torturing myself, and I don't know what to do anymore." His eyes stung and his voice quivered.

Even if I talk to someone, what can they say that would actually help? Sometimes, I wish that—that I had never been born. He allowed his thoughts to continue spiraling, imagining scenes that wouldn't have happened in his past if he wasn't born. How the world would be better without a person like him in it.

Tears that Tay had vowed never to show, gathered at the corner of his eyes. Without a whimper or sniff, two drops fell. He didn't care anymore if people saw as they passed by. He even heard a little boy call out to his father.

"Hey, Dad, why is that man crying?"

"It is rude to stare, son. Let's leave him be. We don't know what is going on and sometimes the best we can do is just leave that person alone."

"Okay." The family walked by and as they did the boy spoke once more. "I hope he feels better soon."

Tay sat there silently, letting his tears stream freely. With his hands clasped in front of him, he leaned his forehead on them and inhaled deeply.

After a while, he took another deep breath. He looked out at the lake and existed. He thought of nothing. He did nothing. He just looked out at the lake watching the sun rays dance on the rippling surface. After some more time had passed, he got up. His heart wasn't cracked as bad anymore. He was able to look out and not see gray tones but there was slight color in his vision. He put his hands in his pockets and made the trip out of the park.

As he walked, he looked around and saw the world continued to move, indifferent to his inner breakdown he just experienced.

He laughed and let out a full smile. *The world is constantly moving, not stopping for anyone.* He looked up into the tree canopies. The breeze shifted the leaves, allowing sunlight to filter through. "I think it is time I did the same," he whispered. With that simple realization, he felt a little better, but he still longed for someone to keep him company.

Just as he was about to walk in front of his car, he was suddenly jolted by a collision to his side. The impact sent both him and the other person tumbling to the ground.

"What the heck?" he began, but the stranger was already scrambling to their feet. They wore a black jacket with the hood pulled over their head, so it was hard to see their face.

"Sorry, sorry…I'm so sorry." The voice was that of a female. She sounded panicked and was breathing heavily like she had been running for a long distance.

He got up and brushed himself off. "Look, just be more careful next time." He looked her over once more and saw that she was uninjured. He nodded to her. "Well, see ya." He turned toward his car and as he got to the driver's side door, he felt eyes on him. He looked up and noticed the girl had taken off her hood and was staring at him, as if she had just encountered a ghost.

"Hey…why are you staring at me?" Tay questioned her. He looked at her face and froze briefly. Her eyes were breathtaking. They were a hazy green and seemed to shine like an emerald but that wasn't the only thing. Tay felt a strong sense of recognition looking at them.

Why do I feel like I know her from somewhere? He held her gaze for a moment or so before he realized they looked like two people in a staring contest. So, he ignored that feeling and waved his hand in front of him.

"Hey. Hello, do you need something?" he asked, his tone edged with impatience, not really caring to sound polite.

At his hand motion, she seemed to snap back to the present. "Oh, yea. My name is Aria Blackwood. What's yours?"

"Tay. Now goodbye." Tay briskly opened his door and got in, tossing his hat in the backseat. He had just started his car when he heard a knock on the passenger side window. He looked and saw it was the girl; he tried to roll down the window slightly but misjudged how hard he pressed the button, and it rolled all the way down.

"Tay, may I have a ride?" she asked. Before he could answer, she reached in, opened the door, got in, and closed and locked it behind her.

"What do you think you are doing?" Tay's voice rose in alarm. "Get out of my car. I don't know you and I'm not in the mood for a prank or anything. So you better leave now."

"Please, I just need a ride." Her voice shook and she gripped her jacket tightly as she just sat there, not moving, looking him dead in the eyes. When he met her gaze, he saw again something familiar in her eyes. Something so comfortable that he momentarily softened his resolve, but he quickly shook the feeling off.

"What do you want?" He turned away from her with a sigh; his tone softened slightly despite his anger.

"Just a ride like I mentioned before," she replied; her voice not shaking as much as before but she didn't move.

"Tell me where to and why should I take you?"

She let out an audible sigh. "Umm. 1124 Jackson St."

"Whoa." Tay turned to look at her; his eyes wide open. "First off, that's all the way in the country. I'm not going out there without gas money."

Aria pulled money from the bag under her jacket. "Will this do?"

"Yeah. Now answer my other question."

Aria looked out the window and looked back. "Can I tell you once we leave the park, please?" She gripped the edge of the window, lifted her head slightly, and looked around frantically. Tay's mouth dried out.

What in the hell have I gotten myself into? Tay rolled up the window.

"Look, just relax. Since I decided to keep you safe for now, I will make sure nothing happens to you."

"Thank you so much, Tay."

He started the car and as they were pulling off, he looked in his rearview mirror and saw three guys in black shirts roaming in the parking lot. They spread out like they were looking for someone. Tay looked at Aria. She didn't look at him, just let the seat all the way back so she was below the window.

Tay didn't drive too fast to get out the parking lot to make sure the men didn't get suspicious. As they came to the stop sign to exit the parking lot, another that seemed to be working with the guys walked up to Tay's car and tapped his passenger window. Aria gripped her seatbelt tightly, as if her life was on the line. Seeing her reaction, Tay was glad the guy was unable to see inside since his windows had semi-heavy tints on them. Tay's heart pounded as he cracked the window. He was gentle with the button this time and let it down just enough so he and the other guy could see each other's face.

"How may I help you?" Tay asked politely.

"Sorry to disturb you but we are looking for a girl in a black jacket. We last saw her running this way. Have you seen her?" The man's politeness was unnerving because his eyes were cold and probing, yet he made no attempt to peer inside the car, only holding Tay's face.

"Sorry, can't say that I have," Tay replied, maintaining a neutral expression.

The man's gaze lingered on his for a moment before he sighed and bowed slightly. "Thank you, sir. Sorry to bother you." He stepped back and allowed Tay to drive off. But Tay could feel the man's eyes on the car as they pulled away.

Making sure that the traffic was clear, Tay pulled off to the right. Once he was a good distance down the road, he looked over at Aria. "Now tell me why you were being chased and don't give me no BS because I can still turn around and drop you off to them," he stated calmly.

Aria leaned her seat up and released the breath she had been holding. "First, let me say thank you again, Tay. I really do appreciate it."

"Yea, you're welcome. Now answer my question. Why involve me in this mess?"

"I honestly don't know who those guys were or why they were after me."

"You expect me to believe that you really don't know them?"

"It's the truth." Aria voice shook slightly as she spoke. "Look, I was stopped by one of them about three or four blocks from the park. He didn't seem pushy, but he asked me to go with him to this random place and I quickly turned him down. As I walked away, I noticed that he was following me."

"So, I tried to make it seem like I didn't notice but once I made it to the next block, two more joined him. I panicked and thought that they wanted some money or something so I cautiously dropped a few bills to see if they would stop and pick them up." She let out a deep breath and hugged herself.

"But they didn't even glance at it and just walked past it. They kept their distance, but I knew then that they were after me. So, once the walking signal at the next block changed, I made a break for it. I ran as fast as I could thinking to get into the park to try and lose them. I was in the parking lot looking back to see if they were behind me and that was when I bumped into you."

Tay listened but didn't say anything after she finished. The silence stretched between them as he navigated the streets, his mind racing with scenarios and suspicions. Every few minutes, he glanced at her, feeling her anxious gaze on him.

"Why would they be after you like that if you don't know them? What aren't you telling me?" he finally asked as they continued the drive.

"I promise I don't know them. I truly was just stopped by one of them and then the rest happened," she explained; her voice rose slightly.

"Ok. I will believe you," Tay replied; his tone laced with reluctant acceptance, and then he turned silent again.

After stretch of silence and the only sounds being the music Tay was listening to, Aria broke the silence asking, "So, how long have you been here?"

"Been where?" Tay asked distractedly.

"Here. As in living—in West Briargate?"

Tay sighed. "Look, I was born and raised here. And I never felt the need to leave."

This made him think of Rin. The time they spent together and knowing that she was here was his main reason for not leaving.

"So, you know almost everything about this city then?"

"No. I don't travel these streets like that."

"Well, how do you know about Jackson Street?"

Tay flexed his jaw . He quickly relaxed and released a soft sigh. "Look—everyone knows Jackson Street. It's the main place in the city where a bunch of rich people live. 'The Platinum Grove,' that is what we call that neighborhood. Which I am sure you know." He side eyed Aria before he looked back at the road.

"Well, excuse me then," Aria replied and huffed as she settled back into her seat, arms crossed.

And this is why I never wanted to get involved with rich people, Tay thought to himself.

An uneasy silence filled the space between them even though there was music playing.

Tay wasn't keen on talking more, but an unanswered question gnawed at him. Gathering his thoughts, he asked in the calmest tone he could muster, "Hey. I don't really care about your situation, but I need an honest answer. Why did you involve me in this?"

"Huh." Aria looked up from her phone.

"Why did you get me involved in this?"

"I." Aria stopped and looked down at her hands. She didn't say anything at first then took a deep breath and turned to Tay.

"I didn't mean to. Honestly, I just wanted to go home. I was scared but when I saw your face. I just..."

"It is ok you are safe now. Please continue."

"Well, I felt safe. Like I knew you from some time ago and I knew you would protect me."

Tay sat on what she said before he asked his follow up question. "So, if you hadn't bump into me, what was your plan?"

"I don't know." She shrugged her shoulders slightly. "Run through the park and hope to lose them. I guess. Then maybe call my dad or mom to see if they could come get me."

"Ok." Tay tried to make his voice seem as soothing as possible even as he tried to understand her logic. "But why didn't you just dial 911 or hit the emergency button on your phone, then run into the park while telling the police what was happening?"

"I don't know," Aria said as she shook her head. "I panicked and was not thinking straight. I just wanted to get away from them as quickly as possible."

As they talked, they came up to their exit. Tay pulled off the highway, stopping at a red light. A final question that had been waiting in the back of his mind since they met unexpectedly spilled out. "Why do I feel as if I know you from some time ago?"

Aria paused. She pursed her lips, looking Tay up and down. "I don't know, but I have the same feeling."

He caught a glimpse of a twinkle in her eyes—a hint she seemed to remember and a hope that he would, too.

But try as he might, no memory of this girl beside him came to mind.

"I guess it will come to me later," he replied as he faced the road. Aria sighed softly; her lower lip puckered out as she leaned against the door. With the conversation lapsed into silence, Tay reached for the radio and turned up the volume. The music filled the car, trying to overpower the quiet unease. Aria, now somewhat settled, pulled out her phone and tapped away at the screen. As he drove, Tay stole glances at her. The mysterious connection he felt between them was both distant and achingly familiar. Like that of reconnecting with a lost friend. But he again ignored that feeling and just drove.

Tay looked around as he pulled into the Wellington View neighborhood. The area wasn't gated but all the houses had their own protections. Not to mention each house was situated on sprawling, well-manicured lots with ponds or dense trees, exuding opulence, making Tay feel increasingly out of place.

"So, what were you doing over on that side of town if you stay over here?" Tay asked, trying to distract himself from the intimidating surroundings.

"I was supposed to go to the movies then hit a club tonight for a Kappa party with a friend from school," Aria explained. "Maybe I can introduce you to my parents so you can take me."

Tay's response was immediate and sharp. "No!" His voice reverberated in the confines of the car, seeming to turn the air thick with tension. Taking a quick deep breath, he composed himself and replied in a calmer voice that still shook some. "Look, I'm trying to be gone before your folks see me or the car."

His puzzlement and agitation was steadily increasing. *Why does it feel like she's deliberately trying to entangle me in her life?* he wondered silently, frustration brewing inside him. He had sought solitude, not complication.

Aria's matter-of-fact response did little to ease his growing sense of entrapment. "Sorry, but it doesn't look that will happen now."

"Huh, and why is that?" Tay said, his annoyance growing as his suspicions were confirmed.

"Because everyone is at the gate," Aria stated, gesturing toward a crowd gathered around a massive iron gate. Tay's eyes followed her gesture, his heart sinking as he saw the group of elegantly dressed family members and house attendants with their eyes seemingly fixed on the car. Immediately, Tay stopped the car, causing Aria to brace on the dash to not hit her head.

"What was that for?" Aria asked, her voice sharp.

"Why are they out there?" Tay's voice was almost a whisper.

"What?" Aria leaned in to hear better.

"I said, why is everyone out front like they are waiting for a freaking princess to come home that ran away?" His voice rose with his frustration.

"Dude, chill," Aria replied, scooting back in her seat as far as the space allowed. "Look, I've been updating my mom about what happened since we drove off and that I had got a ride. I been letting her know my location as we got closer," she explained, her voice steady, suggesting this was the most natural thing to do under the circumstances.

If Tay was thinking clearly, he would have recognized the prudence in her actions, especially given her situation. But clarity was far from his reach at that moment. The sight of so many people arrayed at the front, eagerly awaiting their arrival, sent his heart racing uncontrollably. He reflexively reached for his chest, his breathing shallow.

Mentally, he tried to rationalize what was happening. He was trying to drop her off and disappear— never to be seen or heard from again. *Why are they all out front like this?* he thought frantically. He could understand her mother and father being there, but the entire household?

He glanced at the house, its grandeur struck him anew—it wasn't just a large home; it was a veritable mansion, imposing in its elegance and size. The realization only intensified the tight knot in his stomach. He wasn't just dropping off a girl he barely knew; he was delivering her into the arms of a world so different from his own, where every detail screamed wealth and scrutiny.

"This is as far as I go. Get out and walk the rest," Tay stated, striving for calm, though his grip on the steering wheel grew intensely. He hated being the center of attention in any setting and this was definitely not the time to start.

The well-dressed crowd gathered outside, wearing suits and dresses that spoke of the household's wealth and taste. All except two people in the center, who Tay assumed were the heads of the house. They seemed to be dressed down.

Unable to stop, he looked down at his own attire— faded blue jeans patched with design tears, a red button-up left open over a white t-shirt, and the modest watch on his right wrist and silver chain adorning his neck. His gaze then shifted to the luxury cars in the driveways of the other homes, each gleaming under the midday sun. It made him think of his car. Though well-maintained, it paled in comparison to what was around him. *I don't belong here*, he thought bitterly, a strong sense of alienation washed over him.

"Why did I even agree to drive you here?" he asked more to himself than her.

"Because you are a kind person," she responded gently, sensing his discomfort. His heart raced as he looked back toward her family and workers at the gate, their expectant eyes fixed on them.

"Please, just get out," Tay pleaded, his voice dropping to almost a whisper as he rested his head on the wheel. His hands started hurting from how tight he was gripping it. He was desperate to leave this overwhelming situation behind.

"No, Tay." Aria leaned in closer to him. "You told me you'd drive me home not to the street," Aria countered, her tone reflecting a sense of sincerity.

"Well, it's different now." Tay peeked over the wheel at the crowd still waiting. "Your entire family is out there and I don't have any intentions on meeting them," Tay protested, his reluctance clear.

"Come on, Tay. Pretty please." Her voice dropped to imitate that of a cute child. "Look, the house is right there. Just drive up." Aria placed a hand gently on his arm in a pleading gesture. He glanced at her hand, then her, then the crowd. He felt a weight settling on him. Their eyes seemed to bore into him.

Tay steeled his heart from escaping out his chest as he inched the car forward. All the while telling himself it was to honor his word, but his mind told him that he really didn't care about his word at the moment, this was just the quickest way for him to get this over so he could get away.

As he pulled up to the gate, he stayed on the street, not by choice but because the throng of people blocked any closer approach.

"Thank you," Aria said softly. She then reached across the seats and hugged him. The contact took him by surprise. He flinched in her grasp, not fully prepared for such an intimate gesture in his current state of mind.

She held him like that until he felt his heart stop trying to break through his ribs. "Yea, now please go so I can leave," he muttered as he gently disengaged from the hug and avoided her gaze. Then, unexpectedly, he felt her lips on his cheek. He recoiled in his seat. Startled, his foot pressed down instinctively on a pedal. Luckily, it was the brakes.

"What the hell you do that for?!" he exclaimed, his voice loud and slightly higher than normal.

"I thought that might make you move," Aria whispered, smiling as she shifted the car into park. She then stared deeply into Tay's eyes and laid her hand on his thigh. Her approach was playful but edged with an intent that made Tay uncomfortable.

"Enough, Aria. Get out," he said firmly through gritted teeth. He pushed her back slightly on her shoulder to create some space while he held her other hand in place.

"How about you get out first then? Unless..." she asked as she pushed against his hold and inched her hand up his thigh.

Feeling even more uncomfortable, he quickly let her hand go and undid his seatbelt, opened the door, and got out with his head down. As soon as he took two steps out his car, he nearly collided into someone.

Their hands rested on his shoulder to stop him from bouncing away. Their grip was strong, and they didn't move an inch when he walked into them.

Tay turned around and came face-to-face with a tall dark-skinned man built like a linebacker. He wore a charcoal short-sleeve Henley, the top two buttons undone to reveal the fullness of his chest. The shirt tapered down to a pair of olive tech joggers, each leg sporting a sleek cargo pocket. All-white low-top sneakers grounded the look — sharp, clean, effortless.

Tay took all that in within a second before lifting his eyes to meet the man's eyes. His head was smooth and seemed to glisten in the sun. His beard full and precisely trimmed. But it was his eyes that stood out—sharp, steady, and gleaming with something that shifted the air around him. Respect. Control. Presence.

Tay knew then that he was the head of the household.

"Well, how are you, son?" the man asked, his voice deep and resonant, carrying both warmth and authority.

"I… I…" Tay swallowed hard, trying to find his voice. "I'm good, sir. And you?" he said as he edged away from the man, bowing his head slightly.

"Fine. Just fine," the man said with a soft chuckle. His voice was soothing to hear. "But it seems my daughter went too far with her trick." Tay stopped trying to get to his car. He raised his head and looked at this man. His voice wasn't threatening but held a sense of familiarity that reminded him of his dad.

"Well, I'll be." The man gazed into Tay's eyes. It seemed like he was scanning Tay for something.

Tay felt his body lock up, as if frozen in place. "It really is you, isn't it?"

Perplexed, a frown creased Tay's forehead as he found he could move again. Tay steadied himself and looked back at the intimidating man. "I'm sorry, sir. You must have me mixed up with someone else."

"Nonsense, you are Tagen Davis, right?" the man asked.

Tay involuntarily took a step back. A cold sweat started trickling down his back. "How do you know my name?"

The man smiled and looked over Tay's shoulder. Tay turned his head and only saw Aria. She had gotten out of the car and was watching Tay. The moment their eyes met, she turned her head away as her cheeks turned a slight shade of red on her caramel skin.

That was when it hit him.

She told them. *But how did she even know who I was? I never gave my full name.*

Aria raised her head and returned Tay's gaze. "You must be wondering how I knew who you were?"

Tay didn't answer. He looked at her, waiting.

"Well, let's just say I knew you from school?"

Again, that feeling of knowing her from somewhere rushed over. The way she spoke was like that of a friend or someone he knew very well.

But is it really just from school? Even though he questioned the meeting place, the feeling of familiarity grew deeper in his chest.

Tay turned his gaze from Aria to the tall man before him. This man also seemed familiar like he met him before but in passing. Or the meeting was so short he just didn't recall. Tay continued staring at the tall and imposing figure, lost in his thoughts.

Somone cleared their throat returning Tay to his senses.

Tay quickly bowed. "I'm sorry for staring, sir."

"Oh, my boy, it is nothing to worry about." The man reached out and patted Tay's back. His pat was tough and caused Tay to cough with each hit even though they were gentle. Once he stopped, Tay stood up.

"Sir, how do you know my name and I'm sorry if this is rude but…" Tay's voice wavered as he stood.

"Go ahead."

Tay took a breath and stiffened his posture with his chest up. His father always told him to never ask a question to anyone looking down. The only ones that did that were ashamed or guilty of something. So, with all the courage he could muster he asked, "What is your name?"

At this, the entire gathering seemed to freeze. No one looked around. Nor did they make a sound. Then the man bellowed out a deep laugh. The tension broke and it was filled with smirks all around.

"Ho, ho. Aren't you a polite one." The man continued chuckling briefly before speaking again. "Let me answer your last question first. My name is Jeff Blackwood. The girl that you picked up is my daughter, Aria Blackwood. And this—" He turned, holding his hand out. The only other person that was dressed down took his hand and he pulled her in close and looked deep into her eyes as if she only existed. "—This is my beautiful wife, Linda Blackwood." He then kissed her hand and Mrs. Blackwood chuckled and gently slapped Mr. Blackwood's chest.

Mrs. Blackwood stood about 5'2" with soft, wavy brunette colored hair. A simple white V-neck tee hugged her frame beneath a cream cardigan, paired with fitted blue jeans and sleek black Gucci slides. She looked casual and relaxed, but the grace in her posture and the quiet precision in her movements revealed years spent in a position of power—and the respect that came with it.

At hearing the name Blackwood, Tay felt an itch in the recesses of his mind. A blurry memory was trying to surface but was quickly drowned by Mr. Blackwood speaking.

"Now, as for your first question," Mr. Blackwood continued with his gaze fixed back on Tay. "It appears you are unaware, but my daughter has had an eye on you since you both were in the same class some years ago," he explained. He paused, stroking his beard thoughtfully. "Now let's see, Aria is twenty-two and she is a year younger than you so that would've been about eleven years ago."

"Eleven years ago?" Tay echoed, his eyes widened, and his voice rose in pitch slightly. He looked around at the maids and butlers whose eyes squinted at him. He quickly cleared his throat and recomposed himself. "Mr. Blackwood, I'm afraid I don't remember much from that time."

"Yes, that is understandable." Mr. Blackwood nodded his head in agreement. "Eleven years a long time to hold a memory," Mr. Blackwood continued with murk in his voice, "But Aria here. That day was special to her and she has not forgotten it once. Isn't that right, dear?"

Aria had walked around the car now and was by her father's side as he finished. Once she realized what he asked, her eyes went wide and she looked from her father to Tay.

"Dad, don't embarrass me like that." She punched her dad in the arm. Mr. Blackwood feigned being hurt by rubbing the spot where she punched.

"Oww. Linda, did you see how she abused her own father in front of her crush."

This time he yelped in earnest as Mrs. Blackwood pinched and twisted his forearm. "What was that for, my dear?"

"Because you deserved that." She looked gently at Aria then to Tay. "Please don't mind him. When it comes to Aria he is more wrapped around her finger than mine."

"That is not true. You are my only love."

"Yes, yes, dear. I know." Mrs. Blackwood rubbed the spot she had pinched. "But weren't you going to answer Mr. Davis' question."

"Oh, right." He turned back to Tay. "I'm so sorry, my boy. As you can see, I love my family dearly. So imagine my surprise when little Aria came home so excited. The smile on her face—it seemed like it might never fade. The sparkle in her eye told me she was in love. Naturally, as a father, I was curious."

"At that time, you two were in the…sixth grade. And if I remember correctly, you sat at the end of the first row close to the window."

Tay remembered the middle school he attended and his favorite seat. He even began to remember different things that happen while he was there. But he still couldn't seem to remember Aria. "You were quiet, spoke only to a select few, yet you maintained above-average grades and were quite popular, might I add."

Tay looked at Mr. Blackwood with raised eyebrows. "Sir, how would you know that about me?"

"Well, I paid a few visits to the school to check in on Aria and since you were in the same class I got to see you, too. Now, I wasn't just looking at you but all her classmates. I had a few people dig into them and their families. As a father must make sure his baby girl isn't in trouble or causing trouble." Mr. Blackwood looked at Aria with a deep smile.

"But sir, I don't remember you ever showing up. I'm pretty sure that if someone of your status was there, I would remember that," Tay questioned, trying to solve how his memory was drawing a blank for never seeing such a powerful man.

"Oh, I was dressed differently then, and I acted like someone else. I know if I present myself normally people tend to try and show their best side. But I rather see them naturally, so I typically came as some random uncle, cousin, or such. And it was during one such visit that you did something completely unexpected."

Mr. Blackwood paused and looked up into the sky, as if reliving the memory itself. "It was November 15. I was visiting Aria during a break. That time I came dressed as a cousin and I saw that she was being picked on by some upperclassmen on the playground. I knew that I couldn't step in for that would blow my cover and I wanted to see how she handled the pressure."

"Though my blood boils even now from hearing and seeing what they were doing to my little girl. After a few moments of no one doing anything and Aria just taking it, I was about to step in but you stepped between her and the group of boys and girls." He looked at Tay respectfully. "From what I saw then, the moment you stepped in between them and her, their ire turned to you. They began calling you names, saying you were parentless and that no one wanted you. Yet you stood there not saying a word. Then someone pushed you from the back trying to get you to ram into the boy in front of you. That was when you reacted. Despite the odds—five against one—you not only defended yourself but also ensured not even a speck of dust reached my daughter." Mr. Blackwood nodded his head approvingly and even some of the house attendants eyes shined with slight respect at hearing this story.

"You walked away barely scathed, leaving those bullies in a state of shock and pain. Even for myself, I must say, that is quite remarkable," he finished.

Tay could only stare, his mind reeled from the revelation. He remembered that day vividly—the main reason being his long-standing grudge against those bullies. They had called him names, destroyed his homework, wrote in his notebooks, and left nasty notes in his locker. He took all of it for a few months, but the last straw was when they had said his parents must have been criminals and that was why they were killed.

That was the day he went around the school on break, trying to find them. He found them in a half circle, huddled like they were looking at something. He walked in front of them and stood there for a moment— no one saying a word. He vaguely remembered there being a girl there with silky black hair that looked soft like a pillow, but he didn't remember her name. She even grabbed his hand then and thanked him, saying something like she wanted to be his girl later. But Tay didn't really pay attention to that because the next day the girl was in a different school, and he never saw her again—that was until now.

By the end of the story, Aria had mustered enough courage to move from her father's side to stand by Tay, looping her arm around his.

"You remember, don't you?" she asked, her voice soft and filled with hope.

"Yes. I...I remember. So, you were that girl?" he questioned, looking at her now. She did have the same lustrous black hair as the girl.

"Yea. Sorry that I waited so long to say this but thank you for saving me that day."

"Yea. No problem," he replied softly. His gaze drifted from her to everyone that was out and realized something was off. Even for a rich family, the way the maids and butlers seemed to always be on guard sent a shiver down Tay's spine. Like in a moment he would be in danger.

"Excuse me, Mr. Blackwood, but who are you really?" Tay asked, driven by a sudden surge of curiosity. At his question, the attendants' demeanor shifted subtly; everyone except Mr. and Mrs. Blackwood and Aria looked at him with warning eyes that said, *make the wrong move, and you'll regret it.*

"Son, it seems you have sharp eyes, and you think quickly. But I cannot answer that question," Mr. Blackwood responded gravely. "At least not here."

In that moment, Tay understood. Though the memory was still fragmented, he remembered overhearing his father telling his mother about a feud between two groups, the kind that never made it to newspapers or the internet. And he remembered clearly a phrase his father said to his mother with full confidence, "The Blackwoods will never fall, not with us here."

Eyes wide, Tay quickly extricated himself from Aria's grasp, got on one knee, and bowed his head.

"Forgive me for not recognizing you earlier, Mr. Blackwood. But now that I have returned your daughter, I must take my leave. And to your daughter, I bid you farewell," he said in one fluid breath, his voice laden with sincerity and respect but there was a small undertone of fear. He felt his neck begin to sweat and chills running down his spine yet he didn't move.

It wasn't that he couldn't, but the world the man before him was in didn't allow for lesser people to move unless they were given approval.

"So, you figured it out." Mr. Blackwood observed, a greater note of respect in his tone.

"My dad taught me well, especially since you were his senior and partner," Tay stated, his voice steady despite the steady increase of pressure he felt on his shoulders.

"I see. So, you really are the son of Henry Davis," Mr. Blackwood acknowledged, his tone somber.

"Yes, sir." Tay kept his gaze fixed on the ground as his body tensed and sweat rolled down his arm as his heart pounded in his chest. He swallowed hard before continuing, "Sir, forgive my saying so, but I wish to live a peaceful life, not one shrouded in shadows as before."

At his words, he felt even more intense pressure bearing down on him. He knew it was the stares of the house attendants, as if they had daggers pressed against his skin. The air tensed, and he could hear the subtle rustle of hands reaching for concealed weapons.

No one moved, however.

"It is your choice to make, and I will not be the one to ask you of such a thing. But I would dishonor your father if I did not tell you this." Mr. Blackwood reached out and laid a strong and comforting hand on Tay's shoulder. "Though you may no longer wish to live in this lifestyle, you will see that once you set even one foot back in this world, the road to living a peaceful life is harder and more elusive than you might think. For your sake though, I hope that you will get to live the life that you want." Mr. Blackwood straightened up.

"Well, I hope you do come visit from time to time. My daughter, I presume, would like that." As if on cue, Aria grabbed Tay's arm again and pulled him up, resting her head on his shoulder and smiling.

"I will consider it, sir," Tay replied, his voice low, still not meeting Mr. Blackwood's eyes.

"Dear, we must go. The food is getting cold, and I even cooked this time," Mrs. Blackwood called out, her voice light, breaking the tension in that moment.

Mr. Blackwood looked at her and smiled. "Yes, my dear. I believe I would like to enjoy your meal while it is still warm." From that statement, everyone walked to the house—everyone except Aria.

Tay remained there, eyes looking to the ground, head bowed. Aria quickly let him go and ran to her father. Once beside him, she whispered in his ear. Tay felt Mr. Blackwood's gaze on him once more.

"Please don't. Please don't ask me," Tay whispered to himself so faintly it was barely audible, a silent plea for respite.

"Tagen, I have a favor to ask of you," Mr. Blackwood began as he walked from Aria back to Tay.

"Yes, sir," Tay responded.

"First, look at me, my boy. I prefer respect by looking at your eyes." Mr. Blackwood's voice softened. Tay lifted his head, meeting Mr. Blackwood's gaze. The eyes that looked back at him were strong yet gentle, offering a sense of calm Tay hadn't expected. In that moment, he didn't feel judged as a thug or a statistic, but as a person, an equal. It was disarming and unexpectedly reassuring. Tay felt his own eyes fill with a mix of admiration and wonder. Here was the type of man he aspired to be—commanding respect not through intimidation but through integrity and presence.

Despite the comfort those eyes offered, Tay remained acutely aware of the precariousness of his position. He knew a single misstep could turn the house attendants against him, potentially ending disastrously though such an outcome would likely never be witnessed by the Blackwood family.

"My daughter wants to go to this party tonight. Normally, I would send an escort to watch over her, but if you were to consider going it would be less suspicious."

"Sir. If I may ask a question," Tay began, his tone respectful though his eyes wandered over the crowd behind Mr. Blackwood.

"Go ahead." Mr. Blackwood gently encouraged.

"Why me? I understand that I may have done a good deed by returning her to you from the earlier incident, but I am sure the young lady has many more capable people in her circle that can do a better job than I could."

Mr. Blackwood crossed his arms and seemed to be in thought. He then looked back at Tay with that gentle smile. "Though that may be the case, this is a last-minute request and as I see it you are a better choice than having someone that would seem to be more of a chaperon than a companion in this situation."

"May I give a request, sir?"

"Speak freely, my son."

"If this is all you request, I will oblige," Tay answered, his voice steady despite the tension knotting in his throat. After a slight swallow, he added, "I only request that this be the last time we come in contact with each other."

Upon hearing this, the attendants turned toward him, their postures tense. Some fingers subtly brushed the hilts of concealed knives, ready to spring into action. However, before anyone could advance, Mr. Blackwood raised his hand, halting them with a single calm gesture.

"If that is your wish, I will honor it," Mr. Blackwood responded, his deep voice resonant with an unexpected warmth but loud enough for the attendants to hear clearly. His smile was broad and genuine, not born of scheming but of a heartfelt joy. "Though I believe my daughter is another story."

Aria rushed to Tay, wrapping her arms around his neck in a tight embrace. "Thank you! Thank you!" she exclaimed; her voice bubbled with excitement. "Okay pick me up at nine. See you then!" She hurried off toward the house, her father and mother shook their heads, smiling merrily as they walked back to the house followed by the attendants.

"Yea," Tay muttered to himself. His eyes lingered on Mr. Blackwood's back until the group was behind the iron gate.

Once the gate closed, Tay turned sharply; his steps quick and purposeful as he made his way to his car. He slipped inside, fired up the engine, and sped away, the tires biting the pavement as if in haste to escape.

"What the hell just happened?!" he asked aloud to the empty car, his voice echoing slightly in the confined space. "Why did I accept? I know even the smallest steps here can tether one forever." The weight of his decision pressed down on him as he navigated the familiar roads back to his home.

He didn't know how long it took to drive home, for he barely remembered the drive. His mind was a tumult of apprehension and regret, trying to figure out how this day went from despair to a protection job. His drive home was haunted by these thoughts, and when he arrived, he was consumed by a mix of exhaustion and dread.

He went inside and without undressing, Tay collapsed onto his bed. The day's events replayed in his mind on a relentless loop. He forcefully calmed his mind and felt his tiredness finally claim him. His last conscious thought before his eyes shut was a whispered hope, "I hope I forget that deal."

Tay had a dream he never had before. His father stood in front of him, arms folded across his broad bare chest. They were back in the old underground training room—the stench of old sweat ever-present. His dad's favorite workout mix thumped loudly over the speakers, the bass resonating through the room.

"You may not like the tasks or even the goals but by doing these, it will help make you into the greatest of them all," his father's voice echoed, resonant and firm throughout the hollow room.

"But, Dad," Tay protested, his voice higher, younger. "I just want to be normal."

A burly laugh erupted from his father. "If you ever find 'normal,' let me know," he replied, his tone light despite the words. "Now, let's add twenty more pounds."

"Dad, come on! I just got used to 150 pounds. I'm only twelve. Can I have a break, please?"

"Breaks mean giving up. You've only got twenty minutes left. Push through it, then you can eat and rest."

"You said that same phrase two hours ago."

"Did I now? Well, we are behind. Time for sparring—and we're taking it to the next level." Despite the grueling training, Tay felt a smile break across his face. It was these moments alone with his dad that Tay truly treasured and that deepened their bond. Suddenly, the weight in his hands and the echo of the music faded. The training room dissolved into a bright day at a park, the sound of children playing in the distance. Tay was now older, his hands empty, and before him stood his ex.

"Rin?" Tay whispered in disbelief. She turned, her eyes meeting his—red-rimmed and streaked with tears. "What's wrong, babe?"

"Tay, I'm sorry, but I cannot take it anymore," Rin choked out, tears still trailing down her cheeks.

"Baby, it's ok. Just tell me what's going on," he urged, stepping forward to comfort her. He reached out to touch her shoulder, but she gently pushed his hand away.

"Just—Just leave me alone." She turned her back to him and walked away. Tay immediately reached for her, only for people to appear between them. Tay felt his heart crack again. Why did his dream have to cause him to feel the lost again. He wished he could at least rectify or get closure from the situation. He saw a glimpse of the people separating them—faceless— their movements eerily coordinated in the shadows, reminding him of one dreaded possibility.

"Phantoms?!" he exclaimed, the word a bitter taste in his mouth. These faceless figures represented a time in his life when happiness seemed within grasp, only to be cruelly snatched away. They embodied his deepest fears— that any joy he dared to embrace was destined to be ripped from his hands. No matter his efforts or how fervent his partner's intentions, the outcome was inevitably marred by loss. The more he dwelled on the life he might have had, the more his rage burgeoned.

Instinctively, his body went into motion—punching, kicking, thrusting— aside the shadowy figures, but he couldn't catch up to Rin. He finally came to a stop, heaving, as the last vestiges of Rin's image disappeared into the crowd like a light swallowed by the darkness. All that remained were the sinister silhouettes.

"It will never stop, will it?" Tay spoke aloud to no one, tears flowing from his tightly closed eyes as he caught his breath.

"Your life will never go how you want it," a hollowed voice said from his right.

"No matter who you meet in your life, you two will never see eye to eye," another sneered from beside that one.

"Shut your mouths," Tay whispered to himself. His fists clenched so tight that his hands shook.

"You've grown soft and tried to live a fantasy," a voice jeered from behind him.

"I rather die than live in that cruel world you people come from," Tay retorted as he reached to his sides and pulled out two guns, one silver and the other black, standing up.

"Awe look, he's trying to act tough." All the phantoms laughed. "What does he think he can do with those toys against all of us?" the one directly in front of him chuckled.

"Then stay there and watch," Tay said darkly as a smirk crept on his face. He opened his eyes, flipped the silver gun to hold the muzzle, and flung it at the last one that spoke. The gun hit it in the head, causing his gun to fly into the air. He shot with trained precision, hitting his targets' vital points as he ran to the one he hit with his other gun. Tay reached in front of that phantom just as the figure regained its balance. With the momentum of his run, Tay delivered an uppercut to the phantom's stomach. As it doubled over, he kneed it in the face, sending it sprawling back. Without stopping, he rolled over the fallen figure, scooping up his gun. Quickly, he turned onto his stomach and fired a shot into the phantom's head. Quickly, Tay got up and crippled the figures in his way. Tay's vision was red with rage and he ran through the crowd unleashing his furry. As the last one fell back from a shot to head, Tay stood ready, his senses sharp for any signs of further threats. Even though his breaths were quick and heavy and sweat covered his body causing his clothes to stick to his skin.

Suddenly, a flicker of light caught in the corner of his eye. He spun, pointing both guns, but froze before he could pull the triggers. There, in front of him, was Aria.

Tay noticed a sudden change; his sleeves had transformed. He looked down and saw he now wore a beige tux with a sky-blue tie. Shocked, he looked back at Aria standing there in a white wedding dress, one hand extended.

"Why are you here?" he asked, stowing his guns behind him before taking her hand.

"That is a silly thing to ask, honey. It is because I agreed to marry you," she replied, her voice light and full of warmth. She stepped in close to him and wrapped her arms around his waist. She then looked up at him and smiled. "I'm glad you asked me to be your wife."

Tay's face became a mixture of puzzlement and disbelief, but before he could say anything, her lips met his in a gentle kiss. The kiss felt too warm—too real—to be a dream. Yet he knew that was what it was, a dream. As they kissed, he felt his gun being taken from his back followed by a loud bang behind him. He turned quickly, seeing a man with a sniper rifle fall from the balcony. He looked back at Aria, her smile radiant despite what she just did. She got on her tip toes and whispered in his ear, "Time to wake up."

Tay opened his eyes slowly and pulled his phone from his pocket and saw that the time was only 7:00 pm. Tay rolled on his back staring at the ceiling in the dark.

"I really shouldn't take her," he muttered. He rolled over on his stomach and tried to go back to sleep. After just lying there for fifteen minutes and his mind refusing to quiet down, he sighed heavily. He pushed himself up and went to the living room. With nothing to do, he decided to do a light workout. Turning his back to the sofa, he placed his hands on the ground and rested his feet on the sofa's arm. He did five sets of thirty push-ups while alternating with five sets of forty-five sit ups. After finishing, he went to get his jump rope from the top shelf in the washroom.

As he rummaged for the jump rope, his hands bumped a box. Puzzled, he pulled it down. Once it was in his hands, he recognized it instantly—it was his father's gun box. Forgetting the jump rope, he went back to the living room with the box in hand and sat on the floor, placing it on his lap.

As he looked at the box, Tay's thoughts drifted. His brother had rose to prominence in the underworld, and his sister had become an unmatched assassin. They both followed in their parents' footsteps. But Tay? He was trying to find normalcy in a world that seemed to deny him. The more he tried, the more impossible it seemed. His friends, though dear, inevitably became liabilities and in worst cases, hostages. This always caused him to wander back into a world of actions and plans he desperately wished to leave behind, thus showcasing how naïve his dream was. This repeated cycle forced him to keep a cautious distance from those he would love to call friend, leaving him feeling alienated and incomplete.

"Father, what am I to do now?" Tay asked, voice wavering as emotions swirled inside him. He gingerly opened the box. Inside laid his father's gun embossed with his personal symbol on the handle—a sword in a stone with an eagle resting on the hilt. Tay rested his hand on top of it. Its cold feel was comfortable and solid just like his dad. Lifting the gun from the box, Tay felt a sense of familiarity from its weight. His mind eased as he felt that his father was standing beside him telling him that he would be ok. He let out a breath he didn't know he was holding as his body relaxed. He held the gun between his hands and rested the top of the muzzle against his forehead with the barrel pointed to the ceiling. He slightly bowed his head and closed his eyes as he spoke words of gratitude.

"Thanks, Dad," Tay whispered to the gun. "I love you."

As he put the gun back in the box, a sense of comfort and security washed over him. His muscles ached as he got up from sitting down for so long after he had just warmed them up. As he put the box back on the shelf, the smell of sweat wafted up his nose.

"Oh God, whoever said their natural musk was attractive clearly must be lying if this is my natural musk." Tay chuckled as he went to take a shower.

His shower was warmer and more enjoyable this time than when he showered in the morning. He even sang a bit as he cleaned himself off. After drying off, he wandered to his closet with his towel around his waist. He looked through his options and took his time to figure out what outfit he wanted to wear for the night.

"Hmm, I want to look good since I'm going out but I was always horrible at picking outfits. Rin was my fashionista and I depended on her for getting me together."

At that thought, Tay felt his heart seize up and almost caught in his throat like swallowing a chunk of food and not chewing it completely. He took a deep breath.

Even if she is now gone it doesn't mean it was all bad. He exhaled slowly as he looked for solace in the hurt.

Dude, relax and know that you just need to move on and try to be more open and honest next time. Besides, she would die laughing if you pick something weird. As he thought this, the tightness in his chest began to ease and the lump in his throat loosened. Once he was fully settled, he looked back at his closet. "Now what would be a good choice?"

He decided to go with a pair of black straight-fit jeans, paired them with a red button-down shirt with sleeves rolled up, and a white fitted shirt underneath.

He laid his clothes on the bed, assessing them to make sure he wanted to wear this outfit.

Yep, that is good for now. I'm not going to impress anyone anyways. The earlier thought of Rin made his actions become bitter and lack any true emotions. He still pressed forward doing anything he could to ignore the stabs in his chest, even if it was now minor compared to earlier.

Next, he took out his favorite red and white mid-top sneakers to complete his outfit. He looked at his shoes and sensed comfort and familiarity in them. They not only physically grounded him but now they were acting like an anchor, keeping him tied to land. For accessories, he went to his dresser and took out his black and red-accented watch, a silver chain, and silver studded earrings and placed them on the bed with his outfit.

"Man, I feel like I'm going to be looking fresh out there. Plus, this outfit is easy for me to move in," Tay said to himself, giving his sign of approval though his actions were forced to help him keep moving forward.

Now that his outfit of choice was laid out, he decided to cool off some more. So, he did some stretches to dissipate the heat from his workout and shower.

After a while, he checked the time again and saw that it was 8:05 pm. He got dressed and walked out the door, locking it behind him. He turned and noticed the moonlight pouring over the yard and the street. He looked up to see the full moon. Its beauty captivated him, making him momentarily consider staying on his porch to drink and admire the night. His heart seemed to still as he gazed upon the moon. The quiet night on the street made the scene even more mesmerizing.

This caused him to remember he was going out for a job, not for an enjoyable night. With that sobering thought, he reluctantly walked to his car. He decided to take his time getting to Aria's place, not minding and even considered praying that something happened along the way to prevent him from going. He pulled off and zoned out to his music and without noticing, he had run through the gears, reaching a fast pace.

Why am I rushing? he thought as he came back to himself, feeling the wind on his face and blowing his hair. *Maybe I just love the way that driving fast in this car feels.* Enjoying the feel, he kept going and entered the neighborhood in thirty minutes. As he pulled up to her street, he saw someone was standing outside the gate. He squinted and realized it was Aria. He checked his clock and saw that it was just 8:40. *Why is she out there?* he wondered, slowly pulling up in front of her.

"I knew you would come early," she said as she walked to his car and leaned through the window.

"Yea, well, I just hate being late and having others wait on me." He tried his best not to stare but her shirt and the way she was resting on his window made her cleavage more pronounced, as if she wanted him to notice.

"Typical, but I like that about you." She smiled brightly with a hint of something more than just a friendly invitation. She tilted her head slightly; a lock of her hair fell into her face, and she slowly moved it behind her ear looking at him with an alluring gaze.

"So, you want to head out or is there something else you need to do beforehand?" he asked, his senses alert to the surrounding area, feeling as though they were being watched.

"I would love to leave now but my father wants to talk with you," Aria said, standing up with a sigh and raising her hands in a gesture of resignation.

"Ok, let me in and we'll go see him," Tay replied, though the thought of being locked behind a gate where he didn't know anyone made him uneasy.

"Hmm. How about we take a walk?" Tay looked at her, eyebrow raised.

"Don't look like that. Besides," she stated, a light blush coming to her cheeks as she tapped her index fingers together making a field goal. "Walking will take longer, and I would get to stand beside you a little longer."

"You do know that we don't truly know each other, right?" Tay pressed, attempting to put some distance between her past affections and the current situation.

"I wouldn't be so sure. I know a decent amount about you from school," she replied with a mischievous smile, which only made Tay more cautious. "Relax, it was just typical girl gossip of who is dating who and who the hot guys are. Honestly, you would be surprised how much your name came up."

Just as Tay opened his mouth to make a snide remark, Aria countered. "No, I wasn't the one that brought you up. Why would I do something to make other girls notice you more?"

Tay conceded to her point. He got out, locking the door. He walked around to Aria and gestured with his arm pointing out. "Shall we?" With that, they walked through the side gate. As they stepped through, one of the gate attendants stood there waiting.

"Keys, please," was all the attendant said as he held one hand out.

Tay hesitated but did as

requested. "Thank you."

Then the guy went out the gate and Tay heard his car come to life. He didn't move as the gate opened and his car drove by them. Watching his car being driven by someone else, a tinge of irritation flared up in him. Aria noticed and walked in front of him and twirled around.

"So?" she asked as she faced him again.

"So. What?"

"What do you think of my outfit?" Tay looked her over and was relieved his darker skin hid his blush. The soft glow of the lights from the driveway mixed with the pale moonlight above, casted a gentle sheen across her ebony skin, making her appear almost luminous against the night.

She wore open-toed, hollowed-out black high heels, and ripped black high-waisted skinny jeans that hugged her curves. Her bold, deep red blouse—with a knot tied at the side that stopped at her navel—featured a daring V-neckline that showcased her cleavage. Over it, she draped a lightweight ivory cardigan. Her outfit made her look stunning. Her jewelry was simple yet elegant—a gold chain with a heart pendant that delicately rested just above her cleavage and gold leaf-adorned earrings.

As Tay's gaze returned to her face, he noticed her smoky eyeshadow, which accentuated her striking green eyes now even more captivating in the dim light. Her eyes, framed by long and full lashes, held his attention effortlessly.

Tay was momentarily at a loss for words, taking in the full image of her beauty. The only thing he could think of was...

An angel...

Even his heart seemed to agree as it thumped loudly in his ears and pounded behind his chest.

"Tay?" She stepped closer, a hint of nervousness in her voice.

"You look beautiful," he said, his voice low but filled with awe.

"Hee-hee, thanks. You don't look too bad yourself. Going more for the comfortable approach? And look we match!!" Aria beamed, her enthusiasm brought a lighter note to the evening.

"Yea. I'm not here to impress anyone. And I guess we do," Tay responded, his gaze finally breaking away from her as they continued walking. They walked for a couple more minutes before reaching the end of the driveway and ascended the stairs leading to the front door.

Once at the front door, they were greeted by two guards in black suits. Despite the attires attempt to conceal their frame, it was clear they were well-built; their stances exuded an air of quiet strength. They looked at the two of them, bowed to Aria, and then cut their eyes to Tay. Their eyes sharp and assessing, as if testing his mettle.

After a tense moment, one stepped forward. "Mr. Tagen, we have been expecting you. Before we can allow you to enter, we must perform a search. Please stand with your arms out, finger spread, and legs apart," he instructed, his voice deep and commanding. Tay complied, standing in the requested position as he was thoroughly patted down, and his belongings were searched, namely his wallet and cellphone for that was all he had on him. While he was being searched, Aria leaned against the wall and looked at him, as if admiring him. Tay's attention drifted to Aria's hair, noting how deep black and curly it was. It stopped just below her shoulders. He then imagined that if she straightened it, it would probably reach the middle of her back.

Once satisfied, the guard exchanged a brief nod with his colleague. They both stepped aside, signaling Tay could proceed. Aria pushed the door open and entered ahead of him, Tay following closely behind, his mind alert and ready for whatever awaited them inside.

The first thing he noticed about the interior was its striking brightness. A grand chandelier hung centrally in the room above a round table, which hosted a solitary flower vase the size of Tay's torso. Its light reflected off the pristine marble floor, lending the foyer a dazzling brilliance. To the left, a marble staircase with elegant, black iron railing curved gracefully to the upper floor, flanked by portraits of Aria and Mr. and Mrs. Blackwood ascending alongside it. The railing continued across the landing.

Behind the centerpiece of the foyer was an archway that seemed to lead to an expansive living room. While on the right was a set of dark oak double doors, suggesting the other side was either an office or sitting room.

As Tay took in his surroundings, he felt a hand interlace with his, startling him. He looked to see Aria holding his hand in both hers. She smiled gently at him and led him through the doors on the right.

Upon entering, immediately he saw an expensive heavy oak desk facing the door. Along the right wall were two bookcases, settled between them was a cabinet that held a selection of whiskey glasses and whiskey bottles. At the desk sat Mr. Blackwood, looking through mail.

"Welcome back, Tay," Mr. Blackwood greeted him distractedly, not looking up as he finished reading a letter.

"Thank you, sir," was Tay's courteous reply. He looked over Mr. Blackwood and noticed his shoulders looked squarer and sharper than before.

But it was somewhat dimly lit in the room, so Tay brushed it off as a lighting trick.

After a moment, Mr. Blackwood set the letter aside, finally looking up and addressed Tay. "Well, I would like to have a word with you alone," he stated, switching his gaze from Tay to Aria.

"Can't I stay, Father?" Aria pleaded.

"No. This is something I must discuss with Tagen," Mr. Blackwood replied firmly, using Tay's first name, which instantly made Tay tense. The way he said his name was different from the heartwarming moment they had earlier that day.

"Yes, sir." She sighed as he poked out her lower lip; her eyes downcast. She turned to Tay, offered him a soft smile. "Well, I will see you soon." She added a playful wink as she reluctantly released his hand.

She walked to the door, but Tay's gaze never strayed from Mr. Blackwood. As soon as the door clicked shut, Mr. Blackwood hurled a letter opener at Tay. Instinctively, Tay swayed back, allowing the knife to pass over his head and thud into the door. When Tay straightened up, Mr. Blackwood had already vaulted over his desk, his right fist aimed at Tay's head.

Swiftly, Tay deflected the punch and seized Mr. Blackwood's wrist. For a supposedly built man, his wrist felt weak and somewhat flimsy. As Tay noticed this, he also saw a silver object in Mr. Blackwood's hand. Without hesitation, Tay pulled his wrist back, stepped behind him, and pinned his arm to his back. With his free hand, Tay pushed the back of Mr. Blackwood's head down, forcing him to bend forward so that he was facing the ground.

An object dropped and clattered on the floor. This broke Tay's concentration as he looked to see what it was.

It was just a fork.

But that distraction was all Mr. Blackwood needed. He ducked and spun, sweeping Tay's feet from under him. Tay released his hand and stumbled backwards onto the desk. Just as Tay regained his balance, he saw a gun in Mr. Blackwood's hand.

Reacting instantly, Tay dove toward Mr. Blackwood's feet. He rolled, picked up the fork, and kicked the inside of Mr. Blackwood's knee, making him buckle and fall to one knee. Tay continued his momentum and caught Mr. Blackwood's neck behind his leg and slammed him to the ground. Sensing movement to his right, Tay only thought was another attacker. So, without hesitation, he threw the fork into a dark corner of the office by the bookcase where a curtain was draped.

"Okay. That is enough," a voice said from behind the curtain. From it emerged the real Mr. Blackwood with a broad smile on his face.

"I am happy to say that, Tay, you passed. Please wake our head butler, Eric. I fear you may have knocked him unconscious."

Tay looked down to see a fake bald mask had slid to the floor and revealed a head full of hair. Tay quickly got up and held the butler up. He looked at the face and sure enough with the mask removed he saw it was the head butler. Tay quickly shook him awake. Eric slowly came to, and he looked around dazed.

Tay apologized profusely as he helped Eric to his feet. As Eric stood, holding his head where it had impacted the ground, he bowed to Tay and Mr. Blackwood, then turned to walk out on unsteady feet. After ensuring Eric made it out the office, Tay turned to look at Mr. Blackwood.

"Why such a test, sir? And why have a real gun?" Tay hand shook from the thought he had tried to fight to win and possibly kill. If Mr. Blackwood hadn't moved when he did, Tay might have stabbed Eric with that fork.

"To make sure my girl is in good hands," Mr. Blackwood replied, touching his cheek.

"As for the gun. It was empty. I made sure before I gave it to Eric. Can't have you accidentally getting shot." A small smirk played at the edge of his lip. "But I needed to see how you reacted under real pressure. And I have to say, you didn't disappoint. I'm glad you still remember everything your father taught you," Mr. Blackwood said as he walked back to his desk.

Tay's eyes narrowed at the mention of his father.

Mr. Blackwood knew Tay didn't want to be part of their world anymore.

And yet—he tested him. He put Tay in a position where he had no choice but to remember.

His father.

The training.

The joy of fighting with his dad and learning and laughing.

And even remember the wetness of the blood of those he had to fight.

The blood of his father in his last moment.

The heat of the fire as his only home was burned down.

Tay's hands curled into fists. His eyes stung. He looked up at Mr. Blackwood, ready to lash out. But then—he saw it. A cut. A trickle of blood running down Mr. Blackwood's cheek. Tay's expression shifted instantly as he quickly dropped to one knee and bowed his head.

"I am truly sorry about that cut and questioning your judgement," he apologized sincerely, voice tight. His heart thudded like a drum.

Oh shit! I injured Mr. Blackwood! I'm fucking dead!

Tay closed his eyes tightly as he waited to hear his verdict.

"Oh this…" Mr. Blackwood touched his injured cheek, seeing the blood on his hands. He just smiled even more. "This isn't anything to worry about. I'm just amazed at how quick you realized it was me and altered your aim," Mr. Blackwood said, his voice still full of admiration and praise as he sat on the edge of his desk.

"Thank you for your kind words," Tay replied, still kneeling.

"Aria, come here," Mr. Blackwood said. Tay looked around, eyes in a scowl. He was sure he heard her walk out the room but the way Mr. Blackwood spoke it was as if she was in the room with them.

"Yes, Daddy?" she said excitedly, popping up from behind a chair to the left of the door. She walked to where Tay knelt and stood beside him.

"You found yourself a great man," Mr. Blackwood stated, smiling warmly at her. He then turned back to Tay. "Tay, please stand up. We are equals in this house." Tay stood up but his eyes still looked at the ground.

"Come now, my boy, look me in the eyes."

Tay lifted his gaze to meet Mr. Blackwood's. "That is much better. Given how you performed, I will permit Aria to go to this party only if you accompany her," he continued. Tay felt like there was a meaning behind those words, but his thought was thrown off by Aria's voice.

"Please, Tay, go with me? Everyone is going to be there, and I bet you will have fun." Her voice was sweet and pleading.

"Sir, I came here just to take her there and bring her back. I would like to readdress that I have no claim as to become part of your world," Tay said without thinking. *What am I saying?* Tay reprimanded himself as he continued to look Mr. Blackwood in the eye, unwavering.

Mr. Blackwood met his stare evenly, his expression turning somber before he smiled. "I understand, Tay, and I give my word that I will not involve you in any situation of my own making. But the two of you go on and take care," he said, rising and placing a hand gently yet firmly on each of their shoulders. He looked them in the eye in turn before walking them to the door.

"Have a great night, and I'll see you when you get back," Mr. Blackwood said, his expression that of a father proud of his daughter's choice in a companion.

"Yes, sir. I will take care of her," Tay assured as they stepped into the foyer.

"I'm sure you will, Tay. Now, Aria, make sure you behave yourself and don't cause trouble for Tay."

"DAD!!!" she exclaimed, blushing. "Why are you trying to make me seem like all I do is give him trouble?"

"Well, there was that time in school and then there was today at the park where you ran into Tay and then there is now you asking to go out with you tonight," Mr. Blackwood teased as he ticked up to three fingers.

"Okay. Okay. I get it, Dad, sheesh." She walked up to Tay and wrapped her arms around Tay's. "Then I will just cling to his arm and that way I won't get into trouble."

Mr. Blackwood burst into laughter. "You do that, my dear. He will make sure you are protected, and that trouble stays away."

As Tay watched this family's chemistry, his heart stung and it was hard to swallow. He saw his mom and dad. The way they used to play with him, his brother, and sister. The happiness they had. His eyes watered as his heart sank into his stomach because he no longer had a chance to have moments like this with them.

Tay softly cleared his throat and fought to keep his tears from falling for the third time in one day. He refused to let these strangers see weakness in him.

Aria turned to look at Tay and saw the water in his eyes.

"Tay, are you okay?"

"Yea. I just had something in my throat." He cleared it louder and shook his head to clear his eyes. He then looked back at Aria with a smile.

"Okay. Well, I do hope you have fun with me tonight."

"I will have as much fun as my task will allow."

They walked out the front door and Tay stopped. He didn't see his car but a limo in the driveway.

"Would you mind if I take my car?" Tay asked.

"Why would you want to ride in that if you could ride with a higher status level?" Mr. Blackwood turned to face Tay.

"That is the reason." Tay looked himself over and looked at everyone else. "Though this family is high class, I don't believe showcasing your money at a night club when you want me to protect your daughter is a smart move. Plus..." He glanced at himself, took a deep breath, and stood tall as he faced Mr. Blackwood. "I am not comfortable in that riding style," Tay answered.

"Hmm, if that is the case please go ahead," Mr. Blackwood conceded with a small smile, and he signaled the housekeeper to get Tay's car.

"Thank you, sir."

"Not a problem. I am proud that you didn't try to take the chance to ride in a status that could hurt your task. Others your age would have jumped at the chance to show off."

"Well, I just want to be comfortable truthfully."

As Tay's car pulled up, Aria tightened her grip on his arm. Tay looked at her and nodded. They walked to the car, and Tay courteously opened the door for her. After she was seated, he closed it gently, gave a respectful bow to Mr. Blackwood.

"See you later, Mr. Blackwood."

"You too, Tay. And don't let the task I gave you feel that strong. Please go and have fun with Aria tonight. I believe she would like it if you both enjoyed tonight." Mr. Blackwood winked at him.

Tay looked at Mr. Blackwood momentarily and then looked at Aria before he walked around to his side and got in. Tay drove cautiously out the gate and through the neighborhood, but as soon as they left the neighborhood, he sped off.

As they got on the highway, the only sound in the car was the hum of the engine and the soft sounds of the radio playing. Aria was fidgeting in her seat like she was sitting on pins and needles. Tay kept his eyes trained on the road. He still thought about the so-called test Mr. Blackwood had given him.

Why test me so? If he knew my father, he should know how he raised me. Tay still couldn't figure it out. Maybe it was just to confirm he didn't let his skills get rusty. But even so, that was a deadly way to find out. *Hell—I almost killed them both on reflex.*

Tay's grip on the wheel tightened as he replayed the test again. Now he wanted this task to be finished more than ever.

Aria unable to take the silence anymore turned and fully faced him. "Hey, Tay."

"Hmm," Tay spoke reflexively, barely registering that she had just spoken.

"Look, I just want to say sorry about my father. He is very picky about who I hang out with," Aria explained.

Tay didn't reply at first, just let her statement hang in the air before glancing at her. "You really don't know. Do you?" Tay asked as he shifted to the highest gear and pushed his car further.

"Don't know what?" Aria looked at him, puzzled.

"Tell me, who do you think your father really is?" Tay probed, needing to confirm his suspicions. "And don't lie because I can tell."

"He's a businessman and he has competitors who would kill to take over what he has built," Aria responded, her gaze fixed on Tay.

"I knew it." Tay's grip on the wheel increased slightly. "So, I can't avoid this fate no matter what," Tay murmured to himself.

"What's wrong?" Aria inquired as Tay swerved to pass a line of cars.

"Nothing, just get ready; we're almost there," Tay said, easing off the gas to take the exit. After another five minutes of driving, Aria spoke up again.

"Tay, pull over there for a minute," she said, pointing to a secluded dirt road near the club.

"Why?"

"Just do it, please."

Confused but compliant, Tay pulled over, the car now surrounded by trees.

"So, why are we here?" Tay asked, his voice tinged with frustration as he put the car into park.

"Because I want to know about you."

"Why? I am just a bodyguard."

"No, you're not. You are more than you realize," Aria replied softly, gazing gently into Tay's eyes.

"If you say so," Tay responded, his tone dismissive as he turned his head away from her. He was tired of her attempts to get closer. "Look, I'm only here on a job; there's nothing else to know about me," he said, unbuckling his belt to get out, but Aria caught his arm.

"Why are you avoiding me?"

"Because I don't want a new relationship. I'm still not over my last one."

"May I know what happened?"

Tay hesitated for a moment. He thought of telling her why his potential fiancée broke up with him and the danger of being with him would bring to her just to get her off his back, but he rejected the thought and the hassle that would come with it.

"Let's just go, please," he pleaded, pulling his arm free and stepping out of the car. Aria followed him. Halfway to the club, she slipped her hand into his just as they walked into the clearing where others were already gathering. A few people looked their way and snickered. Annoyed, Tay was about to pull away, but she tightened her grip. Tay sighed, silent for a moment. Despite his resistance, there was familiar warmth in her hand made him partly want to hold on tighter, but he stifled the impulse as just a weak attempt to have someone to bounce back from his breakup.

They approached the club's front entrance and bypassed the line. The bouncer recognized Aria immediately, nodded, and waved them through without hesitation. Inside, they faced another security check where an officer was stationed with a metal detecting wand.

"Please place all items on the tray and stand here," the officer instructed.

The two did as they were told. After getting checked and collecting their items, the two went inside the main area. The scene was bustling with activity—the DJ was getting everyone hyped, playing recent hits. The floor was full of people dancing in groups or as a couple under strobing and swirling lights, and the bar was half full with three bartenders serving drinks.

Just as Aria reached for Tay's hand again, a strong male voice called out to her.

"Hey, Aria! How are you, ma?" A lean but dressed up young man with a drink in one hand approached them.

"Hey, Jaron," she replied, her tone less than enthusiastic. "I'm great, thanks. How's the party?"

"It's ok, but at midnight it's going to be live as hell." Jaron gaze lingered on Aria, and he drooled over her. Tay coughed loudly, drawing his attention. "Anyways, who's your friend?" Jaron asked, nodding at Tay as he took a sip of his drink.

"I'm sorry, this is Tay. I invited him since he was in town," Aria introduced as she hugged him and placed a hand on his chest.

"Hey, Tay. How are you doing?" Jaron smiled, extending his hand in greeting, but his eyes had turned cold.

"I'm good, Jaron. Thanks for asking," Tay responded with a polite smile, shaking his hand. "Well, you two have fun. I'm going to be at the bar," Tay said, removing Aria's hand and quickly weaving his way through the crowd of people standing on the edge of the dance floor as he made his way to the bar.

He found an empty seat between two girls. The bartender noticed Tay rather quickly and delivered a drink to the woman on his left and then turned to him with a warm smile.

"What can I get you, hon?" she asked, her southern accent pronounced.

"Just a rum and coke and a glass of water," Tay replied, pulling a $20 bill from his pocket.

"Coming right up," she said, taking the money and preparing his order. As Tay waited, he turned and glanced over the floor until he found Aria. He found her now laughing with a group of girls at a table on the edge of the dance floor. She seemed to be enjoying herself. He nodded his head and looked over the rest of the room.

His eyes drifted some more until they landed on Jaron, who stood in the corner near one of the speakers by the DJ's booth, surrounded by a group of guys, all eyes occasionally flicking toward Aria's group.

"Here you go," the bartender said, placing his drinks down. Tay turned to take his drink and upon lifting it up he noticed the napkin had writing on it: **Evelyn Lewis – 328 9176 at 3am.** Tay couldn't help but chuckle slightly as he pocketed the napkin. *Why not? At least she's not trying to desperately hit on me.* Just as he took a sip of his drink, Aria came over and grasped his arm.

"Hey, Tay, come dance with me."

He finished his sip and looked at her. "No. I don't want to dance." He didn't move and took another sip of his drink.

Aria tugged on his arm slightly. "Come on, Tay, just sitting here is no fun."

"Well, I'm not here to have fun tonight."

She pouted as she gripped his arm, pressing her breasts on him. "Come on, Tay." She leaned in and spoke into his ear. "Do you want to have some fun with me?" Her voice dripped in seduction, where she was teasing out an idea for more fun after the club.

Tay felt a shiver run down his spine. His hand twitched in his pocket and he felt his blood rush to areas he didn't need it to. Tay closed his eyes and took a deep breath.

This girl truly knows how to play with a man. Tay opened his eyes and turned his head, only to see Aria's face right in front of his. Their noses touched and he could feel her breath on his lips. He looked into her eyes and lost the words he was about to say. Tay slowly pulled away from her and glanced over her shoulder. He saw her friends giggling and all he could do was shake his head.

Well shit. Now they must think we are going out or something. This thought caused Tay to look back in Jaron's direction. And just like he thought, he saw him staring at them, eyes furrowed and his lips in a tight line.

Dammit. I don't have time for this headache.

"I think Jaron wants to dance with you," Tay said, eyes never leaving Jaron as he stood straight and took another sip. "He hasn't stopped looking this way."

"I know. That's why I need you," Aria confessed. Her grip tightened on Tay's arm. "Look, he and I dated a while back and he can't move on, but I'm over him."

With her tight grip, Tay was able to feel the tremble in her hands. Tay got up, finished his drink in one swallow, and placed the empty glass on the bar. He left the water bottle.

I'm going to need more alcohol later to complete this job.

Aria let his arm go and slid her hand in his, a bright smile on her face like she was on cloud nine as they walked to the dance floor. The sensation of holding hands with Aria brought a strong sense of familiarity just like at the park. Tay could have sworn he truly knew her. It felt like he knew her from a time in the past beyond that school incident. Like she was someone important to him.

There is no way that is possible. I would remember someone as beautiful as her. Tay shook his head to clear the thought as they reached the dance floor. She walked in front of Tay, raised his arm, and twirled into him with her back pressed up against him.

She leaned her head back and gazed at Tay. Her smile seemed to light up the room to him. "Ready to have some fun?" Just as she asked this, someone came up behind them.

"Hey, mind if I cut in?" a man asked as he rested a hand on Tay's shoulder.

Tay didn't have to turn to see who it was. He knew it was Jaron and he started to reply, "Sure..."

"No," Aria spoke over Tay as she nestled deeper into him. "We are dancing now. So, leave us alone please."

"Sorry, how about the next song?" Jaron asked as he walked around to look Aria in the eyes. Tay slowly tried to push Aria off him but she pulled his arm tighter and held him firm as she leaned into him even more. Tay could smell the sweet fragrance of her shampoo as it wafted into his nose and felt her butt press up against his region, getting him more excited than he should be.

"Jaron, we are over. There is no more US, and we are barely friends now. So please understand and leave me alone," Aria said gently but her eyes were firm. "You are a great guy but not the one for me."

Jaron's eyes dropped to the floor. "So, you are leaving me because you think he can do better?!!" His voice rose at the end as he pointed at Tay. His jaw was flexed and eyes narrowed as he focused on Tay.

"No, I'm no good for her either," Tay quickly responded, waving his free hand in rejection. "I'm only a friend nothing more."

"Tay." Aria stepped away and turned to him still holding his arm. Her voice light and cheerful. "I want to dance over there with my girls," Aria said, ignoring Tay's comment and Jaron's glare.

"Well, go over there," Tay said, trying to edge away and deescalate the situation. "I'm sure you and your girls will have more fun without me."

"If you won't come with me." Aria then stepped closer to Tay and spoke softly into his ear again. "I guess we can have some intimate fun right here then."

Tay coughed. "I guess I could go see what your friends were talking about earlier."

Aria smiled and pulled Tay with her. As they put some space between them and Jaron, she said to Tay, "Tay, remember, we are having fun so forget about Jaron and my dad's mission for you, because you are mine now for tonight." She leaned into his arm as they walked. "And I want to make this night a special one for both of us."

Tay shook his head. *She will never give up,* he thought to himself. So, he just went along with her. But shortly after joining Aria's friends, Tay heard a sound he could never mistake. Even with the loud music playing, a gun click stood out to him clearly.

Suddenly, the music stopped and everyone seemed to get eerily quiet.

"You can't have her," a voice came from behind Tay. Though Tay didn't feel the gun, he knew it was pointed at his head.

"Dude, I don't want her," Tay tried to explain, staying still.

"Jaron, calm down. Don't do something stupid," Aria said with a trembling voice.

"You stay out of this," Jaron snapped, pointing the gun at Aria.

"Man, you may want to point that gun away from her," Tay said calmly, his body relaxing slightly.

"Really, how bout I shove it down her throat, because if I can't have her then you sure as hell can't," Jaron said, moving closer to her with the gun still aimed at her face.

"This just isn't my day," Tay muttered. "Look, you take one more step, and you'll wake up in the hospital with your buddies over there each with a bullet in y'all leg."

"Ha ha." Jaron chuckled. "Very convincing, considering you don't have a way to stop me. Now, be a good boy and run home before I shoot you in your head." As Jaron said this, he took one more step, and just as he was about to set his foot down, Tay caught it, then pushed him back, throwing Jaron off balance. Continuing to spin while ducking, Tay swept Jaron's legs from under him. Tay stood and punched Jaron in the stomach as he fell. Jaron gasped as he hit the floor and pulled the trigger, shooting himself in the leg.

Tay quickly got up, ran to Aria, and pulled her to her friends. "Y'all run now. I will find you once I'm through." Tay ran back through the crowd that was heading for the exits and found one of the five boys that were with Jaron.

"Why are you doing this?" Tay asked, getting in a fighting stance.

"The boss orders are absolute," the boy said and charged at Tay. Just as the boy was about to get on top of him, Tay kicked the boy in the head, then continued to spin and kicked his heel into the boy's back, causing him to run into the wall. The impact was followed by a bang and a dark spot on the boy's right leg. The boy fell to the ground unconscious. Apparently, storing a gun in the front of your pants wasn't a great place to keep it if you weren't going to use it. Tay turned and scanned the rest of the group and saw one guy run for Aria and her friends while the other three came at him.

He sighed. *This is so boring. Why did this have to turn into a stereotypical club fight?*

Just then, one guy reached him with a knife in hand and slashed randomly. Tay caught his arm just as the boy was about to do a backslash and twisted his wrist. The boy screamed as he dropped the knife.

Another attacker took the chance to approach Tay from the side as he threw a flurry of punches. Tay dodged all the strikes but had to let go of the guy's wrist to do so. Tay saw an opening and punched his current attacker in the face. The boy blocked it but it was a feint, and he didn't see Tay's leg move shortly after he blocked. Tay's kick connected with the back of the boy's knee, causing it to buckle.

Tay brought his foot down; he pushed his elbow into the boy's chest. As the boy gasped in pain, Tay followed his strike up by spinning and hitting the boy in the head with his heel. The boy's face went slack and his eyes rolled to the top of his head. He fell to the floor unconscious and as he landed on the ground the gun in his front pocket went off shooting him in the leg, too.

Do all these guys have a gun in their front pocket?

Tay was tackled at his waist from behind as he thought this but held his balance. He turned slightly and drove his elbow into his attacker's spine, causing their grip to loosen. Once freed, Tay twisted and slammed his knee into the boy's head. For good measure, Tay grabbed his attacker's arm before he fell backwards and slung it over his shoulder. He pulled down as he pushed his hips back and flipped the attacker over his shoulder. He slammed onto the floor. There was another bang and crimson-red flowed from the attacker's left leg.

Are they really that dumb?

Tay found this fight to get dumber and dumber. Not once did anyone think to take out their guns and try to shoot him. Though he was grateful because that meant the only casualties would be themselves and not any bystanders.

Tay quickly looked around and spotted the last dude about to catch up to Aria. With all his might, Tay ran as fast as he could through the crowd that was still trying to squeeze through the exit to get out. Just as he was about to reach the girls, he felt a presence behind him. Tay ducked and avoided a knife that was thrown at his head. The knife continued flying to hit the last attacker's arm as he was reaching out to grab Aria. A happy happenstance but Tay would take it.

Tay rolled backwards, and in a crouched position, Tay kicked both his legs out hard, hitting the boy who threw the knife in the stomach.

He gasped and stumbled back. Tay stood up and turned to see the barrel of the gun at his nose. Quickly, Tay palm-struck it up to avoid being shot, then delivered a swift, heavy punch to the boy's stomach. He doubled over, grasped his gun too tightly as he gasped for air, causing himself to shoot his left leg. As he screamed from the pain, Tay delivered a haymaker to the side of his face and the boy went unconscious.

Finally, someone not stupid enough to forget that he got a gun.

"That's four, now time for the last one," Tay said as he spotted him with a gun to the back of one of Aria friend's head. The knife that was in his arm gone.

He must have pulled it out and thrown it down somewhere.

Expecting the girls to be cowering, Tay was surprised to see that Aria stood tall, eyes burning with fire.

Wow, she has some grit after all, Tay thought as he quickly darted in and out of the reaming crowd. Just as he got to the scene, he saw Aria about to run at the dude. Tay immediately jump kicked the gun out the guy's hand, causing the guy to look up. Tay landed between the guy and the girl and elbowed the guy in the stomach As the guy crouched over, Tay slammed his knee into the boy's head then he delivered a spinning side kick to his stomach, making the guy stagger. Tay finished him with a heel kick to the head, making the guy spin and fall hard on the floor.

Tay waited but didn't hear a sound. He rolled the guy over but didn't see a gun on his front side. Tay looked around and saw the gun he kicked a few feet away. He walked over, picked it up with a napkin, checked the chamber, and came back before he shot at the boy's leg.

The girls and boy screamed. Tay pistol whipped him, knocking the boy back unconscious.

"Tay!! Why did you do that?" Aria screamed as she walked up on Tay.

"I told Jaron that they would all have a bullet in their legs before the fight was over." Tay shrugged. "I am a man of my word."

Aria sighed. Tay placed the gun in the boy's hand and crumbled the napkin up in his fist.

"Though I have to say I didn't plan that he wouldn't shoot himself. Man, I'm rusty," Tay said more to himself as he gathered the girls and ran out.

Once outside, Tay said to Aria's friends, "You all go home." Tay grabbed Aria's hand and ran for his car. As he did, he heard an extra set of footsteps behind them. Aria did too, because the moment Tay let her hand go, she ran right while he ran left. Still hearing the footsteps after him, Tay ran deeper in the woods. Finally, he stopped and listened. After a moment, Tay couldn't hear the steps anymore.

Now this is exciting.

He stayed still until he heard a gun click. He knew then the stalker was to his front right. Tay ducked and sprang toward a clearing in the trees where he believed his pursuer to be just as he heard the gun go off. He was right in doing so. Once he made it to the clearing, he saw a figure in the shadow of the tree. Tay reached out and grabbed the hand holding the gun, pulled the person in, and punched him in the stomach. Following up with his elbow, he delivered a blow to the forehead, twisted their arm, making pursuer drop the gun and flipped the guy over his shoulder. Once the guy hit the ground, Tay punched his throat, rendering him unconscious. Then there was another shot. Tay looked around; it seemed close.

Dammit. Better find Aria and make sure she is alright. Tay got to his full height and took off toward the car.

Once he reached the car, he stopped and looked around. He noticed Aria was in the passenger seat. He continued his search. There was no one else around and no sounds were made. He carefully got in the car. Once inside, Aria immediately wrapped her arms around his neck and hugged him tightly.

"Tay. I—I was so scared." Her voice trembled.

"It is ok. We are both fine now." Tay held her and smelled her sweet fragrance, and it sparked a memory of his mom and how she liked to have floral smells for her shampoo, too. He unknowingly hugged her tighter and she buried herself in his embrace.

They stayed like that for a while. Aria being comforted by Tay and Tay basking in the familiarity he was feeling from her.

Why is it that in random moments since I met her I keep thinking I know her and she is someone important to me? Someone almost like Rin.

She pushed away from Tay, causing him to return to reality. She still held his arms and trembled slightly. "Why did they shoot at us?" she managed to ask after breathing for a while.

This caused Tay to remember the second shot he heard. "I'm not sure why? It could have just been instincts or just emotions of wanting to seem tough." Tay paused for a moment, looking Aria over to make sure she was alright.

"Hey."

"Yes." Aria looked up into Tay with eyes that said he was her safe place in this moment.

"I know this may be hard after what just happened, but did you hear that second shot?"

"Yea I heard."

"Did you hear where it came from. Did anything happen around you?"

Aria paused, not saying anything.

"Aria, are you okay?"

"Yea, just was thinking about your question and I'm sorry I don't know where it came from but it wasn't close to me, though."

Tay let out a deep sigh. His shoulders dropped and the tension in his neck eased. She was safe.

I'm so glad nothing happened to her. I don't know... Tay paused that thought. *I'm glad... Glad about what. That she isn't in danger. Tagen, get your head on straight, this is a job. She isn't Rin. And she can't replace her.*

Tay looked back at Aria. She looked so innocent yet her father was such a powerful man. It really made it hard for her not to truly know the type of person her father was.

"So, Aria, your father—did he never tell you anything about what he does for a living?" Tay asked, gently letting his arms drop from her hold.

"Told me what?" Aria sat back, looking at him. Her body was still tense as she gently hugged herself.

Tay let out a deep breath. "You will need to ask him when you get home." Tay started the car and was about to pull off.

"No, I don't want to go home, take me—"

"Like hell you aren't going home. My task is over," Tay replied sharply and with heat in his voice. This was not what he had agreed to. It was just supposed to be a night at the club. Not a shootout. Tay's hand tightened on the wheel. Even if it was an easy fight, gang fights were one of the few steps he wanted to avoid. Mr. Blackwood's words played back in his mind.

"You will see that once you set even one foot back in this world, the road to living a peaceful life is harder and more elusive than you might think."

Dammit. Did I just take that step with this? Let's get her home now and be done with this.

"Please," Aria said, her head down as she hugged herself tighter, voice breaking. "Can I please just go to your place?"

Softening his tone, he replied, "Look, your dad can protect you more than I can."

"Please, I'm scared," she said in a whisper. "I feel safer with you right now." She looked up at Tay with tears rolling down her face. Tay's heart squeezed slightly with a sense of guilt. Was he really going to let this girl go home without at least comforting her.

"I…" Tay looked out the front window, the urge to scream pushing to escape his lips. He took a deep breath and released. He leaned over and pulled out a blindfold from his glove box.

"What's that for?" Aria asked, wiping the tears from her face.

"Just put it on." Tay handed the blindfold to her.

"Ok, but why?" Aria took the blindfold cautiously then looked at Tay.

"Look, I'm not going to do anything to you. I just don't want you seeing where I live."

"Why not?"

"Truthfully, I feel like you would pop up unannounced if you knew."

"Tay, I'm not a stalker," Aria said defensively as she sniffled slightly.

"Then for my own sanity, please do this."

"Fine." She put the blindfold on then turned to Tay. "Are we good now?"

"Almost. Hold out your hands."

She held out her hands and felt something clasp around her wrists.

"What are you doing?" Aria asked as she frantically tried to pull away. But the cuffs jerked back as if they were tied to something.

"This is only to keep you from being tempted to pull off the blindfold. I will take them off once we get to my place."

"Why the hell do you have these things in your car anyway?"

"The less you know about that the better," Tay replied in a disheartened tone. Tay reached over Aria's lap and pulled the reclining lever.

"Lean back. It will take about thirty minutes to get there so just take a nap."

Reluctantly, Aria leaned back. Once she was situated and looked comfortable, Tay drove off. Traffic was light since it was so late at night. As they got on the interstate, he saw two ambulances taking the exit on the other side, likely heading to the club. After about twenty-five minutes, he finally pulled up to his house.

Parking in the garage, he got out, went to Aria's side, raised her seat, and undid the handcuffs. He stowed the handcuffs and helped her get out of the car, making sure she didn't try to remove the blindfold. He guided her, telling her where to step as they walked through the house. He took her to the guest room. Once inside, he let her hands go and went to lock the door as Aria took off the blindfold.

Aria looked around the room just as Tay turned from the door. After she took in everything, she went to sit on the sofa.

"Tay, will you come sit beside me?" Aria said, tapping the space beside her. Tay leaned against the door, looking her over.

"Stand up and turn around." Tay didn't move, looking Aria in the eye.

"What? Don't trust me?" Aria stood up.

"I was taught trust no one even if you want to." Tay twirled his finger around in a circular motion. Aria turned around slowly as Tay looked her over.

"You're good. Well, go watch tv or something. Once you have calmed down, I will take you to your parents," Tay said as he turned back to the door.

"How about we talk?" Aria started quickly before Tay could walk out. "I still don't know much about you. And I would appreciate it if you didn't leave me alone just yet."

"It is fine. There's no one but us here. You don't have to be afraid," Tay answered, trying to not stay in the room. Even without what his father taught him about always being vigilant, he could tell she wanted him, and that strong feeling made him uncomfortable.

"Come on, let's play truth or dare," she suggested teasingly.

"What do I look like? A kid?" he replied nonchalantly.

"Sorry." Her voice sounded meek. "I guess I'm still trying to get over the shock of having a gun to my face." Her voice shook, and her eyes watered.

She is good, Tay thought to himself. *She really knows how to play on the heartstrings to get others to do what she wants.* Tay moved to her and laid a hand on her shoulder.

"Will you be okay?"

"Yea, but I just want to stay here tonight. Is that okay?"

"Call your dad and ask him," Tay replied exhaustedly.

"Sure." Aria quickly pulled out her phone, wiped her eyes, and dialed her house phone.

"Hi, Dad...I'm good...He's here...That's why I am calling... Thanks, Dad...Love you, too."

Based on the flow and how quickly the conversation went, Tay could surmise the results.

"Ok, I will go get my stuff and you sleep in here."

"Will you stay in the room with me?"

"Hell no. I am not your man, just a bodyguard of a very powerful man," Tay replied, annoyed.

"Please, just until I calm down."

"No means no. Now stay here. I need to clean up since you are here."

"Why don't I help?"

"Why do you insist on following me around?" His patience was wearing thin.

"Because I am scared to be alone!" she yelled, tears flowing again. "You are my only comfort right now. Please don't abandon me."

There was a split-second pause. Tay was taken aback by her outburst. He stood there, looking Aria straight in the eyes. He saw fear, insecurity, and helplessness in her. He knew he couldn't leave her like this. But there was something else being covered by those emotions. The longer he looked, the more he felt he had seen those eyes before.

"Fine, I will stay only until you fall asleep," Tay said, sounding defeated. He turned to go clean his room and felt Aria half tackle-hug him from behind.

"Thank you," she whispered, holding onto him for a while. Tay turned around and held her close for a few minutes.

"Now let me go so I can go clean up," Tay said gently, pushing her away but still holding her shoulders. Though she held her head down, he could still see the tears rolling down her face. Unconsciously, he wiped them away with his thumb. He lifted her head up and looked into her eyes once again. They seemed like jewels shining in the sun, as if they found a new hope.

Tay had to pull himself away for his heart raced. He turned around and continued the walk to his bedroom. Thoughts clouded his mind as he walked the short distance. Why did all this happen? How did it turn into this? Wasn't he just depressed about his ex-girlfriend earlier? *Why does Aria make me feel relaxed and comfortable when she is around? How does Mr. Blackwood know my father?* Questions filled his mind so quickly that he walked in a daze to the point he didn't hear Aria walking behind him. Or rather she walked in step with him and just outside of his personal area to where he couldn't notice her. Tay walked into his room and immediately turned on his lights and saw Aria as he turned to close the door.

"Whoa!" He jumped back slightly. "What are you ... Never mind," Tay said. Somehow, he knew he wouldn't be able to win. "Just sit on the bed while I clean up."

"No, I'm here to help," Aria said as she began picking up Tay's clothes from last night.

Tay shook his head while slightly, smiling. *I guess it isn't too bad to have her help me around the house,* Tay thought as he went to make his bed. But his smile slipped as he remembered how Rin used to help him clean up their old apartment. Without another word, he kept cleaning doing his best to ignore Aria across the room.

Once they finished straightening up, Tay's stomach reminded him all he had was half of a burger, some fries, and some drinks.

"Hey, stay here. I will cook something for dinner." He turned to walk out then stopped. "Actually, why don't you go take a shower and relax. Here, let me show you where the towels are," Tay suggested before he turned to walk out the door. Aria clasped his hand, stopping him.

"Can I just stay with you and watch you cook?"

"Come on, my place is…" Tay faced her and was once again transfixed by her eyes. He couldn't understand why he wanted to be closer to her when he barely knew her. Yet there it was—the temptation to pull her in and hold her surged within him, but he resisted.

"What would you like to eat?" he asked, turning away embarrassed and shocked at how vulnerable and comfortable he felt with her.

"Hmm… it doesn't matter," Aria replied, squeezing his hand as they walked to the kitchen.

"Though I would like to help you cook," she added teasingly.

"Okay," Tay agreed.

The two went into the kitchen and no matter what, she stayed by his side, never letting go of his hand.

"You know it will be sort of hard to operate when you are so close," Tay stated as he tried to free his hand while keeping her from hitting the counter as he reached for a pot.

"Sorry, Tay," she said with a playful smile as she purposely bumped into him. Tay bumped into the counter and looked at her returning the smile. "So, how can I help?"

"Well, for starters, how about you decide what you'd like to eat," Tay said as he placed the pot on the stove and opened the cabinet, still holding Aria's hand.

"How about greens, corn, and chicken?"

"Are you going to give me room to cook then?" Tay asked, holding up their joined hands. Aria snuggled closer to him, bringing her face almost level with his. Her eyes sparkled with happiness. It was then that Tay realized a portion of what he had seen before in her eyes.

Can such a feeling be so strong and look so pure? he thought to himself. He couldn't take his eyes off her now. "Hey, do you truly want to eat?" His voice soft and calm, with his free hand he stroked her cheek.

"No. It was your suggestion, so I didn't turn it down."

"Well, I got another idea." Tay's heart began beating faster.

"And what would that be?"

"Follow me," Tay said as they walked out of the kitchen. Now that he was more aware of her, he realized just how natural it felt to have her hand in his, as if he did this many times before. The two went back to the bedroom and they finally dropped hands.

"Lay down on your stomach."

"Hold on. I'm." Aria's voice shook, and she stepped back a little with her hands covering her mouth. "I'm not ready for that!"

"Do you trust me?" Tay asked gently as he stood in front of her looking into her eyes.

"Yes," Aria whispered, her eyes searching his.

"Then just believe in me for now. I promise I won't hurt you." He took both her hands in his and led her to the bed. She cautiously laid down on her stomach and felt Tay straddle over her. He then whispered into her right ear. "Hope you enjoy this. It has been a while since I last did something like this."

Tay then massaged her neck and shoulders— applying enough pressure for her to feel it but not too much to where it hurt.

"You are really good…" A soft moan escaped her lips as she let herself relax from the amazing experience she was having.

"Glad this is helping you relax," Tay said as he continued massaging the tension out of her body.

This sensation…

Tay couldn't shake it and fell into a trance. His hands moved without him thinking and he massaged one area below her shoulder blade and Aria let out a loud moan.

"Damn, Tay… This is amazing," she said in between gasps. Tay didn't reply but his hands kept moving. He went from one spot to the next, hitting zones on her body that released tension and loosened her body.

Why does it feel like I used to do this all the time to her? It was like he was reliving a memory from the past. Suddenly, Tay looked up as he thought he saw a white figure pass by in the corner of his eye.

"Mo—" Tay started as Aria moaned again.

What was I about to say? Did I really just think my mom was about to walk in.

Just then, Aria spoke up as Tay's hands hadn't stopped moving.

"When and where did you learn to do this? It's…so…good. You could work as a massage therapist."

Tay chuckled. "Thanks. Honestly, I don't really remember when I learned to do this. My experience came from when I gave my girlfriend and mom…" Tay suddenly froze, his heart in his throat and teeth clenched.

That was when it felt like that time when I gave my sister a massage so that I could give mom a better one. Mom had walked in on us. Then all Tay could think of was his mother. *They stole my mom from me.* Tay let the memories of his mother play through his mind. He hadn't thought of her in a while because every time he did he couldn't help but cry.

Aria felt his hands shiver and something wet dropped on her back a few times. She quickly realized it was tears.

"Tay? Are you okay?" she asked carefully. There was no reply.

She felt Tay get up and slide off the bed. He started walking to the bedroom door.

"Tay? Tay! What is wrong?" Aria asked urgently as she slid off the bed to follow him. Tay's mind had reverted to the time when his mother was still alive. He could feel her skin in his hands, the smell of peaches and floral wafting from her hair, the gentle sound of her laughing at something on TV.

Then.

The emptiness of no longer having her around to protect and care for him. The feelings he experienced from losing not only her but his family. He was too young to know what to do or where to go; all he felt was a sense of being lost. Being given to others to take care of him but only being seen as a burden. His heart grew heavy and beat rapidly in his chest. His mind thought only on those times and the emotions he felt. Until the only feeling left was the pain of rage, of knowing someone took his family from him. And the encompassing resolve to know that he would see them burn.

While his mind played these events over and over, he walked through the house in a trance. He entered the room across from the guest room. He had turned this room into his personal gym. There was a standing punching bag along the left wall.

Without being aware, Tay stood before it and stared at it.

"Tay?" Aria asked cautiously as she peeked in. Just then he swung hard at the stand and it swayed left and right. And just before it settled, he began to kick, punch, elbow, and knee the bag. He threw all he had at it, not leaving any emotion behind. His rage, his fear, his sadness, his pain. He threw them all at the bag. The force he applied with each strike left indents in the bag as it swayed. But his eyes flooded with tears.

"He killed her," he mumbled through clenched teeth. He was remembering how his mother died right in front of him and his father. The more he remembered, the more force he used. He screamed as he delivered a powerful kick that caused the bag to tip over and slide a few feet before stopping against the wall. Tay stood there breathing heavily. Then Tay came to himself. He looked around to see where he was and once he realized the punching bag was laying sideways by the wall, he let out a defeated sigh and closed his eyes.

Shit, I did it again.

There was a thump behind him. He quickly turned in the direction of the sound, narrowed, and stood in a fighting stance. But the only thing he saw was Aria sitting on her butt. She looked, as if she saw a monster. Shaking his head, he walked over to her, took a knee, and held out a hand.

"It will be okay, and I am sorry," he said, his voice taking on a soothing tone.

Hesitantly, she took his hand and got up, slightly shaking but not saying a word. Tay knew then that he had to take her home. He was so vulnerable with her that he let his guard down. This girl that he thought he knew nothing about felt so familiar to him. She brought emotions out of him that he had kept hidden from most without even trying.

I need to figure out why I'm so relaxed with her. But for now. He looked at her state again and clenched his teeth. He had just scared another person away.

"Come on, it is time I take you home." He placed a hand on her back to steady her but she flinched at his touch.

Damn , fucked up again. And she was practical throwing herself at me. This wasn't the first time that he let his emotions take control in front of someone. But he swore to himself that he would only ever let that happen when he was alone after how he traumatized one of his dear friends. Holding her hand, he led her back to the guest room. Once there, he gathered her belongings and all she did was stand there dazed, unmoving like a zombie.

After making sure he had everything, he took her hand once more and tried to place a hand on her back again. This time she didn't react. He blindfolded her again, walked her to the garage, and into the car. He drove off once they were settled.

After driving for a while, Aria moved enough to feel the cuffs tug at her wrist. That seemed to bring her back to the present. She tugged again harder this time. She looked around and realized all she saw was darkness.

"Umm? Tay? Tay?! Where are you? Help me! Please help me!!" she shouted as she tried to tug even harder, attempting to stand in the seat.

Tay quickly pulled over to the side of the highway and reached over and placed a hand on her hands.

"Aria it's me. Calm down, you are in my car," Tay replied in a calm voice, trying to soothe her.

"Where are we?" Aria asked, voice still high and breaths came in quick gasps.

"On the highway," Tay answered as he reached and pulled the blindfold off her and uncuffed her hands. "We are almost to your house."

"Huh, but why? My dad told me I could stay," Aria said, puzzled as she blinked and focused on Tay.

What is wrong with her? Tay wondered. "Aria, tell me, what is the last thing you remember."

"Um..." She froze and looked at the roof of the car as she thought. "We were going to cook dinner but then you got an idea." Aria's eyes lit up. "Oh, yea, you were giving me the best massage of my life." She looked around like she was trying to determine where they were at from the landmarks. "So how did we get here?"

Did she get amnesia? Or is she just playing? He could not tell. "Something…" Tay swallowed, looking around for the words to say. "I had something come up and I have to take you home. Sorry," Tay apologized as he settled back in his seat and started driving again. Aria sat there in silence for the rest of the drive. Once they pulled up to the gate, Tay parked and went around to let Aria out. She got out with her things and looked at Tay, her eyes red.

"Well, I had a great time and I'm sorry that we couldn't enjoy the rest of the night together," Aria said, her eyes becoming glossy.

Tay looked away, feeling disappointed he messed up not only his night but hers as well. "Yea. I'm sorry, too. Maybe another time then."

"Sure, well. Goodnight," Aria said weakly. She walked closer to Tay, but he didn't react. She got on her toes and kissed his cheek. This caused Tay to look at her again but not with eyes of disdain. He stared at her, searching again for that sense of familiarity and comfort. Just that one kiss made him long to please like he would have done for Rin.

She smiled softly, wiped her eyes, and walked up to the gate. Once she was at the gate, she looked back at him, waved, and then walked in.

Tay stood there in a daze. He wanted to run after her and say he was sorry again and tell her that he would definitely make it up, but he knew he would only be doing it out of pity. Teeth clenched, he closed the passenger door, walked to the driver side, got in, and drove off.

He had been speeding a lot today, and this time he did it to vent his rage, but the drive was too short to quell the emotions swirling inside him. Once he got inside his house, he went straight to his room, threw his stuff on the dresser, and laid on the bed. He screamed into his pillow. A day that started horribly just had to end horribly as well. Just his luck.

"What's the deal with today?" Tay asked as he rolled onto his back and looked blankly at the ceiling. The events of the day played over in his mind. He thought about things he could have done differently, especially how he could have handled the situation at his home with Aria. As he replayed the whole day for the third time, he finally remembered the number he was given.

Might as well, he thought. Pulling the napkin out of his pocket, he looked it over.

Call at three, it said. Looking at his clock, he saw it read 3:02 am. "Well can't hurt to try." He got up, went to his dresser, grabbed his phone, and called. On the fourth ring, she answered.

"Hello." Her voice was lively and sweet.

"Hi." His voice cracked slightly. "Hi, this is Tay. Is this Evelyn?" Tay asked as his face heated up. There was a soft chuckle on the other side.

"Yes it is."

"Hey. Um, I'm the guy from the bar tonight." Tay smiled softly and rubbed the back of his neck.

"Oh. Hey, hon." Her voice rose and he heard the surprise in her voice. "I'm sorry it took so long to answer." Tay heard a door swing close and keys placed down. "I just got home."

"It's cool." Tay went and sat on his bed. "So, what are you up to?"

Instantly, he wanted to face palm himself.

Idiot, she just told you what she was up to. Just getting home.

"Nothing now, just about to relax." She paused for a moment. "Though I am glad I'm still alive."

"Yea." Tay grimaced. "Sorry about that."

"What do you have to be sorry about? It isn't your fault." There was the sound of water running in the background.

"Thanks for saying that. I feel like I have been saying sorry a lot today."

"That is no problem."

The two held the phone to their ear not saying anything. After a little while, Evelyn spoke up.

"So, Tay."

"Yea."

"Not to cut this conversation short—but I was wondering can we meet up later and talk in person?"

Tay's eyebrows shot up. He pulled his phone away from his ear and looked at it before placing it back.

"Would that be ok?" Her voice seemed to shake slightly.

"Sure, I'm down. When and where?" Tay asked as his voice rose slightly, sitting up straighter.

"How about the restaurant off of Lauren and Scott street round noon?"

Tay paused to think of what was at that spot. "Oh—that is a nice spot. Alright I will be there." A broad smile spread across his face.

"Alright, see you then. Goodnight, hon."

"Yea. You, too." Tay hung up and set his phone down.

"Yes!" he shouted as he threw his fist up in the air and collapsed backwards onto his bed.

He thought of the sorrow of Rin breaking up with him, the struggles of the rest of the day in dealing with the Blackwoods and Aria, then the club fight, and the incident at his home with Aria. Finally, something normal and nice. At least now his day didn't have to end on a sour note. He changed clothes, laid back in bed, finally relaxed, and went to sleep still smiling as he awaited the sun to rise again.

He woke up to his phone ringing. Squinting at the clock, he saw it was 10:30 am. Yawning, he sat up and stretched and looked at his phone still vibrating on the nightstand. He picked it up and saw it was from a number he didn't recognize. He put the phone down and let the call go to voicemail, thinking they wouldn't leave a message. But his phone buzzed again. A message. He picked the phone back up and he had four new voicemails. He rubbed his eyes in disbelief, he looked again. Yep, it was four new messages from last night. He couldn't think of who would call him so late and expected him to answer. He opened the first message and put it on speakerphone as he got up to take a shower.

"Hi, Tay. I know it's late, but I had to call…Oh this is Aria. Um…I just wanted to say thanks for a great night. I had fun and it meant a lot to me. Maybe… Maybe we can hang out again some time. I would really like that. Well…Um, I guess will talk to you later." Her voice quivered at the end and there was some kind of crinkling noise. It reminded Tay of paper though it was so soft he thought he imagined it.

"Well, didn't expect her to call me. Not sure if I want to hang out with her again either way but… Maybe I will give her a chance. But for now, I have a so-called date to get ready for."

The next message started playing as he turned on the shower and undressed.

"Hi this is Aria again. I really want to hear your voice tonight if that's ok. So, call me soon." This time, Tay definitely heard the quiver in her voice and there was the crinkling noise again.

"Why is she calling me? Is she that desperate to be with me. And what the hell is that noise at the end of each call?" Tay muttered as he stepped into the shower and began washing himself.

The final message began to play. "Tay…" She was crying now. "Pl—pl—please call me soon. I'm sorry if I frightened you." She sniffed and this time Tay distinctly heard it. The noise sounded like papers being crinkled or shuffled. "I just didn't know how to act. I got weak cause I didn't have my medicine today. And I end up having these episodes where I zone out then have a slight loss of memory. So please forgive me. Give me a call soon." Her voice seemed frantic and had an odd echo unlike the other messages.

But all Tay could think of was, *And here I thought I had frightened her. And this desperation is such a turn off.* He rinsed off, turned off the water, and stepped out to dry himself off.

"Tay…give me a call," she said, sniffing.

"Okay that's enough," Tay said as he started deleting her messages without fully listening to the last one.

"Did she really just write all of these down last night to try and get sympathy from me or something?" Once done, he finished drying off and put on lotion before walking to his closet.

"Well now that that is done, what should I wear? The restaurant she was talking about is sort of high class, but I don't want to be too fancy for a first meet up. So, maybe I should dress just business casual." With that, he looked at his button-down shirts, slacks, and shoes and put something together. Now that he was fully dressed, he gathered his wallet, keys and phone, and headed out the door. He whistled as the garage door rolled up. He got into his car, started it, and was about to drive off when his phone rang. He answered it without looking.

"Hello," he said just as he pulled out his driveway.

"Tay!! I finally got through to you," Aria said excitedly but there was something underneath her excitement and her breathing was labored. Tay barely heard it so he ignored it, trying not to imagine what she was doing.

He instead rolled his eyes, his patience for her dwindled even further. "Look, Aria, I'm busy now. I really don't have time for this," he said, his irritation evident.

"It's okay," she replied quickly, her voice wavered as she spoke. "Well, I won't hold you up, but my dad wants to talk to you first."

"Hold on…" was all he could say before he heard Mr. Blackwood's voice.

"Tay?"

"Yes, sir," he replied, trying to be as polite as possible.

"How are you doing, son?"

"I'm great, sir. And you?"

"That's good, good." There was a slight pause and Tay felt something was weird about the way Mr. Blackwood spoke. The confidence behind his voice wasn't as strong today.

Did he catch a cold or something?

"Well, I would like to thank you again for taking care of my daughter and her friends last night. I truly appreciate that you kept them safe."

"It was no problem," he answered, but something in the way Mr. Blackwood spoke made Tay feel he wasn't calling to just say thanks.

"Well, look, I know I said that I wouldn't bother you after that, but there is one small task I would like for you to do for me." Tay's face crinkled up and, in that moment, he was grateful they were having a phone conversation and not talking face-to-face.

"Sir, I greatly appreciate you for considering me, but I will have to pass on this one," he said, keeping his tone as respectful as he could.

"Oh, and why is that?" Tay was confused by the question. Didn't they already have a conversation about this before.

Is Mr. Blackwood really so forgetful? Tay thought. This made Tay feel uneasy about this call. He knew in the world Mr. Blackwood lived in, your word was your bond and if you forget something like a promise then that was beyond disrespectful and could start a war.

"I think…" Tay's instinct pulled at him not to give the full truth. Something about this conversation didn't seem to sit right in his gut. "I found a path that will give me the life that I want," Tay answered cautiously.

"Really? Well then, best of luck to you," Mr. Blackwood said, his voice sounding genuine and warm.

"Thank you, sir." The sudden warmth made Tay even more guarded. "Well, sir, I have to go now."

"Okay then, son. You take care now." Mr. Blackwood hung up.

What is this feeling of uneasiness in me? Tay thought as he continued driving to the restaurant. He tried to push the call out of his mind and focus on the date he was about to have.

Then it hit him.

Am I uneasy because of this date? Am I truly doing the right thing? Shouldn't I take more time to heal? The thoughts kept coming, reminding him that he was just dumped yesterday. He had even turned down another girl who wanted to go out with him because of the breakup. Now, here he was, heading to a restaurant for a date with a girl he had barely spoken to beyond giving her his drink order.

Having arrived at the restaurant, he parked his car. He felt his heart start to beat faster as he stared at the front door. He knew he still longed for Rin, but he also knew if he didn't do this, he would never get over her and he would not be able to find the happiness he desired.

I need this date to turn out good. He unconsciously added more pressure to himself and his date. He rubbed his palms, feeling the sweat building, took two deep breaths, and calmed himself.

Once settled, he got out of the car and entered the restaurant. The moment he walked through the doors, their eyes met. She stood up as he walked to the table. Tay noticed she was shorter than him, and if he had to guess, she may be about 5'2" with umber skin, which shocked him because due to the club lights, he envisioned her having a slightly darker complexion.

Her brown hair was styled in elegant, voluminous waves that cascaded down her back. The top section of her hair was pulled back and secured with a hair clip, which allowed him to see her glowing smile and honey-brown eyes.

As he walked closer, he took notice of her outfit. She wore a sleek, white blouse with a subtle satin finish, the sleeves were held up by buttoned straps. The blouse was paired with a high-waisted, dark navy skirt that stopped just above her knees, accentuating her wide hips and full butt. The skirt also revealed her strong, defined calves. She completed the outfit with black pumps, adding a classic touch.

Once he reached the table, she extended her hand, causing her slim, silver watch to jangle. Instead of shaking it, Tay gently embraced her, as if he would a friend, trying to make the meeting feel more casual before taking his seat. Evelyn was perplexed for a moment but then hugged him back. They broke apart and she motioned to the seats

"So, how is your day going so far?" Evelyn asked, sitting back down, her cheeks flushed from the unexpected hug.

"Honestly, I just woke up. So it is just getting started. And you?" Tay replied, locking eyes with her and giving a warm smile.

"Mine is okay," she said, her voice softening.

"Hmm. Did you order yet?" Tay asked, glancing around the elegant restaurant.

"No, I was just seated."

"Ok, well, choose anything you want. I am buying," Tay stated, picking up the menu and scanning it quickly.

"Oh, you don't have to. Really," Evelyn insisted, her blush deepening as she reached for her menu.

"No, it's no problem. I would be honored to cover the bill." He looked up from his menu at Evelyn.

"But why is your day just okay?" Just then, the waitress approached their table.

"Hi, my name is Taylor, and I will be your server today. What may I get y'all to drink?" Taylor smiled, her eyes bright and welcoming.

"Water with lemon for me," Tay said, giving her a quick nod before returning his attention to the menu.

Evelyn turned to Taylor and answered, "Raspberry tea for me, thanks." She then looked back at Tay, her eyes narrowing slightly, as if trying to read him.

"I will get that right out. Would you like to go ahead and order an appetizer?" Taylor asked. She took out her pen and notepad, ready to take their orders.

Tay glanced at Taylor. "Honey barbecue wings with bleu cheese and ranch, please," he said, smiling gently at her, then looked around the restaurant again before glancing back at his menu.

"I'll take the spinach and artichoke dip, please," Evelyn added, her voice steady.

"Okay, I'll be back shortly," Taylor said.

As Taylor walked away, Evelyn sighed softly. "My day was just okay because the club laid me off. Now, I'm looking for a new second job," she confessed, her tone tinged with frustration.

"Sorry to hear that," Tay said, genuinely empathetic as he looked up, noticing the way she studied him.

"It's cool. Other than that, my day's going well," Evelyn said, trying to keep her tone light.

Taylor returned with the drinks. "Here's your raspberry tea and your water with lemon," she said, placing the drinks down carefully.

"Thanks," they both said in unison. This caused the two to chuckle softly.

Taylor waited for them to settle down, smiling at their interaction. "So, are you two ready to order?" she asked, taking out her notepad.

"Yes. I'll have the chicken alfredo with a side salad," Evelyn said, sliding her menu to Taylor.

"The primavera chicken with light sauce," Tay added, handing his menu to Taylor after she finished writing down their orders.

"Okay, I'll have your wings and dip out soon," Taylor said before walking away.

Evelyn looked at Tay, her eyes studying him once more as if trying to solve a puzzle. Tay didn't notice as he scanned the restaurant for the third time, taking in the elegant décor and the bustling atmosphere.

"What are you doing?" Evelyn asked after taking a sip of her tea, her curiosity getting the better of her.

Tay saw the inquisitive look in her eyes and decided to give her his full attention. "What do you mean?"

"You're looking around this place like you're on the lookout for something or someone," Evelyn observed, her brow furrowed slightly.

Tay smiled apologetically. "It's just a habit. I always like to know who's coming and going. Sorry if it seemed rude."

Evelyn dropped her shoulders and let out a soft sigh, understanding dawning on her face. "No, it's okay. I was just curious." She chuckled slightly. "You just had me a bit on edge there."

"Oh." Tay scratched behind his ear as he looked down. "I'm sorry about that."

Taylor then returned with the appetizers. "Here you go, and your food will be out shortly."

"Thanks," Evelyn said while Taylor placed her dip and chips in front of her. Once Tay's wings were in front of him, Taylor looked at the two of them.

"Is there anything else I can get you at the moment?"

"No. I believe we are good for the moment. Thank you, Taylor," Tay replied with a slight nod. Taylor nodded back and walked away. Tay felt uneasy and looked back at Evelyn. Her eyes gazed at him as if measuring his every movement.

"So, what else you do besides work at the club?" Tay said, trying to change the mood.

"Oh, I work as a supervisor at Compass International Bank," Evelyn replied nonchalantly as she placed her napkin in her lap.

Tay stopped halfway into a bite of one of his wings when he heard that. From what he heard of before bankers, especially the supervisors, they made good money. They rarely, if ever, had a second job. Hence, why he stopped eating and looked at her with a raised eyebrow midway to taking a bite.

He looked at her and she looked back at him. The sight before her caused her to almost snort with laughter. She quickly covered her mouth and turned away as she tried her best to muffle her laughter.

Tay looked down at his wing and thought of how he must have looked to her in that moment. He chuckled at first but her laughter made him want to laugh even more yet he steepled his fingers and kept a slight scowl on his face as he stared at her. Despite his scowl, he liked the fact he could make her laugh.

After she collected herself, Tay relaxed his posture. "You have a great smile and laugh." This made her cheeks glow a rosy color and she looked down.

"Thanks."

"It's no problem. But now I'm curious. If you work there, why work at the club, too?"

"The club is mainly for connections. And mixing drinks has always been a hobby of mine." Evelyn took a sip of her drink, smiling. "Plus, it's fun. You get to meet all sort of interesting people." Evelyn gazed pointedly at Tay.

Being labeled as an interesting person made him cough slightly. He put his second wing down and used one hand to hide his mouth as he coughed before he continued chewing, all the while he looked away from Evelyn. Evelyn smiled as Tay glanced at her from the corner of his eye. The smile she wore was so bright to him and brought him so much joy to see. He didn't realize it, but he smiled softly. After he finished his bite, he stated, "Seems you really enjoyed working at the club."

"I do. It lightens my day after I worked hard. It's almost like a form of stress relief."

"Stress relief, huh? I guess everyone has a different way of finding relaxation. So, what is your favorite drink to mix?" Tay asked, genuinely interested as he continued eating his wings.

"Oh, definitely! I enjoy watching how the drinks I make blend together and seeing the customers' reaction at times. As for my favorite to mix." She sat back, crossed one arm over her stomach, rested the other elbow on that arm, and tapped the corner of her lips. This caused Tay to notice the slight red tint on her lips and how full they were. "Well, I do like the classics with a little twist. My favorite would have to be lavender gin and tonic. It is simple, but the lavender gives it a unique flavor. Not to mention the lavender flower on top makes it look cute," she answered, her eyes lighting up as she talked about her passion.

"That sounds like an interesting drink. I will have to try it sometime soon," Tay said as he wiped his face having finished his last wing. He leaned back in his seat and asked, "So, any other hobbies?"

Evelyn picked up her napkin and dabbed her lips as she finished chewing. She set her napkin back down and she answered, "Well, I enjoy hiking, reading, and video games in my free time. It helps me to get a break from the routine and the hustle of the day-to-day, and even a break from reality." She took a sip of her drink. "What about you? What all do you do? And what are your hobbies?"

"I'm a personal trainer and a martial arts instructor."

"Hmm," she said, eyebrows raised, hand in front of her mouth as she finished chewing. "That sounds like a lot of work. What type of martial art do you teach?"

"I teach Taekwondo along with some Brazilian Jiu-jitsu. It is truly enjoyable and the flexibility along with the agility that you learn with it comes in handy."

"Oh, really. Well, maybe you can give me a couple of lessons some time."

"Sure. Just let me know when and I will look out for you to join my class," Tay said as he took a sip of his water.

Evelyn looked at him. "Well, I was thinking more of a private lesson," she said softly as she took another bite of her dip. Tay choked on his water and coughed. He used the clean side of his napkin and wiped his lips as he coughed to clear his throat. Evelyn wiped the edge of her mouth and looked at Tay in a seductive manner.

"Umm. Www-e-ll," Tay stuttered. He cleared his throat with a soft grunt.

Evelyn started laughing. "Calm down, Tay. I'm joking."

Tay chuckled. "Oh, okay."

"For now, anyways," Evelyn whispered, taking another sip of her drink.

"Huh?" Tay asked.

"Nothing. So, what are some of your other hobbies?" Evelyn asked to keep the conversation going.

"Other than that, I enjoy reading, biking, and video games, too. I haven't really tried hiking. I might be up for trying if you are willing to show me some of the trails that you frequent," Tay suggested.

"We can definitely make an arrangement for that," Evelyn replied with a smile.

Taylor returned with their food. "Here is your chicken alfredo." She placed the plate in front of Evelyn. "And here is your primavera chicken. Would either of you care for some cheese."

"Yes, please," they both replied in unison again. This time instead of laughing, they stared at each other, blushing slightly. Taylor smiled and started shredding cheese over Evelyn's plate first then Tay's. She then gathered their other plates before she asked, "Anything else you would like?"

"Just two refills, and that will be all," Evelyn said to her with a smile.

"Sure thing. Well, you two enjoy."

With that, Taylor walked away. Tay looked toward Evelyn. "Would you like me to say grace, or would you?"

"You can," she answered.

Tay blessed their food, and they started eating, continuing the conversation. They learned more about each other and enjoyed each other's company. *Maybe this can work,* Tay thought as they were halfway into the meal. Tay felt a weight settle in his stomach. He looked up to find Evelyn studying him. The thought of Rin surfaced, and he wondered if he should tell Evelyn about his past.

Evelyn noticed the focus on Tay's face and his presence seemed to be down than before as she took another sip of her drink. She set the glass down. "Tay, what's wrong?" she asked.

Tay wiped his mouth with his napkin and looked at Evelyn, taking a small breath. "Can I tell you something personal?"

Evelyn leaned forward slightly, her voice soft and comforting. "Sure, I'm listening."

"Look, I am truly enjoying my time with you. You are an amazing person from what we have talked about so far. But I feel I need to be honest about something."

Evelyn gazed at him, her eyes darting to look into one of his eyes then the other, as if searching for something. "Okay, I'm not here to judge. I'm here to get to know you," she replied, reaching across the table and grasping his hand.

The way she held his hand made Tay feel comfort and even more guilt at what he was about to say.

"Okay." Tay took a deep breath. "I was dumped yesterday, and I'm still somewhat fixing myself from it." Evelyn still held his hand and looked into his eyes. "I don't want you to think that you are a rebound date, but I had to let you know that. Having you here is a balm to me. I am enjoying getting to know you and would love to know more. That is the truth. I just had to let you know."

Evelyn placed her other hand on top of Tay's hand that she was holding. And she smiled. "Honestly, Tay, I'm happy that is what you wanted to tell me. I truthfully thought that you were about to say that you and the girl from last night were dating and that you only came out with me to get a side chick."

Tay flinched slightly. "I would never do anything like that. And I was only with that girl from last night because her father asked me to escort her." His voice was frantic.

Evelyn chuckled. "I can tell from how you are being open with me," she said, her voice light and joyful. "Though I have to say she really wanted you. I'm sure if you were to give her the time of day, she would be in heaven," Evelyn teased.

"Please don't joke about that. Her clinginess is so bothersome to me. I even told her to stop, but she refused and that is how I got tasked with being her escort," Tay said, sighing with exasperation.

"Calm down, Tay." Evelyn tapped on his hand gently to calm him down. "Hey, can I tell you something?" Her voice dropped slightly.

"Yeah. What's up?" Tay said cautiously.

"I also had a breakup last week." Evelyn looked at Tay, her eyes seemed to lose their shine a little. Tay could see that the breakup was still affecting her. "So, when I gave you my number I was honestly not expecting you to give me a call. I mean, you are so handsome that I thought you were out of my league. The reason I wanted to get off the phone last night was because I was in shock and I couldn't think of what to say, so I just dove straight to the main point."

"Well, thank you for being honest with me. Also, I don't think I look that good. Though, you are beautiful."

Evelyn slightly turned her head away and withdrew her hands but Tay still noticed the soft warmth blooming across her golden-brown cheeks and the way she bit back her smile. "Well, thank you," she said, looking down then she looked back up at him with a broad smile on her face. "Well, let's finish eating before the food gets cold."

"Yeah," Tay replied, happy they both were able to be honest with each other and there was no weird tension between them. They continued eating and made small talk, even laughing at each other's comments.

When Taylor brought out the bill, Tay paid it, but Evelyn left the tip. They got up and walked to the door.

"Well, I had a good time." Evelyn smiled, taking his hand as they walked out the door.

"Me, too." There was a slight pause and Tay said, "Umm, Evelyn." His voice shook slightly.

"Call me Lyn."

"Ok. Lyn. Can we…" Tay cleared his throat. "I mean would you like to hang out again some other time?"

"Definitely," she responded instantly. She walked closer to him and wrapped her hand around his arm.

"Sweet. Ok, I will call you later on tonight."

"Looking forward to it," she said as she inched in again. "Well, here's my car."

"Alright, talk to you later," Tay said as he turned toward her. Their faces were centimeters apart. They stood there just gazing into each other's eyes. Tay let go of her hand, pulled her in, and hugged her. But the moment he let go to walk away, she placed her hands on his cheeks. She stared at him and brought his lips to hers. They kissed slowly. It was a gentle feeling, and as they pulled apart the warmth remained on his lips.

"See you." Evelyn quickly got into her car, started it, and drove off. Tay followed her with his eyes. Once she was out the parking lot, he quickly walked to his car. He got in, started his car but just sat there with his hands on the wheel.

"Wha… What… What was that?" he said as he gripped the wheel. "Was that for real? Did she just kiss me?" He pinched his cheek. "Ouch!!!" he exclaimed. He knew then that it wasn't a dream. "Yes!! Oh, hell yes!!!" He smiled brightly. He felt his phone's vibration against his leg as it rang. He took it out, silenced it without a glance, then placed the phone into the cupholder.

"Please, God, don't let this be a test. She feels like the one I need in my life. I just want to live normal and be happy," Tay prayed, looking up at the clear sky. He put his car in drive and drove off, a smile gracing his face and his heart feeling light. The date made yesterday feel like it was just a bad dream.

Tay pulled up to the gym, still light from the date with Evelyn. He replayed the lunch date, thinking of how they talked about their interests, their friends and family, and even their troubles. And through it all, she seemed to be very understanding and looked at him like a normal person. Tay touched his lips, still feeling the lingering sensation of Evelyn's lips pressed to his. He smiled as he got out his car and gathered his bag from the trunk. He locked his car and headed to the door.

He walked into the gym and was greeted by the sights and sounds of members cheerfully chatting, weights clinking, and the occasional grunt of exertion. He readjusted his bag on his shoulder and looked at the front counter. There was no one there. Tay assumed that whoever was on shift must be out walking the floor, making sure that the gym looked decent. He knew that this task would take a while, so he went to the locker room and changed into his martial arts uniform. Once he finished, he hefted his bag and went back to front counter to see if the front counter person had returned.

As he reached the desk, he saw his best friend, Phillip, walking around the corner, heading back to the front counter. Phillip was taller than Tay and well-built; his biceps looked huge in the polo shirt he wore. He was carrying a printer from the side office. When he saw Tay leaning against the counter, he threw his head up in greeting. His veins stood out against his sun-kissed skin as he set the printer down. He let out a sigh and shook his wrist out before running his hands through his almond brown hair to comb it back.

After he fixed his hair, he looked at Tay. "Bro, how you been?" Phillip greeted him, reaching out his hand. The two clasped hands over the counter.

"Man, chilling. You know me," Tay said in a nonchalant manner.

Phillip raised an eyebrow and replied, "Yeah. You are right. I do know you. That's why I asked." Phillip looked Tay over carefully as he waited for a response. Tay purposefully turned away, leaned back on the counter, and looked out the door.

"So?" Phillip pressured.

"So what?" Tay said as two girls walked by him. One looked in his direction, and he gave a smirk as they passed.

"Dude, stop playing. You know I can read you, and I know something's happened."

Dang, nothing gets by him. Tay thought, smiling. *Well, that's one of the reasons he is my best friend. Besides, he is the only one that hasn't left me despite all that I told him about. And we both are dealing with similar problems.* Tay faced him and started recounting all that had happened recently.

Tay trusted Phillip because he wasn't just a best friend—he was one of the few who understood the world Tay came from. Phillip was part of the underworld—what outsiders would call the mafia. He was a member of the Summers family. They were a small family but were growing into a major player.

Tay's parents had been deeply tied to the Blackwoods, serving them like a sword and shield while the Blackwoods supplied money and protection. Together, they'd once controlled a five-state region. Even after Tay's parents were gone, the Blackwoods were still standing. That said enough about their strength and their reach.

But Phillip was the only person in the field who knew Tay had a background in that world.

Well, besides Mr. Blackwood now. But that never stopped Phillip from befriending Tay, and they became a support pillar for each other. Tay wanted out. Phillip knew that and he did everything he could to help Tay live like he was free—even if the past never really let go.

That was why Tay could talk to him. But even now, in public, it had to be in code. Tay shared his story in between Phillip greeting members coming in with a warm smile. When Tay finished, Phillip noticed a member waiting and motioned for them so he could help them. Once the member was at the tablet signing in, Phillip turned toward Tay. "Man, that's a lot to happen so close together. So, how are you handling all that?"

"Bro, honestly, I don't know. I want to say that I am happy about the outcome of things, but I also feel scared that it could vanish just as easily as it did with Rin. I just don't know what to do at this point."

"Look, man, don't stress out so much," Phillip consoled Tay. "From what you said it sounds like you found someone you may be able to live the kind of life you want with. For that, I'm happy for you. But this Aria chick needs to go."

"I know but the thing is her father." Tay trailed off as he glanced sideways at the member still putting in their information. Then he leaned in closer, causing Phillip to do the same. In a soft voice, he whispered, "Her father is Mr. Blackwood."

Phillip jumped back slightly, looked around, then leaned back in. "Are you sure? I mean couldn't it just have been someone else with the same name?"

Tay nodded. "I'm sure. He looked just like the picture from the newspaper two years ago."

The two looked at each other for a moment. Phillip, in disbelief, searched Tay's eyes to see if he was going to say 'got you' or something. When Tay didn't, he sighed, casting his eyes to the ground briefly before looking back at Tay. "So, dude, how are you going to get out of this one?" Phillip's voice held hints of resignation, which brought home how trapped Tay felt.

He remembered the request for one additional favor from Mr. Blackwood before he met Evelyn. A chill crept up his spine. "Man, you know that there has never been anyone to truly oppose him. And even those that did end up giving into his will eventually." Tay looked up and leaned back as he grasped the counter. "Honestly, I just haven't been thinking about it too much. Trying to focus on other things."

The member came back to Phillip, signaling they were done. He greeted them with a smile and finished setting up their account. "Here you go. If you need anything, just come and ask me or anyone that you see with a name tag like this, and we will be more than happy to help."

As the member walked into the main section of the gym, Phillip looked at Tay. "Okay… So about you not focusing on the issue. I wouldn't bet on that strategy, but I hope it works out. Just be careful," Phillip advised, his voice etched with concern.

"Thanks, man," Tay answered, smiling. "On a work-related note, is the room free?"

Phillip checked on the computer. "Yeah, it is open. And one last thing, I don't know much about this Evelyn, but seems you may be on the right track with her. As for that Aria chick." Phillip just shook his head. "Dude, be careful. I don't think she means harm but she really wants you to notice her."

"I know." Tay rolled his head and eyes. "I mean, how could I not notice all the hints she was giving. And then the voicemails this morning."

"Yea…" Phillip paused and looked at the ceiling. "It is just—something about those messages don't sit right with me. Especially that crinkling noise you heard."

"Tell me about it." Tay rubbed the back of his neck. "I thought she was reading off a script she wrote or something."

"Then there was the vibe you got from Mr. Blackwood." Phillip looked at Tay, as if studying him then hung his head with a sigh. "Bro, I don't know what you plan to do but I wish you the best of luck. And know I'm always here for you."

"Yo, I appreciate that, Phil." Tay turned to face him then they clasped hands over the counter, their grips firm. "See you around."

"Yea, see ya," Phillip said as they let go. Tay and Phillip knew things for them could change at any second. Still, they were the only true friends they each had left.

Tay hung his bag back on his shoulder and walked away, thinking of what kind of mission Phillip had. Though his friend did well to hide it, Tay felt his nervousness, and that scared him. The thought of not seeing Phillip anymore created a hole he didn't want to feel.

"Wonder when he will be back?" Tay whispered, then took a deep breath and released it as he headed to the second floor where his room was. The walk gave him time to clear his mind and refocus himself. Once he reached the room, he was centered again. He entered the room where sandbags hung on one side, and on the other side was a weight rack and benches.

"Well, time to get to work," Tay said to hype himself up as he set his bag down, took out his speaker, and played his workout mix. He changed clothes then began his pre-workout routine.

Once his muscles were loose, he racked the dumbbells and went to the bench. He placed two 45-pound plates on each side of the bar and laid down. By his fifth rep, his biceps began to burn slightly.

"Man, if this is burning already, I need to work out more," he muttered as he held the weight up before he pushed through that set of ten. Next, he hung upside down on the pull-up bar with a twenty-pound dumbbell behind his head and did ten crunches. With each rep, he controlled his breathing and movement. He breathed in new air and energy and released out all the stress…the hurt of Rin's departure and worry of dealing with the Blackwood family and all other emotions he had built up over the past few days.

Once done, he alternated between the bench press and pull-up bar until he completed four sets of ten reps each. His arm throbbed and abs were sore, but he enjoyed the burn because it meant he was developing himself.

"Burning means progress. And progress means growth," he whispered as a reminder to himself to keep pushing through no matter what he faced.

He then grabbed his jump rope and began jumping. Only the sound of the rope hitting the ground echoed throughout the room at a steady rhythm.

He finished his pre-workout with sweat rolling down his back and his forehead.

"Finally, time for dummy sparring," he said as he changed the playlist to something more upbeat. He settled himself in front of the sandbags, took a breath, and delivered a right jab to the bag in front of him. He began a furry of kicks, punches, and elbow strikes to all the bags until he was through the line of sandbags. Once through, he turned and looked at the swinging bags and went back through them, punching, kicking and even kneeing them, working on his combos while doing his best to stay aware of the bags and not get hit by them. He kept this up for a good minute before he started taking hits.

"Dang it. Concentrate, dummy!" he chastised himself as he refocused and delivered heavier blows while trying to maintain form. But it didn't help. He just kept taking more hits. So, after about three more rounds down and back, he stepped out of the sandbag area, breathing heavily and his body drenched in sweat

He slowly walked to his bag to get some water and relaxed for a bit. The cold liquid was an instant balm to the dryness in his throat.

"Ahh, that feels so good," he said after taking a long sip. He sat there and rested the cold bottle against his head as he watched the bags swing.

What was that paper Aria was rustling in her voicemails? And why did Mr. Blackwood feel so strange in that call?

Tay sat there in a daze as his mind replayed the voicemails, scanning for any hidden meaning, or clues in the way she spoke or acted.

Could she have been in trouble? Was she asking for help... but couldn't say it?

The bags continued swaying until they went back to their resting position. The only sound in the room was his music blasting. Tay let out a slow breath and chuckled softly.

"Yea right. Let's not kid myself. Her father wouldn't let that happen. And besides… she was in the safety of her own yard when I left." He exhaled sharply as he got up and went to pull out the standing punching dummies. He set them up in a circle and stepped into the middle. He looked at all the dummies, closed his eyes and breathed, then opened his eyes and started throwing combo after combo mixing together his kicks, punches, knee, and elbow strikes along with back hands. Each time he attacked, he tried to move quicker and to strike harder to make the dummies rock back and forth.

He kept going until his alarm blared. It was time to clean up and get ready for his class today. After he set up the room, he took his shirt off and wiped the sweat off his chest and back before putting his uniform top on. As he was tying his belt around his waist, there was a knock at the door.

"Come in," he said as he finished tying his belt.

"Good afternoon, teacher," a little girl and boy said as they walked in and bowed to him.

"Good afternoon, Tom and Rei," Tay replied as he smiled and bowed back to the two kids.

"Well, I see you are in high spirits as always," said a young lady behind them, voice bright and sweet.

Tay stood up to see one of his older students.

"It is a pleasure to see you too, Regina," Tay answered as the two slightly bowed to each other and smiled.

Regina stood up and took a step closer to Tay. "Come on now, I told you call me Gina," she said looking up at him with her hands clasped behind her back and a sly smile on her face. At twenty-years-old and just five feet tall, she exuded youthfulness, enhanced by her radiant skin and playful, bright hazel eyes. Her brown hair was straight and pulled back into a ponytail to keep out of her face. She looked petite, partly because the uniform was slightly baggy on her. Tay couldn't deny she was cute but that was all he felt for her —cute like a younger sister.

"Can't do that." He greeted the other students with a bow as they entered the class.

"Why not?" Regina walked to his side and stood as close as she could to him while waving at the others.

"Well, would you prefer Ms. Hughes then?" he teased while walking to the door, glancing to make sure there were no stragglers. Once he was sure that was everyone, he closed the door. The moment he turned to his right, Regina was in front of him. "Whoa!" he exclaimed, instinctively jumping back and raising his hands in defense. The children's laughter reminded Tay of his surroundings, and he quickly lowered his hands, glaring at Regina. "Ms. Hughes that will be twenty push-ups," he said sternly.

Regina's face fell as she realized she had crossed the line. "Yes, sir," she replied as she dropped to the floor. As she began her push-ups, Tay took a knee beside her.

"Why would you do something like that?" he asked, his voice softer.

She paused in a plank position, eyes still looking at the floor. "Because I don't like that you keep trying to push me away," she answered before resuming her push-ups.

"Sorry, but that is the only other name I can call you," Tay said as he stood up and straightened his uniform.

Regina finished her push-ups and stood up breathing heavily. She looked up at Tay's eyes filled with determination. "Why is that? Is my age that much of a problem?" she asked, her voice steady despite her exertion.

"No, you are my student, and I don't want to mess up our instructor-student relationship," he replied matter-of-factly. He placed a hand on her shoulder and said softly, "Besides, a pretty young woman like you will find someone much better than me." He walked past her to the front of the class. Once there, he turned to look over the class and noticed Regina was still in the back. "Regina, please come join us," he called out.

She sighed softly. "But I want you," she whispered. She took a small breath, turned, smiling and said loudly, "Yes, sir," and ran to her position in the front of the class. Once everyone was in position, he began to teach.

Over the next hour, he taught them as much as he could about Taekwondo. He released the students that didn't sign up for his Jujitsu class and continued instructing the rest of the class for the next hour. The older kids were picking it up quickly, the younger ones not so much. But they all were doing great, at least in his opinion. Once his last class ended, Tay straightened up the room. When he was done, he gave the room one last look-over and walked out the door. He locked it, turned to leave, and immediately bumped into someone.

"Sorry," Tay said quickly as he reached out to steady the other person. He looked the person over and saw that it was Regina. "Oh, Regina. Did you forget something?" Tay asked as he turned to unlock the door. Regina laid a hand on his just as he stuck the key in the slot.

I really have to stop bumping into people. It tends to bring me trouble when I do.

"No. I just have a question," Regina said, her voice soft and wavering, as if she wasn't sure about something.

Tay looked at her hand on his and then into her eyes. He could guess what she wanted, and though he didn't want to entertain the idea, he figured he better be up front. "What is your question?" Tay asked as he removed the key from the door, which caused Regina to pull her hand back. He then readjusted his bag on his shoulder and really looked at her.

First, he noticed she had let her hair down from the ponytail she had in class. This prompted Tay to look her over some more and he noticed she changed clothes, too. She wore jean shorts that had a rolled hem that showed off her toned legs. Her top was a floral off-the-shoulder blouse that stopped at the top of her shorts in the front and dropped to her thighs in the back. The top highlighted her smooth skin and gave a presence to her modest figure. Tay found himself in a slight trance.

She really is beautiful. Though...

Regina brought her hands together in front of her and twiddled her thumbs, eyes downcast. She took a deep breath and looked up at Tay. "Would you please come hang out with me sometime?" Regina asked quickly, her voice shaking.

They looked into each other's eyes, a silent moment stretched between them. Finally, Tay began to speak. "Look, you are beautiful..." he started.

"You think I'm beautiful?" she interrupted, a huge smile on her face, her sun-kissed cheeks turned a slight red.

"I never said that you weren't," Tay reassured her.

"Then would you be willing to come hang out with me now?" Regina asked, her voice steadier and her eyes sparkled with hope.

"Look..." Tay began. Immediately, Regina's eyes dimmed, and her shoulders dropped slightly. Tay knew he had hurt her, but he needed to be honest with her. "I already am talking to someone."

Regina bit her lower lip, as if to hold back a remark. She let out a soft breath and said softly, "I see. I was too late then."

Tay looked at Regina's crestfallen face, his heart ached, and he wanted to console her. "Honestly, you are a great girl, but I can't help but see you as my little sister or my student," Tay stated softly. "I know that there is a man out there that will make you feel like you are on top of the world and will keep you happy and satisfied. More than someone like me could."

Yeah, like I could ever bring true happiness to anyone. The image of Rin crying popped up in his mind and he turned his head away from Regina as he pulled flexed his jaw. Then a smell like that of peaches hit Tay and he could help but think of food. This made him this of the date he just had with Evelyn and the right side of his mouth curled up slightly. *Well, maybe. Just maybe this time will be different.*

He looked back at her and asked, "I am confused about something, though. Why are you so determined to be in a relationship with me?"

Regina sniffed slightly and cleared her throat. "To answer that, I guess I have to tell you why I like you." She looked at him and smiled softly, the smile not reaching her eyes. "It was my first class here two years ago," she began. "I honestly was so nervous, and I felt out of place. I'd been wanting to learn self-defense, but I figured I was too old for a class like this. But I wasn't old enough to spend hundreds of dollars on a personal instructor, so here I was." Her cheeks turned red again as she recounted her experience. Tay just stood there and nodded slightly, encouraging her to continue.

Regina took a deep breath and continued. "You actually greeted me downstairs at the front desk. You had this air about you that was warm and comforting like I didn't have to worry about anything if you were beside me. You said hello and asked me what was wrong. I guess my face must have shown I had something on my mind." Regina looked down, eyes wandering not wanting to look at Tay. "And I just ended up telling you the truth. That I was scared. Scared that I wouldn't fit in and scared that one day some guy would try to push his luck with me." Regina looked up at Tay and smiled. "I told you about how it happened to a friend of mine and she went down a hole of depression and never was the same since. You at first just listened but at the end." She paused and closed her eyes, as if seeing the memory back then. "Your demeanor changed, and you looked ready to run out and fight. I was honestly surprised that I could tell all that to a stranger and that stranger would get that upset for me and my friend. You then looked me dead in the eyes and asked me. Would I like to learn how to defend myself?"

"Yeah." Tay nodded as he followed along with her story. "I remember that day. You looked like you wanted to change something about yourself but didn't know how to go about it."

"Well, I did, and you just happened to be the one that I unconsciously trusted." Regina walked to the railing and leaned on it. She glanced over the gym floor, watching the other members workout.

Tay walked next to her and turned his back to the railing and leaned back, elbows rested on the top rail. He turned to look at Regina. She looked more composed now.

She continued, "Well, you know that after I started taking your class. I sucked." Regina chuckled lightly and Tay did, too.

"You weren't that bad."

Regina looked at him and playfully punched his arm. "Oh really. I remember you having to tell me to stay behind after class more than a few times just to correct my form."

"Well..." Tay tilted his head and raised his eyebrows as he looked at her. "I mean. You can't defend correctly if you hurt yourself in the process." They smiled at each other and laughed.

"Yeah, you were right." Regina held onto the rail and leaned back, stretching before she stood back up. "You helped me get better and the time I spent with you felt like my sanctuary. There were times I tried to distance myself from you and I focused on improving at home so that I wouldn't take up more of your time or come to depend on you," she said as she turned to look back out over the floor.

"Oh, so that was how you got better in just a month's time. I thought you was getting lessons from someone else."

Regina stood up and put a hand to her chest feigning offence. "Sir, I will have you know I have never cheated on you."

"Well, I greatly appreciate that," Tay said, he gave her a slight side bow.

"So, I felt good at first thinking I made a major accomplishment. But I felt hollow. I found myself wishing that you would ask me to stay after to train more. I wanted to talk to you more. I wanted you to know more about me and I wanted to know everything about you. Like how you were so strong when we were only three years apart?"

At that phrase, Tay felt his heart throb and sting. He thought of how he got to where he was. The things that happened in his past. And he remembered that his parents weren't here anymore. The compassion that they gave him that he would never feel again. But the lessons they taught him continued to live on through him. He struggled to keep his face neutral to not show his hurt.

"It was then that I realized I wanted more than to just take your class. I wanted to be around you," Regina said. "And that is how we got here."

"Well, I must say you are very courageous and determined. I can promise that any guy would truly be blessed to have you in his corner."

"Yeah. But the man that I want to stand beside won't let me stand there," Regina teased, she poked Tay in the side. He flinched slightly.

"Oh, are you ticklish?" Regina asked, her hands wiggled as she got ready to tickle Tay more.

"No, Regina," Tay said as he took a step back. "You don't want to do that."

"Oh, but I do," she replied as a mischievous smile appeared on her face. She lunged toward Tay. Tay juked past her and ran down the stairs. As he reached the front desk, he saw someone else was working the counter instead of Phillip. He quickly approached the desk and extended his hand, holding the keys to the room for the clerk. The clerk jolted back in shock.

"Sorry, was in a bit of a rush," Tay apologized to the clerk. He just nodded in response. Just as the clerk took the keys, Regina bear hugged Tay from behind.

"Ha! I got you," she exclaimed. Tay looked at her. Her smile made him feel more relaxed. They laughed and stood apart from each other.

"I'm glad we can still talk like this," Tay said, appreciative of Regina's strong spirit. He held out his hand.

"I am, too. Thanks for always being there for me," Regina said as she clasped his hand. "But though I'm happy for you, don't you think that just because of you are talking to someone now means that I'm going to quit. Until you get married, or someone can distract me from you. I will keep trying." She shook his hand, pulled him forward, and kissed his cheek. With cheeks now truly red, she let his hand go and walked toward the door waving to him.

As she walked away, Tay sighed, relieved that things ended somewhat neatly. He appreciated her understanding but knew her actions could complicate things later. He stood still for a moment and looked at the door before he gathered himself and headed out as well.

– Chapter 10: A Risky Intervention–

Once settled in his car, Tay heard his phone vibrate in the cup holder. He looked at it and saw he had three missed calls. There were two voicemails and two texts. He first checked the call log. His eyes widened in surprise as he saw his brother or sister had called.

After their parents died, they were all placed in foster care. It was in this foster care that an attorney came and found them and had them all except Tay change their names. Tay even asked the attorney to quickly find families for his brother and sister and to hold a funeral for his parents and his brother and sister. The attorney was hesitant at first but due to Tay's desperation and determination to remove his brother and sister from the life that his parents led, the attorney agreed. So, within a week or two his brother and sister were given to two different families.

Tay was the last to be given a family, but he made sure he wrote to his brother and sister regularly at first. Then he switched over to texts and calls as to not leave a trail for anyone that would try to go after the rest of his family. Even while in foster care, Tay remembered to follow the plan his mother and father taught him if something were to happen to them. So, to see he had an encrypted call from one of them made him smile from ear to ear.

And his happiness didn't diminish even when he looked at the next caller and saw it was Aria. Though he just disregarded her call and looked at the text messages, these messages were not important as they were ads from his phone company.

He quickly went to his voicemail and listened to the message from his brother or sister. As it played, he was surprised to hear it was actually both of them together.

His smile grew knowing they were still close.

They must have planned the call and was trying to do a three-way.

They told him that they missed him and couldn't wait to see each other again at the next meet up. It was then that Tay remembered it was almost that time of year where they paid tribute to their parents' grave at an undisclosed location to keep others from disturbing it. Tay felt his body turn to lead slightly like the earth was pulling him down. He missed his family too, but he knew he couldn't risk certain people knowing he had family left. Especially the people who killed his parents.

So, he deleted the number and the message from his phone. He was glad that the message was short and from one of the disposable numbers his brother had set up for them before they all split up after the last meet up.

Next was Aria's message. Tay remembered how odd her last messages sounded but he couldn't find any clues as to something being wrong so he disregarded them and went about his day. But Tay couldn't shake the feeling that something was off. So, he played her message.

"Tay, please..." Then there was silence. She didn't say anything else for a few seconds. Tay rolled his eyes.

Not this charade again. What is this girl playing at? He took the phone away from his ear and was about to end the message when she spoke again but this time her voice was a soft whisper like she was scared of being heard. "Please help me. Jaron's father has me captive and is demanding you to come get me." Her voice shook and cracked as she spoke through short gasping breaths.

Dear God, please don't let her actually be in trouble.

"His address is 2513 Abram boulevard. Please…" Then there came a loud thud like a door being kicked in.

"You dirty little wench!!" a boisterous voice called out. There was a smack and the sound of the phone clattering to the ground. "It is because of you that my son is in the hospital along with his friends." Given the flow of the conversation, Tay assumed the man speaking was Jaron's father.

Dammit. I knew something felt off but because I wanted to distance myself from someone I thought was a headache I ignored her when she was in real trouble. Tay chastised himself for thinking this was another one of her tricks to get him involved with her.

"It was his own fault for pulling a gun on me and my friends," Aria yelled, her voice quavered even more. It sounded to Tay like she was about to cry. Unconsciously, his face wrinkled, jaw flexed, and his free hand balled into a fist.

"Shut up with all your lies," Jaron's father exclaimed. Suddenly, all Tay could hear was Aria gasping. "I know you called that little shit." Jaron's father's voice was low and carried a menacing undertone. "And he better get here soon, or you will be the one to face my wrath." There was a sudden crash and the call dropped.

"Damn her," Tay said through clenched teeth as he gazed at his phone. He threw his phone in the passenger seat, disbelief at the situation washing over him. "Why does it seem like she is always in trouble and I'm having to save her?" he asked the air, his voice rising slightly as he thought what the message meant for him. He placed his hands on his head and began to massage his forehead and temples as he began to think of what he had to do. Then he remembered he had delivered her safely to her house. He even saw her walk through the gate before he left.

"Hold up." Tay paused as he quelled his frustration slightly and reconsidered what was happening, becoming confused. "How did she get taken? Did she walk back out that late at night?" he questioned as he replayed last night's events in his mind. "Better yet, why couldn't her dad protect her?" Tay asked. He realized that there was one way to get answers, though he had hoped to avoid interacting with the Blackwoods again. He took a deep breath, picked up his phone, and called Mr. Blackwood.

The phone rang twice before someone picked it up. "Blackwood's residence," the voice was that of the butler.

"Hello. This is Tagen Davis. I would like to speak with Mr. Blackwood, please," Tay said and marveled at just how proper he sounded and shook his head.

Got to find joy in the small things. But this isn't the time.

"Mr. Blackwood is busy at the moment. May I take a message?" the butler responded, voice leveled and almost emotionless.

"Sure. Please tell him to give me a call. It is regarding his daughter, Aria."

"Oh," the butler said. Then there was a slight pause, but Tay didn't miss the small drop of venom that the butler let slip into his voice. "In that case one moment please." The butler's voice had regained its professional cadence. The phone was set down, and seconds later, the next person to speak was Mr. Blackwood.

"I can't believe it was you who did this. I thought I could trust you but apparently, I was wrong." Mr. Blackwood's words threw Tay for a loop.

Does Mr. Blackwood really think I kidnapped his daughter? Tay was at a loss for words and just held the phone.

"So, how much?" Mr. Blackwood asked, his voice tight and low, like a tiger getting ready to attack. Tay couldn't believe they would suspect him. His thoughts raced.

Why would he assume I took her? Did someone plant the idea in his head? Tay replayed what he told the butler without giving an answer.

"Tagen Davis," Mr. Blackwood said, his voice strained to remain calm. "I am asking you HOW MUCH!" Mr. Blackwood snapped, unable to keep his irritation down.

The sharp tone of Mr. Blackwood's voice brought Tay back to the present. "Sir, I don't have her. She left a voicemail on my phone," he answered briskly, his voice steady despite the hundred thoughts going through his head.

"Then, where…Where is my daughter?" asked Mr. Blackwood as he continued to strain to keep his voice neutral. Tay knew then that the situation was far more serious than he had thought.

"Jaron's father has her, sir," Tay replied calmly and as politely as he could. Mr. Blackwood didn't say a word, so Tay continued. "Sir, can I ask something?"

"Fine, but you must answer my question, too," Mr. Blackwood agreed, his voice unnaturally calm.

"Yes, sir," Tay replied politely. He took a breath; he knew that what he was about to ask something that could be seen as disrespectful. "Sir, I just have to ask. Why didn't you watch her after I dropped her off last night?"

"What do you mean after you dropped her off? She never came home. So, I assumed she was still with you at your place," Mr. Blackwood replied, his voice unchanged.

Tay's eyes widened at this revelation. "No, sir. I dropped her off at the gate and watched her go inside before I left."

Mr. Blackwood paused again after he heard this. "Tay, tell me what happened last night." His voice low and calm but Tay could sense the danger behind his voice.

Tay recapped the night to Mr. Blackwood. He even told him about the moment where he thought he scared Aria because he remembered something painful. When he finished, Mr. Blackwood remained silent.

"Umm, sir," Tay started, his voice shook slightly with uncertainty.

"Sorry. Now here's my question: what did her voicemail say?"

"That Jaron's father wants to pay the person back for what he did to his son and friends," Tay answered, trying to keep the situation from escalating further.

"So, why don't you go?" Mr. Blackwood asked, his voice controlled, but a hint of desperation seeped through.

"Sir, with all due respect, I'm not involved in this. I was just following your orders, so it's your responsibility to handle it."

Mrs. Blackwood interjected, her voice breaking slightly. "Tagen. This is Mrs. Blackwood. I respected your parents when they were alive. They were good friends of ours. But right now, my daughter's life is on the line because of your actions. If you have any decency, any respect for your parents' memory, you will do this."

Tay took a deep breath, trying to steady his racing heart at the mention of his mother and father.

"I'm trying to live a different life now. Getting involved means putting everything I've worked for at risk. That's why I was calling to inform you of all I know so you can come up with a plan."

"This is not just about you, Tay!" Mrs. Blackwood snapped. "This is about an innocent girl who is suffering because of something she didn't do. You owe this to her, to us. And if you won't act, I will."

"I'm sorry that I can't help out more," Tay started.

"Don't say sorry—" Mrs. Blackwood said with emphasis on each word. "How about this?" Her voice changed to a polite tone once more. Tay's heart jumped in his throat and sweat began to bead on his palms. "I know about your brother. And I know where he is currently staying."

Tay flinched, pulling the phone away from his ear. He looked at it briefly before returning it to his ear and replied in an eerily calm manner, "I don't have any family left. They are all..."

"Don't give me that bullshit!" Mrs. Blackwood screamed before she released a tense breath and spoke in her polite tone again. "Jerome Alphonse Davis will die tomorrow unless you go now."

"Woah, now Carrie, settle down," Mr. Blackwood said cautiously.

"Don't you tell me to settle down. My daughter is out there with that man and you want me to settle down! You know what he did to us before. And now he has my baby girl." Mrs. Blackwood sniffed and began breathing hard. "Bring my daughter back. Bring my little girl home," Mrs. Blackwood said as she cried. Slowly her sobs grew more muffled, as if she was being taken away.

Mr. Blackwood's voice returned, calmer but still filled with tension. "Tay, please. We're not asking for ourselves. We're asking for Aria. She needs you."

Tay felt the weight of their words pressing down on him. He knew what he had to do, but the fear of being pulled back into the shadows he had tried so hard to escape was overwhelming. Yet the thought of Jerome and the threat of losing him was even more terrifying.

"Fine," Tay said, his voice barely above a whisper. "I'll do it. But this is the last time."

"Thank you," Mr. Blackwood replied, genuine relief evident in his voice. "Just bring her back safe."

Tay ended the call, his mind a whirlwind of thoughts and emotions. The foremost thought being...

How the fuck did I get involved in this lifestyle again?

He threw the phone in the passenger seat, programmed the navigation, and sped off toward the address. As he drove, his mind calmed and focused on only one thing—to murder the one that dared to make him have to live this life again.

A short time later, Tay screeched into the neighborhood of his destination. Due to the location of the neighborhood being a few miles to the northwest of the Blackwood's, Tay could guess that there was bad blood between the two since their domains practically bordered each other's. As Tay drove, he scanned the neighborhood for any threats, but he saw nothing out of the ordinary. Still, he drove cautiously to make sure he didn't draw unnecessary attention.

When he reached the house, he noticed the house was almost as massive as the Blackwood's. It wasn't gated but had a long driveway with trees evenly spaced on both sides. Tay was grateful that it was still light outside so he could see if anyone was hiding among the trees.

He calmly drove up to the front door, parked, and got out of the car locking it behind him. He walked up the stairs and noticed the French double door design. As he walked to the doors, they opened revealing two husky men that walked out to greet him.

"May we help you?" the one on the right said as he moved in front of Tay. Tay didn't answer. The guard placed a hand on Tay's shoulder. "Hey, I'm talking to you."

Tay grabbed his hand and spun so his back was to the guard and threw the man over his shoulder, slamming him to the ground. As the man hit the ground, Tay heard a metal object bounce on the porch. Ignoring the sound, Tay turned to the other man who was stunned by the sudden move and left himself wide open. Tay stepped up to him and delivered two punches to his sides, followed with a jump spin kick to the head. The man hit the door frame and slid down unconscious.

"No. You can't," Tay said to the unconscious guard. He noticed the metal object that hit the ground was a gold colored L insignia pin.

Guess they needed a way to show who they are loyal to, Tay thought as he walked past the guards and into the house.

The house was spacious with a foyer the size of a guest room. It led to the living room straight ahead, a hallway to the left, and stairs on the right. Tay headed toward the hallway. Upon reaching the door, he heard a noise. Tay paused and listened again, hearing the sound more clearly without his movements. He could tell it was a buzz, like an electric charge.

He looked at the doorknob, leaned down slightly, and heard the electric current running through it. He stood up and stepped back. He softly bounced on his feet before he delivered a jumping side kick to the door, causing it to swing inward. The person behind the door gasped from the current going through their body. Tay then shoulder rammed the door forcing the doorknob into the other person. He pushed his way through and looked around. The room was an office with a window facing the front yard. Besides the furniture and the now unconscious but still jerking person on the ground, there was nothing of importance in this room.

Where could they be? Tay thought as he walked out of the room. He checked all the rooms on the first floor. No one was there and he couldn't find a way to a basement either. So, he went back to the foyer and upstairs. Once at the top, he was greeted by a maid and butler.

"Oh, a visitor. I was wondering what all the noise was downstairs," the butler said as he and the maid bowed. "Welcome to the Lackston's home."

The butler stooped and tapped the maid on her shoulder. "Marie, I shall take it from here." She raised her head and left without a word. "Sir, my name is Carl. I am the faithful butler to the Lackston family. May I inquire as to your visit on this night," the butler said, facing Tay after the maid left from their sight.

"Where is Mr. Lackston? I have important business to discuss," Tay replied with irritation filling his heart.

"Sorry, but Mr. Lackston is out at the moment," Carl answered, his voice and eyes filled with disdain as he stood tall and looked down his nose at Tay.

"Liar," Tay responded. "I know that he is here. Now let me through," Tay said as he tried walking around Carl but was cut off.

"Sir, I must insist that you leave," Carl stated, a smirk crept on his face.

"I will leave after we talk. Now move!" Tay said as he pushed past Carl.

"Sir." Carl reacted and laid a hand on Tay's shoulder. "It would be wise for you to leave now." Carl applied slight pressure, causing Tay to wince.

"No, I will not." Tay grunted as he pried Carl's hand off him. Carl punched at Tay's face, but when Tay let his hand go to guard, he was hit in the stomach instead with Carl's now free hand. Tay gasped and reached for the hand that struck him, but Carl pulled it back. Tay tried to cross jab, but Carl blocked it and stood back in a butler stance with one hand down to his side and the other across his stomach, as if holding a towel.

The next thing Tay saw was Carl's foot and hand twitch. Then pain. His nose and right cheek hurt from colliding with Carl's knee. Tay staggered back, nose dripping blood. He wiped the blood away with the back of his hand and reassessed Carl. Carl's experience and lack of fear was evident as he smiled at Tay.

"So will you leave now?" Carl said, his voice full of ridicule.

Tay smiled back. Despite the injuries, he couldn't deny he was getting excited at the challenge of fighting someone better than him. Suddenly, Tay rushed at Carl. Once within a step of Carl, Tay punched, causing Carl to lean back, and followed through with a spinning roundhouse. Carl ducked. Tay then did a dropkick, making Carl jump back. Tay charged in and delivered an elbow strike. Carl stumbled, holding his stomach.

"What do you think?" Tay said as Carl stood up.

"It appears that you have some skills." Carl grunted as he regained his composure. The two smiled at each other briefly before running at each other. They exchanged blows up and down the hallway, each attack echoing in the confined space.

Tay felt the speed of his attack drop and his lungs burned as they overworked to keep his energy level up. This caused him to drop his guard. Carl took the chance and punched at Tay's face. Tay sidestepped, caught Carl's wrist, then swung him into the side rail, causing Carl to flip over it and hit the foyer floor with a loud thud.

Tay didn't look but leaned back against the wall to his left, resting his hands on his knees to catch his breath. Once he had control of his breathing, Tay went to the middle door down the hall. It looked like it was the master bedroom. Once at the door, he laid on the ground and knocked by the doorknob. Immediately, guns fired, riddling the door with holes that would have surely killed Tay had he been standing up. Tay stayed down and rolled to his back, waiting for someone to come verify he was dead. The door opened slowly. Once he saw a head stick out, he kicked the door closed, slamming the head between the door and the frame. He jumped up, threw the door open, and used the person who opened the door as a shield as he went inside the room. He took the gun from their hands and shot at the line of people firing at him the moment he entered the room.

Once the shooting stopped from the others being incapacitated or dead, Tay let the dead body fall to the ground, then realized it was Marie that he had used as, a shield. He felt a small sense of guilt and hate for himself for not realizing it sooner, but he didn't waste any time grieving. In this line of work, it was either kill or be killed, and she was on the wrong side today.

He walked to the bed the others were protecting as he killed the injured ones with a bullet to the head. He walked up two steps to the bed's landing, and there stretched out with hands and feet tied to the bedpost was Aria. Her face showed dried tears. She was gagged and unconscious, her shirt half-torn and her pants nowhere to be seen.

At the sight of her state, Tay's blood boiled. Fury at himself for ignoring her cry for help surged through his being. "I should've listened and just came to get her," he whispered quietly as he started undoing the ropes. Just as he was working on the last rope, the window to the balcony opened.

"I wouldn't do that if I was you," a voice spoke out. Tay turned to see a figure walk into the room. He was slightly shorter than Tay, but stood with an air of fierce authority. He was shirtless, revealing a chiseled chest and abs with bulky arms and broad shoulders. His pants hugged his thighs, showing toned muscles underneath. He was smoking a cigar; the smoke curled around his face, one hand casually behind his back. His eyes gleamed with a cold, calculating light as he looked Tay over. Then his gaze shifted to Aria behind

Tay and a small, sinister smile crept up the side of his face. His body language exuded the confidence of a seasoned predator eyeing his next meal. The immediate thought in Tay's head was this was Mr. Lackston.

"Am I to presume that you are Mr. Lackston?" Tay asked, trying to keep his voice steady.

"Yes, that is me," Mr. Lackston said, releasing another puff of smoke from his cigar.

"Why have you done this?" Tay asked, his voice tight with anger.

Mr. Lackston laughed a harsh, joyless sound. "Why you ask? This girl was the apple of my son's eye. He would have done anything for her, even going against me. I tried to stop him from seeing her, but he was firm in his resolve, and that impressed me," Mr. Lackston said evenly, as if he was just having a casual conversation. He took another pull of his cigar and walked to the dresser on the left side of the room where an armchair rested. Tay followed his every move, his hand relaxing, knowing he would need to focus if this came to a fight, which seemed inevitable.

Mr. Lackston turned and sat in the chair, body relaxed. "So, I allowed him to date her, only for her to break his heart not even three months later. He tried to get back with her many times, even tried to be friends. Still, she played with his heart and made him believe there was a chance to get together again. And then last night at the club, she decided to bring you along to harm my precious son and his friends." Mr. Lackston stated the last sentence through gritted teeth, his eyes piercing through Tay. Tay felt a sense of dread creep up his neck. Then Mr. Lackston's face relaxed. "So, since she decided to punish my son, I decided to punish her. It was only fair," Mr. Lackston said, his voice was light. He drew on his cigar again and knocked off the ash in the tray on the dresser beside the armchair.

"What have you done?" Tay asked, not noticing his hands had curled into fists.

"Oh, nothing much. I just took something precious from her that she can never get back," Mr. Lackston said, his voice tinged with a cruel smile.

Tay's eyes dropped to the sheets between Aria's legs. And there was a mark he had overlooked in his haste to free her—a deep red stain that he would never mistake for anything else.

It was blood.

"You had no right," Tay spoke softly, his voice trembling with barely contained rage.

Mr. Lackston laughed as he stood up from the armchair and walked over to Tay. "I had every right. My son was shot in the leg along with most of his friends. But after that, he ran into the forest, pursuing that tramp and her so-called mate, who turns out to be you. He was put unconscious and short through the back. Fortunately, the ambulance was on the way before that happened and found him in the forest before he bled to death."

Tay remembered the night vividly. *So, his son was the one that I ran into in the forest,* Tay thought.

"So, who was the one to do it?" Mr. Lackston asked as he took a seat next to Aria on the bed. His voice was calm but carried an underlying threat. "I asked her, but she didn't answer. So, I made her a proposition: tell me or bear me a child to replace the one you almost took from me. She still refused, saying she didn't know." He drew on his cigar, letting out a thick cloud. "So, I tied her down and cut off her shorts. I must admit she is beautiful, and her screams made it all the better. So, I tried teasing her and next thing I know I see blood on my fingers. Oh, how excited I was." A sinister laugh bellowed from Mr. Lackston. Tay's fists tightened so hard, his hands shook slightly. His vision tinged with red as he focused on Mr. Lackston's face. "And then..." Mr. Lackston continued.

Unable to hold back any longer, Tay turned and punched Mr. Lackston square in the cheek, sending the cigar flying across the room landing on the carpet. Mr. Lackston fell to the floor on one knee.

"Don't say another word!" he roared, his voice shaking with fury.

"So, you seem ready to fight. Good, but you must know." Mr. Lackston got up off the floor, brushing himself off. "You need to hear the whole story first before making a move."

Mr. Lackston rushed at Tay, feinting a punch but instead kicking at Tay's knee. Lifting his leg, Tay blocked the kick, countering with a swift jump kick to Mr. Lackston's back. Mr. Lackston stumbled forward, gasping. "You are very good," Mr. Lackston said.

Mr. Lackston snatched up his fallen cigar and hurled it at Tay, who instinctively dodged. Mr. Lackston capitalized on the distraction, rushed in with a heavy punch to Tay's chest. Tay caught it with both hands, pushed down, swiftly lifted his knee, and collided with his head.

Mr. Lackston staggered backwards, disoriented Tay pressed the attack with several punishing hits to the ribs and chest. After a last punch to the right rib, Tay did a spin side kick that pushed Mr. Lackston into the air off the landing. He crashed onto the floor beside the bed, the air knocked out of him. Tay followed Mr. Lackston, stomped on his chest, and heard a loud crack, but Tay didn't stop. He straddled him and delivered a barrage of punches to Mr. Lackston's head—one, two, three—fifteen strikes in total before he finally stopped. He breathed heavily, face drenched in sweat as he stayed on top of Mr. Lackston to ensure he was down before he stood and went over to Aria.

He finished untying the last restraint and wrapped her in the cover. As he did, he saw her bag halfway under the bed. He knelt and picked it up and noticed her pants underneath as well. After collecting both items, he rifled through the bag to make sure there was nothing suspicious inside and make sure her things were in there.

He saw her phone and wallet and even took out the wallet to verify her ID was there before he slung the bag over his head and across his body. He shook out the pants to put them on her but they were practically cut open on one side. Tay glared at the unconscious Mr. Lackston on the floor. His rage bubbled to the surface. For a moment, he wanted to finish what he'd started and make sure Mr. Lackston never drew another breath. But he forced out a long exhale, crumpled the pants, and dropped them.

"Not worth the effort or the risk." He turned back to Aria. He looked her over once more and thought of the trauma she must have experienced at Mr. Lackston's hands. A pang shot through his gut and he pressed a hand to his stomach as if he'd just taken a blow.

If only I had taken her calls seriously.

"Let's get you home," he whispered, his exhaustion seeped through his voice. "This time, all the way."

He picked her up in a princess carry before leaving the room. As they descended the stairs, he looked over the railing and noticed the butler was gone.

Tay looked around in a panic.

Please don't let him sneak up on me now.

As Tay was looking around, he heard a piercing beep cut through the silence. It was an unnatural sound—sharp and insistent— not from an alarm or appliance. It sent a chill down Tay's spine.

Shit!

His heart raced. There was no time to investigate. He adjusted Aria in his arms and took the remaining stairs two at a time. The beeping grew louder, faster—each beep coming closer together until it was nearly constant.

"That damned butler must have tripped something. I need to get out of here quickly."

Once at the front door, Tay didn't bother with the handle. He kicked hard at the seam where the two doors met, and they burst open. Without slowing down, he sprinted toward his car, his legs burned from the effort.

He barely had time to lay Aria in the passenger seat when the house exploded. Tay was thrown off his feet and landed on his back, hitting the gravel. His ears rang as he slowly got up. He shook his head and then stopped due to the headache that ensued from the motion. He just sat there for a little until he could see straight again. And the moment he did, he wished he hadn't.

The house was up in flames. Tay stood up and slowly walked to his car, looking at the house. No one was running out screaming and no one was coming to see what had happened. It was only him and Aria. Tay continued looking at the house, the heat and image reminding him how his family died. And how no one was saved except for him and his little brother and sister.

"Time to go," Tay told himself softly. He took off her bag and placed it in her lap before he closed the door. He walked to his side, got in, and drove off.

It took a while, but Tay made it back in the Blackwood's neighborhood. As he approached their street, he saw police cars, news cars and vans, along with other vehicles that lined both sides of the street nearly blocking all forms of traffic except for one lane in the middle of the road. Tay stopped at the intersection one block before the house. A policewoman with short, dark hair and a serious expression approached his window, shining a flashlight in the car. Tay rolled down his window.

"Good evening, officer," Tay said in a polite tone.

"Good evening," she replied, her professional smile not reaching her eyes. Tay then realized how serious Mr. and Mrs. Blackwood were when he called earlier. "May I see your driver's license, please?"

"Sure thing. Mind if I reach under me to get my wallet out?" Tay asked, keeping his hands in her line of sight. The officer gave a nod. He slowly leaned forward, took his right hand, and pulled his wallet from his back pocket. He opened it up in front of the officer and pulled out his ID and handed it to her.

She looked at his name. "Tagen Davis?" she asked, looking at him with a slight furrow in her brow.

"Yes, ma'am," Tay said, his voice shaking as his heart raced slightly.

"Would you kindly step out of the car?" she said, placing her hand on her stun gun.

Seeing her reaction, Tay reached out the window and opened the door. He stepped out with his hands raised. As he got out, he heard the officer talking into her walkie talkie. "I need a second patrol to come to the intersection of Burbank and Arbak." She looked back at Tay and said, "I will need you to walk with me."

"I will gladly walk with you, but can we wait for your partner so they can watch over Ms. Blackwood, who is asleep in my car? She hasn't woken up since I found her."

The officer's eyes went wide. "You're saying she's in the car?"

"Yes, ma'am," Tay replied. At this, the officer shined her flashlight back on Tay, scrutinizing him more closely. She noticed the bruises on his face from his previous encounters.

"What happened to you?" the officer asked cautiously, her eyes narrowed as her hand firmly grasped the handle of the stun gun.

"I'm willing to discuss everything, but can we do this in front of Mr. and Mrs. Blackwood?" Tay asked, his hands still in the air. Out of the corner of his eye, he noticed a figure walking quickly toward them. Tay tensed up slightly, ready for anything, but kept a cool demeanor to not alert the officer in front of him. The officer stared at him, not seeming to notice the figure. The figure walked under a streetlight to reveal a young police officer.

"Lieutenant Stokes. I'm here to relieve you," greeted the young man, his voice eager and his stance overly stiff, betraying his inexperience. It was clear this was his first time in the field.

Stokes shook her head. "Thank you, Corporal Thomas. Mr. Davis and I will be heading into the house. Please move the car to the side of the street and keep an eye on the person sleeping inside."

"There's someone in the car, ma'am?" Thomas asked, his eyebrows raised as he looked at the car over Tay's shoulder.

"Yes, apparently asleep. We'll stay right here until you've moved the car."

"Yes, ma'am," Thomas said as he turned and walked to the car. As he was about to get in, he noticed Aria. "Lieutenant, you might want to know the passenger's identity. It looks like Mr. Blackwood's daughter."

"That's why I called you, corporal." Stokes said, her voice sounding slightly exasperated. "I'm taking Mr. Davis to verify with Mr. Blackwood. So please move the car and stand guard."

"Oh okay. Should I call another officer to stand guard over the car?" Thomas asked, his voice shaking.

"No, I won't be long," she said as she walked to Tay's side. Corporal Thomas got in and drove the car to the street adjacent to them and parked it under the nearest streetlight. Once parked, he rolled down the windows and got out. He walked to the center of the intersection and stood with his feet slightly shoulder width apart and hands clasped behind his back, eyes darting around.

Tay studied him before looking back at the lieutenant. "Are you sure he'll be okay?" Tay asked genuinely concerned for the corporal and Aria.

Lieutenant Stokes just shook her head as she let out a low sigh. "Come on, let's get moving before my corporal decides to ask me more questions." She set a hand between Tay's shoulders and guided him forward as she fell in a half step behind him. "Also, you can drop your hands."

Slowly, Tay lowered his hands to his side as they walked down the street in silence. As they approached the front gate, a throng of news reporters swarmed toward them, shouting questions. The flash of cameras was so bright in the night that they momentarily blinded Tay. Stokes kept her pace, ignored the chaos as she stuck to the outer fence and walked through the gate.

On the other side of the gate, two officers searched Tay before he and Stokes continued toward the front door. When they arrived, Tay noticed the police chief was the one guarding the entrance. He looked at Tay and then the lieutenant; his jaw muscles flexed as his nostrils flared.

"Please tell me that you didn't bring another random boy claiming he knows the whereabouts of Tagen Davis and The Blackwood's daughter," he spoke softly, his voice exasperated. Without a word, Lieutenant Stokes gave

Tay's license to the chief. The chief took it, slightly rolled his eyes. He glanced at the license and looked up briefly disappointed before he studied it more closely. He even held it under a blacklight as he searched for signs of forgery. After a two-minute search, he looked up at the lieutenant.

"Great work. Was there anyone with him?" the chief asked.

"Yes, sir. A female, whom he claimed it to have been Ms. Blackwood."

"And why isn't she with you?" the chief questioned as he arched an eyebrow.

"Sir, she was currently incapacitated and couldn't be roused. So, I called for a switch to not only cover my spot but to also watch over the car as I brought Mr. Davis here. I plan to return shortly in the event that she wakes up."

"I will have to say your thought process isn't bad, but might I make a suggestion." The chief stood tall and looked at Tay. "Why didn't you just have this man carry her?" the chief asked with his chest puffed out, as if that was the most logical solution.

Tay looked at the chief, dumbfounded.

Yes, Tay could have carried Aria up to the door no problem, but that would also mean if she woke up in his arms, she would be that much more of a headache to deal with. Besides, who would make a person walk almost a half-mile carrying someone when they are being accused of abduction?

Lieutenant Stokes' chest rose slightly then deflated at the chief's words. "Truthfully, sir, that thought didn't cross my mind. I will do better to ensure that the potential perpetrators carry their hostage with them into the house of the family that is accusing them, so that the family can become even more distraught at the potential sight of their daughter, who could've been hurt or abused, making the family want to have immediate justice against the perp," she stated in one breath, her tone flat and controlled.

Tay blinked wide-eyed. Her words were sharp, but she wasn't being reckless—she was defending procedure, even when it meant correcting a superior.

But Tay felt it.

The tension. It didn't come from her. It radiated from one person—and it wasn't authority he was feeling. It was insecurity.

He looked at the police chief again, noting the man's slack jaw and delayed response.

This doesn't feel like a unified force. This feels like a scramble—rushed bodies reacting to pressure they weren't prepared for.

Then it clicked.

The chief isn't here to lead. He's only here to be seen helping the Blackwoods. To get some points for showing alliance.

Tay couldn't help it and chuckled softly.

The chief blinked and sent him a sharp glare. Tay coughed, covering the sound.

The realization that the Blackwoods had enough weight to summon the police force, and enough power to make even the top brass walk on eggshells, sent a chill through Tay.

Clearing his throat, the chief turned stiffly to Stokes.

"You make a valid point. Again, great job lieutenant. You may return to your post. Alert me if the girl wakes up and wants to talk."

"Will do, sir." With that, Lieutenant Stokes turned on her heels and walked back to her post. Once she was down the stairs, the police chief fully faced Tay.

"You look pretty banged up. Did she put up that much of fight, or are you that weak?"

Tay stared at the chief. His eyes widened at the latter then narrowed, his pulse   thudding   loudly   in   his   ear.

This man really is stupid. How did he even make it to chief? Tay thought, maintaining a neutral stance.

"Good thing you aren't talking. If you had, I would have taken great joy in shutting your mouth up." The chief's words were harsh and menacing, though that type of threat didn't faze Tay. He'd heard worse from street thugs and rookies with something to prove not to mention his dad had trained him to not be swayed by those types of remarks. "Be glad the Blackwoods want to talk to you before we can take you in for questioning." The chief sniffed dismissively before he turned away and walked to the front door.

Tay barely managed to suppress an eye roll. He had faced his share of police drama before, but that was usually from new recruits trying to act tough—not from someone in a high position like the chief.

They walked through the doors and into the foyer. There Tay saw police officers scattered throughout, mingling with people in suits. Tay paused to take in the chaotic scene. Despite their formal attire, they exuded a presence that told him they were people who thrived in the underworld. On reflex, Tay tried to diminish his presence as much as he could while staying close enough to the chief so the chief would know he was still behind him.

The chief, for his part, didn't shout as they entered. Instead, he stood in front of Tay and scanned the room. "Ah ha," the chief exclaimed. "You stay here and wait until I return," he said as he turned and walked into the maze of people.

Now alone, Tay moved to the side of the door frame and leaned back, as if he belonged there. No one glanced his way as he waited for the chief to return. After two minutes, the chief came back with another man in tow. Tay looked him over and realized it was Mr. Blackwood's butler. Tay relaxed but as they approached him, something felt off about the butler to Tay. He decided to play it safe. Tay kept his relaxed posture but decided he would speak, as if he never met the butler before.

"Mr. Eric, this is Tagen Davis. He's here to talk to Mr. and Mrs. Blackwood about their daughter," the chief said, voice carried a strong sense of respect toward the butler. Tay was relieved the chief spoke softly, as to not alert everyone in the foyer. However, Tay noticed a few picked up on the conversation and looked in their direction.

The butler sighed. "Ralph, I hope that for your sake that this boy is the real deal. The Blackwoods are tired of these boys trying to earn credit for giving out false information." The butler's voice was the one Tay had heard on the phone carrying the same discontent and uncaring attitude.

"I've verified him myself, and I'm confident that he's the real Tagen Davis," the chief said, flashing a bright smile, as if he was the one to find Tay and brought him in.

"Very well. I'll take it from here," the butler said, dismissing the chief. The chief gave a slight bow and walked out the door. The butler, Eric, never stopped looking at Tay. "So, you are the infamous Tagen Davis. You better prepare yourself—the Blackwoods are not in a mood for falsehoods."

"Thanks for the warning but I don't plan on lying to anyone," Tay replied confidently.

"Hmm…" The butler looked Tay over one more time. "Be sure to remember that. Now, this way."

The two of them walked toward the stairs, the crowd parted before them, as if instinctively knowing to let them through. As they walked, Tay looked over the faces of the men and women gathered. They each held a gaze that let him know they had seen their share of bloodshed and fought for a cause. For this many people to be present for the Blackwoods emphasized just how strong the Blackwood family was. Tay couldn't help but think as to why the Lackston family would antagonize such a family who could rally such people at a moment's notice.

Once on the second floor, the butler took Tay down the left pathway with the railing being the only safeguard from falling to the first floor. They walked to the second-to-last door on the right. Once at the door, the butler faced Tay.

"He is in here but mind your manners."

"Sure thing, but what was your name again?"

"Eric," the butler replied before he left without another glance back. Tay looked after him until he disappeared beyond his sight halfway down the stairs. Tay looked in the direction Eric went even after he disappeared.

Something about the butler didn't sit right with Tay and the unsettling feeling gnawed at him, as if begging for him to undo the secret. Tay shook his head to clear it so he could confront the Blackwoods. He turned, knocked on the door, and waited for a reply. Nothing. He grabbed the knob and tried to ease the door open, but instead he stumbled in. The door swung open from when someone had forced their way in, breaking the latch from the frame.

As Tay regained his balance, he realized he was in a library of sorts—the walls were lined with books. He took a breath, expecting the familiar scent of old pages, but instead the sharp metallic tang of iron filled his nostrils.

Tay's senses sharpened instantly. He sniffed the air again and moved deeper into the room. As he walked past the sofas, the scent of iron grew stronger. In the center of the room, he stopped and listened intently. Then he heard it—a soft drip that hit the floor.

He turned and peered behind the sofa on his left and froze. Mr. and Mrs. Blackwood were laid out on the floor; she on top of him, both in a dark pool of blood.

Just then the butler reappeared—and froze.

Both men stared at each other, eyes wide in shock. One, in shock from the scene of seeing the heads of the household dead. The other...in fear as he was caught with two dead people only after having been brought to them.

"You! You murderer!" the butler shouted, his voice carried down the hallway alerting the police force in the house.

Instinctively, Tay bolted past him, knocking him to the floor as he dashed out of the room. There was a commotion downstairs—people looking to find out who had shouted. Tay frantically scanned his surroundings, looking for an escape. He spotted the attic door on the other side of the stairwell. Tay sprinted toward the door as the butler appeared in the hallway.

"Murderer! Someone—stop him!!" the butler yelled. This drew the crowd's attention and made everyone look up. But Tay was already past the bridge-like walkway and hidden by the wall on the right side of the house. He kept running until he made it to the rope for the attic.

He yanked the rope and stepped to the side as the ladder slammed to the floor. Quickly, he climbed up, pulled the ladder up and closed the hatch behind him. Tay held still, not breathing and just listened. Footsteps pounded the ground beneath him, and he knew it was only a matter of time left before someone thought to search the attic.

There was no light to be found in the attic and there was a strong smell like ammonia mixed with flowers. It was a weird combo. Tay kept low and felt around, only taking a step when needed until he found the light switch on one of the beams. The dim light flickered to life, casting an orange glow in the space. As Tay eyes adjusted to the light, he saw guns, knives, and other weapons along with antiques that were fakes to replace the real ones. But none of that mattered.

The main thing that truly got his attention was the body that laid on a tarp on the floor, as if thrown without a care. Flies buzzed around it and the skin was a pale gray color. Even the cheeks had already started to sag slightly. But that wasn't the thing that troubled Tay.

No, it was that Tay knew this man.

It was Eric. The butler from the other night that fought with Tay. But…

"If this is Eric." Tay glanced at the attic door. "Who was that downstairs?"

He stared at the decomposing body as he tried to work out how this could have happened.

"The Blackwood family is strong. So, I don't see anyone just randomly trying to mess with them. And yet here is their butler," Tay whispered to himself as he studied the body in more detail.

"Exactly how long has this guy been dead?" Tay slowly approached the body still careful not to make a sound as he walked across the floorboards. He then realized the smell was coming from this body.

"If the body is already giving this bad of a smell it must have been here for at least three days. So why hasn't anyone noticed the smell?" He looked around and noticed someone had placed a plugin beside the body in a weak attempt to delay the smell from drifting downstairs.

"So... That wasn't Eric that I fought yesterday?" Tay reached out to the body but hesitated before touching and balled his outreached hand. "Then who the hell did I fight?"

"And how did Mr. Blackwood not realize that his butler was dead and replaced?" Tay whispered through clenched teeth. His thoughts were sharp but filled with confusion about this whole situation.

He looked back at the attic door and he noticed around three sides of the entrance moth balls had been placed as if to deter others from noticing the smell coming from the body.

So that is how they explained the smell to keep others from searching the attic?

But before he could think any further, muffled voices rose up from below.

"Did y'all find the killer?" a male voice asked. It sounded like the fake butler.

"No, but we think that he may have found a way to get outside the house." This was the voice of the police chief. "There are many opened windows so he could have escaped through them."

"If he jumped from the second floor he will definitely be injured and moving slowly. You must capture him and make him pay for killing Mr. and Mrs. Blackwood."

"Don't worry we will capture him."

The two then walked away.

He had to get out—now. He looked around cautiously and found a rectangular vent on a wall behind the dead butler. He carefully walked toward it as he prayed that the floorboards wouldn't creak. Thankfully, he made it without incident. He peered through the slits and saw that it led outside. Not only that, but just a few feet he saw a thick tree in the distance.

Tay turned to look for something to pry the vent open, but the moment he did a strong smell invaded his nose. It wasn't the smell of death but of something like a light coating of vinegar in the air that tickled the edges of his memory, but he couldn't place it. With time getting short, he disregarded the smell and went back to his task and found—nothing.

With no more time to waste, he side-kicked the vent and found that it broke away easily. The wooden vent flew out of its slot and broke into splinters as it hit the ground. He climbed out, balanced himself on the ledge of the sill, and jumped to the tree close by. He managed to grab onto one of the thicker branches and praised God it didn't break. He quickly climbed down the tree. Once on the ground, he saw the broken vent and grabbed the pieces of wood to keep others from knowing how he had gotten out of the house.

He stood up just enough to peer over the bushes that surrounded the house. He was on the side of the house, and strangely enough there were no police roaming this area. Tay breathed out a soft sigh.

He wasn't seen. He quickly gathered himself and focused on leaving the estate. With the wood pieces still in his hand, he made his way to the front gate while sticking to the darkness made between the trees and the fence, grateful it was dark outside now.

Tay managed to get to the gate unnoticed and saw the two guards who had searched him when he walked in with the lieutenant earlier, were gone. The gate was left unmanned. But Tay knew two things about this type of scene: either there were guards lined up on the other side or there would be no one there. So, Tay looked around for another means of escape.

He scanned to the left of the guard station and saw a lone tree in the corner against the brick wall that enclosed the estate. Tay couldn't help but smile.

Seems like I'm doing a lot of climbing today, Tay thought to himself as he darted toward the tree.

He took off his shirt, wrapped the planks, and strapped them to his back before he began his climb. Once he was at the point where he could jump on top of the wall, he peered over it and saw that he was right next to his car. He looked at the intersection and didn't see Corporal Thomas or Lieutenant Stokes. Taking this chance, Tay jumped the wall and landed with a roll. His back stung as the wood had scratched through his shirt into his back. He ignored the pain, got up, quickly dumped the wood planks and his shirt on the ground, and went to his car. He opened the door and saw both Aria and his keys were there. Thanking God again for small miracles, Tay started the car and popped his trunk. He took a can of lighter fluid and his gas tank.

He poured gas on all but one plank of wood. He then poured lighter fluid on the edge of that plank and set it so that in the middle of the gas-soaked pile. He lit the lighter fluid. As the flame caught on the wood piece, Tay ran to his car. He got in the car and drove off. Just as he turned right on the next street, there was a loud explosion and the sky behind him lit up a bright orange.

Tay skidded to a stop, quickly got out the car, and looked back at the Blackwood's estate. The house was ablaze, and the orange glow of the fire danced in his eyes. Suddenly, the scent he smelled from the attic came back to him, and he remembered why it seemed so familiar—it was acetone peroxide and natural gas. His dad made him memorize almost any chemical that had a scent dangerous to him while he was blindfolded so the scent would be more than pronounced to him. Tay knew it was only by chance he noticed it when he was by the vent that led outside due to a small draft. But knowing that now caused Tay's heart to sink into his stomach. He feared for the people inside as he knew they didn't notice. They were too busy with each other and searching for him to pay attention to their surroundings.

Tay numbly took a step back to the house; his eyes fixated on the flames. Another small explosion occurred and Tay shielded his eyes as the glow brightened momentarily. After a moment, Tay slowly turned to look back at the house. His breathing sped up and became sharp and deep as the sight of the flames overtook his vision. Tay grasped at his chest where he felt a stabbing pain. But there was no knife, no one was around, and he knew the pain from within.

Not again. No, not again, Tay thought to himself. He unconsciously took a few steps toward the flames, his vision swimming. He stumbled as his foot hit the curb of the road. He caught himself before he fell. When he looked back up, he saw his younger self in front of him staring at the flames. He was outside his old house as the fire consumed not only the place where he called home, but the people that he loved, too. Beside his younger version stood two younger kids, a boy and a girl. They cried while holding onto the younger Tay. But Tay didn't cry.

It was then his rage and his desire to protect his younger siblings came into confrontation with each other. He wanted to hunt down the one that stole his family from them. But he knew what his father always told him.

Rage only leads to destruction. Protect what you can and live the life you want. We have lived ours and you should do the same.

It was those words that had made Tay decide to leave the shadow world and do everything to protect his only family. Suddenly, the younger Tay turned around and looked at him, eyes hard but with a sense of sympathy in them.

"You don't need to be here. You have someone to protect," the younger version of him said softly as the glow from the fire behind him intensified. Tay closed his eyes and monitored his breathing to stable himself. Once he felt calm and grounded, he heard his younger self tell him in a whisper, "Go and live."

Tay opened his eyes, seeing only the flames from the Blackwood's estate. He turned and got back in his car. Twice in one night he watched a house burn and twice he was reminded of the time he lost his family. Tay breathed deeply and let the breath out slowly, composing himself. He pulled out his cellphone and he texted his brother to go get his sister for she was in danger and for them to come home now. His brother replied quickly with a, *Yes sir. See you in two days.*

He hated having to uproot their lives once again to make them leave everything behind and start over again. But he knew that they knew he prioritized their safety first.

Tay drove. He didn't have a true destination in mind. The only thing he could see were the flames from both the Lackston's and the Blackwood's homes. The memory of how his own home looked constantly overlapped them. He tried to focus but he couldn't shake the feeling that this was all a repeat of that night. And that the one that caused his home to burn was the same that caused these two flames.

After a while, Aria began to stir. He pulled over to the side of the road, slipped the blindfold over her eyes, removed the cover enough for him to cuff her hands. Though she was now safe, he didn't want to risk her hurting him or herself until she was calmed down. After he did that, he saw the gag ball still in her mouth from Mr. Lackston—a sight that filled him with a wave of revulsion. He looked at what he was doing and he felt bile rise in his throat.

Though I'm not doing this for the same reason as him. Tay gagged and he swallowed to clear the feeling. *Now I feel like I'm doing the same thing as him.*

He undid the handcuffs but left the blindfold on. He gently took the gag ball out of her mouth. The moment it wasn't touching her tongue, he heard a soft click and a beep like a timer had started.

His grip tightened briefly around the straps of the gag and his throat flexed as he swallowed the scream he wanted to let out.

What is up with things exploding all night tonight? He threw it out the window and drove off.

I'm tired of this shit. He had barely pulled away when a sharp explosion echoed where the gag ball landed, which jolted Aria awake.

"Hmmm… Where am I?" Aria asked in a stupor, her voice weak. Tay didn't speak. Aria seemed to have forgotten what happened to her or maybe her mind was blocking it out. She turned silent and sat there not moving. Tay drove another fifteen minutes before he parked into the garage. He turned off the car, got out, and walked around to Aria's side. He opened the door, but she still didn't move.

"Time to go in," he said as he reached to take her hand, but the moment he touched her, she began to fight. Her arm swung around, as if to desperately protect herself.

"No, please. I'm begging you don't take that from me. Tay is the only one that can have my first," she cried out. Tay pulled back, puzzled. *Why me of all people?* He wanted to ask, but he knew now wasn't the time for that. His priority was to calm her down so they could go inside.

"Hey, Aria, calm down. It's me, Tay," he said softly to soothe her as he caught and held her wrists.

She stopped struggling, her breathing labored, and her hands shook. "Tay?... What...What are you doing here?"

"I will explain everything, but first, let me take off your blindfold." Tay slowly reached toward the blindfold. The moment he touched her head, she flinched slightly but held still. Tay slowly lifted it off her head. Once it was completely off, she blinked multiple times before she focused on Tay.

"See? It's me," Tay said gently as he offered her a small, reassuring smile. "As for why, I'm here... Well, I didn't have much of a choice. Your parents were worried that you were in danger, and from the messages you left me, I felt obligated to help. So, I rescued you."

Aria looked at him as she processed what he had said. For a minute, they stared at each other, letting the silence hang between them. Then Aria eyes glossed over. She sniffed and threw herself onto Tay and wrapped her arms around his neck. "I was so scared," she cried out, tears freely fell from her eyes.

"I know, but you are safe now. No one will hurt you here," Tay said as he took a knee, embraced her, and stroked the back of her head to calm her down. They stayed like that for a while—wrapped in each other's arms as Aria released the fear and frustration she held inside. Slowly, her sobs subsided. Aria pulled back and rested on her feet as she wiped her eyes.

"Thank you, Tay, for coming to get me. I'm so gratefully for you." She smiled warmly at Tay, cheeks still damp from her tears and eyes still on the verge of crying again. "So where are we now?"

This question made Tay's heart sink. He turned his eyes down and remained silent for a moment, not sure how to tell her this was her new home.

"Tay?" she asked, her voice shaking.

Tay looked up at Aria. "Look I… I got something to tell you."

Aria leaned forward and placed one hand on his and the other on his cheek, her touch warm and comforting. "It is okay. You know I can keep a secret."

Her words made it even harder for Tay to say what he needed to. He swallowed hard. "Aria… Your parents… They are dead. Along with your butler, Eric."

Aria stared at him in disbelief with a confused smile on her face. "Wh— What?"

Tay took a deep breath, centered himself, and continued. "After I rescued you from the Lackston's residence, I drove you back home…" He recounted the events that had unfolded at the Blackwood's estate—the police, the search, and then the explosion that consumed the house. He explained how it seemed like the explosion had been planned, made to look like a gas leak, but that he suspected otherwise. He told her about the house they were now at. "So, this… this is the second safehouse that my family left behind." He hesitated, not comfortable enough yet to tell her about his brother and sister.

Aria just stared at Tay, her hand dropped from his face and her eyes seemed to empty of all life.

"You're lying…" she whispered, her voice hollow, devoid of emotion.

"I'm sorry," Tay said gently, "But it's the truth."

"You're LYING!!!" she shouted as she stood up, her fists clenched at her sides as her whole body trembled with grief and denial.

Tay looked up at her. "I truly wish I was."

"Stop… just stop," she muttered as she shook her head furiously before she turned to the car and got in. "Take me home now."

"I can't."

"Tay, take me home NOW!" she shouted at him, tears flowing from her bloodshot eyes, her voice rattled with desperation. "Please."

Tay said nothing. He stood up, pulled his phone out of his pocket, and pulled up a news channel. He played the video loud enough for her to hear. *"We are now at the scene where a devastating house exploded occurred earlier tonight. Authorities say that it started out as a search and rescue mission for a 22-year-old girl by the name of Aria René Blackwood. They were getting ready to go to the suspect's house when an explosion went off claiming the lives of Mr. and Mrs. Blackwood, the homeowners, along with many others. Forensics are saying that the explosion was caused by a gas leak…"* Tay closed his phone to end the broadcast.

Aria pulled her knees to her chest, hugged herself, and sobbed even harder. Tay wanted to reach in and comfort her, but he thought of all she had been through that night and now she had lost everything—her house and family. She was like him all those years ago, but she was alone with no one. No one except for Tay. He walked to the back passenger door, turned, and leaned against the door. He stuffed his hands—now fist—into his pockets and listened to her cry. Her pain gnawed at him; each sob made him clench his teeth harder.

After about five minutes, Aria's sobs softened. She sat there, curled up, her breathing uneven. Tay looked at her, and the realization hit him—he couldn't force her to stay. No matter how much he wanted to protect her at that moment, he would respect whatever decision she came to.

Tay inhaled deeply, steeled himself, and spoke softly. "If you want to go, I can take you wherever it is you want. I won't hold you here. But… at least accept some cash before you go."

"Tay…" she said still curled up, her voice fragile.

"Yes?"

Aria slowly uncurled, turned to set her feet outside the car. She leaned forward and stared blankly at the floor. The tears had stopped, but her expression was like someone watching tv and not really there.

"Tell me why," she said so softly that it was almost a whisper.

"Why what?"

"Don't play dumb," she said as turned to look at him, her eyes no longer empty but blazed with a fierce fire—a fire that told a story of revenge and retribution. "Why did they die? Why would anyone want to kill them? Why am I alive? Why…" She trailed off as she bit hard on her lower lip and clenched the side of the seat to keep herself from shedding anymore tears.

Tay looked at her, not sure what to say. So, he went with what he knew. "I don't have all the answers, Aria. I wish I did. But I do know this—you're alive because your mom and dad made sure you were. And I'm here… because your mom convinced me to protect you. She made sure I wouldn't abandon you."

There was a heavy silence as Aria stared at Tay, her eyes searched for something unspoken. Tay held her gaze and waited patiently.

"So, what is your decision?" Tay asked softly.

"May I…" She hesitated, then turned and looked at the floor again. "My dad taught me a lot of things—how to protect myself, how to be brave when I needed to be. But the most important thing he taught me was how to live my life without regret. He used to say he lived most of his life regretting everything he had done, until he met my mom and had me. From that moment on, he said he had no more regrets. He said that even going to jail wasn't something he regretted—because it had toughened him up, made him the man who could protect the ones he loved."

Aria paused, her voice trembled slightly as she continued. "He told me that if a shadow from his past ever came to claim him, he wouldn't regret that either. He would fight—and fight hard. And if he passed away, he wanted me to know that he had lived his life. He told me that I should live mine. He told me never to let rage and revenge consume me, because then I'd miss out on everything important in life. He told me to live. To find peace, find joy again. And... to find love." Tay listened to her. Her words sounded oddly reminiscent of what his father had told him.

"So, I guess what I am saying is that I don't want to live by the rage I now feel. I know that will never honor my parents' memory. So, if you are okay with it, I would like to stay with you," she finished softly, her eyes filled with a quiet resolve.

Tay searched her face and saw a genuine desire to live without being led by rage and revenge. Relieved, he let out a soft sigh. "That's fine. I don't know how much I can do for you, but I'll do what I can. All I ask is that you look after yourself, too. Try not to rely on me too much."

Without warning, Aria jumped out of the car. The cover fell to the ground as she hugged him tightly. "Tay, you are the closest person I have to a true friend."

He hugged her back, but responded with a gentle skepticism. "I doubt that. You probably have a few people you could call true friends."

"No, I'm serious," she insisted, her grip tightened around his waist. "No one else would do what you're doing for me now."

"How about you check your phone first before making assumptions like that," he suggested to try and put some distance between the relationship she was steadily trying to form.

Aria let go of Tay, went to her seat to get her phone out of her bag. Tay's eyes followed before he quickly turned away, his heart racing at the sight of her exposed figure. He glanced at the discarded cover, bent down, and picked it up just as she turned back.

"What is wrong, Tay?" she asked, puzzled at his refusal to meet her eyes. "Anyways, here. I want to show you the messages from my so-called friends," she said as she stepped toward him, phone extended. Tay took a step forward and draped the cover over her.

"For now. Please wear this. You are a bit too revealing." He then took the phone from her just as she looked down. She saw the state of her outfit and quickly clutched the cover closed around her.

"Thank you."

"No problem," Tay answered as he read through the messages from people who had been around her only for her money but claimed to have been friends. Not one had checked in on her, even though her house had been all over the news.

"See? That's what I mean."

Tay shook his head slightly, still not entirely convinced. "You're just trying to make me feel special. Besides, it's late—they could be asleep and might see the news in the morning."

"No... Well, yes. I do want to make you special because you are to me," she admitted with a small smile. "But even when they know, they don't show any true emotions. You're the only one I know I can trust."

"I appreciate that, given the situation. But don't forget—you barely know me. You still need to keep your guard up around me," he said, his tone a mixture of seriousness and caution.

"Tay, ever since that day in grade school, I trusted you. And it grew more when you stepped in to defend me and my associates."

Tay sighed inwardly, wishing it had been someone else who had caught her eye. He knew having her around might complicate things—especially with there being a real possibility of something with Lyn, and his hopes for a normal life.

"Look," he began, searching for the right words, "I need you to understand something."

But before he could continue, Aria interrupted, "Tay, I already know about the girl you're interested in."

Tay blinked, caught off guard. His confusion quickly turned into suspicion. "Wait, were you spying on me?" he asked, a scowl on his face.

"No," Aria answered as she shook her head. "I just saw her hand you her number at the club. But something didn't seem right about her."

"Yeah, well... whatever." He turned away from her and walked to the back of his car.

"Tay, I'm not trying to get in your way," she said gently. "I just want you to be careful with her. And... I'd still like to stay with you."

Tay paused and thought about his siblings and all the complications ahead. After a moment, he nodded slowly. "I know, I already told you—you can stay. We're not going to kick you out after all that happened."

"We?" Aria asked, puzzled.

Tay said nothing, instead opened his trunk. Aria walked up beside him, looked at him pointedly as she waited for him to answer, but he didn't meet her eyes. He pulled out a backpack then went to the backseat and got all his stuff. Together, they walked into the house.

The moment they stepped inside, Aria froze.

"Where are we?" she asked as she ran to catch up to Tay who just kept walking. They walked into the kitchen that was big enough for a family reunion. Tay set his backpack on the island and finally turned to face her.

"This is my place," he said simply.

Aria's brow furrowed in confusion. "Then… What was that other place we were at the other day?"

"That's my other home," Tay responded as he turned to his backpack, unzipped it, and took a few boxes out. He opened one and took out a key before closing the box and putting everything back in the backpack.

"Why… How can you afford two houses? Especially one like this?"

"Does it matter?" Tay shrugged, turned, and walked into the foyer. There were two sets of grand stairs that followed the curve of the walls to the next floor. Aria followed, still in awe at how huge and beautiful the house was.

"Tay… Why do I feel like I have been here before?"

Tay froze mid-step, the question hitting harder than he expected. He closed his eyes and tried to ground himself.

She just had a traumatic experience. She's latching onto anything familiar. That's all this is.

He counted to five in his head, then turned to face her. "That's not possible. This place has only ever belonged to my family. Not even childhood friends came here."

Aria didn't respond. She slowly walked to the wall and ran her fingers across the crown molding, her eyes drifting over the staircase and down the curved hallway.

"No… I swear I've been here before. It's not just déjà vu. It's like… I was here once—when I was really young. A long time ago."

Her gaze lingered on the architecture, like the house itself was pulling at something just beyond her reach..

Tay sighed as he continued walking. He wanted to be attentive to her, to comfort her. But her questions were beginning to drain him. Without pausing, he headed down the hall on the right and stopped at the second door on the left. He inserted the key and opened the door. "This is your room for now," he said, his voice carrying a hint of exhaustion as his eyes glazed over the room and his shoulders hung. "There should be some extra clothes in the dresser that you can change into. Not sure if they will fit."

"Thanks," Aria said as she walked in, glanced around before she turned to face Tay, who lingered at the entryway. "Um… Where will your room be?" she asked, her voice soft and expression bashful as she looked down.

"Please. Don't start that," Tay said as he shook his head. He then turned and walked back down to the foyer. Aria watched silently as he made his way up the staircase on the left. Once he left her field of vision, she closed her door softly behind her.

Tay walked up the stairs, lost in his thought of what the future held. He worried for his brother and sister and how they would react to not only having to start over but having Aria here. Upon reaching the second floor, he turned right. He walked down the hallway, zoned out and barely noticed the doors he passed. Each one was decorated from when him and his siblings were kids. He glanced over them as he passed.

One door had stickers of Naruto, another door was Sailor Moon, and the last was chemistry beakers and such. He hadn't seen those doors in over a decade… but they still held the same energy. Still made him feel like an older brother who was supposed to protect his siblings from everything. Tay's hand twitched and a lump formed in his throat that was extremely hard to swallow. As he swallowed, it was like swallowing a whole object and it burned and scratched going down. Being back here meant to him that he failed.

He continued walking until he came to a double door. Another weight seemed to settle on his shoulders, which caused his legs to weaken. He slowly shuffled the last few feet to the door. He stood in front of it and looked at it.

After a time, he slowly reached for the knob. As he grabbed it, he let out a deep sigh. "I wish I never had to come back here," he muttered under his breath. He turned the knob and slowly opened the door and flicked the lights on.

"Wow. So, this is your room," Aria said from behind. Tay jumped and spun to face her.

"Why are you here?" he asked, his voice laced with irritation as he tried to turn the lights off. But Aria stepped in front of him, cover still on her, blocking his way.

"Look this is my room. Congrats—you found it. Now, please get out and go change," Tay said as he turned to the side with one arm extended to let her out, eyes hollow and his voice flat.

"Tay, why are you so adamant about pushing me away so much?" she asked as she stood there, her gaze steady as she refused to leave until she got an answer.

"Because the life you are living in... I don't want any part of it anymore," Tay replied thick with emotion. "Whether you know about that kind of world or not."

Tay's thoughts drifted to his old life—his mother waking him up, training with his father, brother, and sister. And then how it had all been stripped away from him. Now, all he had left was his little brother and sister, and a broken life. He even thought of Rin and how she broke up with him because of his past lifestyle. He then thought of Evelyn and feared that the same thing would happen again crept inside his mind. "I can't handle the torment it causes. And I'm barely holding together the life I got," he added, his voice trembling as tears welled up in his eyes. He looked down, fighting them back. He had sworn to himself that he would never cry again, that he would never show the hurt and rage inside him—because to him that was a sign of weakness.

"Tay, look... I've had feelings for you for a long time now," she spoke softly as she relaxed her body posture and slowly walked toward Tay. "You mean more than the world to me. And I will do whatever it takes to show you that." She was now one foot away from Tay and reached for his hand.

Tay looked down at her hand, feelings inside him warring with each other. Her touch brought a sense of comfort and security, but it also unsettled him with how she could sway his emotions so much.

"Look... I'm going to live my life how I want. If you're in it, you're in it, but with the way things are I don't see myself being with you." He lifted his eyes to meet hers, only for his heart to throb in pain.

"I know," she replied, her voice steady and her eyes showed a strong determination. "But I am not going to go anywhere unless you are with me." Aria released his hand and clutching the edges of the cover, she opened it up and wrapped Tay in the cover with her, hugging him tightly. "I'm sorry for barging in like this. But I'm glad you're the one I can depend on." Tay's arms momentarily raised, as if to hug her back but he froze midway and dropped them back to his side. Her embrace was a balm to the day's events. Even if he was irritated with her when they first met, something about her now made him want to keep her around.

She released him, stepped back with a warm smile that reminded him of his mother as she covered up. The smile was gentle and caring yet held a strength to say 'You can depend on me.' As she walked out of the room, she paused at the door and glanced back. "I'll show you how committed to you I am one day. So be ready for it." A devious smile tugged at her lips before she disappeared down the hall.

Tay closed the door behind her and locked it. He leaned against the door and exhaled loudly, his mind a whirlwind. He thought of how her touch had made him feel comforted and wanted, but there was something obsessive about her that kept him wary. No matter how hard he tried, he just couldn't seem to distance himself from her.

Tay looked around his room. Almost everything was covered in plastic yet there was not a speck of dust to be found anywhere. Though he hadn't lived here in a long time, the will of his parents had a specific clause in it to use some of the funds they left behind to maintain this house in case it was ever needed. The staff came on a quiet rotation—cleaning, restocking, and preserving everything while leaving his parents' bedroom untouched. Though the will expressed that it hoped that there would come a time when the house would be needed. And as he looked around, he noticed the same old game posters from when he was eight still adorned the walls. He thought back to that time—the life he had once believed would last forever.

"I was so naïve back then," he muttered, shaking his head. "Thinking that my family was untouchable."

Setting his other bag down beside the bed, Tay tore the plastic off the furniture. Once he uncovered the bed, he collapsed onto it, letting out a long breath. The familiar feel and scent of the sheets offered some comfort, and for a moment, he allowed himself to relax. Then he felt a vibration against his leg. Rolling over, he pulled it out and saw his brother's name flash on the screen. He sat up and answered the call.

"Hello."

"65, 25, 7," and the call ended.

Tay thought for a moment and realized that his brother was on I-65, just 25 minutes away from exit 7. "So, he's almost there to get sis. Great," Tay muttered as he laid back down. His eyes grew heavy as the weight of the day finally hit him. He tried to get up, but exhaustion took over, and in the next moment, his eyes closed, and he drifted into sleep.

Knock! Knock! Knock!

Tay opened one eye as he groaned.

"Tay. Tay. Are you awake?" Aria asked through the locked door. "There is someone at the front door." Tay sat up and wiped his eyes. He looked around and realized he was in his old room. Aria banged on his bedroom door again.

"Tay, come on. Open up. There really is someone at the door."

He got off the bed and walked groggily to the door. He unlocked the door, and as soon as he opened it, Aria stumbled into him. He caught her and they looked into each other's eyes briefly.

Her eyes seemed to shine to him just like the night before the club.

She is so beautiful. Tay felt his heart speed up and he unconsciously pulled her in closer. Then he heard the banging on the front door. The rhythm of the knocks cleared the lingering fog that clouded his mind. He swiftly stood Aria up and ran out of the room.

What the hell am I doing? Tay placed a hand to his heart as it still raced. *Why do I act like that around her? What about her makes me feel so comfortable I don't want her to leave my side?* Tay tried to clear his head as he made it to the stairs. He heard the knock once more and bolted down the steps and jumped down the last six. He landed hard on his feet, lost his balance, and fell to his hands. He scrambled to stand as he steadily approached the door.

Once he had his hand on the handle, he paused and slowly peered through the peephole. He saw two figures and due to the darkness of the early morning he couldn't see their faces. But one held up a small box with a silver gun emblemed etched into it. Tay recognized the box and opened the front door and there stood his brother and sister in cloaks that shrouded their faces.

Tay stood there stunned. They really were here. Finally, the family was together once again.

"Come in," Tay said as he backed up and let them in. He looked them over as they passed. They limped slightly and seemed to be holding themselves as if they were hurt. Tay closed the door and locked it behind them before he turned to fully see them. They took off their cloaks gingerly and Tay felt his eyes burn and his heart raced as he saw the condition they were in.

"Tay, what is going on?" Aria spoke up from the last step on the stairs. She was able to fully see them now that their cloaks were off. She saw all the marks on their clothes. She knew those marks weren't from falling down. "Tay, who are they and why are they so messed up?"

Tay shot Aria a sharp glare, his eyes flared with his frustration. She flinched; fear filled her eyes. He noticed her reaction and closed his eyes then took a deep breath to calm himself.

Don't blame her. She didn't cause this. Relax and hear what happened.

When he opened his eyes again, they were softer but still held a fire that was ready to ignite if the need arose. He looked at his brother and sister. "Shayla, Tim, this is Aria," he said as he extended his arm toward her. "She will be staying with us for a while." Tay turned to Aria and he noticed that she had changed clothes. She wore a summer dress with shades of blue floral designs and halter straps tied behind her neck. "Aria, this is my brother, Tim and sister, Shayla." Tay then looked back at his brother and sister.

Shayla was the first to meet Tay's eyes. Though her voice was soft, her words cut through the silence. "Tay... they tried to follow us again."

Aria stood frozen momentarily after the brief introduction but came to her senses after Shayla spoke. She turned to Tay. "Tay, may I talk to you?" she asked in a soft yet determined voice.

Tay turned his back to her. He gently grabbed his sister's arm and wrapped his arm around her back.

"Let's talk in the living room," Tay said softly as he guided his brother and sister. Aria followed at a safe distance but stopped at the entrance to the living room. Once Tim and Shayla were seated, Tay sat on the sofa across from them and looked them over one more time before he asked, "So, what happened?"

"As I walked into the club to get Shayla, I saw some new guys at the bar flirting with her. The moment I tried to take her out, one reached for something behind him. So, I quickly pulled her with me and ran for the car," Tim answered methodically as he cradled his ribs.

"Tay, I'm sorry. It's my fault. I was wearing heels and couldn't break them, and we ended up getting caught," Shayla's voice quivered as she stared down at her hands squeezing them together.

"Shayla, it is okay. You're here now and that is what matters," Tay said in a comforting tone as he leaned forward to look at her. She looked up upon hearing his words and was met with eyes filled with love and care. She nodded. Tay looked at Tim. "So, who were they working for?"

"All I remember was an 'L' on their collar," Tim said as he looked at Tay. Tay held his gaze. He instantly thought of Mr. Lackston, but that couldn't be right.

Tay knew he burned in his own house last night. Either way, Tay pushed that thought out his mind for later. His siblings needed him right now.

Tim looked toward Aria, who still lurked by the entrance way. Tay noticed his glance.

Guess this is as good a time as any, he thought to himself as he sighed inwardly.

"Aria, come here," Tay said, patting the cushion next to him. Aria moved quickly, a small smile playing on her lips taking her place beside him. Tay noticed the way she leaned slightly toward him, her posture relaxed but hopeful, as if sitting next to him brought her comfort and joy.

Again, Tay felt a spark. Just having her touch him sent a shock through his body and he felt the need to wrap an arm around her, as if it was the most natural thing to do. Tay glanced at her, and for a moment, he thought he saw a glint of something in her eyes. She seemed more controlled but it looked like there was a soft hunger in her eyes. Tay thought of Mr. Blackwood and he knew he would have taught his daughter something in case of emergencies.

Let's test this out.

Once Aria settled beside him, Tay shifted his attention back to his siblings. His voice grew firm when he addressed them. "I will only say this once. You two stay right there," he ordered Shayla and Tim. His tone didn't leave any room for argument. His expression softened slightly when he looked at Aria as he remembered the night she just had. "Aria, I have a favor to ask of you."

Her eyes beamed as he spoke. "Oh, what is it?"

"I know you had a hard night last night but I need you to do something for me."

Her face turned somber and she pulled her lips tight before relaxing. "Ok…what can I do?"

"Did your father ever teach you something to do in case of emergencies? Like if you found yourself around other people how you should introduce yourself."

"Um—he did." Aria looked from Tay to Tim and Shayla. Her eyes stayed on her for a moment longer than the guys before she looked back at Tay. "Why do you ask?"

"I need you to introduce yourself the way your father taught you."

Aria searched Tay's eyes, as if asking if she really had to. Tay nodded. She bit on her lower lip then reluctantly stood up. She curtsied before speaking. "Nice to meet you all. My name is Aria Renee Blackwood, daughter of the late Jeff Oscar and Linda Joyce Blackwood." She finished then sat down.

"Blackwood," Tim and Shayla said together under their breath as they turned to gaze at Aria.

"Why… Why did you bring her here?" Tim said through clenched teeth, his hands twitched as he shook to keep himself from standing up.

"Because she's just like us now," Tay said calmly as he looked to Tim and held him in place with his eyes. "Look, her parents were killed the same night she was kidnapped and raped. The person who kidnapped her was Mr. Gerald Lackston."

At this, Tim backed down but still flexed his jaw. "I can understand why you would do that. But you remember it was because our parents were grouped with the Blackwood family that they are dead now."

Tay shot Tim a look that made Tim flinch and sink into his seat. Aria, on the other hand, looked at Tay with eyes wide open.

"Tay, is that true? Were my parents one of the reasons for your parents' death?" Aria squeezed Tay's hand and he felt her arm shake.

Tay looked into her eyes and he saw the fear that her family had something to do with his pain. Tay shook his head.

"Though our parents were really close as your father mentioned before. They aren't the reason for our parents' death. I firmly believe that from how proud my parents were to have yours as friends." He placed his other hand on her shoulder. "So don't think about it that way." Tay looked up and gazed at Tim and Shayla. "Either of you."

They all nodded in agreement. "Now back to why Aria is here. After all that happened I felt she needed a place of comfort and somewhere safe to stay."

"I can understand that but why here?" Tim asked.

"I honestly don't know. I just felt that she will be more comfortable around me after all that happened. And I sort of want her around."

Shayla smiled. "So, you are saying you guys are close to dating?"

"No," Tay said instantly. Aria looked at their hands together and her cheek became rosy.

Tay face palmed. "Look. I have someone that I am interested in. And she seems to be very understanding." He then looked to Aria. "And I won't deny I feel something familiar about being around Aria but it isn't at the level of wanting to make you my girl or anything."

"Not yet. But it definitely seems to be soon with the way you two are still holding each other's hand," Shayla teased. Even Tim chuckled as Tay looked down and released Aria's hand. Aria looked sad for a moment, but her cheeks were still rosy.

Tay cleared his throat. "Look, we have gotten off topic. What I was trying to say was before was that now that I hear what happened to y'all, I'm not convinced that the man I took down was really Mr. Lackston."

This caused everyone to stop playing around and the room fell into a deep silence.

Tim was the first to break the tension. "Tay, why do you think that?" All emotions drained from his face.

"When you said you saw an L on the collar of the people that were after you. The man that also caused severe harm to Aria was the first to come to mind. Not to mention the fight we had seemed too easy to be really him."

"Wait—hold up," Shayla interrupted, her voice rose as she tried to piece it all together. She looked from Aria to Tay; her brow furrowed in confusion. "From the top. Tell us everything that happened."

"Okay, but listen carefully. I don't want to have to tell it again," Tay said. His voice carried a sense of authority his siblings knew all too well. He leaned in and recounted the events that took place since he met Aria. When Tay mentioned his date with Evelyn, Tim and Shayla froze. Their eyes locked on him, beamed with joy and curiosity as they interrupted and demanded details about Rin and what happened with her and how the date went. Tay kept throwing glances at Aria as he told them about the date, but she didn't move or seem affected by what he said. At least not until he told them about the kiss at the end.

Aria flinched and huffed a little at the mention of Tay being kissed on the cheek. Tay looked her way but she returned his gaze with a gentle smile. Her eyes smoldered with a heat that sent a chill down Tay's spine.

He hesitated to continue about what happened with Rin.

Well, might as well. Not like we will ever get back together again. Before he went on, he looked at Aria, knowing that telling about Rin would also mean letting everyone know how he and Aria met.

In the end, he shrugged and he decided to just tell the truth. He told them of the breakup call and how that led him to the park that day. Tim and Shayla exchanged looks, their suspicion of Aria clear. But Tay quickly dispelled any doubts by explaining how the Blackwoods acted when he dropped Aria off. Reluctantly, they nodded though their uncertainty lingered on their faces.

Even with their suspicions, they congratulated Tay for the step he took toward getting back to something resembling a normal life. After that, Tay completed the recap as he said, "And now, here we are."

Tim and Shayla reeled from the revelations, but Aria's face showed her discomfort with the unexpected company. She nudged Tay gently.

"May I speak with you privately now?" she asked softly.

"We will be right back," Tay said as he stood up. He took her hand and led her into the dining room.

"Well, what is it?" he asked once they were alone and let her hand go.

"Tay, how are they your brother and sister? Your family died—leaving only you. I was at the funeral, so I know," she pressed.

Tay did indeed remember seeing the Blackwood family there and they had a little girl with them. He assumed she was their daughter or something but he didn't really pay attention as he was distracted by the last sight he would see of his parents. He sighed. "Look, you don't know anything," he said, frustration crept into his voice. "Yes, there was a funeral. But there were no bodies."

"Then why do they have different names from what was written on the program?" she asked, determined to figure out who they were and why they claimed to be Tay's family.

Tay raised an eyebrow at the level of detail that Aria's memory held. "First off, I don't know if I should be impressed or creeped out that you remember a program from back then no matter how infatuated you seem to be with me," Tay said. "Look, they are my brother and sister. And I can prove it."

I don't know why I'm even doing this—just to satisfy her curiosity, Tay thought. His mind swirled with frustration and a need to prove his siblings' identities to Aria. Without hesitation, he called out, "Jeremy." Tim's head snapped up, alarm clear in his stiff posture.

"Chanice." Shayla looked up, eyes scanning for the one who called her, her breath caught for just a moment.

Finally, her eyes rested on Tay, wide with something that looked like recognition. But there was more. Her face softened and her gaze turned hollow as her lips trembled. She looked away quickly, covering her face with her hands as her shoulders shook. Soft murmurs came from behind her fingers, but Tay could barely make them out. The only words that reached his ears were, "He isn't here... he isn't here..."

Tay's heart clenched in his chest. He remembered how in the past she would always tell him that his voice reminded her of their father when he called her. Tay felt the guilt of his actions instantly. He hadn't meant to hurt her. It had just... slipped out. But it was too late to try and take it back.

Tay felt Tim's gaze on him, as if he was under a microscope. The rage in his eyes let Tay know he had crossed a line they weren't ready to cross.

"Why, Tay..." Tim's voice was low and dangerous, the words barely escaped his tight jaw. "Why would you call us by those names? Why now of all times?"

Tay looked at Tim resolve to face his judgement head on. He knew he had messed up, but he couldn't think of any other way for everyone to try to trust each other. He hadn't planned it to go like this—he just wanted Aria to stop doubting his family.

Tay took a deep breath. "I'm sorry, guys," he said loud enough for them to hear him in the living room. "I didn't think my actions through. I still remember the promise we made, and I know the stakes. But this house is supposed to be a safe place for all of us. And right now, she needs to trust you. And you need to trust her. If we're at each other's throats all the time, how are we supposed to keep this place safe?"

Tay paused still looking at Tim, whose face was still filled with hot rage. Tay scratched his head, frustrated. He hated being the middleman. "Look," he said, his voice took on a commanding tone. "I can't and I won't be the middleman because you all don't want to trust each other. I also doubt Aria but my doubts of her are different from the doubts you two carry. Either way, we are all now living under the same roof, and I will not have us being on high alert all the time with each other." Tay looked at Tim then to Aria. He briefly glanced at Shayla, who still sobbed softly but he knew she was listening. He turned his attention back to Tim.

"I know it seems like I broke the promise but believe me when I say I did it to help us all in this moment."

Tim's posture didn't relax but he nodded his head. He turned to Shayla, wrapped an arm around her, and cradled her gently. Tay watched them for a moment. Their closeness made his heart ache. He hated he didn't have that close of a relationship with them like they used to before they had to live apart. They used to be unbreakable but Tay's need to protect them drove him to distance himself because he was the oldest and the one who needed to make sure they were okay. This didn't mean he didn't know what was going on with them, just he didn't get the chance to hang out or truly talk to them anymore.

Tay turned back to Aria. "You see," he spoke to her softly, his voice caught in his throat briefly.

"They are my true family. The only family I have left." He turned to walk back to the living room when Aria gently grabbed his arm.

"Tay, please listen to me," she whispered. "I'm not trying to deceive you—it's just I don't think we should trust them. Yes, they may have answered to their true names, but something still feels off," she pleaded.

Tay stared at her in disbelief before he pulled his arm free. His eyes were fierce and left no room for questions and as he spoke, his voice rose enough for his siblings to hear. "Look… You are just clinging onto a lie that I put out back then to protect my family. And I refuse to lose them because you don't want to believe they are who they are. I know my family and I will not listen to any more of your nonsense."

Tay looked up to the ceiling and counted to five. Once calmed down, he walked back to the living room, Aria still in the kitchen. "You two need to go get some rest. Give me the house keys and head to bed."

"Thanks, bro," Tim said though his voice was still strained. He set the keys on the table, helped Shayla to her feet, then they walked toward their rooms on the first floor.

Tay watched them leave then turned to Aria. "You, too. Go to your room. Dinner will be ready shortly."

Aria hesitated for a brief moment before she looked down and sulked to her room.

Tay's eyes followed her until she walked out of sight before he walked to the kitchen. His mind was still clouded on how to handle the situation they were in. In almost a mechanical motion, he opened the fridge and stared at what was inside.

He saw it was fully stocked and even the freezer and flex drawers had plenty in them. Not to mention the detail for the way things were organized made it extremely easy to see what was there and the options Tay had.

He started gathering things to make dinner as he thought of the last time he lived together with his little brother and sister. The times when he would cook and take care of them while their parents were away on a few missions. How he made sure they were taken care of and protected. Though those times were tough since they were alone with only the three maids they had at that time but they were able to make it to be who they are now.

It's nice to be together again, Tay thought as he turned on the oven and prepped the ingredients. The corner of his right lip tugged into a small smile. Despite the situation, he was really happy.

His family was home again.

Tay quickly got into his flow of cooking. He had already prepped some potatoes in foil as the oven beeped to indicate it was ready. His mind was blank as he focused on cooking. And the next step was one of his favorites to cook.

Steak!

The pan had just reached a hot enough temp as Tay finished seasoning the steaks. Just as he was about to place them in the pan, his nose itched. He tried to hold it back but the sensation was too strong. As he looked to the ceiling and stared at a light. He just stood like that, frozen for a moment. No sounds. No movement. Just the itch reaching a crescendo.

Tay sneezed so hard, he bent at the waist and jumped. He sniffed and stood up.

"Whew. Yea boy. If you ain't sneezing it isn't seasoned." Tay laughed and continued making dinner. Tay thought about what he would cook with the steak as he seared the outsides.

Hmm—maybe we will do some fresh snap green beans. And you know what, why not sauté some mushrooms for toppings for the steaks.

"I hope everyone enjoys this meal as much as I'm enjoying making it." And with that statement, he deftly worked his way around the kitchen, not allowing anything to burn or over cook.

He had dinner ready in an hour and a half. The smell was so delicious; he salivated. He washed his hand, set the table and poured drinks. He then stepped back to look over the setup and to admire his work for a moment.

I still got it, he thought to himself before he pressed a button. A chime rang throughout the house, letting everyone know dinner was ready. Tim and Shayla were the first to show. Their eyes widened at the setup.

Tim's frustration earlier dissipated after his brief rest. "Tay, this looks amazing," he said as he walked to his usual seat. Shayla followed him, her eyes glued to the table. Aria was the last one to walk in. Tay's eyes lingered on Aria as she moved slowly toward the table, her steps hesitant and her face drawn. She looked like she hadn't slept, her mind clearly still elsewhere. A flicker of worry crossed his mind, but he pushed it aside for now. There would be time for that later.

"Now that we are all here," Tay began then looked at Tim. "Tim, please bless the food."

"Sure." Tim bowed his head and everyone followed suit. "Lord, we thank you for bringing us together one more time and for keeping us all in good health. We ask that You bless this food that we are about to partake and the drink as well. May we receive the nourishment and strength we need to go about our daily lives. In Your holy name we pray."

"Amen," everyone said in unison.

Everyone picked up their utensils—everyone except Tay. He sat back and looked at everyone. He reached for his drink, sipped, and looked around. He couldn't help but once again think, *my family is home*. Suddenly, a memory came to mind.

He was at the table with his whole family including Shayla, Tim, their mom, dad, granddad and grandma. They had just finished blessing the food and Tay went to reach for the bowl of mac-n-cheese, but his dad tapped his hand and shook his head.

"No, son, you must be a gentleman at all times," his father had said, his voice firm but kind. "So let your mom, grandma, and sister go first."

His dad smiled and Tay smiled back and nodded. His mom chuckled softly and grabbed the bowl he was reaching for and gave him a spoonful.

"See what being a gentleman gets you?" his mom said, her smile warm and bright.

"Come on, Cheryl," his dad said in a playful way, a gentle laugh escaped from his lips. "He needs to learn."

"Well, you heard him," his mom teased. "So, did you learn your lesson?" Tay nodded again as he swallowed his food, the smile on his face stretched from ear to ear. "That is my sweet boy," she said as she dabbed her napkin on his face to wipe away some crumbs. "Now go ahead and take a sip of your drink."

Tay loved his mom and dad. No matter what he went through he knew they were there to protect him.

The memory faded and Tay felt his eyes water. Only Aria seemed to notice his struggle, her eyes catching his briefly, but she said nothing. Instead, she turned her attention back to her food, much like the others.

The quiet of the room was filled only with the sound of utensils scraping against plates or the soft clink of a glass. Everyone took their time savoring different parts of the meal—Tim started with the smothered steak, Shayla with her loaded baked potato, and Aria with the green beans.

"Mmmm! Tay!" Aria exclaimed with a hand to her mouth as she turned to look at Tay. She swallowed her food, eyes still wide as she glanced at Tay. "This is delicious." She then went back to eating.

Tim and Shayla nodded in agreement as they chewed their food.

Shayla smiled softly, she had moved to try her steak as she spoke. "You haven't lost your touch, I see." After she swallowed, she looked at Tay and to Aria. "I'm sure you will make your girl truly happy with meals like this."

Tay followed Shayla's eyes. He shook his head once he saw she was looking at Aria, though a brief smile tugged at the corner of his lip. "Thank you," Tay said as he picked up his fork and knife then cut into the steak. He took a bite, chewed slowly, allowing the taste to linger on his tongue.

It was good—better than he had expected—but there was a hollowness inside him that even this meal couldn't fill. The memory of his family having dinner had struck him hard. He took a deep breath as he savored the food, then followed it with a sip of his drink before he continued eating.

The meal continued in silence. But beneath the quiet, a heaviness lingered, pressing down on them all. As the meal ended, Tay set down his fork and knife, unable to contain the weight in his chest any longer.

"I wanted to make today…" Tay's voice broke and he coughed to clear it. "A very special day," Tay said suddenly, his voice breaking through the quiet.

"Because everyone is here?" Aria asked cautiously. Her voice was soft as though she wasn't sure if she should speak.

Tay nodded, but his expression turned somber. "Yes," he replied, then paused before continuing.

"But… there's more."

The room stilled. Aria set her fork down gently, and Tim and Shayla exchanged glances. Tay closed his eyes and took a deep breath.

"Today is the anniversary of when our family was killed," Tay said quietly, his voice thick with emotion. His fists clenched beneath the table, and his jaw tightened as he fought back the tears threatening to fall.

Aria's eyes widened in surprise, and she started to speak but hesitated. She froze when she saw the look on Tim and Shayla's faces. But it was Tay's who made her hold back from saying a word. His jaw was clenched, brows furrowed as he struggled to maintain control. His eyes burned, the tears now too close to hold back.

A heavy silence fell over the table. Tim and Shayla looked down at their now-empty plates, their expressions darkening as the weight of Tay's words sank in. The atmosphere shifted, becoming somber and oppressive. Tay took a long moment to compose himself before speaking again.

"So, you see," Tay continued, his voice steadier now though when he opened his eyes they were still glossy. "We're all the same. We've all lost family. Aria just lost hers later than we did. That's why we need each other now."

Tay looked around the table with a softened expression. "So, let's come together and enjoy our time with each other. And to do that, I want to celebrate our reunion," Tay said as he looked to Tim and Shayla.

"Tim, would you please get the big black box out the fridge?" he asked.

Tim nodded and rose from the table. His movements were slow and deliberate as though the weight of Tay's words still lingered on him. Tay also stood and went to the cabinet, retrieved a few bottles of champagne—three from 1998, one from 1989. As he set them down, Shayla's eyes flickered with curiosity despite the somber mood.

"Tay, how did you get those?" Shayla asked.

Tay offered her a faint smile. "We all have our secrets, don't we?"

"True but these are all ten years old at least." Her eyes still wide at the choice of champagne he brought out.

"Well, when the maids are the only ones here for years, it makes it easier to bring things in without them being touched." Tay winked at Shayla.

Tim returned with the large box in hand. Tay set his bottles down and cleared the plates. Shayla and Aria stood at the same time, exchanging polite smiles before they helped move the plates. Once an area was cleared, Tim set the box down as everyone else took the dishes to the sink then returned. Tay looked at Tim and Shayla. "Shayla, Tim… would you do the honors."

They lifted the lid to reveal a beautiful double layered white icing cake. Tay popped open one of the 1998 bottles, the sound echoed throughout the floor. And with that, the mood in the room moved slightly, a sense of celebration took over the downcast vibe.

"Let's have a good night," Tay said. He filled the glasses and passed them out. Once everyone had a glass, Tay held his out. "A toast…" He raised his glass up and everyone followed suit. "To happier days now that we are together again. May we not hold anymore secrets… and learn to live normal lives."

He looked at each one of them and held their gaze for a moment before he looked at the next. After he looked at everyone, he said, "This is the last time we'll start over. From here on, we move forward as a family." Everyone clinked their glasses together softly, but while the others sipped slowly, Tay downed his drink in one swift motion.

Aria watched Tay and knew he was going through something, but since he didn't bring it up, she didn't try to push her luck more than she had that night. They all ate some cake and drank. The champagne was matured enough that everyone showed signs of being slightly intoxicated after drinking half of the second bottle.

Now, everyone was beginning to enjoy themselves and loosen up. Aria and Shayla were actually talking, and Tim had drifted to the living room and was watching TV.

It was the science channel of course. This caused Tay to chuckle.

Tay had walked to the kitchen to do the dishes as he watched his family relax. But despite them being there, the hollowness in his heart did not disappear. The voices of his parents and grandparents echoed in his mind.

The times from when they would have little moments like this and Tim, Shayla, and Tay would just run around the living room tiring themselves out before bed. Tay's face twitched and the memory was a happy one, his eyes squinted and glazed over.

He felt he needed time and space to refocus. So, he finished the dishes along with his glass and went to grab the 1989 bottle from the dinner table. With it in hand, Tay said to everyone, "Y'all continue to have fun and enjoy. I will be in my room."

All eyes followed him until he was in the foyer. He went up the stairs to his bedroom. He walked into his room and closed the door behind him. He didn't turn on the lights but went to the window, opened it, and sat on the sill. He hung one leg freely outside while the other remained bent; his foot firmly planted on the sill. His knee was raised, which he rested his left arm on. In his right hand, he held the bottle, rested it on the sill just beneath his propped-up knee.

Tay breathed in the fresh night air. "It is beautiful tonight," he said softly as he looked at the half-moon partly hidden behind some trees. The moon was big and red, appeared as though it was pressed right against the earth. He raised the bottle, popped it open, and took a sip. The drink had a stronger bite to it compared to the 1998 vintage. Tay turned his attention back to the nature that surrounded the house. He basked in the calmness of the night and felt a presence. It wasn't intimidating but rather gentle, warm, comforting, and most of all familiar. He smiled softly, his gaze now on the stars and voice just above a whisper. "Don't you agree, Mom and Dad?"

A gentle breeze blew through the trees. Tay closed his eyes and let the warm breeze envelop him. He sat there quietly and listened as he occasionally took sips from the bottle.. He heard the song his mom and grandma used to sing to him when his dad and granddad were asleep. Tay couldn't hold back his emotions anymore. Tears flowed freely from his eyes. The song was soft and carried so much meaning to him. He set the bottle down and rested his head on his propped-up knee. He cried like he hadn't before. His family that wasn't taken from him were together. They were able to eat, drink, and sleep under the same roof again. This brought him so much joy but also reminded him of what they had all lost.

"Look, we're all here, together again," Tay said softly through his tears. Tay looked up and for a moment, he saw them. The ones he never could forget: his parents and grandparents. He couldn't stop himself and cried even harder.

"Even you all came back to celebrate," Tay whispered through his tears. "Mom, Dad, Grandma, and Granddad thank you." He stayed on the sill for a little while longer until he calmed down. He picked up the bottle from the sill, took a sip, then poured some out the window—an offering to his family. He stood up slightly unstable, awkwardly walked to his bed, and laid down. He placed the bottle on the floor. As he laid there, he could still feel them—his parents and grandparents—seated beside him, their presence as real as the song on the wind that whispered through the open window.

"I love you all," Tay said, a soft joy in his voice. He smiled as he felt a hand rub his head. It was relaxing, like the way his mom used to comfort him.

"You never really left, did you?" Tay whispered as he closed his eyes, a smile etched on his face as he drifted to sleep.

"Tay," called out a soft voice. "Tay."

Tay opened his eyes and saw nothing but darkness. He closed his eyes and let out a soft moan.

"Hmmm…"

He tried to roll over but realized he was on his feet. Tay thought back to what had happened that night as he checked his surroundings. Tay didn't see anything but darkness. Yet it wasn't complete darkness; he knew that light was somewhere for his eyes didn't strain to look around.

"Tay, come here. I have something to tell you," the voice called out again. This time, he recognized the voice—the warmth it held, the peace it brought him, and the love in the way his name was said.

"Mom?" Tay asked but then realized his voice sounded childish. He patted his body and noticed not only had his voice changed, but his body was that of a ten-year-old. That was all he needed to know to figure out that he was in a dream.

Suddenly, he felt wood flooring under his feet and smelled the scent of a candle burning in another room. The sensations made this dream seem so real that Tay was internally scared he was having an out-of-body experience. He never liked the idea his soul could leave his body and he wasn't dead. But the thing that scared him the most was the assumption an evil spirit could come and enter his body and lock his soul out of his body. He looked around again to find some sort of light to guide him to his mom, but found nothing.

"My son, come here. I need to tell you something," she said, her voice held a sense of impatience, which was rare for her. He never remembered her panicking about anything when she was alive. He listened hard, but her voice was coming from every direction.

"Mom, where are you?" Tay asked as he reached out his hands and felt for something to give him direction. Tay took a few steps before he bumped into something. He placed his hand on it and his heart jumped. He knew this object—it was the living room table. The texture was something he never forgot, especially the engraving where he and his dad carved their initials into it. Tay knew then where he was, even if he still couldn't see. He moved through the room based on his past memory of how the house was set up and avoided other obstacles until he found a door frame. The moment he was in the kitchen, he instantly smelled his father's favorite dish being cooked.

"Tay, come here, honey." This time the voice was from his grandma and her voice was from straight ahead. "You been such a good boy. I am so proud of you."

"Grandma!!" Tay shouted. He moved faster but was still careful not to bump into anything.

"Hey, son, you know the kitchen off limits until I'm done," his father said, his voice was strong and kind as Tay always remembered. He ran in the direction of his father's voice. He bumped into his leg and wrapped his arms around it—so he thought. But instead of the usual heavy fragrance his dad wore, Tay smelled a soft, sweet fragrance that made his tense body relax almost immediately.

"Mom?" Tay asked on the verge of tears, burying his face into her thigh even though he stood up as tall as he could.

"Yes, son," his mother said as she took the scarf off him then rubbed his head. "You really are such a good boy."

Tay's vision was back. They were all in the kitchen. His dad by the stove, Mom sat in her favorite chair by the sliding door as she caressed Tay, Grandma was seated at the table with Grandpa who held his cane by his side as he looked at Tay.

"I love you, Momma," Tay said. He felt himself crying again.

"I love you, too," she said as she lifted his head and wiped his eyes dry with the scarf even though more tears rolled down his face. "Now listen to me." Her voice slightly changed, there was a tone of authority and compassion in it. Tay stopped crying and listened intently. "Tay, please be careful with who you trust and leave behind. She is no good." The first person to come to his mind was Aria and his heart thumped in rejection at the idea. But Tay couldn't think of anyone else his mom could be referring to.

"You don't need to worry. I will keep my distance," Tay replied as he decided to fight his emotions.

"Son—" His mother looked him in the eyes, as if she was trying to say something but wasn't able to. Again, his heart brought up Aria and he felt a joy and peace at the thought of her.

"Mom, you don't have to worry. Though I seem to be developing some type of attachment to Aria. I won't let her jeopardize the lifestyle I'm trying to live and the people that I'm trying to connect with."

His mom's eye dropped but she smiled brightly.

"Cheryl, let him make decisions for himself," his grandma said.

"But Mom—" Cheryl began, her voice filled with concern.

"No, Cheryl. You need to listen to your mother." This time it was his father.

"Henry, of all people you should want to protect him," Cheryl pleaded.

"If only you knew, my dear," Henry responded, his voice carrying something that sounded like guilt and shame. "I wish I could have protected them all correctly."

"Dad, you did great," Tay said as he did his best to comfort him.

Tay's father smiled at him. His eyes looked over Tay's left shoulder. "Jim, don't you think you been silent for long enough."

"Jim?" Tay froze. His heart skipped a beat. That was the name his dad used for Grandpa. Out of everyone in the family, it was Grandpa's voice they all yearned to hear the most. He had always been a man of few words, only spoke when he saw something worth saying. He believed in letting others figure things out for themselves, stepped in only when it truly mattered. To hear him speak now was like witnessing something sacred.

"Tay, listen to your grandpa," Jim spoke slowly, his voice deep and resounding. "You are one of the best to ever be trained and have great potential to be a man no one can control or even touch." Jim's voice carried a sense of pride as he spoke. "But you aim for a dream and that dream is strong. You can succeed in that life if you truly want, but for now, don't stress. Just keep dreaming and embrace yourself." His granddad then looked at Henry. "Henry, stop worrying. You did a great job. Now all you can do is watch your son grow. And Cheryl," he added, his tone softening. "You must tell him about his brother and sister now."

"Yes, Dad." Cheryl looked at Tay. "Baby, now listen carefully. Your brother and sister are..." She was drowned out by another voice.

"Tay," the voice called, sweet and soft. It was familiar. Tay looked around the kitchen to see who called, but it wasn't anyone in the kitchen with him.

"Look at me, dear," his mom said. "Beware—those that are close to you will one day challenge your way of life. Be strong and learn to trust—"

"Tay," the voice called again, this time louder, cutting off his mother's words.

"Be strong for—" his mom continued, but the voice called out again.

"Tay," the voice insisted with slight urgency.

"And one last thing—she is the most important..." His mom tried to finish but the voice cut through one final time.

"Tay!!" the voice yelled into his ear. Tay jolted awake, pushed himself up into a fighting stance on the bed, eyes wide as he looked around for a sign of danger. Not seeing anything, he closed his eyes, let out the breath he was holding, and relaxed. Once he opened his eyes, he noticed it was still night, but what caught his attention was Aria. She was on her knee situated beside his pillow on the floor. She was dressed in a tank top and pajamas shorts that were blue with clouds on them.

"Dang, you sleep hard." She smiled lightly.

"And why does it matter?" Tay asked as he sat down on his bed. He rubbed his eyes and crossed his legs under him then looked at Aria. "Hold up…" He looked at the door and frowned. "Wasn't the door locked?"

"No. It was open." She stood up, walked to the window, leaned on the sill, and peered outside. "It's a beautiful night tonight."

Tay ignored her comment. "What do you want?" His voice was thick with weariness and irritation. He held a hand to his head as it throbbed, but he focused.

What was it that my mother was trying to tell me?

Aria turned to face him, a bashful smile appeared on her face enhanced by the glow of the moon light on her face. "Just to be close to you."

He squinted at her, hand still on his head. "To be close to me?" His gaze traveled down her body and back up. Even in her pajamas, she was undeniably beautiful—sometimes even mesmerizing. He couldn't help but swallow at the thought of her spending time with him. His heart raced once again.

But tonight wasn't the night. The warning from his mother in the dream resurfaced, and he reassessed her with cautious eyes. She was beautiful, yes, but she was also an unknown, and her persistent, almost forceful nature, put him on edge.

"Look, I know you want to get with me but I'm honestly getting tired of you just doing what you want." His voice grew sharper as he continued staring at her. They were silent for a moment before Tay spoke again. "You want to know more about me, right?"

Aria walked over to Tay despite his tone. "Yes, but I promise that it is only because I truly want to be with you."

"Well, here is something you should know. I hate when people try to force themselves on me. Be it physically, mentally, or emotionally. I like my space and living a comfortable life. But there is one thing that truly wreck my nerves."

Aria looked skeptical at him as she sat beside him. "What is that?"

Tay stared into her eyes, as if he was boring into them. "I hate when spoiled inconsiderate people don't know when to mind their own damn business!!" Tay spoke softly but his voice carried a heat to it.

Aria stared back at Tay, fear flickered in her eyes, but disappointment was the stronger emotion on her face. "Tay..." She swallowed as she held his gaze. "You can't be talking about me. Are you?"

"I am," he said through gritted teeth.

"Tay, I don't know what I did to make you..." She reached to grab his hand.

"Don't play that dumb innocent shit with me." Tay snatched his hand away and slid to make more space between them. "You have been nothing but a headache ever since we met. You practically dragged me back to a world where I don't want to live. You hover around me like you want to live in my skin. Most of all, you question whether my only family my brother and sister are real."

Aria stared at him. At his last words, her gaze fell to the floor. Tay huffed.

"I don't get you. Why do you want to be with me? It can't possibly be because of what happened in middle school all those years ago." Tay glanced at her.

She kept her head down for a moment and then looked at him, eyes determined and strong. For a brief moment, Tay felt his anger subside as he looked into her hazy green eyes and how even in the dark they held a glow that entranced him.

"It wasn't just because of the fight at school. Once we got into college, you became someone that I wanted to approach to thank from before. Yet over time that desire to thank you became more."

Aria got up and walked to the dresser. She leaned against it, crossing her arms. This made her breasts look fuller. Tay's gaze traveled to her breasts but he quickly returned to her face. He saw a shadow of smile on her face. He could only inwardly curse to himself as he sat there listening.

"I then began to think more of you. So, I watched you from a far. Ever afraid to approach you but never wanting to let you out my sight."

Tay raised an eyebrow. "You were stalking me?"

"No. No. I never did anything like that. It was just when we were in the same area. I noticed you and the things you would do. I saw your kindness to your colleagues, your protectiveness for the elderly and those that were wronged, how fair you were and listened to everyone before siding with anyone or no one. But most of all, it was how you seemed lonely and looking for someone or something. I could never figure out what it was but in all that I was drawn to you. Then that park incident happened and here we are."

"Really? You just developed feelings for me from wanting to thank me?"

"Yes," she answered immediately as she tucked a lock of hair behind her ear.

Tay hung his head; his anger deflated, like it was barely an ember. "Look. Even after hearing all that it doesn't change the fact that you forced me into things I didn't want to do. So, for now just go to your room and leave me alone until I call for you," Tay said, pointing to the door without having moved from his bed.

She hesitated as she searched his face. She took a deep breath then spoke calmly. "Tay, I will do what I can to make you see that I'm not here to mess up your life." She walked toward the bed, placed one hand beside him, and leaned forward. "I want to make you happier than any man in the whole world." She leaned in closer to where their noses were almost touching. Tay's heart pulsed like he ran two miles. Her sweet scent filled his nose, making him think of how delicate she looked. But Tay held a firm gaze not trying to give her a win. "I will make sure you understand me and my intentions one day soon." She slowly stood up, giving Tay a full view down her top before she walked to the door. Once at the threshold, she looked back once more. "Again, I never meant you any harm. All I want is your affection and heart and for you to accept mine." She smiled softly then left the room.

Tay stood, walked to the door, and this time ensured that it was locked before he returned to his bed to lay down. He stared at the ceiling as frustration gnawed at him.

Why did I even bother to bring her in the first place?

Though he felt he knew the reason, her behavior was making him want to reconsider that justification by the day. He shook his head, closed his eyes, turned to his side, and shortly after he was asleep again.

Tay woke up groggy, and his head ached slightly. The sun filtered in through the blinds, casting plate stripe beams of light throughout the room. Tay turned his head and looked at the clock on the wall.

10:35 am

He pushed himself up and sat on the edge of the bed, not thinking of anything—just trying to reorient himself. He looked around his room and the events of the last few days came back to him. He sighed and dropped his head into his hands.

So much has happened these past few days. I wonder where it is all headed, he thought to himself. But even with that thought, he was sure of one thing and that was he didn't want to go back to the life he had before. His resolve to lead a normal life was even stronger now than before. The only problem was things kept happening around him that seemed to pull him back into the shadows.

He stood up and looked around.

"Well, since this will be our home for a while, I might as well move things around a bit and make it more livable. Though I have to admit the housekeepers did a great job keeping it clean," he spoke aloud to no one in particular. He stretched and a smell hit his nose that caused him to flinch. With his arms still out in front of him, he sniffed again. His nose wrinkled at the smell. "Damn, I need a shower. I smell like gas, sweat, and blood." He ripped off all his clothes and walked to the bathroom. He turned on the shower to let the water get to a nice temperature. While the water was running, he went to the sink, brushed his teeth and washed his face. Thankfully, the house was already prepped and stocked by the rotating staff his parents had arranged years ago — a system that quietly kept the place ready for emergencies like this. Especially since everyone most likely left all their small things at their old place or it was burned away.

The only thing he knew he had to do was take Aria shopping for more clothes. Until then, hopefully she could wear some of Shayla's clothes. They seemed to look close in size, but he knew looks could be deceiving.

Once done, he hopped into the shower and let the water run over him. The sensation was calming and relaxed his mind. He showered thoroughly, scrubbing everywhere to ensure that no stench was still on him.

After he got out, he applied lotion. He could never stand the feeling of being ashy or crusty. It just made him seem like he didn't take care of himself. He went to his dresser and removed the plastic cover and rummaged through his clothes.

"Hmm. I don't really have anywhere to go today so..." He took out some comfortable house wear he knew he could get dirty in. His next task was to rearrange his room.

It wasn't that his room was a mess; he just didn't want the housekeepers coming into the bedrooms and messing with things that were valuable to him and his family. Not to mention the covering kept the dust and critters from habituating in their things. Hence, why there was plastic wrap or coverings on many objects throughout the room even though they had a rotation of housekeepers that maintained the house.

He set to work, removing the coverings and wraps and rearranged his room to suit his style. Once he was done, he felt satisfied though the sound of his stomach growling reminded him he hadn't eaten yet.

"Yes, sir. I know, it's time for food," Tay told his stomach as he left his room and headed downstairs to the kitchen, thinking about what he wanted for brunch. He decided to fix a bowl of cereal even though it was already noon. He didn't feel like making a mess and then he remembered he still had the dishes in the sink from last night. A soft sigh escaped his lips as he made it to the foyer. He went through the living room into the kitchen. The moment he walked in, he saw Shayla in the fridge. Tay walked quietly toward the island behind her. Once he was close enough, he hid below the counter.

"Good morning, sis," Tay said as he popped up from the side of the island to Shayla's right. "What are you doing up so early?" She jumped back into a fighting stance, her eyes wild and full of fear.

It was a stance Tay had never seen her use before, but the thing that confused him was the look of fear her eyes held. Shayla knew fear but for her to be so scared that it showed in her eyes worried Tay.

Why would she be afraid of me like she is hiding something?

But as quickly as he saw it, it was gone.

"Tay, you scared me," she said as she put a hand to her chest and calmed down, but her eyes quickly darted around before landing back on Tay. "What are you doing up? I thought you were still asleep?" She walked back to the fridge as if nothing happened. Tay noticed his bag that was on the counter last night was on the floor by her foot.

"I woke up and cleaned a little. Then I realized that I was hungry, so I came down to fix some food. So, mind if I get the milk?" He walked to the fridge, opened the door wider, and reached for the milk. Shayla swiftly grabbed it before him.

"Not until I get my good morning hug." She winked at him.

Tay smiled as he shook his head. "Come on, Shayla. Aren't you too old for this?"

She pouted. "No hug. No milk. And what do you mean too old?" Her eyes glared at him slightly.

"I'm the baby of the family, remember. Momma said once the baby always the baby." She smiled teasingly at him.

He pulled her in and hugged her tightly. "How was that?" he asked, still hugging her.

"I missed you, bro." She held him tightly with her face in his chest. "I'm so tired of pretending and then starting over. When can we just live a normal life?"

Normal.

He gave a soft chuckle. "Wouldn't that be nice." He placed a hand on her head and slowly stroked a few times before he pulled away gently. "Is Tim awake?"

She shrugged. "I think he is in the training room."

He sighed. "He is always training, isn't he?"

"You know he looks up to you and Dad." She put the milk on the counter then went to get a bowl and some cereal. "But you may want to check up on him. You know he will overdo it at times."

"Yea, you are right. Better go make sure he isn't trying to hurt himself." Tay went to the fridge, grabbed the orange juice, and two parfaits before closing the door.

"I thought you wanted some cereal," Shayla said as she stared curiously at Tay.

"I changed my mind. Enjoy your breakfast. I'm going to check on Tim," he said as he poured a glass of orange juice then put the container back in the fridge. He picked up his bag from the floor, grabbed the juice and parfaits from the counter, and took everything with him to the training room.

As he walked to the training room, he thought over Shayla's reactions.

Something about Shayla feels odd. He glanced over his shoulder to the kitchen. *Maybe it's just because we haven't spent more than a week together every two years. Yea that must be it.* Though he tried to shake the uneasiness, the way she acted seemed so different.

It was like someone being caught not wearing the mask they made.

Tay reached the training room and stood at the entrance. The words from his mother from that dream resurfaced.

No, that can't be it. I'm letting Aria's fear become my own. And using that dream as evidence. He shook his head. *Shayla is my sister. I know who she is. Being apart for so long and Aria are the only reasons I feel this way.*

Tay nodded and exhaled, letting his body relax before entering the training room.

The room itself was almost a quarter of the main floor space in size and was fully stocked with all kinds of training equipment from dummies to fake weapons. Even balancing beams and a small obstacle course. Tay smiled as he looked around. This was where he and his dad trained and bonded.

As he scanned the room, Tim charged at him. Without hesitation, Tay executed a side kick, stopping Tim in his tracks, followed by a spinning roundhouse kick that sent him flying back.

Tim knelt as he landed, clutching his side where Tay had kicked him. He breathed heavily. "Even with your hands full, you can still manage that," Tim said as he stood up and stretched.

"Tim, what do you plan to accomplish with all this training?" Tay asked as he set his juice and parfaits on the table by the door. He walked over to the lockers, placed his bag inside, and habitually changed the lock.

"That's a pretty obvious question, don't you think, Tay?" Tim asked still trying to catch his breath. "I want to catch up to you." Tim took his stance as he got his breathing under control.

Tay half-smiled and whispered, "You are already there. You just don't realize it."

"What did you say?" Tim asked as he beckoned Tay to take his stance.

Tay decided to go with the flow. He didn't take a stance at first but closed his eyes and drew in a deep breath. Slowly, he exhaled, opened his eyes, and got into his stance, ready. "Come!" he shouted.

Tim didn't move. He stood there, as if looking for an opening.

"If you don't come," Tay said with a mischievous smile, "then I will." Tay charged with one arm pulled back queued to strike. Tim quickly brought his arms up to guard his face. He blocked the hit, but the force caused him to lose balance. Tay followed through with a kick to Tim's grounded leg. Tim jumped using a back handspring to gain his balance and create some distance. Tim smiled as he took his stance once more. Tay smiled back. The two rushed at each other and went full force. They exchanged blows for nearly an hour before Tay heard the door open. He looked and saw Aria rush in.

"Tay! Tay!" she shouted as she ran onto the battlefield. Tim was in mid attack, his punch aimed for Tay's side, when instincts took over. Tay jumped back slightly and reached for Tim's arm, but Tim twisted kicking at Tay. Tay grasped the leg and spun. But the sweat on his hand caused Tim to slip from his grasp and fly toward Aria.

"Aria! Watch out!" Tay shouted, hoping she would jump out of the way.

Aria moved so smoothly; it shocked Tay. She laid back and kicked up, hitting Tim in the back making him flip over so he would land on his feet. Afterward, she laid there gasping, eyes wide with shock. Tay ran over to her.

"Aria. Aria, are you alright?" Tay asked as he gently lifted her head. She gazed at him, her chest rose and fell rapidly, her eyes were filled with fear. Swiftly, Tay picked her up then looked at Tim. "Grab my drink and parfaits and follow me."

Tim didn't move. He just stared at Aria; his face held a look that Tay didn't recognize. "Tim!" Tay shouted. That snapped Tim back to reality.

"Huh. Oh, yea I got it," Tim stammered as he rushed to do what he was told. As he went to get everything, Tay noticed how he kept throwing glances at Aria, like he was trying to make sense of something. Tay didn't have time to focus on Tim with what was happening to Aria, so he carried her out the training room with Tim right behind him.

Tay was grateful the training room was on the first floor. He quickly went to her room, opened the door, then laid her on the bed. As Tay was about to stand up, Aria tugged at his hand. Her grip was tight. He looked into her eyes to see that she was staring at him. He grasped her hand back and knelt beside her.

"It's okay. It's okay, Aria. You are safe," he said in a soft and comforting tone. "No one is here to get you. You are fine."

Tay noticed her breathing started calming down. "That is right. Take deep breaths and relax. I'm here."

Aria closed her eyes and breathed slowly. After a minute or two, her breathing steadied and she opened her eyes. She looked at Tay and smiled. He smiled back.

"How do you feel?" Tay asked still holding her hand. She nodded slowly, her eyes still a bit dazed but calmer than before. "That's good. Just lie down here until you fully recover." She nodded again. He slowly released her hand and she let him go, too. He pulled the cover over her and stood. He walked to Tim and took a parfait from him. Tay turned and set it on Aria's dresser. He motioned Tim out of the room. Once outside, Tay closed the door.

He turned to face Tim with an eyebrow arched. "Tim, man, what's up with you?" His tone held a sense of suspicion.

"Hmm," Tim said distractedly, his eyes fixed on Aria's door. Tay moved to block his view. Tim blinked and he finally looked at Tay. "Oh. Umm. Nothing," Tim stuttered, eyes looking everywhere but at Tay.

"You sure?" Tay asked as he looked Tim in the eyes. Tim noticed and tried to look unbothered, but his gaze was distant, almost as if he were looking through Tay. It was clear he was hiding something.

"Yeah," Tim said as he squeezed his right hand with his left. He took a step back. "Well, I still gotta clean my room, so see ya." Tim turned and walked off.

Tay watched Tim until he rounded the corner into the other hallway. *Tim cleaning? That's rare,* Tay thought as he reached back inside her room to lock Aria's door. He walked back to the gym, retrieved his bag, and decided to visit a room he hadn't been to in a while.

He walked up to the second floor, but instead of turning right to go to his room, he went left. He walked almost to the end of the hallway above Tim's room. He stopped and looked at the door in front of him. This was his parents' room. He took off his backpack and unzipped the small pocket and took out a key. After zipping the pocket back up, he slung his bag over his shoulder again.

He hesitated for a moment, his heart beginning to race, then unlocked the door. Slowly, he opened it to reveal a room in pristine condition. This was one of the few rooms he allowed the housekeepers to maintain. He stepped in and breathed in deeply; the scent of lavender and cashmere wood permeated the air. For a brief moment, he saw an image of his father in front of the mirror tying his tie, and his mother at her vanity finishing her makeup. They stopped and looked at him with bright smiles on both their faces. Then the images were gone.

Tay half-smiled as he turned back to the door and locked it. He loved this room, not for its space, but the comfort it gave him. All the decorations were the same as when he last left them, which was how his parents kept them when they were alive. Tay sat down on the bed, careful not to spill his orange juice. His eyes landed on a painting by the bathroom. He stopped drinking and looked at it.

"I truly miss you guys," he murmured to the painting. He sat there, drank his juice, then his eyes closed and he breathed in the essence of the room. Its fragrance and comfort had, in a sense, recentered him. Once he finished drinking his juice, he opened his eyes and started to get up when his phone rang. Tay pulled it out of his pocket and his eyes widened as he saw the name on the caller ID. It was Lyn. A small smile crept over his face as he answered.

"Hello."

"Hi, Tay, what are you doing?" Evelyn's voice was as sweet as always.

"Nothing, I'm just chilling. And you?" Tay asked as he sat back down.

"Well, I was just thinking of you." Tay's heart did a little flip. "And I was wondering if you are free tomorrow night."

"Oh really. Well, you are in luck." Tay smiled bashfully and leaned back with his hand propped behind him. "I am free, actually."

"That's great!" Lyn said, her voice sounded like an excited teenager. "Because there is a movie and an event that I want to go to."

"Cool. Sounds like fun." Tay was so happy. "So, who's all going?" Immediately, Tay froze. *Please don't tell me I just asked that,* Tay thought as he leaned forward and hung his head in disbelief.

"I was thinking it could just be the two of us. Or…" Her voice sounded a bit disappointed. "Do you have a friend that wants to come?"

"No!" Tay almost shouted as he tried to recover. "I just thought you had some friends you were going with already and wanted me to join y'all." But inside, he wondered, *was that really why I said that?*

"Well, no. I just want to hang with you so we can get to know each other some more." Her voice brightened.

"I like the sound of that." Tay got up. "Well, text me where you want to meet and what time, okay."

"Okay, boo. Talk to you later," Evelyn said sweetly.

"You, too, " Tay said and they hung up. He walked to the door and saw feet scurrying. Tay could guess who it was but didn't think too much about it. He was happy and wasn't going to let anything ruin that.

Tay took one last look at the family portrait and said, "Wish me the best." With a wink, he unlocked the door, walked out, and then closed and locked it behind him. As Tay walked to his room, he started daydreaming about his date with Lyn. When he reached his door, he noticed it was slightly ajar. His heart raced. He scanned the hallway—no one was in sight and nothing out of place. He studied the door. There was no sign of forced entry. So, he inhaled and slowly opened the door. He looked around, nothing seemed to be out of place from when he left. His eyes landed on an envelope in the middle of his bed. He walked in, locked the door, and sat on his bed as he picked up the envelope.

He nearly dropped it, surprised by how heavy it was. He adjusted his grasp, opened it, and out fell a necklace and a letter. He picked up the necklace and looked it over quickly before he picked up and opened the note.

Hi Tay,

Hope you are having a good day. Thought I should show you my appreciation for always risking yourself to make sure I was taken care of. I don't know if this is enough to show what you mean to me, but I hope it gets the point across. To you, the one who guarded me and inspired me to become better—thank you for everything.

Tay looked for a signature but didn't see one. He turned his attention back to the necklace again and saw a red gem set within the links. He scrutinized it carefully for about a minute before recognition dawned—it was his grandma's necklace, the one that she gave to Shayla. But something seemed off about it though he didn't know what. The necklace was a symbol that meant a prosperous future and was traditionally given to the greatest assassin in the family. Tay smiled thinking, *Though it is a great gift it belongs to her. I should give it back*.

Tay was about to put the necklace in the envelope when he saw another note inside. He pulled it out and opened it.

Tay,

I know we don't always see eye to eye all the time, but I want to say this with all my heart—Happy birthday BIG BROTHER.

Ever since mom and dad died you have been there for me, and I am sure Chanice too. I love you and greatly appreciate all you have done. Now hurry up and blow out your candles.

At the bottom was a hand-drawn cake with candles that made the number twenty-one. Tay smiled, he remembered how he used to look forward to turning twenty-one when he was younger. He always thought that age meant adulthood—it still did. Tay looked in the corner and saw the date—it was from three years ago. Tay put the notes back in the envelope and set it on his dresser. He had honestly forgotten it was his birthday with everything that had happened. Not that he celebrated it much anyway. He then grabbed the necklace and made his way to Shayla's room.

He was about to knock when he heard voices. He put his ear to the door and listened carefully. The voices he heard seemed to come from his brother and sister, but they were too muffled to make out clearly.

"Did you drop it off?" a voice that sounded like Tim said.

"Yes, he should be coming any second," Shayla replied softly.

What are those two thinking? Tay wondered as he slipped the necklace into his pocket. He knocked on the door, and silence followed. He turned the knob and slowly opened the door. He walked in and turned on the lights.

"Happy Birthday, Tay!!" Shayla and Tim shouted, popping streamer cannons as the lights came on. Tay was momentarily stunned as streamers floated down on his head. Between Shayla and Tim was a cake with a silver and a black pistols design on it. As he took it all in, he was overwhelmed with happiness and tears welled in his eyes. He felt his body tremble. Tim walked up to Tay with a bright smile and rested a hand on Tay's shoulder.

"Whoa, bro. Why are you so stiff?" Tim asked, caution in his voice as he looked Tay in the eyes.

"Come on, relax and enjoy." Tim guided Tay farther into the room.

"One more big one, right?" Shayla smiled. It was so warm and innocent just like when they were kids. Suddenly, he saw them all as kids playing around in the backyard, laughing and smiling like those times would never end. Tay walked to her and pulled both her and Tim into a deep embrace.

"You guys... Thank you so much," Tay said, no longer able to hold back the tears.

"You're welcome, bro. We're glad that we were able to celebrate with you. Though if we had known we'd be meeting earlier, we would've bought a better cake instead of this one," Tim said as they pulled apart.

"Speaking of the cake," Tay began as he wiped his eyes. "How did you even get it?"

"Well, we managed to get it after we arrived in town. Luckily, there was a store still open, and Shayla was the one to remind me."

Tay looked to Shayla eyes full of gratitude. "Thank you for thinking of me, Shayla, but you didn't have to."

"Oh, it was no problem. Though I thought you would've found out this morning when you went into the fridge."

"So that's why you were up so early?"

Shayla nodded as she started lighting the candles. Tay looked between them and smiled brightly.

"Again, thank you both."

"Enough of that. Come on, Tay, blow out your candles and make a wish," Shayla said as she finished lighting the last candle. Tay stepped to the cake. The same number of candles were on the cake as in the drawing from the letter. They burned forming a two and one. Tay closed his eyes and made his wish.

I wish that we can keep times like this, where we are just like a NORMAL FAMILY, he thought as he blew out the candles and looked up at his siblings. They smiled at him and he returned it with a genuine smile. *How long has it been since I could smile like this?* he wondered.

The three of them continued enjoying the celebration. They reminisced about the past and all the places they had been to throughout their life. Tay was thoroughly enjoying himself until he remembered Aria. He got up, put a slice of cake on a plate, and headed to the door.

"Where are you going, bro?" Tim asked, eyeing Tay with suspicion. "You aren't leaving us already, are you?"

"I'm just taking this to Aria. But you and Shayla enjoy yourselves." Tay walked down the hall to Aria's room. Once at her door, he knocked. No answer.

"Aria?" Tay called through the door. Silence. "I'm coming in," he said as he unlocked the door and walked in. It was pitch dark and hard to see anything, so Tay turned the lights on. He looked at the bed, but Aria wasn't there. Tay looked around and saw Aria huddled between her bed and dresser, curled up and shaking. Tay set the cake on the dresser and knelt in front of her. "Hey, Aria, you okay?" he gently asked. She didn't reply but he noticed she was muttering something. He leaned in and listened intensely.

"Someone, please help. Save my mommy and daddy." Her voice was filled with fear and desperation. Tay assumed she was reliving the recent death of her parents, but he found it weird she would call them mommy and daddy like a child would. "Tay..." she whispered. He looked up, thinking she had come back to her senses but she hadn't. She mouthed something but he couldn't make it out. He placed a hand on her shoulder and shook her.

"Hey, Aria, wake up," he said softly

"Hmm..." She looked up groggily. The moment her eyes cleared, and she saw Tay, she jumped onto him, holding him as if she thought she was never going to see him again. "Tay... Please don't leave me." She cried into his shirt.

"Look, I'm not going anywhere." He held her close until she calmed down. "But what's wrong?" Tay asked as he gently pushed her away and looked at her face.

"There… There was a fire, and my mom was lying on the kitchen counter, and my dad was on the living room floor. Neither of them moved, no matter how much I called for them. Then some… someone pulled me outside into the forest along with another boy. They held us there as the fire consumed the whole house, along with my mom and dad. Then it all went dark. And I woke up to see you," Aria explained hurriedly but her voice was filled with distraught and her eyes looked as if tears would flow any minute.

Tay was speechless for a moment, then gently pulled her back into a hug. "It was just a nightmare," he said softly, trying to reassure her. But in the back of his mind, he couldn't help but wonder, *why is it so similar to the exact way my family died?*

"But it felt so real." She sniffed.

"Was it as real as this?"

"No…"

"See? Then it wasn't real." He slowly released her and helped her to her feet. "You're stronger than you think, Aria. Try not to let this get to you so much," he advised as he held her hands.

"Okay. I will try." She released his hands and wiped her eyes then looked up and smiled. "Thank you, Tay. You truly have saved and helped me." The moment he saw that smile, an image of his mom flashed in his mind. He quickly shook his head to push the thought away.

"Anyways, I brought you something." He handed her the cake off the dresser.

"Oh, thank you, Tay." She reached to take it but hesitated and pulled her hands back.

"What is wrong now?" he wondered.

"I have nothing to give you for your birthday."

How does she know... He started to wonder then remembered. *Oh. Right. She is a stalker.*

"Don't worry about it," he said as he placed the plate in her hands. She looked at him again and gave that same smile.

Once in her hand, she picked up the fork and took a small bite. She sat on the bed and finished eating while Tay sat in the chair by her closet. "So how is it?" he asked.

"Really good." She smiled. Again, he saw his mother's face. He felt a rage build inside him.

Why does she have to smile like that? Why did it have to remind me of mother so much? he wondered. *Well, I better leave before I do something stupid.* He started to get up, but Aria grabbed his hand.

"Wait, I know what to give you," she said as her eyes danced with excitement. "But I need you to come with me."

Tay didn't like the sound of that. "Look, I appreciate your effort, but I don't think it wise for me to go with you."

"Okay," she said with a mischievous glint in her eyes. "Then I guess I'll let you have your way with me then." She began undoing her belt to her robe.

"NO!!! STOP!!" Tay exclaimed as he held his hand out and turned his head. His ears heated up so much that he thought they were on fire. His heart raced. "Okay, I will go."

She looked slightly disappointed. "You didn't have to be that forceful with your no," she said as she stood. "Just let me know when you are ready to head out."

"Ok then," he replied. She beamed as he stood and walked out, closing the door behind him.

What is up with her? he thought, puzzled. *She seems to have it together at times, then she's totally different other times.*

Tay walked back to his room, grabbed some clothes from his closet, and got dressed. Once ready, he headed to Tim's room.

"Hey, Tim," he said as he knocked.

There was clanging and hurried footsteps before Tim opened the door. "Yo, what's up?"

"First, is everything okay in there?" Tay said as he tried to peer around Tim.

"Hm…" Tim looked behind him at the mess he would have to clean up later. "Oh yeah, everything's going great," he said as he looked back at Tay. "Did you need something?"

"Yeah." Tay looked at Tim with suspicion but about the mess that was supposedly going great. "I was wondering if you wanted to come with me. Aria wants to take me somewhere."

"Umm." Tim hesitated, then answered. "Naw. I'm good. Me and Shayla got something to do. Besides, I really should clean up this mess."

Tay sighed then chuckled disappointedly. "Cool. Well, y'all take care. I'll see you when we get back," Tay said as he walked off. Once he was back at Aria's room, he knocked.

"You ready?" he called through the door. She opened the door quickly, as if she had been waiting. Tay looked her up and down and was surprised at how beautiful she looked in casual clothes. She wore tennis shoes, jean shorts that stopped mid-thigh with the trim rolled, and a spaghetti strap tank. He forced himself to look at her face even though his mind continued thinking of how her outfit complemented her figure so nicely.

"Well, let's go," Tay said as he started walking to the front door. Aria walked behind him silently. Once in the garage, she stopped a few feet from the car. Tay noticed, turned to her, and asked, "What up?"

"Tay, I need to ask you something," she said, eyes fixed on the ground as if embarrassed.

"Okay." He leaned against the car. "So, what is it?"

"First, promise me that you will answer it and be truthful when you do." She still looked at the ground every once in a while, then would glance up to meet Tay's eyes.

She looks like a little kid that is having their first conversation with their crush. No telling what I will be getting myself into, he thought as he said, "I promise."

"Thanks, I will ask in the car as you drive," she said as she got in the passenger side.

Great. now I can't even lie to her, he muttered to himself.

Tay got in and looked at Aria. "So, where are we going?"

"The house my parents died in."

Eyebrows raised he asked, "Are you sure?"

"I am positive." With that, Tay drove off.

While driving down the highway, Tay couldn't clear his mind. The whole while they sat in silence once again, the radio the only sound in the car. During the silence, he wondered about Aria's question.

What is she going to ask me? He would occasionally glance at her only to see she was looking either down at her hands or out the window. Countless scenarios had raced through his mind; none seemed to be the right one.

Why isn't she asking me yet?

Finally, Aria let out a soft sigh. His heart pounded against his chest, his palms growing damp as he tightened his grip on the steering wheel.

"Tay..." she murmured, her voice low, almost a whisper. She stared down at her hands and nervously intertwined her fingers.

"Yes?" he responded, his mind raced with thoughts so quickly; he didn't have time to process them. Through it all, he kept his eyes trained on the road.

This is killing me. Just what is she going to ask me? was his final thought before she spoke.

She hesitated, drew in a small breath, and slowly released it. "When we get back." She fidgeted with her hands before she turned to face Tay. "...would you... would you please sleep with me?"

For a split second, Tay's mind went blank. He fought the urge to slam on the brakes, his thoughts scrambling to process her words.

Did she say what I think she said?

"What did you just say?" he asked, his voice edged with disbelief and uncertainty.

"I want to be with you," she repeated with more determination and confidence. She placed a hand on his arm. "Even if it's just for one night. I want to be close to you."

Tay glanced at Aria's hand resting on his. Soft. Warm. He didn't want her to move it — and then Evelyn flashed through his mind, instantly snapping him back to reality...And he immediately chastised himself.

How could I forget about the girl I'm trying to win over, for this girl that is... He looked from the road to Aria and looked her over. Her body shape was something that most men crave from their partner, not to mention she gave all her attention to him.

"Aria, I can't—"

"Please, Tay. I need you. I really only feel safe when you are around." Her grip on his arm tightened. He looked into her eyes and saw not only her uncertainty and fear, but the desire to be with him. Yet he felt she was doing this out of need to feel safe from her recent trauma.

He looked back to the road, his heart ached for her. He wanted to pull her close, to comfort her, to lose himself in the warmth of her touch. He didn't know where these emotions came from but he knew she was becoming someone special to him and he didn't know why.

Maybe it is because of all we have been through.

"Aria... I'm trying to date someone else." Her hand fell from his and she looked downcast. "I'm sure that—"

"Tay, please..." Her eyes watered as she interrupted him. "Just give me one night. One night to prove to you that I can be your girl."

Tay let out an exasperated sigh. "I'm pretty sure I asked this before but remind me, why are you so hung up on me?"

"I fear that if I lose this chance then sometime soon. I–I will lose you forever," she pleaded as she stared at him and squeezed her hands together as in a prayer, waiting to hear his answer.

Tay briefly glanced at her and then looked in her eyes and calmed his mind. He looked back to the road and relaxed his hands on the wheel and sighed.

"Look, Aria…" He started as he debated on what words to say. "You are truly beautiful, that almost any man would be happy to not only make you his, but to do almost anything—to make you happy and build a family with you." Her eyes shone brighter, and she leaned in closer to him with each word that he spoke. "The thing is… I am not that guy."

She took a minute to process what he said. "Okay—" Her eyes turned hollow, and her shoulders slumped. "Thanks for being honest," she said as she turned to face the window. Though she didn't make a sound, Tay saw tears roll down her face in the reflection of the window.

Tay looked back at the road, jaws flexed. He hated himself for hurting her heart but he turned that anger into curiosity.

Why me? Why do you constantly think I am the one for you? There are so many other people out there. And I'm almost positive that there is one for you.

He then glanced back at her and felt the disappointment and sadness rolling off her body. His heart ached and his hands gripped the wheel tighter because he was causing her more pain. But he knew if he lied, she would only have been given false hope.

He desperately wanted to tell her all the reasons why it wouldn't work, why he didn't see them as a good match as a way to try to make her feel better. But he knew that was just his way to make himself feel better and a way for him to escape from her feelings and thoughts, so he kept quiet.

"What do I have to do?" she whispered.

"What?"

"What must I do to prove to you that you are the only one for me?" Aria almost yelled as she turned to him, her cheeks wet from her tears. "A true gentleman will never lie and does his best not to make a lady cry."

Tay looked at her, shocked. Her words brought forth a memory of a time when his father had said those words to him and Tim when they made their sister cry.

"How… Why do you know that phrase?"

"Tay, please don't try to change the subject," she said in an agitated voice. There was a brief pause as Tay collected his thoughts.

"There is nothing you can do that would convince me." He glanced at Aria from the corner of his eye. She still looked at him with determined eyes. Tay let out a deep breath through his nose. "We are just two different people. and I don't see any reason for us to be together," Tay said calmly.

Aria scowled at Tay, her lips trembling before she turned to face the window again. "Liar," she mumbled under her breath.

Tay couldn't understand her.

Does she really believe that I'm the only one? Why can't she just try to find solace in someone other than me?

A few moments of silence passed as they drove to her neighborhood. When they arrived, Tay glanced at her. He should have been upset or irritated by her actions to try and pursue him so passionately, but when he saw her in the window he felt that trance state again.

Even when sad, she had a beauty to her. He felt an urge to stroke her head to comfort her. But before he could act, he turned onto her street and parked on the side of the house where he had burned the vent planks before.

He thought of what he was about to do and realized that could have confused her after what he had just said. Yet he wondered why she affected him so. It was unlike any other women he had ever met to including Rin.

At that moment, he thought of the phrase she had spoken, and he turned to her.

"Look, now that we are here, I need to know something." His voice was calm and kind, even though she still glared at him. "Will you tell me how you know that phrase?"

"I don't know," she spoke weakly like she didn't want to talk. "All I know is that I heard it from someone I trusted and loved."

Tay looked out the front window and contemplated how she could have heard that phrase.

My dad did work for Mr. Blackwood, so my dad could've gotten it from him.

As he was thinking, Aria kept talking; her voice grew more confident. "Now it is time for you to answer my question." Tay looked at her, face still strained in thought.

"Hmm."

"Why won't you just let me in your heart?" Her brows drew together, not in anger, but in a desperate plea to understand. Her eyes shimmered—not just from shedding tears, but from a longing that made her expression ache. "Why won't you give me a small chance? I'm sure if you got to know me, you will see that I will be your perfect queen."

Tay gaze shifted from curiosity to sincerity. He stared into her eyes as he spoke.

"The simple answer is, I don't trust you." His voice was calm but matter-of-fact. "We barely know each other. Even if we did, something about you throws me off."

Tay thought of all the times his heart raced and how she made him react differently than he thought he would. "I can't see myself being with someone that makes me go crazy. I just don't see us together like you want without something drastic happening. Which I pray doesn't."

This time, he reached out and placed a hand on her shoulder. "You are a good person and seem thoughtful, especially to those you care about. But you come on too strong. I'm sure that you'll find a man that is the exact type you want and need. Again though, that man isn't me." Tay paused, their eyes held each other's. He pulled away first, his heart heavy with guilt like he was just hurting her on purpose. "Anyways, how about we get out here and walk back?"

"Ok," she said, her voice low and laced with disappointment.

They got out and Aria led the way. She walked to a burned down section of the gate that was a few feet from them and led them to the backyard. Once through the gate, they walked in the direction of the now burned rumble that was the Blackwood's house. All the way, Aria kept up a quick pace and didn't turn back to look at Tay not even once. Tay would look at Aria and was surprised to find himself somewhat upset she wasn't giving him any attention. Conflicted, he looked down at the ground as he tried to sort out what he was going through.

He knew he didn't want Aria— at least he thought he didn't— but he felt hurt when she ignored him or refused to speak to him. He thought back to what happened before they came here. He had wanted to see Aria and give her a slice of the birthday cake his siblings had given him. He even agreed to come back here with her because she suggested it. Tay shook his head.

Have I gotten so used to her being here that I get flustered when she doesn't act a certain way?

He looked up at Aria, who was still walking ahead of him. He noticed things about her that seemed so small. Like the way she walked looked like she was gliding. The way her hair shined in the afternoon light, even the soft fragrance that wafted from her to him as he walked behind her. Tay vehemently shook his head.

No. No. No. I have Evelyn now. She even agreed to give me a try, and she seems more put together than Aria. Besides, I only feel like this because I have been around Aria so much as of late. He nodded to himself, reaffirming his thoughts.

Yeah, that's all it is—familiarity. Nothing more than that. Tay looked up and had to immediately sidestep to avoid colliding with Aria.

As Tay stood by her side, he looked at her then at the house. She had stopped outside the former kitchen area. She trembled slightly as she took in the view of her destroyed home. Tay felt a strong urge to hug her, to comfort her, and to let her know it would be okay—she would be okay. But he ignored it and stood there beside her in silence, hands balled into fists. A wave of rage washed over his body. He thought of how everything was taken from her in one night. Her whole family, the memories she had in the home she grew up in, and the people she had gotten to know and loved that helped her in the house. He felt his teeth press on each other as he felt her lost and in turn was reminded of his own.

Whoever was behind this will surely pay, Tay promised to himself.

After a moment, she walked inside the house, stepping over the burnt planks littering the ground. From there, they went into the hallway. They walked carefully as they avoided the burnt wood and some beams that were either broken or still stood but they looked like they would crumble at any moment. Aria stopped. Tay walked up beside her. She looked down at the floor and Tay followed her gaze. At the spot she was staring at was a rug, still whole but covered in ash and stained black from where parts of it had caught fire. She knelt down, grabbed the edge of the rug and with a strong jerk, threw it aside. The rug landed with a loud thud, shocking Tay.

He turned and looked at the rug with curiosity. He walked over to where it was and bent to lift one corner. As he gently lifted it, the weight and rigidity of the rug surprised him. It felt like metal plates were in the corner. Tay released the corner and it clanged to the ground. He looked back at Aria, who was now brushing away soot on the ground with eyes full of surprise at her strength. Tay walked back to her side and heard a soft click. The next thing he saw was a part of the floor rise up and slide to the side to reveal a metal door with a keycode lock on it.

"What is that?" Tay asked.

"A secret compartment to the house. Only my mom, dad, and I knew about it," she explained. She tapped a few keys. A click sounded and the door swung up to reveal a set of stairs. "This is just an entrance. Once we go in, there will be another exit inside."

Tay nodded as he followed her lead.

They descended the stairs, and the door closed behind them. As it locked with a resounding click, soft blue lights along the floor and ceiling flickered to life, illuminating a long corridor. Tay looked around and felt like he was in a sci-fi movie.

"Welcome back, Ms. Renee," an automated female voice said.

"Hi, Linda. Today, I brought Tagen Eugene Davis with me. He needs to be added to the database." A red light flashed at Tay from down the hall. He flinched, but as soon as the light hit him, it disappeared.

"Registration complete," the voice said after ten seconds.

"What did you just do, Aria?" Tay asked as he patted himself down to make sure he was still whole.

"Just had to put you in the system so the computer, Linda, won't think you are an enemy," she replied.

He was uncertain of what to do or believe. His shock wore off as Aria turned to continue down the hallway. He reached out and grasped her hand. "Ok, it's time to come clean. Who are you really?" he asked as she turned to face him. His eyes hungered to know the truth.

Aria left her hand in his and answered, "As I told you before, I am Aria Renee Blackwood." Her shoulders dropped and she looked around the hall. "Look, I don't know much about my family. They shared things with me but apparently they kept a lot more to themselves." She looked back at Tay. "What I do know is that my father was a computer geek among many things. He had some people build this for him. Saying it was to fulfill his fantasy of having a secret lair." She chuckled slightly at the memory of that time.

"Once it was done, Dad added Mom and me to the system. My dad would then take me down here from time to time to train me for a bit in martial arts.

I even remember visiting your mom and dad a few times before their deaths. Though it was brief, and I was too young to remember much of my time with them, my body doesn't seem to have forgotten what they taught me, especially in self-defense." She tilted her head to the side and spoke softer like she was speaking to herself. "Though it was only recently that I remembered being taught by them."

After hearing her explanation, Tay released her hand. Aria turned and walked down the corridor. Tay followed though he still felt uneasy about her and the situation.

"So, my mom and dad trained you?" Tay questioned, his voice in disbelief.

"Yes. My mom and dad truly loved them, and I did, too. They treated me kindly and pushed me to always do better. It was like having two sets of loving parents look after me. But then one day, they went somewhere and never came back. Later on, I was told that they were dead."

"Yeah. They never came back because after their mission, they came home only to be killed while protecting me, Tim, and Shayla," Tay said in almost a whisper.

Aria didn't hear him and turned to continue down the corridor. They walked in silence for a few more minutes before a metal door stood in their way. Aria approached the door and looked around. After a moment of searching, she pushed a section of the wall and stood back. A red light shone from the top of the door that scanned Aria and Tay.

"Identities confirmed," came the voice of Linda. And with that, the door slid to the right. Aria walked inside with Tay close behind her. Once she crossed the entry way, a light turned on in the middle of a room. There was a sofa, table, bookshelf, and a counter with some snacks on it. Aria walked to the table and rummaged around, searching for something.

When she couldn't find it on the table, she went to the counter and felt around there. As her hands ran along the lip of the counter she spoke out,

"Oh, there it is." It sounded like she flicked a switch and the sound of gears turning filled the room. The countertop opened and inside were two boxes, one long and one small. Aria took them both out and handed them to Tay.

"What are these?" he asked as he took the boxes.

"They are your birthday gifts." Aria smiled and backed up. Tay looked at them, surprised. They didn't have a name on them but if they were from her, he wondered what they could be. He went to the table and put the large one down and started opening the small one. As he looked over the small box, he noticed his family's crest— two pistols crossing above a tree— engraved on the top of the lid. Tay's mouth went dry, and he had to swallow to speak.

"How did you get this?" Tay said, his face slack and eyes wide.

"Your parents gave it to me before they left that day," Aria replied, her voice filled with excitement.

Tay looked at the emblem. A silent rage filled his heart. "I don't believe you," he said softly.

"What?"

"I don't believe you!" he shouted, his rage spilling out.

"Tay." Her voice now tender and sweet. "I know you may not believe me right now, but it is a fact that you are holding a gift from your parents. Just open it and you will see," she urged Tay.

Tay placed his hand on top of the box. He hesitated briefly before he lifted the lid and peered inside. Inside, he saw a necklace. The necklace was beautiful with a carefully crafted gem set in it, and the design looked familiar.

It hit him. The necklace looked like the one Shayla gave him. The only difference between the two was the gem. The one in Tay's pocket was a ruby yet this one was a blue sapphire.

Tay's breathing quickened and was barely controlled. "What is this?" Tay asked, the rage inside his chest grew even hotter as he pulled the necklace from the box. He looked at her with heat in his eyes.

"What do you mean?" she asked, confused. "Your mother told me that is the heirloom for the person to have the best stealth in your family."

"Don't play with me!" he yelled and took a threatening step toward her. Aria jumped back in defense.

"What is wrong with you?" her voice trembled.

Tay put the box down and reached into his pocket to pull out the necklace Shayla gave him.

"This...." He shook the necklace in her face. "This is the necklace that symbolizes the heirloom from my family."

Aria was speechless. Tay put the necklace back in his pocket and thrusted the other necklace into Aria's hand. She took it, still looking shocked.

Tay calmed himself and looked at Aria. "Look." His voice was softer and more controlled. "I appreciate the sentiment but please don't try to pass these off as my family heirlooms. The loss of my family still hurts." He turned to walk away and Aria snapped back to reality. She reached out and grasped Tay's wrist.

"Tay, I..." she stuttered. "Would you please open the other one. I don't know what is inside it or if it's real or not but the man that gave it to me... I trusted him with my heart and life," she pleaded. "Please."

Tay didn't look at her but he grimaced before he let out a resounding sigh. He looked at the long box. He didn't want to open it. He didn't want to be disappointed and hurt again. But he wanted to know what was in it as well.

I doubt it will be another fake heirloom.

He walked back to the table and picked up the large box. There was no emblem engraved on this one. That increased his hope in it being a random gift and not something like the previous one.

This one shouldn't be related to my family.

He opened it and inside was a katana. The handle was a mix of red and black wrappings. There was no hand guard, but the pommel was adorned with a red and black tassel. The sheath was beautifully crafted with the design of a dragon flowing from a waterfall. Though at first he was relieved to see that it was a random sword, he sensed something familiar about it.

He examined it carefully, looking for anything to reveal why he had felt it was familiar. Not seeing anything special about the sword itself, he laid it down with its sheath. He was about to walk away when he noticed why it felt familiar.

He looked at the sword and sheath and realized it was similar to the katana design his father used to have. His father told him the sword belonged to the warrior and protector of the family. Tay went back to the sword and looked it over quickly. Still, he couldn't find anything to make him believe it was his father's.

He sheathed it, missing the emblem on the blade handle underneath the wrappings then looked at Aria.

"Thanks, but I don't think this is real either," Tay said, his voice caught in his throat. He put the katana back in the box and closed it.

"But I'm glad you at least liked one of the two." A half-smile graced her lips, but her eyes showed sadness and hurt.

"So, how do we get out of here?"

She looked at the necklace in her hand and pocketed it. "Over this way," she said as she turned and walked toward a corner of the room. At first, Tay looked confused. All he saw was a dark corner. Then he noticed a computer in the wall.

This is truly like some sci-fi shit.

He followed Aria to the corner. Once at the computer, she started typing. Her fingers moved with muscle memory of the keys location. Tay looked at the keys and noticed they were in three different languages. To him, this was overkill, but Aria kept entering keys without looking at the keyboard. What she was typing didn't appear on the screen, or rather Tay couldn't see anything on the screen. He moved to a different position but the only way to see anything on the screen was to stand directly behind Aria. Even so, the protective screen made it to where the screen was barely visible from his point of view. So, Tay assumed one had to be directly at her height for the screen to be fully seen.

She pushed enter and the sound of gears turning filled the room. Tay looked around and saw the wall by the counter that held the gifts slide open.

"Once we go through here there is one more room and then we can leave," she stated, her voice still tinged with disappointment and guilt. She walked past Tay— her eyes seemed distant and hollow. Tay almost reached for her wrist as she passed him, but he held himself back as to not give her any mixed signals. He placed a hand to his chest for it ached at seeing her like this. As she walked through the entryway, he looked after her briefly before he followed.

– Chapter 17: Darkness Revelations –

They went through the new entrance only to stop just a few feet inside the new room. It was pitch black with the only light being from the room behind them. Yet not even five seconds after they walked in, the wall slammed shut plunging them into darkness.

He felt comfortable although he couldn't see anything. He remembered his training and knew if his sight was gone, he still had his sense of smell, touch, and sound to move around. But before he could take a test step, he heard Aria say something that sounded similar to 'Lights on'. The lights on the floor emitted a dim green glow. The glow was enough for them to see where they could go but not strong enough to show them their way out.

"Follow me," Aria said in a distant voice. She walked ahead mechanically like she wasn't there. Tay looked back at the wall that was now closed. He found himself wondering what other secrets were held in the room behind the wall. He shook the thought away and looked at Aria.

Just as that room has secrets, I wonder what else you are hiding from me.

They walked, turned corners, and sometimes even walked into dead ends for what felt like fifteen minutes without seeing any kind of exit. The layout reminded Tay of a tunnel system made by ants or something.

Each time they came to a dead-end Aria would search the walls and then mutter something like,

"Not this one."

Tay was curious as to what she meant but after the third dead-end, Tay felt his frustration grow. He was tired of being underground and he was beginning to think Aria was lost. By the fifth dead-end, his frustration reached a peak.

"How much longer before we are out?" His voice strained as he fought to remain calm though his foot bounced rapidly on the ground.

"It isn't far but there is one more thing I must show you before we can leave," she replied, facing the wall to her right and feeling around for something.

"And you couldn't have told me that while we were walking around this place?!" His voice rose at the end. He was pissed. Not only did she lead him around but he followed her blindly.

Just then, Aria seemed to have found what she was looking for. She held her hand against the wall with spread fingers. The place under her hand turned a bright blue. Once the light died down, a panel flipped around to reveal a monitor and keypad. She entered in a code and the screen read, "Access Granted."

The wall that was a dead-end lowered to reveal another staircase. Tay looked at the stairs and his frustration flared again.

"More stairs!!" Tay breathed before he turned to her. "Can't we just do this later?" Tay pleaded through clenched teeth, his voice tight. Aria didn't seem to hear him and headed down the stairs. Tay looked at her back, eyes wide as she descended.

"Dammit!" he screamed as he kicked at the ground. He hesitated for a moment and stared at the stairwell. He chased after her with a loud grunt.

They walked in silence down three flights of stairs before reaching a room with nothing in it. Tay hoped this was their destination because now he wanted to leave.

The room was a huge cube. There seemed to be nothing here. To Tay, it looked like a fallout shelter. The lights were too dim for him to see the other side of the room. Aria walked to a corner on the left that was shrouded in shadow. Halfway she turned to see that Tay wasn't following her. She motioned for Tay follow.

He rolled his eyes and let out a loud sigh then walked toward her. Once he caught up, she continued toward the wall. Once at the corner, he saw another hand scanner.

"Again!! Seriously!!" Tay said, his voice tired and distressed. He looked at Aria. "Look, I just want to go home. This stuff has too much for me to understand at this time."

Aria didn't reply. She stood there with her eyes locked on Tay.

"Why are you just staring at me?" Tay said as he took a step back. Her hollow eyes followed his every movement. Tay took a step toward her and realized she wasn't really looking at him but past him. She looked like someone stuck in a dream state but still able to perceive the world around them. When he noticed this, his rage diminished slightly as concern gripped his mind.

"Aria," he called gently to her as he looked straight into her eyes.

No reply.

"Aria," he said more forcefully as he placed his free hand on her shoulder and shook her.

Still nothing.

This reminded Tay of when she freaked out and screamed while he was punching his dummy at his old place.

Is she having another episode because she didn't take her medicine?

Tay tried to shake her once more and waved a hand in front of her face but she still didn't say anything. As he was about to move his hand from her face, she reached out and took his hand and placed it on the scanner.

He flinched and tried to pull his away, but her grip was tight and secure. He looked at how she held his hand and realized her grip made it to where he would hurt himself before he could remove her hand. So, he relaxed, and the scanner scanned him for three seconds.

Once the scanner finished, there was a beep. The room lit up and the whole area could be seen. Tay turned and looked around as certain sections of the room opened up and revealed an old square tv, computer, radio, telephone, and a miniature scale version of the city with active lights and moving vehicles. Beside each was a chest of various sizes. Tay looked around in awe.

"What is this?" His rage and frustration forgotten, his voice soft with wonder.

"You will find out soon," she said.

Tay turned sharply to look at her, shocked to see life in her eyes again. He stood before her and looked her over, his heart racing to make sure she was okay.

"Aria, are you alright?"

"Hmm…yeah…" she said as she focused on Tay. "Oh, I'm great. Why?"

She didn't know she was acting lifeless and moved as if she was in a trance state. Before Tay could ask her more about it, she looped her arm around his and pulled him in the direction of the radio first.

"Never mind me. Now that you are here, I was told by my father to have you to check out all these objects. He said that everything down here will allow you to experience a truly wonderful gift." Her face was beaming as she pulled Tay along. It was like she had forgotten the other room and how she was acting.

The radio was an old wooden style that had a wooden mesh in front of the speakers. The radio looked just like the one his granddad used to listen to on his Sunday mornings in his room. Unconsciously, Tay reached out and started playing with the dial like he did when he was a kid. The familiarity brought a smile to his face. He remembered how he would always get in trouble for doing that by his parents, but his granddad never punished him. He would listen with Tay with a smile on his face.

All the stations seemed to pick up nothing but static. But the moment he took his hand off the dial, the dials moved by themselves. They stopped on what looked like a random station and then a voice came out the speakers.

"Tay." He stared at the radio, his grip on the sword's box slacked enough to let the sword's box fall from his hand. He quickly reached for it and readjusted his grip. He stared back at the radio. "How are you doing, my grandson? I do hope you are doing well?" His grandpa's voice was warm and friendly like always.

"Grandpa..." Tay whispered in disbelief.

"Tay, I hope you are looking after your brother and sister and keeping them out of trouble. Especially Shayla. She was always looking to get into things she shouldn't." The mention of Shayla made Tay's heart race. The feeling of longing and the need to be cared for rushed through him. "There is something you must know. If you are listening to this then everyone is dead except your brother, sister, and of course you." There was a pause before he continued.

"I am happy you all survived. Protect those that are close to you and most of all protect your heart. If there comes a time when you feel that you lost your way, use this." The chest beside the radio popped open and inside rested a compass with a dragon on its cover. "This compass will show you which directions are the best, but it will not give you a definite answer. You must decide that for yourself."

"Sounds just like you, Grandpa J," Tay said with a slight smile .

"Be brave. Use your head and heart and stay strong. You are doing great, and I am so proud of you. Love you, my favorite grandson." The radio clicked off. Tay took the compass and looked toward Aria.

First it is the fake necklace... then this sword... and now voice recording and other heirlooms.

Tay looked at the other objects he had yet to interact with.

If all these are recordings or something like that from my family...Why does the Blackwood family have all this? Why wasn't it left to me or placed in a vault? He didn't feel anger—not yet—because he knew his family worked closely with the Blackwoods to manage their realm but it still felt odd.

Before Tay could ask a question, Aria took hold of his arm and pulled him to the TV.

"Hey, Aria. Wait—" Tay tried to get out but they had reached the TV. Shaking his head, Tay glanced at Aria then back at the TV before he decided to see what would happen next. He felt around the TV, found the power button, and pushed it. The screen flashed to show a huge eye. Tay jumped back at the sight of the eye and took a fighting position out of reflex.

"Hey, is this thing working?" The voice of Tay's grandma asked as the view switched over to the other eye. Tay looked at the eye and noticed how it was a beautiful light green. It was the same color as his grandma's eyes. Tay could still remember her eyes and how they seemed to shine no matter what. She pulled the camera away and showed her full face. His heart raced again but with mirth. It really was her.

Seeing her still looking at the camera puzzled him. Tay shook his head and replied out of habit, "Yes, ma'am." Once he realized what he did, he smiled and looked up at the screen to see her smiling at him. He loved the corny sense of humor his grandma held. But her being on the screen made him wonder even more why Aria had all this information and why her of all people. Yet as those questions popped into his mind, a troubling thought also surfaced.

Are these really my family? How could she have all these moments that were so special to me? What if all this was just a ruse? Though the questions kept popping into his head, he didn't say a word. He scanned the room for the answers, but nothing never came. His grandma continued speaking.

"Dear, you know Grandma loves you and your brother and sister so much and will do anything for all of you. Well, the time has come for me to prove it. Though, there is a high likelihood that I won't make it back. I'm getting too old and my skills aren't as sharp as they used to be. Though, I can still hold my own fairly well. I feel we have encountered a person we shouldn't have. You are still young and probably won't remember me doing this, but I want you to always remember that my love for you and your little brother and sister was real and still will be even after I am gone. My time is brief, so here are my words of wisdom to you." She took a seat in her favorite rocking chair; hands folded on her lap and eyes closed. She drew in a long breath then slowly opened her eyes, no longer showing her silly side but her seriousness. The true assassin she was known as.

"You know life is never easy nor is it ever fair. For everything we want or have comes at a price. Even happiness has its own cost. But there will come a time when you will see what I mean." Tay hung onto her every word. Her body language and eyes made it seem impossible not to look at her and not to want to know what she was saying. As she spoke, Tay tried to remember a time when she was like this that he ever disregarded her words. He found he couldn't remember a time when he didn't listen when she was like that.

"You are truly gifted. Many would love to have some of the gifts that you possess. But don't take them for granted and don't throw them away. Remember that your mind is the greatest weapon. To move requires thought and thoughts are planning of the mind. Your mind is more advanced than most. To help you concentrate when you feel confused, take my glasses."

There was a small chest to the right of the TV. It opened, showing his grandma's spectacles. The lenses was small half-moon shaped and the frame felt light as he picked them up. Tay put them on and found that it fit just right. As he looked around, something strange happened—everything else in the room faded away, leaving only the object directly in front of him, sharp and clear. With the glasses on, there were no distractions, just pure focus. When he took them off, the room came back into full view, but everything seemed to have a sharper image. If Tay concentrated on certain items, details that had escaped him before suddenly became obvious.

"Oh, before I forget," his grandma continued. "From the moment you were born, you showed a thought pattern of a truly mature adult. It was amazing to see how you grew up and the way you viewed the world. Keep training your mind but be careful. Your mind is powerful, but don't let it be the reason you distance yourself from others. A strong mind can solve many problems, but there are times when a strong heart is needed even more. Stay connected, and remember, I love you." She smiled brightly. Her smile held his attention and even through the TV he felt the love she had for him. Then the TV blinked off.

Tay held the glasses tightly. Seeing her face, along with hearing his grandpa's voice, was starting to take a toll on him. He wished for those old days to return. He shut his eyes to keep the tears at bay, his body trembled. Suddenly, he felt arms wrap around him. He flinched instinctively but didn't resist. He knew it was only him and Aria in the room but the sudden embrace caught him off guard. Slowly, he calmed his mind and relaxed as he let the warmth of the hug soothe him. They stood there for a moment, still and silent.

Tay opened his eyes once he was sure that no tears would fall. He looked down to see Aria with her head buried in his chest. Tay gently pushed her off him and noticed the wet marks on his shirt. He glanced at her and saw the tears still falling.

Why is she crying? he thought as he stowed the glasses in his pocket. He reached to her face and swiped her tears. She looked up at him and smiled as she nuzzled her cheek in his palm. One of the traits about her that had captivated him before was how cute she was. Not to mention the constant feeling of comfort that Tay felt from her. She had once more unknowingly put him in a trance. But this time it was because of how eerily similar her eyes reminded him of his grandma's eyes. They were almost the same hue.

You are just imagining things now. She isn't related to you.

Tay shook the thought away as he let her stand there with her cheek against his hand. He once again began looking around the room. The room still seemed sharper than before, but the clarity was slowly fading to what it had been when they first entered.

After a few minutes, she stopped crying and took Tay's hand, leading him to the computer. As they got closer, Tay felt a strong familiarity from the setup. A memory flashed through his mind—him as a kid running to the computer. The height of the desk, the position of the monitor, the keyboard, and the tower on the floor—it was exactly how his father's computer had been arranged. The realization hit him, and he stumbled.

Aria quickly adjusted, caught him, and helped him regain his balance. Her eyes shone at him like the day at the park. His heart stirred with that familiar sense of connection—he knew it was because of their parents' history, but in that moment, it felt deeper. As he stood up, the monitor came on and an input screen popped up. They walked to the monitor to see what it was asking for.

The screen had a basic input for name, date of birth, and favorite food. Tay looked to Aria, thinking this was another security measure her family put in place, but she stood there, unmoving.

"So don't you need to input something."

"Oh, I don't know this one. I was told to never input anything into this computer."

Tay looked at her baffled and that warm familiarity faded. "So why are we standing here then?"

"I thought it was obvious." She looked Tay in the eyes, full of hope.

Tay raised his eyebrows at her.

"Oh. Let me explain." Tay nodded as she began. "When you dropped me off from the park, my dad was truly happy to meet you. He pulled me aside once inside the house and told me that he had something he wanted to show you downstairs for when you dropped me off after the club."

"So, I was curious and my dad told me that if I ever brought you home and he wasn't there, that I should bring you down here. He told me about the scanner and that everything after that were gifts from your family that he had been protecting for years. He even told me that he was hesitant at first to hold all of it as it reminded him of a tragic event. But because your dada and mother were his best friends, he agreed. So, all in all, everything shown down here is meant for you."

Tay kind of figured that but he just didn't want to believe it. Her family had so much stuff that belonged to his family; it hurt his heart. He couldn't help himself and thought again.

Even with that story I find it hard to believe that they would have all this? Why do they have their last words down here instead of it being given to me after their funeral?

Tay approached the keyboard and entered his answers then pressed the spacebar. The moment he did, his mom appeared instead of his dad.

"Hi, my son." His mother's voice was soft, her smile the same gentle one he remembered. Yet, Tay clenched his fists, something felt wrong, off-kilter.

"Tay, please heed my last words," she continued. Her smile remained, but tears slipped down her cheeks, contrasting with the warmth of her expression. "What the mind may block, the body will still remember."

Tay looked at her eyes. They were a bright emerald but they were now shining from the tears that welled up and ended up falling down her cheek even though she continued smiling. "I love you, your brother, and your sister so much. So please watch over them and protect them." Her voice wavered as the tears continued to fall. "And don't forget my words."

The screen blacked out before Tay could even react, leaving him with the weight of what she had just said. Another input screen appeared. This time it asked for hobby, most precious moment, and dream for life. Tay read it twice but each time he felt that this screen was not meant for him. The chest under the computer desk popped open, but Tay didn't reach for it. His mind was a whirl of thoughts. The sight of his mother in such a state pierced his heart. He stared at the monitor, her words replaying in his head.

What the mind may block, the body will still remember. What did she mean by that?

It wasn't until Aria slightly tugged on Tay's sleeve did he come back to himself. He looked at her lost and confusion evident on his face. But the sight of her sparked something. He turned away, too irritated to even look at her.

This is all her fault. She just had to bring me here for my birthday. Let's just grab the things here and leave. Then once we get home she is out. Tay glanced over his shoulder at Aria. She smiled back.

He turned away from her and shut his eyes tightly. *I can't kick her out. She has nowhere to go nor anyone to turn to.* He breathed and managed to calm himself but he still felt his shirt shaking. He looked at it to see Aria's hand was shaking. He realized how seeing and hearing these moments might also be affecting her as well. Especially after he found out that she grew to love his parents, too. Tay placed a hand on hers and looked at her with a gentle smile.

She released his shirt and stepped back, allowing him to kneel down to look inside the chest.

Inside was a diary with a weird lock on it. There were three shapes that showed a way to open it, but they had to be just right. But Tay had no idea what those objects could be. Tay took the diary without a second glance, stood, and turned to the telephone— the next to last object.

He wanted to hurry and leave. Not only did he have to deal with his emotions, but also all the questions forming in his head. He snatched the phone and placed it to his ear. At first, it was just noise—children laughing, static from a radio, a TV commercial. But then the music began soft and familiar, a piano and trumpet. The sound was unmistakable.

He froze.

His body went cold as the memory hit him like a punch to the chest.

He knew exactly where and when this was from. Tay slammed the phone down, only to hear it play on the speakers overhead. He tried covering his ears, but the music played in his head.

He stared at Aria, trembling with rage and strained eyes.

"How? Why the hell do you have this?" his voice cracked as he spoke through trembling lips.

"There…There's no reason for you to have this." He pointed at the telephone. "So why?"

Aria looked at him and didn't say a word. Her body shook from fear and she was afraid to move.

"Stop just standing there and answer me dammit!!" Tay's voice boomed, but the tears in his eyes betrayed the fury he felt.

"Tay, I don't—" she started as she shook her head. "Please…calm down. And let's…" she said, trying to comfort herself and him.

"Calm down?" Tay stared at her, wide-eyed. He laughed—a short, bitter, broken sound.

His lips trembled as he turned away, his hands clenched so tight his knuckles cracked. "You really think this is something I can calm down from?"

"Tay, it will be—"

"Don't. Don't say it."

He turned toward her so fast, she flinched. His eyes glowered at her as his voice rose like a tidal wave.

"Don't you dare say it's going to be alright!"

Tears burst from his eyes like he'd been holding them back for years. His breath shook. His voice cracked.

"You—you and your family—had these pieces of *my* past. These memories of my family. The radio, the glasses, the tv, and the compass. And possibly even this sword!" he shouted as he waved the box with the sword in front of her.

"We thought it was all gone. I thought the fire erased everything. But now—Fuck!" he screamed as he spun away from her.

Aria backed up a step with her hands raised.

"Tay, I didn't know—"

He turned back and snapped at her. "You didn't know! You didn't know that all of this was down here! You didn't know that the next thing to fucking play was a scene from my worst nightmare!" He held his arms out wide, gesturing to the area before turning away and pacing as the music still played overhead.

Aria's face crumpled. "I wasn't trying to hurt you. I'm so—"

"No. No. You don't fucking get to say I'm sorry," he said as he stepped toward her, pointing at her face. She stepped back once more, trembling. He looked into her face and noticed her fear. He felt his heart ache and this time he knew it wasn't from his pain but what he was doing to hurt her right now. He turned away from her and screamed into the room.

"Fuck!!!!" He squatted down and tucked his head as he held his knees. Aria didn't move.

After a while, the music stopped but neither moved.

Tay was the one to break the silence.

"You know, at some point in our recent interactions, I had begun to like you. I was confused about it at first but I realize it now. Through all your actions and words, you were constantly in my head. At first, I was just irritated that you came on so strong. But it started to feel...normal. Like a piece of my life that I was starving was being satisfied." He scoffed as he thought of how she seemed to make him feel certain emotions when she was around. How he was subconsciously happy to have her around. But instead of making him happy like before, he felt nothing but disdain for her at the moment. He got up and walked toward her.

"But now I don't want anything to do with you. You fucked with my mind and my heart but this is just too much. So, when we get back I want you to get your things and get out and never look for me again. You are on your own now."

Tears poured down Aria's face. She looked pleadingly at him with trembling lips. She raised a shaky hand to touch his face but he backed away and turned his head. And with that movement, Aria pulled her hand back, crouched down, and cried.

"Tagen Davis!!"

Tay froze instantly. The voice sounded like it was right behind him. But that wasn't what caused him to lock up. It was the voice's tone. It was strong and commanding, almost demanding but there was compassion in it.

It felt familiar, too.

"Dad?" Tay whispered under his breath.

"Tay…my son." His dad's voice was now calm and comforting. "Why do you let rage control you?" Tay turned from Aria and looked for where the voice came from. There was a speaker under the phone and the voice was being projected from there.

The confusing thing was how would his dad have known he would be enraged at this moment. From the way everything was being presented, Tay assumed all these recordings were from the past. Or rather Tay believed they had to be.

A small pain stabbed at his heart as a new thought formed in his mind.

A thought so unrealistic to him that he felt like a kid for even thinking about it. But it was there. And with it came a hope.

The hope his family could still be alive burned in his heart and with that thought came rage.

If they are alive… Tay stared at the speaker. *Even if it was just my dad, why didn't he come back to us? Why did he let us continue to live thinking everyone was gone?*

Tay stopped his line of thought. *No. They are all gone. Don't think of nonsense.* He shook his head hard to bring himself back to the present.

"Calm your mind and heart and listen to me." Tay noticed his father's undertone. It was like his dad feared something and was set with despair.

"This is the night that I am to die." His father took a deep breath and spoke again. "I have come to accept this as fate. I am disappointed that I can't watch you or your siblings grow up. But my first job is to protect you all the best that I can." His father stopped for a moment. It sounded like he was walking and in the background was the sound of kids playing.

"I have told your mother and grandparents about this. I managed to persuade your mom to run with you and your brother and sister. But I don't know how safe y'all will be even after y'all get away." He paused once more, as if he was remembering something. "But no matter what happens, I will put my life on the line to give y'all a chance."

This confirmed it for Tay. He knew his dad would have stayed to fight as many people as he could to give his mom and them time to escape. His grandparents would have done the same. They believed they lived a great life and always expected to die in battle or of old age.

Tay's hand curled into a fist and his left leg bounced rapidly. Just then, the sound of kids playing faded and became muffled. His dad must have walked away.

"Listen, son, I know living the way we do must have been hard for you. You have strong sense of responsibility and great morals. You put up with it because you wanted to be there for us if we ever needed you to be. I have always prayed that that time would never come. I guess not all prayers are answered." He chuckled sadly. Tay's nose flared from each word his father spoke. His exhales came out loud and deep.

"Tay, my son, I know that you will want to get revenge for me and your grandparents. But I must tell you to let that desire go. There isn't any good feeling at the end of that achievement. It will only start a vicious cycle of killing. All I can say is I am sorry I wasn't strong enough or wise enough to keep this danger from our family. But I will say this, I pray that this event will allow you to live the normal life that you always dreamed of."

The veins in Tay's neck throbbed as his lower lip shook. "When did he find out?" Tay mumbled. He had been careful not to tell anyone of his desire from a young age. He only wrote it in his hidden diary and thought he acted normal enough for his age.

"I imagine you are surprised that I know. Well don't be." His dad chuckled, as if he was remembering the day it happened. "It was your mother who found out first. You left your diary open as you were rushing to go to a party. She was in your room cleaning and just so happened to see it. She was about to close it but saw the title of that page. I believe it was something like my biggest dream. She couldn't stop herself from reading it. Don't blame her. Any parent would want to know what dreams their child have and how they can help them achieve it."

"After that, she came and told me. We were so happy and then swore to do our best to make that happen for you, but we still wanted you to be able to protect yourself. So that is why we trained you the way we did. Son, we all love you and wish that we could be there for you to help make your dream come true."

His father paused. When he spoke again his voice no longer held the strength Tay was used to. He sounded frail. "Well, it is almost time for the show to begin. But before I go, two things. Take good care of my sword. I know you always wanted it, but from this day onwards you have earned it." This caused Tay to briefly forget his simmering rage and he looked down at the sword's box then back to Aria.

"So... it is really... It is his sword..." His words came out as a soft whisper. He instantly felt guilty for not believing Aria earlier. But his emotions once again meddled into rage.

Just another fucking piece of my family that they kept. Tay closed his eyes as his father continued speaking.

"Also, I have one more small gift. Keep both and remember us with smiles."

The chest popped open and Tay opened his eyes.

Upon seeing the chest, he slowly made his way to it from where he was standing with Aria. It looked empty. He put his hand inside and felt around.

Just as he was about to pull his hand out and ask Aria something, his finger flicked something metal followed by a clinking sound. He looked inside again and found a ring. The ring was made from silver and held three gems; an emerald princess cut, a diamond heart cut, and a sapphire oval cut. Tay looked at the ring and thought of the ring his mother always wore.

"This is the ring Dad gave Mom for her last birthday."

Tay knew his mom never took the ring off and yet there it was in his hand without a dent or scratch.

"Tay, this ring is but a key to the past and present. Keep it with you and remember to cherish those close to you like a gentleman should." This time the words came from the chest.

Tay stood there shaking and unable to control his emotions. Sadness, confusion, anger, and pain all mixed together making him unable to think or focus. His father spoke again but this time his voice held more authority in it.

"Now, Tay, go to the miniature scale of the town and place your hand on the lake by the golf course and Aria place your hand on the open grass in the park." There was a click and the call ended, but to Tay this click sounded eternal and final.

He didn't know what to do with his jumbled emotions. Though his mind was reeling and unable to give him any direction, his body moved to follow his father's words and walked to the display. As he moved, he remembered his family with smiles. His dad's strong half smirks, his grandma's gentle goofy faces, his grandpa's wise deep smile, and his mother's...

Her smile would light up the room and was filled with so much joy and love each time she saw him. He felt a smile try to form on his face. But with each face, he remembered the pain of losing them along with anger at not being able to help, which overrode his fleeting happiness.

By the time he reached the display, his mind was plagued by the night he lost his family— by Aria having all this stuff that belonged to his family— but most of all, he thought of why his family would leave such things behind and what was their plan.

As he stood at the table, he snapped back to reality. He looked at the lake and saw a faint imprint for a hand scanner. He looked at Aria and she gave a weak smile, as if she knew his pain. And in that moment, he was suddenly struck by how she reminded him so much of his little sister in the old days.

He thought of how his sister moved— stealthy and quick. He thought of how she smiled and it brought him peace and joy. He thought of how she stuck around him more than necessary for two siblings. Then he thought of Aria. The way she moved, the way she stuck to him, and the way she made his emotions all messed up by being around her.

No Tay. Stop trying to make her into someone she is not. And besides, isn't your sister at home with Tim now.

They looked at each other and nodded slightly as she placed her hand on the table, and he followed suit. The moment their hands were in the designated locations, there was a buzzing sound. It lasted for a few seconds and then the figure of the town changed its shape. They pulled their hands away as the lake drained and the buildings switched positions. The trees moved to the other perimeter of the table until the middle of the display was a flat clearing.

As the table transformed, the walls in the room shifted as well. The walls moved closer as the items in the room disappeared; some were lowered into the ground and others went into the wall depending on where they were placed in the room. Everything stopped moving after a few minutes.

Light shone onto the walls and the clearing in the middle of the table. Tay looked at the table and saw a video of his family. The video was on a short loop and played without sound, but it showed them mingling around with each other happy and smiling. Tay looked around and noticed that each wall displayed a picture of a different family member.. Underneath their picture was their title and even the object that showed their status. They were the gifts Tay had received.

Tay scanned the walls and took in each image. He pulled his phone from his back pocket and took pictures. When he took his grandma's picture, he paused in confusion as he studied her picture. In her picture, he saw the necklace she wore was the same one Aria tried to give him earlier with the sapphire gem. He was sure before that, that the one he had gotten from Shayla was the real one. But now...

Why did she wear a fake heirloom?

Tay pulled out the one Shayla gave him. He looked it over carefully then looked back at his grandma's picture. Suddenly, the necklace in his hand felt foreign to him, as if it was made differently. The weight and brilliance seemed to diminish, and his grandma's necklace gained a more brilliant light about it.

"Aria, how did you get these?" Tay asked, still studying his grandma's picture.

"My dad must have put them here..." She didn't look at Tay but studied the pictures. "He always held onto these in his office. I guess they are the last photos your mom and dad gave him," Aria replied, her voice soft and pleasant like she was reliving a wonderful memory. "I used to look at them every night in his office. When I felt lonely, because my parents were away, I would sneak into his office and take those pictures along with a picture of my parents to bed with me. It made me feel safe and as if everyone was with me, smiling as if nothing could go wrong."

Tay had partially stopped listening after she said that her dad had them. Instead, his mind was flooded with other thoughts, so he didn't pay much attention to her last remark. Instead, his main thought was why?

"I have so many questions and no answers to them," Tay mumbled low enough for himself to hear.

"Tay..." Aria said to get his attention. "Look."

Tay looked in her direction. She was looking back at the table. Tay glanced over at it too and saw everyone had stopped moving and were now looking up. Tay peered up at the ceiling then saw the moon and fireworks. The scene was that night, but what Tay felt at that time was a sense of togetherness, fulfillment, and happiness in that moment.

"When was the last time that I felt this way?' Tay whispered but Aria still heard him.

"Do you think your family wanted you to remember the good times and hold those memories close to you instead of revenge?" she asked, still facing up but glancing at him through the corner of her eyes.

"Maybe," he said. His eyes were glued to the beauty of that night. He brought the sword to his chest and hugged tightly. He wanted to forget about the anger, about the pain of his lost, and with each explosion of fireworks, he felt all his worries and questions slowly melt away.

He glanced back down and noticed his dad was no longer there and he felt a small stab to his heart. Shortly afterward, his grandparents faded away too, leaving his mom, brother, sister, and him alone gazing up at the fireworks with smiles. Tay stared at the video and even though his father and grandparents were gone, he knew they would have thrived with their mom around.

That happiness was never meant to be, though. His family was taken and he struggled to protect his brother and sister. He stared at the kid versions of themselves and looked at his mom who was looking at them as well. The determination in her eyes and the smile on her face melted away the deep hatred and anger in his heart. When he looked at Aria, all the annoyance he felt for her was dissipating. Her familiarity still puzzled him but he knew deep inside he would still be there to protect her.

"I will protect my family with my life. Don't you worry, Mom, we will all make it," Tay whispered below the sounds of the fireworks. He looked back up and the fireworks, smiling. His revenge was just a small ember about to be extinguished and peace held him.

Just then the video glitched and the image became distorted. Though he wanted to embrace the moment more, Tay felt he was in enough control to guide his life and those around him. "Don't you…"

"What is that!!" Aria exclaimed as she held out a hand, pointing at the table and covering her mouth. The scene was now replaced with his family's house on fire and a man with a hood over his face, sword on his waist, and a gun in each hand.

Rage instantly took over Tay.

"Him," Tay said through clenched teeth. The man turned from the flames and looked like he was laughing. The ember inside Tay began to burn again with seething rage and pain, threatening to become a full furnace in his heart. Tay recognized him. He knew him but he couldn't place from where.

"It doesn't matter who you are. I will find and I will kill him." Tay took in every detail he could about the man he knew was responsible for the death of his family. The video cut off abruptly and Tay looked up at Aria. She was visibly shaken. She glanced up at Tay.

"Tay… I'm… I'm sorry. I promise that…" Her words seemed to get stuck in her throat. "I don't know how that got there. I promise you I never would have brought you here if I had known," Aria blurted out as she stepped back, fear showing all over her face. Tay pulled his hand off the table, stood up, closed his eyes, and breathed in and out a few times. He opened his eyes once he was calmer.

"It is okay—I trust that you wouldn't have done this."

"You… believe me?" Her eyes showed relief, but her body still was on edge.

"Yes, I believe you." He smiled softly. "I mean you... I still have certain things that I'm curious about and think we need time to discuss. But I know you have been trying to connect with me so much that it is hard for me to think of a reason you would show me something like this that could have gotten yourself killed. And besides." His mouth was set in a firm line. "I feel like I know the person that planted this here."

"Really?"

"Yea, remember I told you of the butler I saw the night I brought you home?"

"Yea. You said that you believed him to be a fake."

"Right, I believe he got the information from Carl and then messed with this before he made his escape that night."

"So, he and that man in the video are accomplices?"

"Most likely."

They stood there for a minute as they thought over what this meant. But there were still too many pieces that were missing for any conclusion to be made. "Anyways, let's go, Aria."

"Ok." They walked to each other. When they met, she smiled and put her hand in his. Tay shook his head and let it happen.

She smiled even brighter and said, "Come on, Tay, let's go home. For real this time."

"You lead the way and..." He paused for a moment. "Thanks for the gifts." Her smiled seemed to dim a little but she pulled his hand as they walked toward a wall. As they approached, a door slid open to show a new path. They walked into the corridor with a lot of questions and concerns but the most troublesome thought on his mind was why show him all this?

They walked for a few more minutes in silence before reaching a set of stairs. Instead of going up, Aria turned to face Tay.

"Once we get outside, there is one place I want to see before we head back. If that's okay with you?" Aria asked, squeezing Tay's hand tightly. She looked like she was afraid of being left the moment they got outside.

Tay shook his head. "Don't worry. I'm not mad at you anymore nor will I leave you here alone," he answered. She threw her arms around his neck and hugged him.

"Thank you. I promise it won't be long." She let him go and they walked up the stairs. There was a door at the top of the stairs, and the smell of the outdoors drifted in through the seal. Aria opened the door, and they walked out into the forest in the back of the Blackwood's estate. There were no houses to be seen, and the streetlights couldn't be seen through the dense foliage. Only the moonlight allowed them to see their surroundings. He wondered where this place that she wanted to visit was because this forest was thick and lush. They were the only thing visible.

"So, where is this place?" Tay asked, trying to let go of all the things he just experienced. She didn't reply; she had vanished into the woods. "How did she move so quickly without making a sound?" he asked to the wind as it blew by. Tay couldn't make up his mind whether to follow her or not. So, he sat on the grass against a tree and looked up at the sky as it turned from burnt orange to dark blue. The stars illuminated the air just like every night.

Tay sat there, mind whirling as he tried not to think of all he had seen and heard. But the more he tried the more his mind kept wandering back to the events that happened underground. He knew from all the things his parents said that they wanted him to live a normal happy life and he knew that was his ultimate desire. As he thought of them, the flames would also surface along with that familiar silhouette and smile. Anger welled up inside him and he knew as much as he wanted to live normal he also wanted his revenge. He continued looking at the stars before he closed his eyes to meditate.

Tay was jolted awake as his body jerked upright to keep him from falling onto the grass. He shook his head and stretched. He refocused and looked around. Still no Aria. Tay glanced at his watch and realized he had been sleep for about half an hour. Now he was starting to get annoyed.

"How long will she be gone?" he complained. "I'm ready to get home and get in my comfy bed." He stood up and paced to try to keep himself awake. He wanted to understand all that had happened still but the quick nap helped to briefly forget until he noticed the gleam from the metal door where the moon glowed on its corner. Seeing that corner brought his mind back to the events from below.

He knew now why the Blackwoods had all those things from his family. Aria's father had been entrusted with the legacy by his own parents. That much was clear from what Aria said, but that didn't make it easier to accept.

It still annoyed him that his family didn't leave anything behind directly for them. He thought of all the plans that fell through. His parents' plan for his mother to escape. The plan Mr. Blackwood had to show Tay the basement— though this partly succeeded due to Aria— and how no matter what he tried to do in this life to have a normal one, things just kept happening. With each thought, his annoyance turned into irritation.

"Why can't I just have a normal life? I am so tired of these surprises and the feeling of being dragged back into this lifestyle!" Tay shouted to the stars.

"You can't because you know who you truly are," a voice called out over the field.

Tay jumped and scanned the tree lines. He wasn't expecting an answer. "And though you tired of it all… you actually look forward to it for you love each new adventure," a girl said as she walked toward Tay.

Tay squinted at her and thought she was Aria, but the moment she walked into the moonlight he noticed it was Shayla.

"Sis!" Tay exclaimed, surprised to see her. "What are you doing here?"

"I followed you and *that girl*," Shayla said as she continued walking slowly to him. Tay noticed how she put emphasis on saying *that girl*. He felt like there was some deep hatred in her voice.

"Well, she has gone and ran off somewhere." He swept his arms at the trees. "I don't know when she will be back or if she got lost. So, I'm just waiting here." Tay looked back at Shayla. "So, tell me. What did you mean by I know myself, though?"

"It is simple," Shayla said as she leaned against the tree Tay was resting on earlier. "You know what kind of person you are and what you need to be. In other words, you have already accepted yourself entirely." The way she looked from Tay to the forest made him feel uneasy about her. But her body language remained calm, gentle, and approachable. Yet Tay's body was slightly primed to react.

There is no way that Shayla is a threat, Tay thought as he tried to calm his inner suspicions and relax his hand that was in a fist. *Even still, how did she manage to find us?* He turned his back to Shayla and gazed out into the forest again. Just as he turned, he saw Aria running back cradling something in her arms.

"Aria!" Tay shouted. "Finally, you are back," he said with his hands on his hips, a look of utter annoyance on his face although he wasn't annoyed. He just couldn't shake this suspicion of his sister's purpose for being there, but he steadily tried to disregard his thoughts.

"Sorry, Tay. It took longer to find what I was looking for," she said as she came into the moonlight. She looked at Tay and her eyes widened. "Tay, look out!" she shouted as she reached a hand toward him. Tay wondered why she was acting like that but soon felt Shayla press a gun to his back.

"Sis…" Tay said as he raised his hands. "What are you doing?"

"Shut up." Shayla's voice had changed. It was more menacing and harder. "Both of you don't try anything or you and that girl die tonight." Tay now understood why he felt weird about her showing up; he was still puzzled by the fact she didn't silently target him but did it outright. Not to mention her finding them. She wouldn't have been able to follow them through the basement levels. She spoke again, breaking his thoughts.

"Tay, drop all the items in your hands and, you—girl, get over here with that book." Tay released all the items in his hands, letting them fall to the ground. He scowled his face at Aria.

"Book?" Tay asked.

She was gone all that time just to get a book. Now this made Tay angry. Was he really being threatened over a fucking book.

"I…" Aria looked to Tay, held his faze briefly before she dropped her eyes to the ground. "I can't." She hugged the package in her arms tighter.

"I said get your ass over here!" Shayla shouted as she pulled out another gun and pointed it at Aria. Aria looked at the guns—her eyes seemed scared—but Tay noticed something in them that looked like she was studying the guns. She slowly walked toward them, head low.

Who is this girl? Why does her actions remind me so much of my sister when she was a kid?

He heard a soft beep. No one was talking and didn't notice. Tay listened closely without moving to see if he heard it again. Another beep sounded muffled but close enough for him to hear it. It sounded like it that coming from—himself. Tay thought about everything on him and realized the necklace Shayla had given him was in his pocket. He looked at Aria with shock.

She was right… Tay couldn't understand how she was right. *No, this has to be my sister or Tim wouldn't have brought her to our house. But then why is she here.* Tay looked at the brown package Aria was holding. His blood began to boil.

Did Tim betray me and brought home someone dangerous into our home. And why is the book so important that this girl I thought to be my sis would trap me like this? All these questions swam in Tay's mind. One thing he knew for sure was that he was going to get answers one way or another. By now, Aria was standing in front of Tay but to the side.

"Before I give you the book, I must tell Tay something," Aria said, looking at Tay.

"No. Just come here and give me that book!" Shayla yelled. Aria looked at Tay, her eyes trying to tell him something, but he couldn't understand. "Don't make me repeat myself or that will be the end for you," Shayla said and shot at Aria's head, barely grazing her cheek. Aria bent over and clenched her cheek.

"Hurry it up. I don't have time to play with you. You little bitch. Hand over the damn book." The agitation in Shayla's voice was lost on Tay as he stared at Aria. She stood up and let her hand fall to her side.

When he saw Aria's cheek dripping blood, he felt a new surge of anger. Aria focused on Shayla. It was then that Tay noticed how much Aria reminded him of his mother and sister when she was a kid. Her eyes were the same in this moment. When his mother and sister trained with him and his father, their eyes always looked like they were piercing you and holding you in place.

Why must I keep seeing glints of my sister in her, and now my mom too? Shayla pointed the gun dead at the middle of Aria's head.

"What are you staring at?" Shayla asked, sounding joyful, as if she wanted to see blood. "Last chance. Give me the book or die."

Aria didn't move but she looked at Tay. Her face softened and tears welled up in her eyes.

"Tay, I'm so sorry," Aria said and just in that moment, Tay heard his little sister from so long ago. That was all Tay needed to hear. He was done with this charade.

Okay that is enough. I don't care who is who. But I know that the Shayla behind me isn't my sister, he thought as he glanced at the gun that was pointed at Aria. The symbol on it wasn't his family crest but one that had a skull engulfed in flames. Just as he realized this, Aria ducked and juked to the right and darted for the forest, unwrapping the paper on the book. Shayla turned to take aim with both guns. Tay quickly turned, grabbed both her hands, and slightly twisted her wrists enough to make her shoot into the ground and drop the guns. She jumped and using both feet, kicked him in the stomach. Tay released her wrists as he staggered back holding his stomach. She fell to the ground and banged her head. She held her head momentarily as Tay ran at her. She regained her composure and looked at Tay charging at her then rolled to her nearest gun. Tay dove for the other gun and rolled to a kneeling position as they pointed a gun at each other.

"Why did you have to interfere?" Shayla said as she kept her gun trained on Tay, scanning the forest for Aria.

The moment she looked away, Tay picked up a rock and hurled it at Shayla. It hit her in the head. She grabbed her forehead. Tay closed the gap between them and drove his elbow into her stomach with a forceful blow. As she doubled over, he grasped her hand holding the gun then grabbed a fistful of her hair, yanking her head back. "Who are you truly?"

Shayla clawed at his hand, trying to free herself but it was useless. Yet even as she struggled, she smiled at him.

"What do you mean?"

"You are not my sister." Tay twisted her wrist holding the gun, making her drop it. "You will tell me everything."

Shayla winced from Tay's grip. "Big brother, stop. You are hurting me," she said, changing her voice to sound like his sister while still trying to make him release her hair.

"I said…stop….toying with me!!" Tay yanked her up and let her hair go but grabbed her other hand. He stepped in front of her and threw his hip back as he pulled her hands forward. He flipped her over, his shoulder slamming her on the ground. She gasped, losing her breath and looking dazed. "My sis was never so obvious, nor would she have fallen for such an easy trick," Tay said, his anger peaking. Not only did he get played but he was blind to the truth. He didn't like hurting women, but he knew in the world she was from, it was kill or be killed and he still wanted answers.

"Guess hiding it anymore wouldn't be nice would it," Shayla said with a malicious smile once she got her senses and breath back. Tay jumped back as she got up spinning, trying to trip him. Once up, Shayla went for her gun and Tay knelt down and picked up his father's sword. With weapons in hand, each took a stance. Shayla laughed. "What you think you can do with that sword?"

"Why don't you get over here to find out?" Tay tried provoking her.

"Hmm, I rather not. But you know what, I never truly introduced myself," Shayla said as the two walked in a circle watching each other intently. "The name is Shayla Evenest. I am a member of the Lackston family."

"The Lackston family?" Tay almost froze. Shayla took the chance and fired at him as she ran toward him. Tay shifted from side-to-side dodging with his hand still on the sword. "Why are you following orders from a dead man?"

"Dead. Oh dear, you seem to be misinformed," Shayla said as she ran after him still shooting. "Mr. Lackston never was there that night. The man you thought you killed was nowhere close to the true Mr. Lackston's skills."

Her words had confirmed his previous feeling. He knew something about that fight felt too easy when he thought about it. Yes, it was quick and his opponent was tough, but it wasn't a fight he knew he couldn't overcome with his strength. The only issue he had now was he didn't know where Mr. Lackston was located. And to find out where the real Mr. Lackston was, he had to capture this imposter. He took one more jump then drew his sword as he ran at her in a zig zag motion. She could follow him with her eyes but the moment she tried to get aim he was already moving to another position.

"Even if you can follow me with your eyes, your hand is too slow to fire over even take aim of me," Tay taunted as he steadily closed the distance. Shayla was standing still, trying to focus on taking aim. Tay took one swing at her, but she blocked it by side-stepping and pushing his hands down. Her action caused the sword to dig into the ground. She followed up with a kick to Tay's head. Tay caught her leg with both hands and he spun, picking her off the ground and slung her to the side. As she rolled to get up, Tay left the sword and ran at her again. Shayla got up in enough time to see him charging at her full speed. She pointed the gun at him, but he just kept running straight at her. She smiled and shot twice only to see him duck, jump forward, and roll.

She tried shooting at his foot to slow him down but missed, causing only dirt to stir. Tay moved to the side and then back and forth. Shayla was having trouble aiming at him and he seemed to be getting closer. She became annoyed she couldn't hit him. She started shooting blindly. Tay noticed and quickly ran straight at her. He made subtle feints, just enough to trick her into thinking he was about to move—baiting her into wasting another bullet. She took notice immediately and visibly calmed down and took aim only. Tay threw dirt at her, but she still pulled the trigger. There was no sound of impact, but a second later Tay was still running at her. He was just a few feet from her. She hastily tried to take aim. When she locked on and squeezed the trigger, Tay was in her face. He pushed her arm up and punched her in the stomach. She gasped and Tay held the gun, hand released the cartridge, and spun again, slinging her into the tree. She hit the tree with a thud and collapsed to the ground. Tay stood a few feet from her, breathing heavy but still focused.

Shayla managed to get into a sitting position and smiled like she was enjoying every minute of the fight.

"Well..." Shayla coughed and spit out blood as she slowly got up. "Seems, I was never a match for you in the first place." She quickly jumped at Tay. Tay already knowing her moves, was ready. He jumped back and caught her hand holding the knife. He twisted her hand before pulling and driving his knee into her elbow. There was a sickening crack. Shayla howled. Tay slowly walked in front of her. She gasped; tears streamed from her eyes. Tay felt nothing when he looked at her now. "Don't worry, I won't kill you just yet. I still need to get some information from you." Tay kicked her in the head and she hit the ground hard. His eyes locked in the distance of the forest. After he caught his breath, he checked to make sure she was unconscious. Once he had verified, he dragged her to a tree and searched her to make sure she didn't have any other weapons. He searched around the tree for something to bind her feet. He found a sturdy stick he felt would be useful in the coming events. He gently and smoothly removed her belt to bind her feet then took his belt to bind her other arm to her waist as tight as he could. Once he was sure she was tied up securely, he pinched her shoulder's pressure point.

"Ouch!" she screamed. Her movement jarred her broken arm, and she screamed even louder. Once she settled down, she looked around again. Her eyes landed on Tay, who stood about three feet from her with her gun trained on her. She was lost and confused. "What? What happened?"

"Really. As if you forgot that quick," Tay said with a sigh. "Come on, I'm not dumb and neither are you." She moved slightly to not jostle her arm but also like she was trying to reach a weapon. "Looking for these." He tapped the pile of weapons by his side. "I almost had to strip you naked to find all your weapons. And you may not want to move anymore, your arm isn't set and I'm sure the pain is almost unbearable." Tay squatted down and looked her dead in the eyes. "Now I think it would be wise for you to just answer my questions and be honest about it. Because you don't want to anger me anymore than you already have."

Shayla clenched her teeth and snarled. "What do you want?" Shayla asked annoyed.

"Why do you want that book that Aria had?"

"Hmph. Wouldn't you like to know. Why don't you just ask Aria?" She said her name sarcastically, as if it disgusted her. Tay looked at her blankly and picked up the stick with his free hand. He waved it up and down before he tapped her broken elbow gently with it. Shayla bit her lip to stop from screaming.

"Would you like a harder tap or to tell me the truth. Without the sarcasm." She glared at him saying nothing. Tay shrugged and swung hard and swift, the stick broke on her arm. She screamed out loud with tears now coming from her eyes. Tay walked a few steps away to find another stick as she continued to scream out.

This one thicker. He gave it a few swings and found it thick enough before he returned and sat her up. Again, he rested the stick to her broken arm.

"Shall we try again?" His question was void of emotions yet his eyes blazed at her. Shayla swallowed her pain and stared back, breathing heavily.

Tay shook his head. "You know I really hate hitting a girl. No matter how tomboyish she may be." Tay drew back and was about to swing. Shayla's eyes went wide. She spoke before Tay could descend.

"Wait,wait,wait....Please don't."

Tay lowered the stick and squatted down. "Well..."

"The book holds a certain agreement that two families made along with their most kept secrets."

"Why does Mr. Lackston want it?"

"You really aren't as smart as you claim," Shayla said with a chuckle. This time, Tay actually swung the stick hard, hitting dead center on the broken elbow. Shayla screamed. "Why you little shit! Fuck you! God dammit!!"

"I told you no more sarcasm, right?"

After composing herself again, she glowered at him even more enraged. "Fine. He wants it to forever destroy them so he will be the number one family on this side of the nation. Also, to gloat about being the one to bring down the families that were revered across the nation."

To have her as a spy when she leaks information so easily. What a joke plus her attitude doesn't help them but it truly works for me, Tay thought to himself.

"Was your boss involved in the murder of my family?"

"Maybe he was; maybe he wasn't. And what are you smiling about?" Shayla said with a sassy attitude.

Tay didn't realize he was smiling. But he knew why...He now had a potential name to go with the image. "Nothing. Next question." Tay hated what he was about to ask, but knew he needed an answer. "Was Tim a part of this?"

This time she smiled. And it was a smile that made his stomach drop. "Ask him yourself?" She spat out with a soft yet wicked laugh.

Anger welled up inside of Tay. *Why would Tim do this? Why would he let a snake into our midst?* Tay thought as he sent up a silent prayer hoping that there was more to it than that.

Then Shayla laughed. Her laugh caught Tay off-guard and he looked at her at a lost.

"What is so funny?"

"Your face," she said between gasps. She settled and looked at Tay and her smile deepened. "Your face right now is so delicious. I can't help it. I want to see you in more despair."

"What the hell do you know?" Tay brought the stick back to her elbow as he lowered the gun.

She licked her lips, as if she tasted the despair on his face. "You really think your brother betrayed you willingly? No, Tim was stubborn—so fucking stubborn. We had to spend days breaking him down before he finally agreed to help. But you know what? It wasn't fear for himself that got to him—it was the thought of your precious sister. We told him she'd be safe if he just did what he was told. He held out, thinking he could resist, but oh… how he screamed when we brought her up." Shayla seemed to momentarily drown in bliss at the memory. Tay felt his grip on the stick tighten at hearing how they played with his brother.

"And when he finally gave in," Shayla continued. "All he asked for were signs of life from her. Pathetic, really. He never even bothered to ask what his work was for. He didn't care about the consequences, as long as he believed she was still breathing. So, he got to work, crafting poisons like a good little scientist, shutting out everything else. And you know what? He even lost himself in his work. Though we found him cutting himself whenever he felt too much joy from tinkering. We quickly patched him up and got him back to work." The smile on her face grew as she remembered those times.

Tays rage almost burst out and he wanted to break every bone in her body. But then a certain realization that had been staring at him all night dawned on him. If this Shayla was pretending to be his sister then where was his real sister. There was a strong desire to ask but also an even greater fear he already knew the answer. "Now, where is Mr. Lackston?" he asked through clenched teeth.

"Wouldn't you like to know?" Her smug attitude was back but Tay didn't swing the stick this time. He knew if he did it wouldn't be just her elbow but her face, too.

"As much as I am now enjoying this conversation, how many more questions do you have?"

"Why? Do you have somewhere you need to be?" Tay asked a wicked smile crept on his face.

"No." She held his eyes, smiling back. "But you do?"

His smile dropped. "What do you mean?"

"While you are here questioning me. Isn't your friend still running through the woods? Don't you need to go find her and protect her?"

Aria. Dang I almost forgot about her. He scowled at Shayla. But then remembered that this was Aria's backyard. Not to mention there weren't other shots except the ones from Shayla that night. *Besides even if she found someone. I'm sure that she will be able to evade them.* Tay thought of how she was able to evade trouble not only when they first met but also at the club before Jaron and his gang started fighting. *Besides, I still need answers.*

"Don't try to change the subject I want my answers, and you will give them to me. Now how did you find us?" he asked but figured he already knew.

"Sheesh, for a guy that supposed to be smart you sure ask dumb questions." Shayla shook her head.

"How do you think?"

Just like he thought, it was the necklace she gave him. How did he miss such an obvious thing. Tay was upset with himself for blindly believing this imposter to be his sister and that she was being genuine. He was now out of questions but the one lingering in his mind was about his sister. He looked deep into Shayla's eyes and softly asked, "Where is my sister?"

A big smile came on her face and soon she was laughing. "Sure, you want to know?" she asked teasingly.

Tay, without hesitation, brought the gun back up and shot. He missed her ear by only a few centimeters. Shayla smiled harder and laughed even more. "Oh, don't be a little sour puss." Tay rage finally burst. He dropped the stick and walked up to her. As she looked up at him, he punched her in the face four times, making her head bounce against the tree trunk. On one of the punches, he heard and felt her nose crack. He lifted her up by her hair and looked her in her non-injured eyes as he held his gun to her temple. "For your sake, You better pray she is alive."

"Aww the little boy has grown a pair finally." She chuckled while she coughed up blood. "But I must say that game was so much fun. I never knew an assassin was so skilled at evasions. The way she ran and made it seem like she was scared while killing off my comrades one by one until it was two on one. So, I sacrificed my best friend and shot them both. It was such a thrill to watch all that blood spill from both their bodies. Hahahaha!!!"

Bang!! No sounds were heard from her or Tay. He let her hair go and she fell lifeless to the ground as blood spilled from her head. Tay breathing came in quick gasps and shook. He stared at the hole in the tree where the bullet hit from exiting Shayla's head. His jaws was tight. A sound clawed its way up his throat but he tried to hold it in. He couldn't fight it for long and he screamed to the stars.

"Fuck!!!!!"

His body became weak and he stumbled to the tree. His lips quivered.

"I was so stupid! How could I not have known!" he said as tears fell. He slammed his fist against the tree. "Cereal. My sister never liked cereal, but yogurt or parfaits were her thing. And even if she was attacked, she would've been first to speak to talk about how damaged the others were compared to their looks. " He kept replaying everything that had happened until now trying to figure out why he didn't recognize Shayla wasn't his sister. "I'm such an idiot. I am so sorry, sis. Big bro should've been there but where was I. I was falling in love trying to get that to work so *I* could live a normal life. Forget living normal. I will take these blood-stained hands and live in this shadow world the rest of my life to avenge our family." He looked back up at the night's sky and saw a falling star.

"On this day, I will be true to myself for the sake of those around me and for my future." He dried his eyes, went to pick up the sword and sheath along with the other gifts. After he gathered everything, he reached into his right pocket and pulled out the compass.

"Now, where is Aria?" he said, opening the compass. He saw two arrows; one pointed north and the other pointed northeast. He looked at it confused then remembered his granddad's words. "Right, I'm supposed to choose which path to take." He looked at both paths but neither felt right to him. He kept thinking he would be going the wrong way if he followed those directions. He wished his grandma was there to help him understand why neither answer seemed right. Then he remembered her glasses.

"Well, they were always together so." As he put on the glasses and looked at the compass again, he saw the compass was now glowing with brilliance, but the main thing was he saw three arrows instead of two.

Where did that arrow come from? he asked himself as he took the glasses off to make sure he wasn't seeing things. The moment he took them off, the last arrow disappeared. So, he held the glasses to the moon to make sure that they didn't have a mark on them. They were spotless and unmarked. He put them back on, looked at the compass, and at the direction of the arrows now. The first two stayed the same but the last one was pointing southwest. Tay felt in his gut that was the direction he should take.

"Grandma always said believe in yourself and follow your gut," Tay said with a small smile. With that, he closed the compass and put it with the glasses in his pocket.

After walking for a while, he came upon an old-fashioned cabin. Light filtered through the window onto the surprisingly manicured grass that surrounded the cabin. The light danced on the ground, but no sounds could be heard from within. Curious, he snuck closer until he was able to hear soft cries from inside. Tay approached the window cautiously and listened. The cries were so soft and gentle that it was hard to make out.

"I'm so sorry, Tay," the voice whispered.

Tay took a chance and peered through the window. And seated in front of a fireplace was a woman resembling Aria, rocking back and forth as she held something to her chest.

"…Aria?" Tay said lowly.

She sat up and looked at the window. She jumped up.

"Tay!" she replied as she sniffled and wiped her eyes. "Tay, is that you?"

"Yea, it's me." He was relieved he found her so quickly. "Are you okay?"

"Yea, I'm good. And you?"

"I'm good but may I come in?"

Aria moved again; she barely made a sound. Even with Tay right there with his ear so close to the window, he heard nothing. The front door crept opened and Tay walked toward the door cautiously. He knew Aria was inside, but he didn't see if she was alone. He scanned his surroundings as he moved.

Once he reached the front, he didn't go inside immediately. He found a branch by his foot and used it to gently push the bottom ledge of the door. Once opened enough for Tay to slip through, he waited. There was no movement, so Tay looked around the frame and saw only Aria inside in a side corner. He took out the gun and dove inside. He aimed at one corner on the wall with the door then the other to find no one was there. Glad they were alone, Tay relaxed and went to close the door.

Aria ran at him and jumped on him. "I'm sorry. I am so sorry." She cried while she held Tay tightly. Tay stowed the gun and hugged her back.

"Hey now. It's okay. It's okay," he said as he tried to soothe her. She held him and cried more. Tay gently stroked her head. "It is okay. You don't have a reason to say sorry."

"I should've just given her the book. Then you wouldn't have had to fight her."

"She was going to kill us both anyway. So, you did good. Besides, she won't be bothering us anymore."

"What does that mean?" Aria looked up at Tay with a puzzled expression still sniffling, but tears weren't flowing as much now.

"It means that she is dead," Tay said as he wiped the tears from her cheeks.

It shocked Aria. "I am so, so sorry. I really should've given it to her then you wouldn't have to soil your hands with more blood."

"Look. It is all okay. You did the right thing."

"But... But..."

Tay gently pushed Aria away and looked her in the eyes. He saw her pain and how she wanted to make things right, but she didn't know how. But he pushed those aside as he just pulled her in close and gently held her. "No more worrying about it. Okay?"

They stayed still in each other's embrace. Tay felt the tension in his chest melt away. Despite all the times he tried to push himself away from her, the only thought on his mind now was that she was safe and he would protect her and do his best not to make her cry.

He breathed in and was filled with a floral sweet scent that wafted off her. The sense of love and comfort he felt from her was too strong now. It was like Tay saw his little sister in her but he also saw the girl from middle school that somehow fell in love with him. It was like he knew her deeply and not at all at the same time. Before he could stop himself, he pulled her away and kissed her forehead. He pulled away wide-eyed.

"I'm sorry. I didn't mean to," Tay stammered as he moved away from Aria toward a wall, hand on his lips. She walked up behind him and placed a hand on his shoulder. He turned to face her and she looked at him, a warm smile played across her lips and eyes gentle yet shone with a hidden joy.

"It is okay, Tay. Spur of the moment, right?"

"Yea. I'm sorry." Before he could say anything else, she hugged him and kissed his lips deeply. Tay was shocked at her actions but her lips against his felt so...

Right.

His hands grasped her waist and he gently pushed her back. "Spur of the moment."

"Yea, well, I don't think I can allow that to happen anymore." His lips longed for hers but he held himself back. "I have—"

"I know." She cut him off. "I know you are trying to see if things will work out with Evelyn. But I am still going to try my best to make you mine."

Tay could only shake his head. He was happy for the favor, but he just felt there was so much going on. He wanted to have a normal life, but things kept pulling him down another path. He thought of how Shayla played at being his sister and remembered the warnings Aria gave before. Tay felt ashamed he didn't notice the differences before.

"Look," Tay began. "I want to apologize."

"Tay, I told you it is okay. I know you didn't do it on purpose."

"No, I want to apologize for not listening to you before." Whatever Aria was about to say died on her lips. She was bewildered at what was happening. "You were right all along. That…That wasn't my sister." Tay paused as he felt his frustration well up at himself for not recognizing the signs from before. "I guess I wanted my family so bad that I allowed myself to believe what I saw as true." Tay opened and closed his hands repeatedly before he relaxed. "So please forgive me for not trusting you and pushing you away," he said with a slight bow of his head.

"Oh, Tay..." Aria whispered out as she grabbed Tay's hands. "You don't need to apologize for that. You missed your family and wanted to protect the ones you have left." Her grip on his hands tightened slightly. "And that is normal. You have nothing to apologize for." A moment passed where they looked at each other.

"Why don't we have a seat to relax our minds and body?" she suggested as she let go of one of his hands and sat down against the wall. Tay followed suit, not noticing their hands were still clasped. After Tay was settled, he leaned back and closed his eyes. He felt a head rest on his shoulder. The physical touch was intimate yet not unwelcomed. Within a few moments, Tay had dozed off.

Tay woke up after what felt like an hour. He looked around blurry eyed. The fire was still going, and no one seemed to have tried to find them or enter the cabin. Tay noticed Aria was now laying on his lap fast asleep. He chuckled at how natural her presence felt to him. He gently stroked her head. She smiled and shifted a little but didn't wake up. Seeing her like that, Tay imagined how he would feel if he agreed to be in a relationship with her.

He thought about Evelyn and how she represented a new life, one he dreamed of. A life where he was a normal guy and enjoying the subtleties of not having to look over his shoulder almost every day. His mind was messed up and his heart didn't help. His heart longed to keep Aria close, but his mind wanted something that felt more normal, not an image of the past.

He let out a soft breath and gazed out the window across the room. Through the window, Tay saw the stars shining above the trees that waved in the gentle breeze. He tried to relax but he felt like he was missing something. Something so important that if he didn't figure it out now, he would also wonder about it like it was an itch he couldn't scratch away.

"Hey, Aria," Tay said as he gently shook her shoulder

"Hmm." She slowly got up then yawned. She looked around and saw Tay and smiled. "Well, good evening, handsome."

Tay chuckled. "Good evening to you, too." He then swallowed and gazed at her. His tone became serious. "Hey, I need you to be 100% honest with me, okay?"

Aria sensed his mood change and sat up straight. "Okay."

"I need to know who are you? Really."

She was puzzled by the question. "What do you mean?"

"Well, for a while now I have been seeing my little sister in you, but I don't know how that is possible."

"That's nice of you to say."

"Glad you think it's a compliment, but I'd still like an answer."

She took a deep breath then said, "I am Aria Breanna Blackwood by birth but adopted by the Davis family at three days old and I became Chanice Renee Davis."

Tay looked at her as in disbelief. "I know I said I would be more open to what you have to say but this…There is no way that is possible."

"It is." Aria's eyes became somber. Tay studied her face and realized she was being truthful. "Surprisingly, your sister and I are twins, at least in sense of the date. We were born in the same hospital even. I guess we should blame our parents for that one." Aria turned to look at the fire. "This is what I heard from my dad about that day. It was our third night of life when your little sis was rushed to ICU. They couldn't figure out what was wrong, but her lungs and heart were failing. The doctor tried all he could, but she didn't make it."

She paused, as if she was hearing the story from her father again. "What was insane was that I wasn't just next door but the next crib to your sister, and I was taken to ICU as well. For they feared that what your sister had was given to me. It was then my dad talked to the nurses and doctors. He knew what grief losing your sister would cause your father and mother, so he secretly talked to the doctor and nurses to switch the reports so that I would go to your parents. My father told my mom of course and she agreed to it knowing that she would still always see me." Aria then laughed softly.

"Sorry to laugh but your dad was smarter than my dad gave him credit for at that time. He felt something was different about the child he was given and the report that the doctor told him. He had a blood test done by the next day. Though the results took about a week to process, once he knew he confronted my dad about it. My dad tried to come up with a story but that only made your father upset and sadder. But the thing is, he never lashed out at my parents for what they did. Nor did your mom, once your father told her, too." Aria turned to face Tay as she pulled her knees in and rested her head on her knees.

"After that they made a deal. Your parents would raise me, and I would inherit both families once the time came. But your family died, leaving only you and your brother, I was sent back to my real family. The issue was they had made me believe that my real parents were my god parents when I was living with you. So, they had to give me some medicine to help me forget and rewrite some memories. That is also the reason why I seem to have episodes. It is from not taking the meds like I was supposed to and reliving memories from the past. That conflict with the memories I built with my parents. My dad and mom only told me about this once I was in college after I saw you again."

"Why...why am I just now finding out about this?" he asked as he rubbed his forehead.

"My understanding is the deal was voided since your family died and their will stated that you would inherit everything of value from them."

"So, you are my adopted sister in a sense?"

"Yes, you could say that. But I'm more like your childhood friend than anything I would say."

"Okay. That is a lot to take in." He searched her eyes for any sign of a lie.

"I promise it isn't a lie," she stated, noticing his glances.

"I'm sorry for doubting you but I guess..." He let his head hang slightly as he sighed. "Okay, I will take your word for it," Tay said as he turned his gaze to the cabin floor. His eyes landed on the book still wrapped in brown wrappings. "So, tell me this then. Why is that book so important?" he asked, pointing at the half-unwrapped object laying in the middle of the floor.

"I don't know your dad and mine made me promise to retrieve it if both of them were to die. I believe it is their last will or something. But I can't open it. Even with the lock picking skills I was taught by your mom and mine, the book is sealed tight," she said as she stood up and picked up the book. She brought it back to where Tay was seated and sat down beside him.

Did she just say lock-picking skills? When did she learn that? He studied her.

"When did you learn skills like that?"

She looked at him and put a hand to her mouth, eyes wide. "Oh. I forgot to let you know. Just like how you and Tim were trained by your parents, I was also trained by them. Then once I went back to my parents they still trained me to keep my skills up despite my memory lapse."

Tay felt all that she was saying seemed too fictional to be real. Yet he couldn't deny the position they were in currently, so he shook his head. He looked back at the book. It appeared to be like any ordinary diary styled book. How could this hold so much value that mafia lords would fight over it.

"May I look at the book?" Tay asked as he extended a hand. She handed it to him and he finished removing the wrapping. The book looked glossy and there weren't any scratches or cuts on it. In fact, the book seemed to be rather new.

As he continued looking it over, he saw there wasn't a family seal on it, which puzzled him. Almost any and everything important to his family had their seal on it, but he disregarded this fact as it possibly could have been because it was to be a merger of two families. He began searching for the keyhole. The moment he found it, he knew instantly what kind of lock it was though the shape of it took him by surprise.

He had to feel for it a few times because he originally thought it was like an engraving on the book. This wasn't just a book, but it was bound in an airtight container that would incinerate the book inside if the lock was picked incorrectly or destroyed. He suddenly felt relieved Aria hadn't triggered the self-destruct properties of the case.

"This lock needs its key. If a lock pick is used, the configuration will trigger a chemical reaction that will destroy the box and the book inside. So only with its 'key' will allow us to open the box to get the book out without damage."

"I thought so. Glad I always examine before I just try to break the lock," Aria replied.

"Any idea where the key is?"

"No."

They sat there pondering for a minute when Tay heard his watch chime at 6:30 pm.

"Dang, I'm late. We got to go."

"Go where?" Aria asked.

"I teach a martial arts class, and it begins in an hour and fifteen minutes."

The two got up then checked to make sure they had everything before running out the door. They went back to the hatch they emerged out of and saw the items they collected from below along with Shayla's dead body. Tay walked to Shayla.

"Tay, what are you doing?" Aria asked, looking after him.

"We can't leave her body here, not after she had placed a tracker on us. We need to move her to another position so that whoever could be on their way will not find this entrance."

"Okay I will gather the other items then."

"Thanks." Tay placed the fake necklace on Shayla then gathered her in his arms in a princess carry. The two then set off at a quick pace. Once they were out of the forest, Tay saw that they were about half a mile from the Blackwood's house.

He was surprised at how much of the land was still within the property's fence. He looked around for a place to set her down and decided to leave her behind a group of trees, out of sight from the road and any pedestrians.

The walk back to the car was silent. So much had happened and they both were trying to settle their minds. Once at the car, they got in, placed all the items in the backseat, and Tay sped off to get to class on time while he prayed that he didn't get a ticket.

As he drove, his mind was still trying to make sense of everything he found out that evening. He partially wanted to cancel class but he hated making last minute cancellations to inconvenience others. Especially if they were paying for the class.

It will be okay. Just need to go in see Eric and setup. Then I can fall into my normal routine, Tay thought to himself to try to settle his mind and heart. As he thought of the events he experienced, he remembered the ring from his mom and realized something.

Would the ring fit in that lock on the diary? he thought, but he didn't tell Aria. He wanted to be sure of it before he gave a random suggestion.

They made it to the gym with twenty minutes to spare. Tay left everything in the car and ran into sign-in with Aria close behind him. Tay was shocked to see someone other than Eric at the registration desk.

Did Eric not make it back from his last task. Normally he would say something so that I know he is alright, he thought as he walked up to her. *It is odd he didn't leave anything.*

He explained who he was. She looked him up in the system then gave him the keys to his rooms for his session. Once he had everything settled, he and Aria headed upstairs.

"This is my practice room. Once I let you in just have a seat. I need to change, and I will be back shortly to set everything up."

She nodded and with that he unlocked the door, turned on the lights, and went into the instructor's room in the back. He was truly thankful he always kept a spare set of clothes here just for a time such as this. After he changed, he turned to walk out but saw a note on the floor. He picked it up and looked it over briefly. There were no external markings stating who it was from or who it was for. He threw it on his desk and then went back into the room and saw Aria was sitting against a wall studying the book. He wasn't sure why he brought it but he began to set up the room for his class.

"Can I help in any way?"

Tay looked at the clock and saw he only had about five minutes before class started. "Sure. If you don't mind, I have a few things in the bin over there under the table. Would you please set them up along the back wall."

"No problem."

"Thank you." They went to finish up their task. Once Tay was done, he turned to see that Aria was halfway done so he helped her finish setting up everything else. Tay noticed that Aria constantly kept glancing at the book she laid on the floor, as if making sure it wouldn't disappear from her sight. Tay figured the book held a deeper meaning to her than just something left by their fathers.

There was a knock at the door. Tay went to open it, letting in his students as Aria went to the side and sat down watching them file in as she held onto the book tightly.

With each student he let in, he felt his mind stop worrying about the things that just happened. And it settled on the routine he had built over time. He was beginning to smile at all that showed up and felt a peace from them being there. Tay then looked over to Aria and noticed her get slightly surprised at how many adults and kids were taking his class. But there was one that got her attention and that was Regina. From the moment Regina walked in, she greeted Tay with a bright smile and eyes that longed for him. Tay ignored her approach. She pouted and looked around the room when their eyes locked. Sparks flew between them like by some unknown sense they seemed to recognize each other as a rival.

After Tay greeted the last student and closed the door, he turned and saw the two still having a stare off. Everyone felt the tension between them and watched to see how these two girls would carry on. Tay shook his head. He couldn't help but smile because they didn't realize how they were helping him settle down. He clapped his hands, getting almost everyone's full attention— all except Aria and Regina.

"Well, since everyone is here, let's get class started," Tay said as he walked to the front of the room. Tay started with the normal routine, but it was hard with the tense atmosphere. So, he stopped class and told them all to do some sparring to see if that would calm everyone's spirit.

"Aria," Tay called after he had given instructions to almost everyone.

"Yes," Aria said as she looked at Tay, ignoring Regina now.

"I would like you to also get on some gear."

"Tay, are you sure?" She looked at him curiously.

"Hey, don't look at me like that. You know you want to spar," Tay said as she got up to go to the changing room. Tay looked at Regina. "You two will be matched together for the first round."

"What! Why me?" she exclaimed.

"Because the two of you have been staring each other down since you got in here. Not only that, I can't teach with everyone focused on you two," Tay said as he walked to the table in front of the room and got out his sparring gear. In three minutes, Aria was back, and she saw everyone paired off. She found Regina alone and she seemed like she was waiting on her.

"I'm back." She froze as she looked at Tay. "Hold up, Tay, what are you doing?" she said as she watched him finish strapping on his own gear. "I thought that it was me against that girl." She pointed at Regina.

"Yea. It is, isn't it?" Regina questioned.

"No," Tay said as he turned to face everyone. "Everyone but Regina and Aria have a seat for now." The rest of the class complied excitedly. "For this sparring match, I will show you how martial arts is applied in normal fights," he said to the class. He turned to Aria and Regina. "This match is you two against me."

Everyone seemed shocked. Aria was the only one to smile and seemed anxious about this match. Regina was nervous but as she glanced at Aria, she got herself ready.

Tay took his stance saying, "You two better not hold back or I can't say what will happen if you do."

Aria took her stance and snickered. "Same to you, Tay."

"I never hold back," Regina said with as much confidence as she could muster. "You think I will let you show me up in front of my future man. You must be out of your mind," Regina said, getting into position.

That is right, this is just another normal day. Just another normal class, Tay thought as he looked at the two and smiled.

"Kyle," he called out.

A young boy stood up at attention, as if awaiting a captain's order. "Yes, sir?"

"Would you do the honors, please?" Tay asked, not taking his eyes off an eager Aria and Regina..

"Ready? Si-jag!" he yelled, chopping the air with his right hand.

Aria rushed Tay, aiming to punch his stomach. Tay stepped in catching her hand before she could throw her punch. Pushing her arm back, he made her lose balance. He swept her feet from under her and with his other arm crossed in front of her neck, pushing her back and slamming her on the ground. Regina took the chance to kick at Tay's head. He leaned to the side rolling then turned to face her. The moment he was on his feet and saw Regina getting her balance, he jumped at her with his palm out and struck her in the side. She stumbled backwards and tripped over Aria as she tried to get back up. Tay jumped back and looked at the two already down. The two looked at each other, faces full of rage, then quickly got up. They continued glaring at each other almost like they were about to fight each other. Tay strode forward and they turned their gaze on him.

"Stop playing games and come at me seriously," Tay said, his voice filled with anger and disappointment as he took his stance. The girls looked at each other one more time and nodded. They got in their stances and ran at Tay simultaneously. They were posed to punch, so Tay blocked both attacks. Both girls followed up with a kick at different parts of his body. Tay ducked while spinning and kicked both his feet out at the girls' grounding leg, making them fall. Regina twisted, catching herself and pushed up as Aria just fell on her butt and rolled backwards to her feet. Tay quickly stood since he was just sitting on his butt.

They walked in a circle briefly before they started again. This time, Tay quickly stepped toward Aria and punched at her only to have Regina kick his arm up and try to deliver a palm to his chest. Tay blocked it with a crossbody palm strike. Using the same arm, he aimed for an elbow strike toward Aria again. She rolled away to evade the attack just in time. Regina's foot was above Tay's shoulder about to deliver a drop kick. Tay side stepped out of the way. Aria spun and was about to deliver a backhand strike to Tay's head. He caught her wrist and twisted it to pin her arm to her back. Regina had recovered and punched at Tay's shoulder. He released Aria and jumped back, getting back in another stance. The girls regrouped and took their stances as well. Tay smiled because he missed the normal routine of fighting his dad with his brother by his side.

The three continued sparring for the next several minutes. All the students watching were amazed at how skilled they were, but it was Aria and Tay who held their eyes. The two moved with so much precision, it was hard to follow and figure out which move they would do next. But the moment all three stopped, it was only the girls breathing heavy with sweat rolling down their face. Tay, on the other hand, looked like he had just warmed up for the main event.

"Alright class, line up," Tay said as he noticed the time. He went through the rest of his lesson and basted in the sense of solace and comfort of having something normal happen. It felt like he was realigning himself. But then he looked up again and noticed it was already 8 pm. Everyone was tired after the lesson and Tay had them all line up to be dismissed.

Tay looked over everyone and gave a few announcements before he released the class. Everyone left excited and some even upset they didn't bring their camera to record such a spectacle. Everyone was leaving except Regina. She stayed behind and watched Tay and Aria clean up the room.

"Tay," Regina said nervously. "May I have a word with you?"

"Sure," Tay said as he put down the equipment he was carrying. He looked around to see where Aria was, but he didn't see her. So, he assumed she had left to change.

"Well, I heard that you found someone."

Tay looked at her lost. "What are you talking about?" He thought it was Aria that Regina was implying. "Look, Aria is…."

"I'm not talking about that girl," she interrupted, her face a mask of despair and regret.

"Then who?" he asked even more confused now because Aria was the only other girl that showed interest in him that he and Regina knew.

"Really." Regina was shocked. "You can't even guess or remember. How about my sister, Evelyn?"

"What!!" he exclaimed. It never crossed his mind to put the two together. But now that she mentioned it, he did see the resemblance. "Dang. I didn't know."

"Well, now you do." Regina huffed and crossed her arms in front of her chest. "So, you can talk to my older sister, but not me? What is it that she has that I don't, huh?"

Tay didn't want to deal with this, not after all that happened that day to include his mixed feelings about Aria. "Look." He sighed. "I honestly didn't know that you and her were related. And honestly me and Evelyn barely know each other. We are just trying to get along with each other for now."

"That isn't what bothers me." Regina uncrossed her arms and walked up to Tay. Once she was right in front of him, she stared from one eye to the next. "It just doesn't seem fair that you will go out with her, who you just met, when I have been trying to go with you for the past few months." Her eyes began to glisten. "So why? Why won't you give me a chance?"

"Hey, I know it may look like that, but..." Tay paused as he searched for the right words. He sighed again and met Regina's gaze, seeing the hurt in her eyes. "Regina, I had no control in the way that things played out. But I do know that I am still figuring out my relationship with Evelyn. She is kind and understanding and welcomed me with an open mind."

Regina pulled her lips into a tight line. Her eyes were narrowed and seemed about to overflow, and her hands had balled into fists.

"You are amazing. And I truly mean that." Tay reached out and gently laid a hand on Regina's shoulder, his voice soft and gentle. "And I believe you deserve someone who sees you the way you want to be seen. I don't want to give you false hope or string you along."

"Well, from what I can see, Regina is in the right," Aria said from the side.

Tay turned to looked at Aria. He jumped, still not used to how quiet Aria tended to move. "Aria. How long have you been there?"

"Umm, for the whole conversation. And I have a suggestion." Regina and Tay looked at Aria curiously. "Tay, you don't have to forget about her, but it does seem wrong of her. If she knew that her little sister wanted to go out with you, why didn't she tell you the moment that she found out who you were instead of just hooking up with you?"

Tay knew Aria's point made sense. Tay tried to mentally justify Evelyn's actions so he could verbally protect her, but he couldn't come up with anything. Mainly because if the same thing happened between him and Tim, he wouldn't go out with that girl.

"Ok. You both win," Tay said with resignation. "I will talk to Lyn to settle this, but I won't promise that we will not continue to see each other."

"That's cool," Aria said with a big smile. She went to gather some of the other equipment from around the room.

"Yea," Regina said in a low voice. She had a small light in her eyes, but it wavered as if it was about to go out.

"Well… I got to finish cleaning before I lock up. So, see you later," Tay said softly as he turned and gathered the stuff he put down and walked away.

Regina followed him with her eyes. Tay didn't look back but she said softly. "Yeah. See you later." She left and the door clicked behind her with a sense of finality. Tay looked at the door, his heart hurt over what he did but he felt it was the right thing to do. He turned to gather some other things when he noticed Aria.

Aria had followed Regina with her eyes until she walked out of view. She turned and met Tay's gaze. "You know if you keep staring at me like that, I may think you will really forget about Evelyn and just go out with me." She smiled devilishly.

"Yea, not happening." Tay went back to getting one of the heavier objects, but before he picked it up, he glanced at her and whispered, "At least not yet."

"Hmm. Did you say something?" she asked, as if she heard some noise.

"Nope, nothing," he replied as he picked up the equipment and put it away. Aria looked after him as he did and once he had set it down, she called out.

"Tay. I found this letter on the desk in your room. Any idea what it is?"

"Nope but I was going to open it after I got home. But could you open it as I finish this last load?" Tay said, taking the last heavy load to the closet.

Aria opened the letter so slowly that Tay was back before she was halfway done opening it. Once he was back beside her, she handed it to him quickly.

"Here, you finish. I just can't truly open someone else's mail," she said, watching him. Tay finished opening the letter and saw that it was from Lyn. He read the letter and then passed it to Aria.

Hi Tay.

I know that it would have been better if I gave this to you in person but every time I tried to call your phone went straight to voicemail. But all I really wanted to do was give you this card and say happy birthday. I hope that your day was an amazing one and you will cherish it and the rest of your days to come. Oh, and my little sis found out that we going to together, but she seemed to be okay with that. Since she was the one that told me today was your birthday. But take care and see you later.

Aria read it once more and looked at the door. Her face dropped and she looked sad. "Oh, that poor girl."

Tay took the letter and card and placed them on the counter then went to change. As he walked to the room, he was disturbed by the way Evelyn misread the situation with her sister.

Can she truly not see how her sister feels? There was a punching dummy to the right of the instructor door. He punched the face of the dummy so hard that the head broke and spun and faced the wall now.

"Dammit!" He felt even worse about what he said even if it was the truth. He only hoped Evelyn genuinely thought her sister was being nice.

"Okay time to go," Tay said as he walked past Aria toward the door.

"Mmmm." She gave a slight nod as she followed him out.

He turned out the lights, closed the door, and locked it behind them. They went downstairs and he returned the keys to the front desk clerk with a smile as Aria walked outside. Once outside, he saw Aria was leaning against the car looking up at the sky as if deep in thought. Tay wondered what was on her mind but pushed the thought away as he unlocked the doors. He was still frustrated at the letter. They got in and drove off in complete silence.

As they were heading back to the house, Tay's mind was plagued with many things. Aria was his adopted sister in a sense, Shayla wasn't his sister, Regina was Evelyn's sister, Evelyn knew that Regina liked him but still decided to talk to him. It was a lot to add on to the stuff he experienced with Aria that day.

Tay looked over to Aria. She was staring out the window, her face still lost in thought. Tay was about to ask what was on her mind but before he could, she spoke first.

"Hey, Tay."

"Yea. What up?"

"I always wondered. This is the same house design that was burnt down that night, right?"

"Yea. It is." Tay quickly glanced at Aria then looked back at the road. "Why?"

"Well, why did you get it rebuilt and to look exactly like it did before?"

"To be honest..." He began, his voice trailed off as he came to a red light. "I was against having it built to look exactly the same way." He leaned forward and rested his chin on the wheel. "But that's what the will stipulated," he said with a small sigh. "Plus, it would've cost the price of a new house to get it built differently whereas it was already worked out to be built for a set amount with a particular contractor years ago. At least that is what the will said."

"Okay." She turned to look back out the window again. The air between them was somewhat awkward for him. He wanted to know why she asked about that and to ask his own question, but he felt something was different. It was like their relationship was unraveling as acquaintances from school to something more. Tay couldn't figure it out.

It was like they were on the cusps of heading into a dating relationship and he felt his heart jump at the idea. Yet he also felt she was more of a little sister at times. Then there was Evelyn, and Tay honestly didn't know how he was going to handle that situation. But for now, he tried to rationalize his feeling and thoughts about Aria.

Since he didn't have any clear answer to their relationship, he hesitated to bring it up even if he wanted a better understanding of where they both stood. The light turned green, and they drove in silence, though his mind was anything but. He wanted to know if she remembered anything special about the house from when she lived there. Something to help him come to grips with her truly being his adopted sister. His heart pulsed quickly as if her remembering anything was the lifeline he was looking for and needed. His hands grew sweaty as he looked at her once more before taking a breath and deciding to ask anyway.

"Aria?"

She glanced at him, her expression slightly irritated. "Why are you still calling me by that name?"

Tay was momentarily taken aback. "What?"

"Why do you still call me Aria like we aren't close? Did our time in the cabin really mean so little to you?"

"What? No, that isn't the reason why," Tay quickly replied.

"Then why?"

"Because it's your name."

"Tay." Her face softened and she laid a hand on his. "I know you remember more of the past now and I'm sure you remember that I was fonder of Renee or sis."

"True, I do remember more of the past but it is only bits and pieces of how you were part of my family. We were young then, which is why it was so hard for me to not recognize that Shayla wasn't the sister I remembered."

"Even so..." Aria started.

Tay continued, cutting her off. "But I'm not comfortable with us having that type of relationship. I mean, it hasn't even been that long since I found out the truth about my supposed sister and who you really are. So, I don't think I can call you that yet. Besides…" He looked at her as they came to another red light.

"I don't honestly know where I want this relationship to go."

Tay looked at her and saw his sister and Aria herself as a different person who loved him but that also brought up Evelyn again. His mind raced trying to sort out his feelings but nothing seemed to resolve it. The light changed and he was glad for the distraction of driving again.

"Then what about Renee. Since that's my middle name and you used to call me that all the time when we were kids. So that should be more comfortable, right?" Aria countered.

"Same reason applies," Tay explained. "When you came back into my life it was Aria not Renee or my sister."

"I guess." Aria shrugged and returned her gaze to the passing scenery out her window. "Anyways, what was your question?"

"Huh?" Tay answered distractedly before he remembered. "Oh. I wanted to ask what have you been thinking about all this time? And why did you ask about the house?"

"I haven't really been thinking of much. Just a feeling I had, is all."

"A feeling, huh? Well, what kind of feeling?"

"Nothing important." Aria shrugged off the question. "Hey, how would you feel if I go with you to meet Evelyn?"

Tay rose an eyebrow at her before turning his eyes back to the road. "Why do you want to come?"

"Just because I want to." She looked back at him. "I will even recommend bringing Tim if that makes you feel better."

Did the letter give her that much reason to doubt? Or she just don't want me alone with Evelyn. Maybe this is just a type of jealousy, Tay thought before he considered her suggestion. Then he remembered how he needed to talk to Tim anyway to figure out what was going on and why he brought a spy and assassin into their home.

"I will consider it. Though I don't think it is necessary." Tay gripped the steering wheel tighter and unconsciously pushed the gas harder. "Besides, I got some answers I need to get from him myself."

"Okay."

"Now back to my other question."

"Hmm. What was that?"

"Why did you ask about the house?"

"Oh that. Well, I was just curious about why you had it rebuilt to look the same if it held so many memories," she stated in a nonchalant manner.

Tay side glanced at her and felt like there was more to that statement than she was letting on. They drove the final ten minutes in silence. The only thing keeping them company was their own thoughts.

Tay pulled into the driveway but didn't get out. Aria had just taken off her seat belt and was about to open the door when Tay grabbed her arm. She looked back at him.

"What up?" she asked with a quizzical look.

Tay released her arm. "Hey, when we go in let's act like we didn't meet Shayla tonight. I want to see how involved Tim was in this."

"Okay. I can do that but are you sure?" Aria asked, her voice held a tone of concern and passion. Tay looked down, then leaned back in his seat with his eyes closed.

"Truthfully, I'm not."

"Then why not just tell him the truth."

"Because I need to make sure that he is the brother that I remember. And that he had no part in the event that happened tonight."

Aria gently placed a hand on Tay's right hand. "Okay, I understand. Know that I am here for you."

Tay smiled at her and placed his hand on hers. The connection between them felt so natural to him like she knew his deepest thoughts and cared for him. "Thanks. Let's only take in a few things for now."

She nodded and they both got out and went inside leaving the items too large for their pockets in the car. Aria walked behind Tay, as if they never discussed or learned about anything that took place. Tay opened the garage door and heard footsteps running from somewhere downstairs.

"Tay, is that you?" Tim called out, his voice seemed strained.

"Yea, it's me. We just got back," Tay replied as he walked into the kitchen.

"Y'all were gone for a while," Tim stated as he came from around the corner into the kitchen. "Is everything okay?"

"Everything is good. It just took us longer than anticipated to get everything sorted out," Tay said as he and Aria set things down on the kitchen island.

"Well, I'm glad y'all are okay," Tim said with a wide smile on his face. Tay could tell that Tim was worried and even more grateful Tay was still safe and nothing happened. But that led Tay to consider that his brother was in on the plan.

"So, what have you been up to while we were gone?" Tay asked as he and Aria went to the living room. Tim followed them.

"I was just in the training room practicing some new moves," Tim said, his voice held a sense of pride in what he accomplished. Tay sat down heavily, as if drained from being out all afternoon. Aria sat down next to him and leaned back and rested a hand on her head. Tim noticed the closeness between them even in their tired states. "Did something happen between you two?" he asked as he sat on the loveseat across from them.

"You can say that," Tay answered. He looked to Aria, and she looked back at him. Her eyes seemed to shine even though they looked weary. Tay noticed the look of curiosity Tim gave them and he coughed.

"Well, some things have changed, and we have come to understand each other more."

"Really?" Tim said with raised eyebrows and a sly smile. Tay got a bad feeling about letting Tim continue that line of thought.

"Oh, I was able to hear from Mom, Dad, Grandma, and Grandpa," Tay mentioned to shift the conversation.

"Really!?" Tim jumped up from his seat. "Tay, you better not be playing with me."

"I'm not…" Tay started.

"This is truly great news." Tim's eyes shined with a new hope. "Where are they? Please tell me everything."

Tay stood up and walked over to Tim, rested a hand on his shoulder and looked him in the eyes.

"Though, I heard from them. I don't know if they are alive or dead." Tim's eyes glazed over, and his body went slack. "Look, Tim, as long as we remember the memories we have of them and don't forget the love they have shown us, they will never leave us."

Tim squinted his eyes and glared at Tay, his jaw muscles visibly flexed. "Tay, I was expecting more from you than this," he said through clenched teeth as he brushed Tay's arm aside. "I know that. I know that more than anyone else. I could never forget them and I never will. I… I just want them back."

"I understand and I want the same thing." Tay held Tim's gaze briefly before he continued. "But we can't change the past." Tay's eyes were stern but held compassion behind them. "Remember what Mom always told us." He paused briefly. "Don't let your emotions control your actions. You are more than your emotions even when they feel unwarranted."

Tim's hands shook as he looked at Tay. "You know those words so well."

Tay chuckled slightly. "I won't deny, I have forgotten them at times." He thought of how he let the breakup with Rin devastate him and even how interacting with Aria in the beginning perplexed him to overacting. Granted he never said the words, but they were the cornerstone to why he was able to calm down rather quickly at times.

"But it always came back to me when I needed to hear it most." He tried to meet Tim's gaze, but Tim turned away. Tay glanced around the room before he asked, "Speaking of family. Where did sis go?"

Aria's body shifted . Tay turned his head and gave her a silent look from the corner of his eye.

"She said she had to go somewhere. She should be back soon." Tim sniffed and then looked at the ceiling. "Tay, I really miss our old family."

"I know I miss them, too," Tay replied as he rested a hand on Tim's shoulder. This time Tim let it stay there. "But I been wondering hasn't sis been acting weird?" Tay continued.

Tim wiped his eyes with his arm then faced him. Tay removed his hand and let it drop to his side.

"Now that you mention it, I feel like she has been somewhat different. But it is only the small things that I wouldn't notice if I didn't know her for real."

"Like what?" Tay asked as he looked back at Tim.

"Like…" Tim peered up, eyebrows furrowed in thought. "Oh, like how she takes loud and strong steps. She used to always be quiet and quick on her feet, but now… they seem deliberate. Like she's forcing herself to walk in a certain way."

"True. I noticed something like that, too." Tay paused, as if considering what Tim had just said.

"Anything else?" He tried to edge Tim on.

Tim chewed on the inside of his cheek. "Well, now that I think about it, there could be one more thing."

"What did you notice?"

"Well, I'm not too sure if this counts but when we got caught by those guys before coming here the way she handled herself seemed... weird."

"How so?"

"From what I could see before we got our break to run away, she didn't seem quick nor agile. I mean, normally she would run to the fight and be so hard to hit that she would come out unscathed from any fight. But this time she seemed to freeze up briefly before she struck or moved to avoid a hit. But it could have been my imagination. I mean, I was fighting too and we have been away from each other so long that she could have switched fighting styles. Though I find that also hard to believe."

"Hmm. I see." Tay considered that Tim could not have known Shayla was an imposter, and he was grateful, but he still held back his relief just to be on the safe side.

"Why?" Tim asked while Tay was lost in his thoughts. "Don't tell me you think she is an imposter?" Tim glared at Aria.

"Not sure." Tay's voice died as he registered what he had just said. He avoided eye contact with Tim.

"Not sure?" Tim slowly repeated his words. There was a pause before Tim asked softly. "What do you mean, not sure?" His eyes narrowed, not leaving Aria's eyes.

Tay shifted to stand in front of her and met Tim's gaze. "Just that things have been happening around me lately and I am starting to doubt what is real anymore. It has nothing to do with Aria," Tay replied quickly, trying to give Tim some small truths to ease his suspicions.

"Hmmm…" Tim said as he eyed Tay like he was searching for something. Tay faced him with a weak smile, which only caused Tim to look at him with even more suspicions. After a brief tense moment, Tim spoke. "Well, I think I will go get dinner ready. We can talk and eat when she gets back." Tim turned and walked away, leaving Tay and Aria in the living room. Tay felt more tension from having played his hand.

"Sure," Tay called after him. As Tim rounded the corner, Aria stood up and stepped closer to Tay, her glare was like a dagger that pierced his back. He swallowed hard, turned, and smiled at her.

She leaned in close to Tay's ear and whispered, "You slipped up." Her voice was laced with both amusement and reproach. "After all that talk about me staying quiet and look who couldn't keep it together."

"Yeah, I know," Tay said through clenched teeth. His irritation at his mistake evident. He looked away from Aria and muttered, "Dammit, I got too comfortable." Aria had a smug grin on her face like she won a bet. Tay clicked his tongue in annoyance.

"Come on, let's go get the things we brought from your house," he said as he walked toward the kitchen.

They entered the kitchen to see Tim in the fridge taking out food to cook. They approached the island where they had laid everything before going into the living room.

"Hey, Tim," Tay said, keeping his tone light. "Aria and I need to talk. So let us know if you need any help, ok?"

"You're good. Just go discuss what you need to, and I got dinner covered," Tim said as he continued moving around the kitchen. They collected everything on the counter then went back to the car to gather the other belongings before they headed to Aria's bedroom. Once inside, they locked the door behind them and laid everything on the bed. They sorted through everything on the bed, trying to make as little noise as possible.

After they had everything laid out, Tay stepped back, arms crossed, his gaze swept over the assortment. His forehead wrinkled as he wondered why these were left behind. His eyes landed on the book, and he speculated what it could contain that Mr. Lackston would kill them to get it.

Aria noticed Tay deep in thought. "Tay, are you convinced that that is truly Tim?"

"Yes," Tay replied instantly, but he still looked confused. "But something feels off. I'm not sure what it is but it feels like he is hiding something." Tay looked at the lock on the diary and then remembered the ring. He searched the bed but couldn't find it. He rummaged his pockets and felt the ring. He pulled it out, turned it over in his hand, and studied the gems, comparing it to the lock on the diary.

Could it really be that simple? he thought. It looked too obvious, too simple.

He walked to the bed and picked up the diary. He looked over the lock for any traps once more, but he didn't see anything different than before. He checked the lock again to verify he knew what type of trap it was. He sighed. If he tried to pick the lock the diary would be destroyed. But from the shape it seemed that putting the ring's gem in the lock wouldn't trigger anything.

Slowly, Tay inserted the ring into the lock. It fit perfectly. He pressed down and turned the ring slightly.

Click

The case the diary was in vented its gas. With the room being so big, the fumes that dissipated were harmless to them in a small dose.

Tay and Aria looked at each other with a smile on their faces. Tay pulled the diary out and unclasped the lock. A chime sounded—a smooth, mechanical tone, like a device powering on. The diary vibrated gently in his hands, and suddenly a voice projected from within, clear and familiar but with an artificial undertone.

"To all those here please state your name."

Tay and Aria were silent, not sure how to react. Tay found his throat was dry and tight. The voice sounded like his mother.

Could this book have belonged to my mother? As he opened his mouth to speak no sound came out. He swallowed to try again when Aria spoke up.

"Tagen and Chanice," she responded. There was a soft beep—an access confirmation sound—followed by a faint *pop* as the diary opened fully. Instead of pages, the interior revealed a sleek, foldable screen. Tay stared in disbelief. *The thing had been a tablet all along, disguised to look and feel like an ordinary book.*

He ran his fingers over the edges. Even the faux pages had been meticulously crafted—they felt like real paper, and they had ruffled slightly when he thumbed over them. Tay was amazed at the level of sophistication and preparation to make something like this.

The tablet's screen lit up and opened an app called Diary. Without human input, the screen swiped through the pages until it stopped on a page dated April 8, 1981.

Tay and Aria looked at each other before they leaned forward to read the page.

"Today, I met the most amazing person. He is popular with almost everyone at school and a year older than me but there is something about him. I can't put my finger on it, but he seemed more dangerous than anyone I had ever met. And I don't mean that cute bad boy aura—no, it was something deeper, like looking at a lion and knowing that you are the mouse.

So, I was walking down the hallway and talking with my friends. We walked around a corner, and I bumped into him. He looked annoyed at first, but he smiled warmly and apologized. His smile was so bright but held a cold aftertaste. He was truly different from everyone else. And the weirdest part is that despite the chill that I felt, I still found myself wanting to be around him. Then she showed up. She knocked my books out of my hands and laughed with her friends as they walked past. He stared after her briefly and I could have sworn I saw anger in his eyes. It made me want to run away. Could you believe that. I was so surprised that I didn't notice I had actually taken a step back. He then looked back at me and smiled back but there was actual warmth behind it. He helped me gather my books. But beyond his kindness what stood out the most to me was his eyes. They were... mesmerizing. His gaze felt like the calm waves of an untouched ocean washing over me, soothing and endless. For the first time in a long while, I felt completely at peace, as if nothing else mattered.

"But that was the highlight of my day, other than that, Mom made me practice for over four hours without a break. You know how Mom is. Ugh!!! She wants everything to be done her way.

So, after dinner I snuck out of the house to meet the girls for a movie. I deserved a break, right. But here is the scary part. Even though I know I moved quietly, I felt like I was constantly being watched from the moment I left the house, to the movies, during, and on the way home. When I got home, there she was, sitting in her rocking chair, waiting on me like she had been there all night. She didn't even ask where I had been, only how was the movie. It was like she knew where I was or that she had followed me. She even quoted a part of the movie. As punishment, she told me that I couldn't go to the concert this Saturday. I mean, I have been waiting three months to go to that concert. That isn't fair. I would rather cut the yard for a month. But it is getting late, it's getting late, and I'm exhausted. I'll write more tomorrow. Thanks for listening, Diary."

After they finished reading, an uneasy silence filled between them.

"Shouldn't we close this?" Aria asked, her voice low, as if not to disturb the environment. "It feels a little too personal."

But before Tay could reply, the diary swiped through a few more pages then stopped on the date March 24, 1983.

"I personally would like to know more about my parents. I never heard this story before," Tay said as he looked at the diary again. "Besides, maybe my mom left a hint as to who their murderer was." Aria followed Tay's lead.

"Well, my junior prom is coming up, and Derek just broke up with me. He is running for prom king, and I thought that we were a perfect match. But no—he dumped me right before my first prom.

And guess who he is going with? Vanessa. And of course she is also running for prom queen. I even heard that Vanessa was his middle school crush, guess he wanted his night to be SPECIAL. Knowing that they knew of each other from middle school and it stings even more.

But I can't stay down about this for too long because Mom said that after prom my first solo mission will begin. I'm sort of bummed that I won't be able to fully enjoy prom night but I'm low-key excited about this mission. I wonder what it will be. Anyways, something really good happened today. Remember the most popular boy at school, Henry Davis? Well, he came to talk to me. He said he had been looking for me for a while. I won't deny the first thought in my head was that he would ask me out to prom. But I quickly rejected that idea. I mean, he is going to his senior prom. Why would he go with someone that he barely knows? I mean, sure, we do greet each other in the hallway. And we have talked a few times, but nothing more than just a casual conversation. So, imagine my surprise when he pulled me to a side room and asked me to prom!!!! I couldn't believe it. I mean, I was running for prom queen but I had thought to pull out since Derek broke up with me. When I told Henry, he just said don't because he was also running for prom king. Then he told me that I would have to keep the fact that I was going with him a secret until they announce the king and queen. I wonder why. I mean, I know the other girls will be jealous, but it isn't like I haven't had to deal with that when I was dating Derek.

Besides, I may not even get enough votes to even be the runner up for queen. But in my excitement, I forgot to ask him about if he was going to pick me up at least. Oh well, I will ask him tomorrow if I see him. But I'm going to try and see if I can get queen and then maybe I can ask Henry if we can date. I mean, who wouldn't want to be with the most popular, nicest, and most handsome boy in school. He is like a true gentleman. Oh! One last thing, I found out that Monica was the one spreading some false rumors to try to ruin my chance to be prom queen. But thanks to some other people that want me to win I was able to close that case. But Diary you are always there for me listening to what's going on with me. Therefore, you are my one true friend."

Once again it started swiping through pages to the next diary entry. Tay and Aria looked at each other. Tay could see that she was thinking the same thing as him.

Why is the diary showing them these entries? Is there something more than just history lessons? It stopped on May 5, 1984.

"Well, tonight is my last prom and like last year I will receive my mission once I get home.

Why does my mission have to fall on this night? I sometimes wish I could just skip it and enjoy life like a teenager girl. But that doesn't look like it is in the cards for me. But this night will mark one year of Henry and I dating. I won't deny that it has been amazing. He is always my knight in shining armor. Not to mention that he is always dressing so nice that feel I have got to keep up my appearance. Because if I don't I fear someone will take him from me. Even though he tells me that he is just trying to match me, he just looks so handsome that I want to match his aura. But even if he is that amazing, there are still parts of him that I am still trying to understand. There was that time when I went to visit him on campus one day. I was surrounded by a bunch of college guys that wanted to kill me but played it off as them trying to have sex with me. I mean, I could have handled them. I just would've tried to get them somewhere secluded, and I would handle them. But Henry actually stepped in the moment he saw them gather around me.

He didn't do anything more than just speak to them. He didn't yell or cuss them out, but the way he stood and talked——he seemed so powerful that everyone took a step back. And I mean everyone. I was holding his sleeve and even I felt my feet shuffle slightly. I looked up at him and saw his eyes turn cold as ice but seemed hungry. As if he lusted for battle or to see their blood. That I even shook. But I am truly grateful that he stood up for me. Because I know that if this happened and I was with anyone else they would've ran and left me to handle this by myself. As to why were they trying to kill me? I don't know. And I haven't been able to dig up any dirt as to their connection with any of my past missions, but they haven't shown up again since then. Anyways, tonight is special just because it's my last prom and I want to make this night special. Oh, Mom is calling me so I guess he here. Wish me best of luck."

May 20, 1984

"I just got back from my second major mission. And I got to say it was full of surprises. You will never guess what happened. Well, first off, the mission was a success. But there were some close calls. After I completed my main task, I was trying to leave when I misstepped and tripped an alarm. I began to run and had to take so many different routes that I lost track of where I was. I then found myself cornered and out of energy. I could barely move my legs or arms from all the running and fighting I had done.

In front of me were twenty men and they were after my blood, which I couldn't blame them because I just killed their leader. Three of them tried to rush at me. I knew that I had nothing else to give so I just braced myself for the pain and eventually death. But someone jumped in and knocked all three away as if they were nothing. And I heard a voice ask me if I was ok. The voice was so familiar that I instantly thought of Henry. I missed him so much and being so close to death, I thought I was beginning to hallucinate. Then this mystery guy slightly turned and smiled at me. His smile was warm and loving but had a deadly chill to it. It was that chill that I knew so well. There was no denying it. It was Henry. Henry had stepped in to save me again.

In retrospect I know I was happy, but I should have been wondering what he was doing there and how did he know where to find me. He never told me anything about his past that would have made me think that he had some sort of hidden life. But seeing him there in front of me, made me realize that he knew about my lifestyle. How? I don't remember ever telling him anything about that. I had so many questions for him but then wasn't the time.

But after that, I passed out only seeing him running into the mass of enemies with a malicious smile on his face. When I awoke, I was in the hotel and with a note on my dresser saying we will talk later. I want to see him again but that will have to wait. There is one more thing that is truly special that happened today. I saw another car when I got home from school. So, I thought it was business that my mom was having. To not bother them, I snuck in my room using the tree outside my window. Once I climbed into my room, I saw a man sitting on my bed. Instantly, I was ready to fight but the cologne that he had on seemed familiar. He stood and walked into the light. It was Father. Dad had finally come home. He had been gone for almost all of my high school years. And he brought many gifts for me and Mom, but the best gift of all was to have a family dinner again. Just the three of us together. I missed that. I missed having a normal life."

The diary kept swiping through, showing his mother's thoughts, past events, family secrets, and mainly her desires. It even recounted the event of Chanice's birth. But the main entry that caught Tay's attention was on August 8, 1998.

"Today, Henry had a meeting with Mr. Blackwood. I think it is about Chanice—or rather Aria. But he came home looking devastated, and I soon understood why. On the 12th of this month, we'll have to fake our deaths. All of us—Mom, Dad, Henry, and me. Then we are to continue to train Aria some more.

Tay and Tim already are progressing faster than we anticipated. It is as if mastering the techniques was second nature to them. Still... I wish Tim would follow his heart and become the first doctor of this family, instead of trying to emulate his brother. But they both put their whole heart into practicing. I hope that will be enough for them to survive without us. I will thoroughly miss not being able to hold them, but if staying in the shadows is what it takes to protect them... then I'll endure it."

Tay stared at the entry, his mind a fog.

"So that night was just a charade? A farce? Nothing more than an overacted movie?" Tay said softly. His teeth clenched together as he tried to come to grips with the fact that his parents could still be alive, but he couldn't pull himself to believe it.

The night of their supposed death played back through his mind. He saw the blood. He knew it was real. His father had trained them to be able to tell the difference as to not be caught unaware of an enemy lying in wait. But this entry made him start to second guess the reality he built around his family being dead. The dream he had clung to for so long—the hope his parents were still alive—was suddenly within reach. But his mind couldn't process it. He shook slightly.

Aria noticed and took his hand in hers. Her touch was soft and gentle but gave him the feeling of ease to know he wasn't alone in this. She was there and she wasn't going to leave him.

"No," she said in answer to his questions. "I don't believe that night was a charade."

Tay looked at her and narrowed his eyes. "How can you say that?" His voice tight with suppressed emotions. "Look, it is right there in black and white. We have yet to find any evidence of their existence since that night. Not even a strand of hair."

"Because…" Aria looked away briefly then looked back at Tay, eyes firm with resolution. "Because after the 12th they never showed up as they had planned."

"How do you know that?"

"I feel like I have been slowly starting to remember more about my past as the days go on."

"How is that possible?"

"Well, remember the meds that I told you I was on before?"

"Yea. What about it?"

"Well, when I was with my dad, I took those meds to prevent me from remembering any time I spent with your family due to the trauma they thought

I would experience. At least until the effects of the meds wore off," she explained.

"So, you remember everything now?"

"Yes. Well, I believe I'm remembering more since I don't have the meds anymore," Aria answered. Tay looked at her with suspicion etched on his face. "Look, Tay. When your mom took me out every week it was to go to my dad's place to know him and practice. But she made me take some pills. First, they made me forget certain memories that happened over a period of time, and they would be rebuilt with others. So, in a way it was like I forgotten I was Chanice Davis, and I was born again as Aria Blackwood when I was gone. But there were side effects. If I missed even one dose, everything—*everything*—would unravel. My brain could shut down completely, leaving me... like a vegetable or at worse I would have two different personalities warring for rights to my body."

"So how... How are you able to remember now? How are you still fine?"

"Thanks to your family training my mind to such an extent, I was able to merge most of the memories together to become who I am now."

"That barely explains anything."

"So, when I was with your family I remember your mom would have me do two things at one time. Like drawing a square and a circle at the same time. Or playing two people like your grandparents in chess and needing to have an answer to their moves within three seconds or I lose. There was even the extra tough challenge of drawing two separate paintings at the same time while blindfolded."

"Then that's why you fainted that night when I first brought you to my place?"

"Yea..." She looked at the ground and blushed slightly. "Sorry. I had forgotten to take my medicine that night. And I have to be off the meds for a while before I can establish myself again. That is also why I am able to remember things I shouldn't, like what I was like at three or five."

Once she finished, the diary vibrated and swiped through its last few pages turning to the last entry, which date read August 12, 1998. The words were blood-red. Aria noticed first and gasped.

"Tay, look at the diary," she said, pointing to the diary. Tay began reading it. His heart dropped with each word that he read.

"We were tricked. The assassins we thought that were from the Helm family to slightly wound us never showed. It is Earl Lackston. But why? He was Mr. Blackwood's right-hand man after Henry. Could Mr. Helm have turned on us and joined Earl? No, he never would do such a thing. The way Earl fought Henry, it was like he was after something bigger. Could he...."

It trailed off and suddenly picked up.

"I never knew Earl was so strong. But I hope the children got out and are safe with everyone else. Looks like this will be my last entry I write. I just pray that when my kids grow older that they will live the life they want. I want to say I love..." The entry ended.

The proof Mr. Lackston was the murderer of his family was clear. Tay felt his anger rise. He clenched his hands so tightly that his fist shook. Soon it wasn't just his fist but his whole body vibrated with rage. Aria noticed and moved closer to wrap her arms around him.

"Tay, calm down. He will get what he deserves in time. So please calm down." She held him close despite the fact he had stopped shaking. They didn't move for a bit until Tay reached up and laid a hand on her head.

"Thanks for being there for me… and helping me get through all this." He turned to her, took her hand, and held it gently then stroked her cheek. Her smile deepened as a blush shone through her tawny skin. He felt his heart pulse from her image.

"You are so cute and thoughtful." The words spilled from his mouth before he realized what he said. They broke eye contact and Tay's ears began to heat up. He knew he was spending too much time with Aria, but he didn't mind as much anymore. She was slowly becoming someone he felt safe to be around. And more than that, she was becoming someone he wanted to have around.

"Well, I truly hate to see the man I love in so much pain." She gave a mischievous smirk with her head slightly tilted, making her eyes alluring to him. "And I hope I can help ease your burden somehow."

He couldn't help but laugh under his breath as he watched her. "Unless you are talking about repaying me for that massage from a few days ago, I can't think of how else you could possibly ease my burden."

"Oh, I can think of some special ways for us to ease all the burdens of the past days," she said, sliding her hand into his and lacing their fingers as she stepped closer. Tay's eyes settled on her face. She put a hand on the back of his head and leaned in.

Their lips met but Tay didn't pull away. He pressed into her embrace, kissing her deeply as his heart raced.

His body craved the warmth she exuded, aching to melt against her. The security, peace, admiration, and love she poured into him quieted his mind. And in that moment, he finally realized just how deeply he cared for her. It wasn't just familial love but the undeniable pull between a man and a woman.

He held her tighter and she held him back just as firmly. That was all Tay needed to know, that she truly did want him. Not just a part of him but all of him. The sides he showed daily, his flaws that he tried to bury, even the shadows the dark world forced him to face. That made him feel whole.

They pulled away from each other after a while. Tay's eyes were closed. He wanted to give voice to what he felt, but he bit his lips and swallowed his words. He breathed out and opened his eyes to see she was still watching him.

Her gaze and presence made his heart fight to jump back into her embrace. He stepped back instead.

"As much as I would probably love that now…" Her eyes were beaming with anticipation. "I don't think now is a good time."

"That is fine. Just know my offer is available whenever you want." Her eyes danced up and down his body.

Tay gave a slow shake of his head. He glanced back at the diary and saw it was off and had closed by itself. He studied the cover, not seeing anything outstanding like before. He released from Aria, reached out to the book, and rubbed his hand on the cover.

Was that really all this had to give was just diary entries? He drummed his fingers on the cover. *That can't be right. Especially if Mr. Lackston was trying to get this tablet.*

As he continued tapping on the cover, he heard a difference in the sound of each finger tap. He brought the diary closer, tapped on it again, and listened closely. The tapping around the edge sounded sharp and solid. The sound in the middle of the book was different and hollow. Tay wondered why was there a void space in the cover. He searched for something to write with.

He set the book down, tapped it, and traced the outline of the sound.

Once he finished outlining the shape, he noticed the shape looked familiar, but he couldn't place it.

"What could be in there?" he asked as he stepped back to look at the outline. Something about the shape of the outline jogged his memory. He closed his eyes and thought of any possible way to get the object out without damaging the electronic diary. He could only see cutting it working but that would damage the tablet, too.

He became frustrated at not being able to solve this problem. He knew there was a relatively simple way to solve it, but his mind was drawing a blank. He closed his eyes, took a deep breath, and released it slowly. He then heard Aria humming a familiar tune. He thought about where he could have heard it before and after a minute of listening it came to him.

It was a melody his mom and grandmother would hum when Tay, Aria, and Tim were kids to put them to sleep. Tay's body relaxed and his mind went to a memory of him watching his mother do an art project. She loved to make little things and get him, Tim, and Aria together to do small art projects. This memory showed his mother making wax figured sculptures. The sculptures looked so real and polished; you wouldn't assume they were wax.

He walked back to the dresser and examined the outline. As he traced his finger, he searched for any clue of it being a wax cover. As he reached the bottom, he found a small scratch. He examined it closely and smiled. He went to look for Aria's hair dryer. Once he found it, he placed the tablet on an old shirt and turned the hair dryer to its highest setting.

"Tay, what are you doing to Mom's diary?" Aria's voice rose to a near-shout as she reached for the hair dryer.

Tay grabbed her hands and held her back. "First, keep your voice down." He looked toward the door and listened. The only sounds were the muffled clinks of pans moving in the kitchen. Tay turned back to Aria and released her hand and placed a finger to his lips. Softly he whispered, "Just trust me and watch."

He carefully let the hot air from the dryer wash over the supposed leather cover. After about three minutes, the outline melted but it never lost its shape, like the cover was originally leather but a small portion was cut out and then replaced with a waxed top. Seeing that his assumption was correct, he smiled broadly. Aria's eyes were wide from shock and disbelief.

Tay chuckled. "Aria, close your mouth." She snapped it shut and swallowed to ease the dryness of her throat.

"How did you come to this idea? How did you even know if it would work?" Aria asked still in shock.

"From your humming."

"My humming?" she asked.

"Yea, your humming reminded me of a time with my mom," Tay said as he kept melting the wax.

"You see, my mom used to love building wax models and candles. She even made us each a charm."

"Oh yea! I remember those. But they were lost when the house burned down."

"True, but still didn't change the fact of her hobby was creating things with wax. So, once I thought of that I was like what if…And I had to look at the diary one more time to make sure. That was when I found small scratches that didn't have the leather feel to it underneath and from there I was certain I was right."

They sat in silence as Tay continued heating the wax until it flowed down the diary. Once it was gone, there was a clear plastic film attached to the leather and through it a key. Tay turned the hair dryer off and set it down. He touched the film. Though it was warm, it felt thick like it was tape instead of plastic wrap. Tay picked up the pen he used earlier and poked the tape. He tried to be gentle at first, but the tape only dented slightly. He increased the pressure until the tape gave way.

He put the pen down and tore the tape away. He pulled the key out and examined it. The bow of the key was designed with his family's insignia— a circle with a sword and pistol making a X, in the top section of the X was a dagger and at the bottom was a beaker with bubbles rising from it. Tay flipped it over and saw a campfire in the middle with words engraved around the edge. He looked closer and saw it said:

The warmth of the family reveals the past and guides the future.

This phrase puzzled Tay. So, he extended the key to Aria.

She took the key and looked it over. She also read the inscription only for her brows to crease deep in thought.

"Guess you also don't know what that key could go to then?"

Aria shrugged her shoulders and shook her head. "Sorry, no idea," she said with a sigh.

Suddenly, gunshots rang throughout the house. Tay and Aria reacted immediately. Tay went for his sword and guns on the bed. Aria stowed the key in her pocket and opened her top drawers to grab a gun, four small blades, and some wire. They quietly ran to the door, cracking it slightly to hear what was going on.

"Where is he?!" a female's voice demanded.

"I don't know and even if I did, I'd never tell you!" Tim shouted. There was a smack like metal against flesh.

"It seems that you have forgotten your place." The female's voice carried a menacing tone. Then there was another shot. And silence. Tay feared for the worst. His grip tightened on the sword as he fought the thought of losing someone else dear to him. A new voice came. This one was a male's voice, soft and gentle, as if they were playing bad cop and good cop.

"Why are you tormenting yourself? All you have to do is tell us where your brother went?"

"And why should I tell you?" Tim asked though his voice was strained, as if he was fighting back severe pain. "Don't you have that necklace with the tracker in it with Shayla?"

"Yes, well you see," the male's voice said, as if talking to a dear friend. "The tracker was found with Shayla's dead body in a forest behind the Blackwood's house. So, you can only guess what that means."

"It means that your dumbass brother has the book!" the girl shouted. "Now tell me where he is." Her voice got low and venom dripped from it. "Or the next shot will be in your chest or better yet your head."

The guy sighed. "Tim, don't make this harder than it needs to be. Besides, she is serious." The guy sounded like he was casually walking around. "You of all people should know that she is a trigger-happy fool who will do any mission that allows her to shoot at something." He paused, as if he was considering something. "Though I will have to say this time is different since it was her sister that was killed."

The longer this went on the more Tay felt the urge to rush out and help his brother, but the training instilled in him made him stop and listen to get all the details he could. Not to mention having Aria by his side was a plus to ease his mind. But even with that there was only so much he could stand before his body forced him to move.

Once he gauged that he got all the information he could from the interaction, and before they killed Tim, they made their move. He slowly opened the door, making sure it didn't creak. He peeked down the hallway to make sure no one else was there. Not seeing anyone, Tay stayed still a little longer.

"Look, I don't know where he is. All I know is that he went out with that girl some time ago and they haven't come back yet," Tim said. From the way their voices carried, Tay knew they were on the second-floor landing.

When did Tim get up there? Tay didn't dwell on that thought but instead he and Aria quickly walked out of the room, closed the door softly, and quietly ran into the kitchen. Tay opened the door leading to the garage and slammed it shut making it seem like he had just gotten back home with Aria. He began slamming the drawers and cabinets in the kitchen. Aria stood by the living entrance to see if someone was coming in their direction.

"Tim!" Tay shouted as he continued rampaging through the kitchen. "Where are you?" There was the sound of several footsteps rushing down the hallway upstairs. Tay and Aria gathered in the living room to hear which direction the steps were going. It sounded like they were going to the end of the hallway, which was where Tim's room was. Aria took the chance and motioned for Tay to follow her into the hallway they came from. As soon as they made it to the foyer, they heard footsteps coming back down the hallway. They rushed into a closet in the foyer beside the stairs just as the footsteps reached the stairs. As they gently closed the door, they heard the intruders rush down the stairs and pass them, heading to the kitchen. Once Aria and Tay heard them in the kitchen, they quickly ran up the stairs. Tay yelled out once they were on the second-floor landing. "Come on, Tim!! Stop playing!! The people after us are close. We need to go now!" Tay took Aria's hand and headed to the room on the opposite side of the hallway from Tim's room. Just as they closed the door, footsteps sounded like they were on the second floor, too.

"Tay, where did you go?" Tim shouted back.

"I'm in Mom and Dad's room," Tay called out as he locked the door and made his way to the back of his parents' room, pulling Aria with him.

Tay looked around the room for his dad's weapon trunk. Aria walked beside Tay and whispered, "Really?"

"What?" Tay said as he continued scanning the room for the secret slab of wall that hid the trunk.

"Where are you, Tim? Is that all you could think of?" she said, keeping her voice low so it didn't travel. Tay found a mark he had placed to locate the section of the wall that hid the trunk. He went over to the wall and pressed the mark that caused the wall to pop out. He slid it over to the side to reveal a metal trunk imbedded into the wall. He knelt down and opened the trunk.

"Hey, I was trying to stay on my toes," Tay replied softly with a small smirk. He pulled out the blanket covering the weapons. He laid it on the floor to soften the sound of all the weapons and ammunition he took out of the trunk. "If you didn't like it maybe you should've said something then."

"Maybe I will," Aria said in a playful tone.

"Tay, are you there?" Tim called as he tried the locked door. Tay and Aria got their weapons ready and slowly walked to the corners closest to the door.

"Yea. We are stuck in here," Aria said. Tay looked at her with his eyes wide. "Really?"

"Aria?" Tim voice sounded with disbelief. "Why are you there, too?"

"Tay was showing me something and when we tried to get out the door was locked. "

"What do you mean locked? Isn't there a locking mechanism on your side of the doorknob?"

"I tried that but it is broken," Tay said as he jiggled the doorknob to show he was trying to get it open. "I believe the spare key is in the kitchen. Will you please go get it and hurry," Tay said, trying to sound urgent.

There was a shuffle of feet on the floor that grew fainter with each second. Tay slowly laid on the ground and looked under the seal to see if there was anyone there. He saw two pairs of feet. One looked to be sitting on the floor and the other paced back and forth. From the sound of those steps that person was carrying a gun on each leg. That figure would occasionally face the door. Their shadow showed they were pointing something at the door. Tay assumed it was a gun, but the person never shot. Tay could only gather that it was because of the person sitting down. If that person could stop the other from doing anything without saying a word that let Tay know they were the one in control.

Tay signaled Aria not to move as he undid his belt and looped it on the doorknob. He played with the knob and after a few seconds bullets rained through. After thirty seconds of continuous firing, the bullets stopped then the girl yelled through the door.

"Tay, you bastard. I know you and that tramp are still alive in there. Hurry up and come out so I can get revenge for my older sister, Shayla, who you murdered."

"Ugh!! Who are you?" Tay asked, unmoving and making his voice sound like he was deeply wounded.

"She is Alice Evenest. Sort of emotional and quick tempered. And I am Leon Walter," Leon stated cooly, as if he was introducing an associate to a friend.

"What do you people want?" Tay asked, coughing to keep up the act of being wounded.

"First off, would you kindly stop playing like you are about to die. We all know you dodged that spray of bullets."

Tay cracked a smile and replied playfully. "Well, I thought that I could pull it off for a little bit longer but oh well. So, back to my question." His voice turned hard and threatening. "What are you two here for?"

"If I had to guess I would also say that you already know what we want but I will say it anyway. You killed a member of Mr. Lackston's family and just left her body to the elements. You must pay it back with your life for that. Then there is the matter of her uncompleted mission, which we are here to finish," Leon replied.

"Are you that desperate for something that you know absolutely nothing about?" Aria asked as she tied sheets together that were in her corner.

"Desperate—No. And I don't care about its contents. All that matters is that my boss wants it and that is plenty for me," Leon said, as if he was speaking facts that didn't concern him. Tay heard a foot tapping.

"Enough with all this chit chat! " Alice half-shouted, speaking through gritted teeth. "All I want is to kill the fools that killed Shayla."

"Regrettably you are right, Alice," Leon said as the floor under him creaked. Aria looked at Tay; they nodded to each other. "So, here's the deal. Either you two are going to come out here or…Alice will kill your only family left, Tay." Leon's voice was still calm but held more of a commanding edge to it. There was a sound like someone was being yanked and fell to the ground with a thud. Then there was a sound of a person being kicked in the stomach.

Tim coughed as he spoke. "Brother, I am so sorry." His voice was weak and Tay could hear him crying from pain. "They… They said that they wanted you and me to join them because we would make a great addition to the family. I… I didn't know about this. I just wanted to make you feel useful again, to stop the hurt I've seen in you," Tim pleaded.

This hurt Tay more than anything. He swore to never let his brother or sister cry again. He looked at Aria and she glared at him with eyes saying, *Don't you breakdown now. Get. Him. Back.*

Tay gritted his teeth and began racking his brain to find a way to get them all out of this situation. Then he remembered a training simulation their father put them in that was almost identical to their current situation.

"Tim, do you remember three nights before your seventh birthday?" Tay called out. "Do you remember the gift Dad gave you?"

"Wha—what?" Tim voice shook, as if scared. "What do you mean? Why bring that up?"

A sword was drawn from its sheath and Leon spoke. "Don't you dare think about escaping," Leon threatened Tim.

"Stand up," Leon ordered. Tim hesitated for a beat before grunting to stand. Tay heard the scuffle of feet and a sharp crack. Tim cried out as something—probably Leon's fist—struck him, followed by the sickening thud of his body hitting the wall. Tay's fist clenched tighter. He wanted to burst out now and help Tim, but he had to trust Tim would remember the lesson.

Tay heard Tim taking quick deep breaths. "I couldn't escape even if I tried," he gasped. "But there is one thing you should know," Tim said.

"Oh really," Leon stated sarcastically. A gun clicked, as if someone was readying to fire. "And what would that be? Your brains splattered on the floor or your brother and company rotting in your beloved parents' room?"

Tay knew the last statement would anger Tim. Tim loved his parents the most out of everyone.

Come on, little bro, keep it together, Tay thought.

"It's about the book you two want so bad?" Tim said, his voice shaking. Others might take that shake in his voice to be fear but Tay knew he was just overly excited and was trying hard to keep his calm.

"The book." Alice's shadow walked toward Tim. "You know where it is?"

"Isn't it obvious," Tim said as he chuckled still gasping slightly. "If my brother wanted to hide something he would hide it somewhere he would remember, and that place is…" Tim took a breath. "Up both your asses." Just as Tim finished, there was the sound of a gun hitting flesh and a body slamming on the floor.

"Get smart like that again and you will lose your life," Alice said as she stomped on Tim repeatedly.

Leon watched for a little while then said, "Alice, calm down. Go check the room just to be sure the others didn't try to escape."

"But Leon…" Alice started but fell silent instantly.

"Oh. And while you're in there see if they have the book. I need a word with Tim," Leon said, not giving Alice a chance to talk back.

As Tay saw Alice's shadow heading toward them, he slowly got up and peeked through one of the bullet holes in the wall. He saw a lanky figure with hair pulled back into a ponytail kneeling over another. Tay guessed the one on the ground was Tim so the one kneeling was Leon. Tay noticed blood flowing over the floor from where Tim laid.

Tay's vision narrowed and all he saw was Leon. Without a second thought, Tay raised his gun to another hole, aimed for Leon's back, and pulled the trigger.

Leon jumped to the side, as if expecting the bullet. The bullet flew between Leon and Tim and grazed Tim's cheek.

Time was up and Tay knew they were in for a fight. He rolled to the side just as Alice burst into the room, causing the doors to burst open.

"Aria!" Tay shouted as he stopped rolling and managed to get to his feet and looked in Aria's direction. Aria ran at full speed tackling Alice as hard as she could. Then Aria jumped back and kicked Alice in the face, making her stumble back further into the room. Aria followed her.

Tay stood up and just as he got to his feet, he saw Leon walk in. Leon looked toward Tay and smiled.

"A pleasure to finally meet you," Leon spoke in a polite tone, but his eyes were sharp and scanned all over Tay. He was slightly taller than Tay and he was well defined without bulky muscles. Tay could tell each muscle was hard and toned. Leon carried an unsheathed sword in his left hand and had a gun on his right hip.

Tay repositioned himself and took a defensive stance. Leon smirked and held his sword at the ready. They looked at each other for a brief moment. A vase shattered from the girls' fight and they rushed at each other.

Leon swung his sword at Tay, aiming for his neck. Tay leaned back to avoid the slash as it came across. Tay continued backwards to perform a backhand spring while kicking out, aiming for Leon's chin. He grabbed the sword he had laid on the ground. Leon leaned to the side and ducked while spinning and kicked out with his left leg. Tay brought his sword up and stopped the kick. The two jumped back and pulled out their guns and took a shot. Tay's bullet grazed Leon's right arm while Leon's grazed Tay's cheek. They landed apart, guns still pointed at each other.

"You do know that only one of you need to die to satisfy Alice's hunger for revenge," Leon advised as they stood still.

"Hmph. Yea but I rather neither Aria, Tim, nor I die for someone that was only trying to kill us anyway."

"While I do concede your point, revenge can only be sated with more blood. Preferably of the one who caused the death."

"Then you will need to do better to kill me."

Leon smirked and opened fire. Tay ducked only for Leon to kick him in the head that sent him crashing into the wall. Tay looked up just as Leon shot again. He spun to the entrance before bolting down the hall. Leon followed, taking shots as he ran.

Just as Tay made it to the stairs, a bullet tore into his shoulder throwing him off balance. He barely drew his sword in time to deflect Leon's strike to pierce his head.

Tay punched Leon in the face and he fell to the ground. He ran at Leon, delivering a knee to his head. Leon fell back again but this time he rolled and swiftly bounced back to his feet.

Tay realized the fighting space was too narrow and quickly turned, headed downstairs.

Once in the foyer, Tay heard Leon yell from behind so he side stepped to the right. Leon's attack hit the floor but he quickly raised his sword to block Tay's.

They danced around the room, trading blows and cuts. The fight seemed to continue forever but only lasted minutes. It ended when Tay managed to deliver a deep cut on Leon's left leg. He took a heavy punch to the face that left him reeling and off balance.

The moment he looked back—Leon was gone.

Tay looked around cautiously. He noticed drops of blood on the floor, leading to the living room. But after the first few feet, the blood blended in with the dark wood flooring. Silently, Tay walked in watching where he stepped so he wouldn't give his position away. He listened, waiting for a hint to tell him where Leon was hiding.

Once behind a sofa that hid him from the foyer and kitchen entrances, Tay called out. "Leon, come out so we can finish this." Afterward, Tay switched hiding spots.

"Should you really be worried about me when your brother is bleeding all over the place?" Leon said. His voice echoed throughout the room.

Tay looked at the window and saw a shadow holding a knife move from the kitchen to behind the love seat. Tay didn't remember seeing Leon having nothing but a sword on him. Then it clicked for Tay. Sword and knives, Leon was an expert at handling blades. People who handled knives or swords had great reflexes, eyesight, and were very limber. Tay thought over the fight so far and knew he should've done more damage to Leon. But at the last moment, Leon shifted just enough to make the strike less lethal. After processing it all, Tay thought it was best to keep a safe distance. As he started moving, two knives struck the sofa behind him. The knives pierced deeply and protruded just barely missing his right and left arm.

Leon knew his position.

He laid on his stomach and peered under the sofa only to see Leon jump on top. Tay rolled forward as Leon jumped and stabbed down where his chest had been. Once on his feet, Tay jumped at Leon swinging his sword upward, trying to stab his chest. Leon blocked the strike with his sword and he brought up the knife to stab at Tay's neck.

Tay caught his wrist, putting them at a standstill. They struggled briefly to overpower the other before Tay dropped to his back and pulled Leon with him. He kicked up and threw Leon over his head and he rolled to his stomach. Leon landed with a thud and gingerly rolled over.

They stared at each other for a moment before they slowly stood.

The world seemed muted to Tay. He no longer heard the girls fighting upstairs because it was drowned out by his concentration. The only sound he heard came from the frantic drum of his heart beating in his ears. Slowly, the racing drum calmed and Tay felt grounded.

He jumped at Leon. Leon smiled and jumped backwards and threw two more knives. Tay deflected one and turned his body to the side evading the other. He surged forward again just as Leon landed.

This time Leon lunged forward to meet him. Their swords collided, causing small sparks to fly. They held each other in place, eyes locked on the other trying to anticipate the other's move.

Tay was the first to move as he swept at Leon's forward leg. Leon picked it up quickly and before he could put his foot back, Tay continued his sweep but aimed for the back leg. Leon jumped up and Tay took the chance to deliver a punch to Leon's side.

Leon tanked the blow but stumbled as he landed and this time he hit the wall. Tay thrusted his sword only to be parried to the side and slid through the wall. Leon kicked Tay in the back and slammed him into the wall.

"Now die!" Leon shouted as he tried to backstab Tay in the head with his knife. Tay spun into Leon as he pulled his sword out the wall. The knife grazed his back as he slid between Leon and the wall.. Once he had space, he faced Leon and took a step back. Leon rushed at him, smiling murderously.

Leon thrust his sword forward, piercing through Tay's left shoulder. Tay screamed before gritting his teeth, headbutting Leon then kicking him in the stomach. Tay grabbed the sword, pulled it out, and threw it down. He grabbed his shoulder as it burned worse than any stab wound should.

Leon stumbled back and landed on the sofa. He shook his head and looked at Tay. He smiled, got up, and jumped off the sofa, running at Tay. Tay already knew the long distance wouldn't work because Leon's knives could reach every corner of the room. So, Tay held up his sword and winced from the pain and grabbed the handle with both hands. He swung downward with his sword as Leon swung upward with his knife. The impact sparked and clanged throughout the first floor and they were pushed back from each other.

"I know all your moves and how you dodge. I study the way you trained intensely," Leon said with a bloody smile. "There is no way you can kill me now."

"You never know what could happen in battle," Tay said calmly though he felt with each passing second. His vision was getting hazy, and his sense of touch was numbing in the side he was stabbed in. Tay saw a yellowish-green liquid gather under Leon's blade .

"Poison—" Tay said, forgetting to keep his balance and stumbled backwards to the wall.

"It seems you noticed," Leon stated as he twirled his knives, looking calm and unbothered. "All of my blades are covered in a homemade poison made by no one other than your brother." Leon walked to one side. Tay moved in the opposite direction to keep the distance. He felt the poison with each movement in his shoulder beginning to burn and spread to his back and arm.

"Getting him to make such a thing wasn't that hard. All I had to do was promise not to kill you. And he was faithful like a little puppy. I could even whistle and he would come like a good dog. And though I am breaking my promise, I'm sure he will forgive me for using it on you. Besides, I was trained for the sole purpose of killing you by any means necessary." Leon started laughing.

Tay's body shook after hearing all that. Tay knew Tim wanted nothing more than to see him smile again even if it meant he would make himself lower than a servant to a scumbag like this.

"You can only imagine the thrill of controlling someone without having to damage any of their body parts. Being able to learn his darkest secrets and use that to my advantage and make him obey me silently. No revolts or act of treason. Such a wonderful and stupid kid he is. Thinking I was his friend or that I would even try to help him out," Leon continued.

"Shut your mouth!" Tay spat out. "You know nothing of my brother and what he is capable of." Tay's grip on his sword tightened. "I will admit that he is very easy to go with the flow only because he trusts people too much. He tries to look for a way to make people smile without the pain. And you— you used him and played with his mind." Tay snarled the last part through clenched teeth.

"And for that. you must die." Though Tay sounded tough, he felt the pain in his shoulder now all the way to his fingers and almost to the middle of his back. He blocked out most of it with his adrenaline as he ran at Leon.

Leon swiped his sword, aiming to cut Tay in half. Tay slid on the ground to evade the attack. He thrust his sword upward only to have Leon flip over him. Tay quickly got up, but his arm and hand were completely numb now, which caused him to drop his sword.

Leon charged at Tay. He pulled out his gun with his good hand and blocked the sword attack. Tay looked into Leon's eyes and saw the joy he felt seeing Tay played with mentally and physically. Anger rose in Tay's chest and he pushed back. He tried kicking Leon in the side, but Leon dodged his kick with ease. Tay stumbled to the side, his vision getting blurrier in one eye.

Tay tried his best not to focus on the pain and numbness. He turned and tried to pressure Leon. He aimed to hit any part of Leon, but his attacks became sluggish and Leon dodged them effortlessly. Tay became frustrated and lashed out any way he could but he was still unable to land any heavy blows.

"The reason you can't hit me is because you learned too many types of martial arts and didn't focus on mastering one before moving to the next," Leon coaxed Tay as he nimbly eluded a spinning back kick.

"Though your father was a great man. He was even more widely known he was a fool. To think someone like you would be able to become his replacement," Leon said, dodging Tay's punches and kicks at this point.

Tay stopped and stumbled back. Blood dripped from his nose and his vision grew blurrier with each breath he took. All he could see now were practically outlines. Leon seeing that the poison was nearing its final phase, smiled. "You should just give up and just accept your fate of dying by my hands. You're fighting a losing battle."

Tay ignored his remarks and built up his will to run at Leon, trying his best to do some type of damage. Leon evaded his attacks with so much ease. Leon aimed for Tay's vital spots, trying to finish this battle quickly. Tay took many hits but made sure his vital areas were not damaged by shifting to the side. After several blows, it seemed like Leon would come out as the victor.

Suddenly, Leon swayed but was still able to fight without much trouble. The fight raged on more with Tay missing but now Leon was just barely connecting. Leon swayed increasingly and stumbled more, running into the wall and furniture. He looked at Tay with a shocked expression.

Finally, the hits from the beginning of the fight are starting to take effect, Tay thought as he watched Leon.

"Huh?!!" Leon swayed as he tried to stand back up. "Why is my vision so blurred and I can barely stand?" Leon said as he tripped over his feet and fell on the sofa for support. Tay barely holding on himself, took the opportunity to attack Leon. He slammed the hilt of his gun into Leon's chest then gave an uppercut to Leon's chin using the top of his gun's muzzle. The move caused Tay to fall forward onto the sofa. He was spent, but he knew he had to continue pushing Leon back while he had any strength.

So, he pushed up and continued attacking Leon, each move draining more of his strength. Leon was barely able to dodge or counter. The scene looked more like two drunkards fighting than two skilled members of the mafia.

Just as Tay felt his strength was about to give out, he swung his gun into Leon's stomach. When Leon doubled over, he kneed him in the face. This made Leon fall on his butt. Tay stumbled but managed to kick Leon's head, making him sprawl out on the floor.

Tay stood briefly before his legs gave out and he toppled to the ground. His head hit the floor hard. All he saw were bright white dots and his hearing was fading. He managed to turn his head so he could breathe, but that was all he could do.

He tried focusing through the white blaze. He could make out Leon slowly rising to his feet. Tay tried to move even a finger but his body didn't respond. He was spent. He only lasted this long because all his misses were so close to Leon. They helped twist Leon's senses. But now he couldn't manage to move his head anymore. He calmed his mind and resigned himself for what was to come.

"Tay!!" someone screamed from the foyer. It sounded like it was Aria but he couldn't see. His vision was completely white now and he couldn't hear what was going on around him. He only had one thought.

Damn. Death by poisoning. What a shitty way to go.

Then the world around him went black.

Tay woke up to the sound of repeated beeping. He tried to open his eyes but he barely cracked them before he shut them again. The light from the room was so intense that it felt like his eyes were ablaze. So, he relaxed and inhaled. He heard someone shuffle to his side, but they didn't say anything.

Tay felt his mind try to tense his body up but he found he couldn't move anything. He felt his heart rate spike and his breaths came in quick gasps. The beeping he heard earlier spiked in time with his heartbeat.

What is going on? Why…. Why can't I move? Tay thought frantically. He heard a voice in his ear.

"It is alright, Tay. No one is here to get you. I promise." The voice was female and gentle. It brought a small sense of peace to Tay's mind. Tay took a deep breath and let it out slowly. He repeated this motion three more times before he felt his heart settle and the beeping did, too. A hand stroked his forehead like his mother did when she would care for him while he was sick.

The hand stayed on his forehead for a moment before pulling away. Tay heard footsteps and a door open then close. He heard the muffled sound of someone talking angrily. He tried opening one eye this time, but the light was still too bright that he shut it and focused on breathing. The beeping reminded him of something and he started thinking of where he could be.

That beeping sounds like a heart monitor. This bed doesn't feel like mine nor does the clothes, Tay thought to himself. He thought about how the door sounded when it closed. *I must be in a hospital.* As he came to this realization, Tay felt his consciousness fade, as if he had overexerted himself. He tried focusing on the conversation outside his room.

"We can't let him go now. We haven't even identified how the poison was made." Tay figured that that was a nurse or a doctor.

"Please, doc. He needs to get special treatment," a female voice pleaded. Tay assumed it was Aria.

"Look, whatever that poison was had a bad side effect on him. It looks like he may have had an allergic reaction to some part of it. Not to mention that the poison itself was destroying his inner organs at the molecule level and only aiming for a certain type of enzyme. We managed to trap the poison and begin healing some of the organs but without a way to fully kill the poison he will take a while to recover. I am just surprised that he hasn't died yet," the doctor explained.

"That's why I am saying release him so I can take him to his personal doctor."

Tay smiled—or at least, he thought he did. It was hard to tell in his half-conscious state. *She's still fighting for me. And who is this personal doctor she is talking about?* With that thought, he dozed back off to sleep.

When he woke up again, he slowly opened his eyes. To his relief, the light was mellow enough so he was able to fully open his eyes. After adjusting to the light, he gazed around. To his surprise, he saw that he was in his bedroom. There was still of the beeping of the heart monitor to his side. He tried moving his fingers and found he had not only feeling but mobility in them. He slowly began working motion throughout his whole body. As he worked his lower extremities, he found they were not as alert as his upper body.

He found the strength to sit up and take in everything. The moonlight was shining through the window with a brilliance he rarely saw. It felt warm and welcoming, as if showering him with a love he had lost. He saw someone resting their head on the edge of his bed close to his thigh. He blinked his eyes many times to focus on the dark figure. Partly straining his eyes, he studied the figure. From the angle it looked like Aria. His vision was still slightly blurry. He reached out his hand slowly and stroked her hair once.

She stirred from her slumber. Tay pulled his hand back just as she sat up and stretched. He was finally able to fully focus and felt a sense of relief and happiness. It was Aria.

"Good evening," Tay said gently.

"Good evening," Aria yawned out. She rubbed her eyes and looked around. When she didn't see anyone to her left side, she slowly turned her head to face Tay.

Tay smiled at her. "Good evening, Aria."

"Tay!" she yelled and threw herself on Tay. He hugged her back. She pulled back and kissed Tay deeply. This surprised Tay but he didn't react immediately. He realized how he wanted this moment and melted into her embrace and kissed her back. They pulled away and held each other for a minute or two.

"You're finally awake?" She cried as she held him.

"Yeah. Well, this is the second time," Tay replied with a small smile.

"Second time?" She pushed back with a puzzled look. "When was the first?"

"When I was at the hospital or at least I think I was there."

"Why didn't you call out to me to let me know?"

"At that time, I wasn't able to move anything. And the light was so bright that I couldn't keep my eyes open. Besides, you were talking to the doctor and you two seemed to be really into your conversation."

Aria sighed and rolled her eyes. "Don't get me started about those doctors. It was a pain in the ass to get them to let you go. If it wasn't for Tim talking to them, I doubt they would have released you. But the doctors were surprised you made it because those blades had a strong toxin on them."

"I know." Tay thought about how the poison had affected his body and the numbness he felt at that time. He was surprised he fought like he did with that poison ravaging his body. He forced the memory out of his head and focused on Aria's eyes. They shone with so much passion, longing, and relief. She was genuinely happy he was alive.

"Now, I am curious about some things," Tay said quizzically.

"Hmm. About what?"

"Who is my personal doctor that you were so desperate to get me to?" Tay asked. "And how long have I been out? But most of all, what happened to Tim and those other two?"

"Those are all reasonable questions but why don't I let your doctor answer them." Aria grinned and looked at the corner by the door. There was a subtle movement Tay didn't notice before. Someone was there, but with it being so dark he couldn't make out who.

"It is great to see you recovering so nicely." The voice was that of a female, but it was familiar. Tay was somewhat disappointed because he thought Tim would have been the one to look after him. But this new person confused him. He couldn't figure out who she was or how she was connected to him or his family.

"Thanks, and will you step into the light so I can see you."

"Now that is hurtful," the girl said as she walked into the light. "To have forgotten me even if we only went on one date so far."

"Evelyn?!" Tay exclaimed. He tried to jump up but Aria held him down. "What are you doing here?"

"Tim and Aria invited me after they got you out of the hospital," she said with a bright smile on her face as she continued walking closer. Tay moved his gaze from her to Aria, disappointment flickering across his face. "I am thankful that you brought a doctor to see me but… why her?"

"Tay. look. I was surprised when Tim called her, too," Aria explained, her eyes lingered on Evelyn for a moment. "All he told me was that he had a friend that was really good with this type of treatment. The moment he said your name, she didn't ask any questions and just came over once Tim texted her the address."

"I know it's a little strange," Evelyn said, as if reading Tay's thoughts. "Technically, I'm not a practicing doctor. I went to college for chemistry—pre-med track actually. Did a few rotations as a hospital intern, and that's how I met Tim. We bonded over late-night study sessions and his insane ideas for mixing field medicine with urban tactics."

She gave a soft laugh and shrugged. "But… my parents weren't exactly thrilled. They pushed me to take a more 'stable' job, so I went into banking. Still, I never let go of the knowledge—or the habit of checking in on people who mattered."

Tay blinked. "So, you're… a banker who moonlights as a medic?"

"A banker by day, club bartender by night, and a chemistry nerd for life." She grinned, flashing a dimple. "Don't worry. I'm not here to start prescribing anything. Just wanted to make sure the treatment Tim gave you worked the way it was supposed to. He may have trusted me with it, but I still worry…" Evelyn glanced between Tay and Aria. She saw the closeness between them and her smile faded.

"You asked why me. Well, I'm technically not your doctor. I was more involved in helping develop your medicine."

Tay gave a slow nod. "Ok. I mean, I'm still shocked that you are here. But I can sort of understand why you came. Though I'm still confused as to why you felt so confident to be able to lend a hand to Tim. I mean, he is very strict when it comes to who helps and the way that they can help."

Evelyn turned and leaned against the bed post and looked up to the ceiling. "To answer that I will have to tell you a bit more of my past."

Tay and Aria kept quiet with their gazes trained on her. She peered at the two and let out a dry chuckle. "Very well, since y'all seem to want to know…"

She cleared her throat and looked toward the dresser. Her eyes relaxed, as if she was eyeing at something far away.

"I originally went to college as a chemistry major taking a pre-med track. I loved it—the process of creating medicine, understanding how it works in the body... it just made sense to me. That's where I met Tim. We were in study groups together, and we bonded over his insane ideas—mixing field medicine with urban tactics. I thought he was out of his mind at first, but after seeing his results I understood how brilliant he was." Her face lit up as she reminisced. Tay noticed her smile grew deeper with each word she spoke.

"We started spending more time together outside of the study groups. We ended up developing a few..." She coughed slightly.

"Let's just say unauthorized items." She paused briefly. "Oh, they weren't anything like street drugs but more of caffeine shots or vitamins mainly with a few that we did under our instructors' guidance." Then her face slipped and looked like she had eaten something that had just turned sour, and her jaw flexed. "But once my parents found out, they thought that I would go into selling drugs if I stayed on that path. So they forced me to do something more public and more respectable." She threw up some air quotes then shook her head as she sighed. "Hence, I became a banker."

"But that must have been years ago. And I'm pretty sure your manager role at the bank wouldn't have been enough to get all the chemicals you would have wanted," Tay stated as he searched Evelyn's face, wondering who she really was.

"You are right, it doesn't. But banking and bartending? They tend to go hand in hand. The club gives me connections. And the bank gives me creditability. I'm then able to leverage those connections and more to help me gain favors and material to help fund my simple chemistry home projects."

"Well, either way Tay and I are grateful you never stopped your dream hobby," Aria stated to remind them she was still in the room. Tay faced her, and she met his gaze, eyebrows lifted. He just chuckled.

"It is no problem. Besides, it was Tim that did all the work. Though I have to say…" Evelyn paused. "You are truly an amazing person to be able to live in such a lavish house." Her gaze settled on Tay and Aria as she continued walking to the bed. "Not to mention that you have so many people around you that want to make sure you are cared for." Evelyn and Aria locked eyes as she reached the side of the bed. Tay could have sworn sparks were flying. Aria looked determined not to blink or turn away. Evelyn's gaze fell to the floor under her pressure. To his surprise, Tay wasn't disappointed at all. Instead, he felt joy that Evelyn backed down and Aria won whatever that little fight was.

"So," Tay started, easing the awkward environment developing. "Why are you here, Evelyn?"

Evelyn looked at Tay puzzled. "What do you mean?"

Tay felt his face burn as he realized how his words sounded. "I mean—is there something still wrong with me that you wanted to stay around for?" Even as he said these words, he felt his heart drop. He knew his wording made it seem like he didn't want her around.

A weight settled on the bed and Tay looked up to see Evelyn. Her eyes bored into his and he felt a cold sweat forming on his back. A gentle warmth spread across Evelyn's face. "I'm here because I wanted to talk to you. And there is always the chance that one treatment will trigger another reaction even if it works against the main ailment," she answered cooly.

Tay's eyes cast downward to avoid her gaze only for his eyes to shift to her shirt. It hung down and revealed a godly view of her breasts. Tay realized he was staring and quickly looked to the side. Evelyn smirked playfully at Tay.

Aria gripped Tay's arm so tight that he felt her nails dig into his skin. Without making a sound, he ignored it as justified punishment.

Tay cleared his throat. "Well, thanks for coming and taking care of me. I hope you enjoy your time here," Tay responded as normal as he could given the situation. "So, Evelyn, would that make you my personal doctor?"

"Why? Do you want me to be?" she answered as she sat beside him as a coy smile tugged at her lips. Even in the moonlight Tay saw her eyes dancing from the ideas she was conjuring in her head. Aria's grip on his arm grew tighter and he flinched. He glared at Aria and saw rage build up in her eyes even though she was half smiling.

"Look, I just want the truth. But either way I am glad you are here," he said calmly.

"Ok," Evelyn answered in a down tone before continuing in a normal voice. "Well, to answer your question that is yes and no. I am not your only doctor," she stated just as Tim walked in.

"I am, too," Tim said, his voice brimming with more confidence than Tay heard from him recently. Tay knew Tim was extremely gifted in the medical side of things. He balanced out the team's dynamic with Tay the fighter-tactician and Aria the efficient silent killer.

"Tim, I am so glad you are okay," Tay said as he tried to get out of the bed to give his brother a hug, but he almost ended up just rolling out of bed. Aria and Tim were the ones who caught Tay. "Guess I am not quite healed yet." Tay chuckled.

"You are almost there." Tim smiled as he helped him back into bed. "But it seems you still rather call me by my birth name more than that other name."

"I am sorry," Tay said for he kept on forgetting that fact.

"Don't be. I prefer my true self over my fake life now more than ever," Tim said, shaking his head. Tay thought of all that they had been through and he agreed. Being true to yourself was better than trying to force yourself to be something else. Tay caught Evelyn looking at Tim with dreamy eyes like she wanted to be with him. "Oh, and Aria told me everything," Tim told Tay.

"Everything?" Tay said in a questionable voice as he looked toward Aria to confirm.

"Yes everything," she replied though she shunned away so Tay could barely see it. He concluded she didn't tell Tim about the big crush she had Tay or maybe it was something else. Tay knew he needed to clear up some things with Evelyn but not while the others were present.

"Anyways, you would have been out for almost two weeks on tomorrow. If you had been able to stay here after that attack you would have been back on your feet by now. Those doctors didn't know a damn thing about the toxin. And they pretty much left you to heal on your own." Tim's fists were clenched so tight that his arm shook. He had to take a few deep breaths to calm down. Once he did, he looked at Tay. His eyes held a sense of guilt and pain.

"But I am sorry for making such a killer poison. I told them that I would only make it if they never used it on anyone truly precious to me. So, I thought I could trust them. I am so sorry again," Tim pleaded, his voice caught in his throat as he bowed to Tay.

Tay reached out a hand and placed it on Tim's shoulder. "Tim, please don't bow to me nor apologize. I know you believed that trust is what holds a mafia family together not fear. To a point, that's true. But that is only for its real members. Not necessarily for the outside members that once belonged to another family or were pulled from the street," Tay explained.

"True but..." Tim kept on with tears spilling from his eyes.

"Hey hey. Not another word about that." Tay locked eyes with Tim and smiled. "You are my brother and I will never hate you. You were just trying to look out for the ones you love and build a stronger family because we know what it feels like to be alone with no one to turn to but ourselves. So don't beat yourself up over this." Tim sniffed and nodded his head.

"Thanks, Tay."

"It is nothing." He patted Tim's shoulder twice before removing his hand. "But I would like to know the details of the two that attacked us."

Tim wiped his eyes. "Ah, you don't have to worry about them. Aria took care of Leon and Alice the moment she thought you were dead." Tim then leaned forward to whisper in Tay's ear. "I hope you never play a fake death on her. She went almost ballistic thinking she lost you."

Tay chuckled. "I know not to play that kind of joke now. Thanks." Tay glanced from Tim to Aria and then to Evelyn. He caught her again staring at Tim and her eyes shone with a longing. She must have felt Tay looking at her because she turned to him eyes clear of any desire. But Tay realized what he saw in that moment and he had an idea. "Aria and Tim could you leave so me and Evelyn have a word alone please," Tay said, his eyes never leaving hers.

"Why do we have to leave?" Aria asked, her voice taking on a defensive tone as she readjusted her grip on Tay's arm.

"Sure. Take all the time you need," Tim replied, taking Aria's arm and walking out the room. The moment the door closed, Tay sighed. He thought of how he wanted to tell her that things had changed, and he now knew he wanted to be with someone else.

Tay waited for a minute, as if listening for a sound to show that Tim and Aria were listening outside the door. When he didn't hear anything, he said, "Lyn."

"You don't have to say it." Evelyn grinned and shook her head. "It was my sister, right?" Evelyn said, looking from Tay to the window. Tay thought she would sound more depressed. But her voice didn't sound disappointed or hurt though her body did give a hint of it.

"So, you already knew?" Tay asked with a raised eyebrow.

"I know what I did wasn't exactly fair play but when I saw you that night I didn't know you was the one she had a crush on." Evelyn got up and walked to the window. She opened it and leaned on the sill.

"Look, I like you and she likes you. Well…" She chuckled. "You could even say loves you. I am sure you would live a happier life with her but I wanted a chance before you kick me out your life completely." Tay sensed the hurt in her words, but he knew he couldn't comfort her because that would just be pity.

"Hey. Look, I am not saying we can't be friends. But we just can't be serious for a few reasons," Tay said as he turned to slide his feet off the bed. She turned around halfway to face him. "One, is because of your sister. I know she cares for me and if we were to go together, she would never forgive you or me for that matter. I know this may sound like a sucker move but I don't want to mess up the two of yours relationship." Evelyn nodded her head in understanding.

"The second is I believe I met someone that completes me. You are truly a great person and your man; whoever he may be…" Tay looked over his shoulder when he heard a small scuffle. He ignored it and continued. "He will be more than just a lucky guy to have someone like you at his side."

Evelyn's head dropped as she released a soft chuckle. "Somehow, I can understand. Even though I don't know truthfully anything about your life and for you to come back like this. I am not sure if I could handle it." She walked to Tay. Once in the light, Tay saw strength in her eyes. "But like I said before I did want a chance and if being your friend is the best way for me to prove myself then so be it. You are different from other guys and your presence is something that seems to ease those that come around you. I guess that's why I thought you could be the one for me."

"Sorry for putting you through this," Tay said as he held her gaze with compassion. He thought of Rin and how she must have felt after years of experiencing the same thing. He was glad he could talk to Evelyn like this. He didn't want to be let down again.

"Don't be, but I guess I will give you a call later once you are feeling better and maybe we can hang out?" She walked toward the door.

"What, are you leaving already?" Tay said, watching her.

"Yea. You are getting better but we're only friends now. So there isn't a real reason for me to stay but I will be sure to give you a call later on," she said as she placed her hand on the doorknob. She paused, as if waiting for Tay to say something else.

Tay felt bad for even thinking he really wanted a relationship with her, only to show her the real way his life worked so soon. He felt like he used her to make himself feel better. But then he thought of how she looked at Tim. "Well, you never know. I'm sure there is a man extremely close by that can make you feel more at ease than I could. You just have to open the door for him," Tay said as he glanced up at the ceiling.

She stood there. After a few seconds, she sighed and said, "Thanks, Tay, for at least being there and allowing me in." She pulled the door open and screamed. There was a thud. Tay turned and saw that Tim fell on her. Tim quickly scrambled to his feet.

"I'm so sorry. I was rushing and had just grabbed the handle when you pulled it open," he said as he reached out a hand to help her up. She grabbed his hand and he pulled her to her feet.

"Oh, don't worry about it." Even though her voice sounded normal, Tay noticed a rose color on her cheeks.

Yep. A much better couple, Tay thought as he looked at them. He looked up to see Aria smiling brightly. They locked eyes and she winked at him. Tay shook his head as he thought of what happened. He assumed they had stayed by the door and as Evelyn opened it, Aria pushed Tim through. As Tim and Evelyn stood awkwardly, not trying to look at the other, Aria walked in.

"I'm glad you weren't hurt." She had a satisfied look on her face.

"Yea, thanks. Well, I better get ready to go. See you around."

"Yea, see you," Tay replied.

Evelyn walked off, giving off an uneasy air. No one said anything for a moment and listened to Evelyn's steps as she headed toward the door. "Hey, is everything okay?" Tim asked Tay.

"Come on, man. Don't act like you two weren't listening to the whole conversation." Tim's face flushed.

"Yea, well we just wanted to make sure you were ok."

"Okay, tell yourself that. But, Tim, do you mind going to make sure she is okay and that she gets home safely."

"Hmm. Why?"

"Come on, dude, you have to have seen the way she looks at you."

"What are you talking about?"

Tay shook his head in disbelief. "Please, tell me you saw it," he said to Aria.

She nodded. "Well, anyways, Tim. I can't really move and you are the only other male figure in this house, so please go make sure our female guest is safe like Dad taught us."

"Alright, alright. I will go." Tim left and closed the door behind him. Tay was baffled at how his brother didn't see it or notice it. Aria came to the bed and sat beside Tay.

"What happened while I was unconscious?"

Aria shrugged. "I don't know the full story beyond what we were told earlier. But from what I could see, I guess she admires his determination and drive, especially when it came to saving you. There were many times your symptoms spiked in the beginning and he was determined to do anything to save you. He even kicked me out since I couldn't help. Evelyn was always there, though."

Tay nodded along. "I kind of guessed something happened like that but there has to be more."

"Well, she did watch over him for the full two weeks. Forced him to take breaks, made sure he ate and slept, and even helped him with shifts of watching over you. There were a few times when she would go to his room and put a cover over him because he fell asleep at the desk trying to make another compound to aid in your recovery. She would then look over his notes and continue to make the compound. I could have sworn she looked so happy and impressed with his work. I honestly am surprised she still tried to change her feelings to direct them to you instead of Tim."

"That makes sense. She still felt that we were trying to get together and therefore probably didn't want to betray my feelings for her. I won't deny that's what it felt like when I had to tell her about us. I felt horrible at first until I saw her looking at Tim. It made me feel better knowing that she was looking at someone else."

"Yea, but how are you feeling now?" Aria reached for his hand and held it.

"I'm feeling better. Thanks." Tay looked at Aria and smiled. "Hey, I need you to do something for me."

"What is that?"

"Please go get the diary and the key quietly and quickly. And while you are gone, check in on Tim, please."

"Sure, I will be right back." She kissed Tay on the cheek, got up, and left through the window that Evelyn left open. Tay didn't hear any noise as she scaled the tree outside his room. After about three minutes, she walked back into the room through the door. She closed it gently behind her before she went back to her spot on the bed beside Tay. She told him what Tim was doing while giving the key and book to him. Tay nodded his thanks and turned the diary over in his hands.

"Why are you keeping this a secret from Tim?" she asked.

"Because I want to know everything before I tell him. And he still seems uneasy about the whole situation. I want to make sure that what we learn won't cause him more distress," Tay said, looking at the book. He knew it was an excuse so he could keep something to himself.

"You do know it's better to let him know as you find out so he won't think that we are still holding back from him," she said, as if reading his mind. She sat beside him, waiting for Tay to open the book.

"True," he said, opening the diary. "Maybe I will after this." The electronic screen flickered on.

"Who all are present?" the diary asked once again.

"Tagen and Aria," Tay replied.

"All entries have been read. Do you possess the key?" Tay turned to Aria and she held out the key.

"Yes."

"Please present crest for image scan." Tay held the key by its shaft so the bow with the etched crest was present. There was a soft humming and then a chime. "Scan complete. Retrieving entries."

The screen showed a book closing and another opening. It flipped through some pages before it stopped. Tay set the diary down and they read together.

Dear Aria and Tay,

This is both your fathers. We have some important information to pass to you two. The Blackwood's house has been forever strong in the light but was weak in the dark. The Davis' house is the exact opposite. So a merge seemed to be the best course of action for us both. We got along well and have always been there for each other but the time to truly bring the families together as one is now upon us. Reading this means that both heads of the families are dead and you two have acquired the heirlooms from the Blackwood's basement. Now, please listen to the last words of these dead men.

Aria, you have loved Tay ever since that time in grade school. Make sure you keep him close and never let any woman steal him from you.

Tay, this is your dad. I know you hide your heart as to protect yourself. But I implore you to give the key to Aria. Though she was once your adopted sister. She has no blood relation to you. And I have seen the way you two look and act toward each other. You two are meant to be. So, protect her and keep her close. You will regret it if you ever let her go.

They stopped reading with shocked expressions. Their fathers plan had worked though they would never know. Even after all these years of not being in contact with each other, that one fateful incident at the park brought them back together and even made their relationship grow into something more. Tay chuckled softly and laughed then Aria joined in.

"Well, I got to say they not only read our hearts, but they also knew we would get back together again."

"Yea, scary how all this played out," Aria agreed as she wiped a tear from her eye.

Once they got themselves settled, they continued reading. They noticed it wasn't the rest of the entry but an arrow pointing to the bottom of the diary. They saw a small compartment open and inside were two bands with an engagement ring. Tay took them out and looked them over. The compartment closed once they were removed and the screen displayed the rest of the entry. Tay was still focused on the rings, though. The engagement ring looked familiar, but the bands didn't. Aria shrieked at the bands then covered her mouth.

"Do you recognize these bands?"

"Yes." Her eyes were wide. "They were the wedding bands of my mother and father. They said they lost them and ordered new ones."

At her words, Tay realized the engagement ring looked familiar. It was the ring his mother used to wear. *This is all too much. They knew that we would get together and that we would grow closer to each other. All of this feels unreal,* Tay thought as he examined the rings.

Why should I marry her? He eyed her. She was still observing the rings in amazement and was lost in her own thoughts. *I mean she is beautiful and I feel a strong connection to her. But beyond that what is there?* Tay dropped his head and closed his eyes. *We have been through a lot in a short amount of time. She was irritating at first yet no matter how illogical it seemed; I just couldn't leave her alone. I mean even now I feel complete with her here and her touch makes my heart excited and calm all at the same time. Now I can't imagine myself without her.* He opened his eyes and looked up. He met her eyes and saw happiness and love. He wanted to affirm those feelings, but held himself back and peered at the screen again. They continued reading.

"Tay, if you feel like she isn't the one tell me, will you ever find someone so willing to follow you, help you, even give up everything for you like her. She is your light in the darkness. Plus, can you truly let her go or have you ever been able to," his dad's voice said.

"Damn you, Dad," Tay whispered. He was right. He needed her and he couldn't let her go no matter how many times he tried to leave. He kept reading.

"This book will show you three what to do to restore and combine our families. And in doing so, you will find the things you all most seek some faster than others. Now, for the first step—the sorting of heirlooms.

Aria, you will have the necklace of assassins and the glasses of clairvoyance— wear them proudly.

Tay, you will keep the sword of courage along with the ring of wisdom and inheritance. Use them as I would for the family.

And finally, Tim…"

Tay stopped and felt bad he hadn't included Tim in this. Especially since this book was for the family. But then Tay heard a squeak from the door. Tim was leaning against the door. "How long have you been there?" Tay was shocked because he didn't hear Tim enter nor did he feel his presence.

"Ever since you started reading that book," Tim answered somewhat annoyed.

"Tim. I'm sorry."

"Tay, just save it. Look." Tim sighed and walked to the bed. "I know you like to make sure of things and have been the one to hold us together until now. But these past two weeks with you out have shown me that I can't be a bystander and let you have all the responsibility for this family. I can contribute, too, and I want to. I don't know what I need to do for you to let me ease your burden but I'm your family and family stick together."

Tay was stunned speechless. Tim was right and Tay knew it. He was so used to having to deal with everything; he left his brother out. Not only that, he allowed Aria to stay. Tay felt his heart drop into his stomach and hung his head. Tim placed a hand on Tay's shoulder.

"I didn't say that to make you feel bad. I just want you to remember you don't have to hide things from me. I'm not the young little brother from before. I can handle myself and I want… No, I need to handle family issues, too. We are all in this together."

Tay pulled Tim in and hugged him. "Thank you, man. I truly appreciate you being here for me."

"Any time."

"Well, since you are here let's see what gifts are yours," Tay said as Tim sat on the other side as they continued reading together.

"Tim, you will receive the compass for direction and my gun for protection. All three of you bring a truly special gift to this family and all which is needed to help this future family become the best it can be. So please try to get along with each other. Remember, though we may not be here we are always with you. We love you all. Eugene Davis and Terrance Blackwood."

They exchanged glances. "So, what do y'all think?" Tay asked.

"What do we have to lose?" Tim shrugged. "I mean, our parents are gone and we don't have anywhere else to go and it is becoming hard to live the way we are nowadays."

"I don't mind." Aria was shying away, as if embarrassed. Tay could only guess why.

"Well, I still need to think about it," Tay said.

"Sure, take your time," Aria said still cheery.

"Tim, could you leave me and Aria alone for a little bit. Sorry, but this is something I personally need to talk to her about," Tay said.

"Sure, man. And I can guess what it is," Tim said as he lightly pushed Tay on the arm before he got up and left. Once he closed the door, Tay listened. "Tim, I know you are still out there." There was a scuffle and steps that grew softer.

"Aria."

"Yea," she answered, face full of anticipation.

"First, what I'm about to ask isn't what you think." Her face dropped slightly. "But it doesn't mean I'm not considering it. I just need a bit more time. Ok?"

"Sure, take all the time you need."

"Thanks, but what I want to ask you is what is a normal life to you?" Tay asked.

"What?" she asked, tilting her head with a perplexed look on her face.

"A normal life, what does that phrase mean to you?"

She closed her eyes and thought for a minute or two. Once she opened her eyes, she said, "To me a normal life is just a life where you feel most comfortable. Such as the life you were born into in a sense. Why?"

"Well, answer these two questions." He looked back out the window, watching the tree sit still in the night air before eyeing her. "Is it possible to stay excited about a normal life? And do you remember the way we used to play when we were kids?"

"I believe it is up to you to keep yourself entertained for we never know what life has in-store. And yes, I do." Her face brightened as she recalled the past. "You always were my knight, fighting to keep me safe even if you worked in the shadow. No matter what, you always smiled at me, hiding your tiredness or hurt. Even when Dad trained you far beyond your limits you played with me as if you had more energy. But what I remember most is when I was hurt, scared, or sad; you were always there to comfort me. Your arms felt truly warm and your scent so addicting and comforting."

"Come here," Tay said, holding out his arms. She buried herself in his grasp. Her smell reminded him of the sister he loved and how she would playfully tell him that she would marry him when they were younger. Now it was him that was considering that very question in his heart and mind. Without thinking, he pulled her up so their eyes met. Her eyes sparkled and danced with joy. They were so beautiful that Tay slowly pulled her closer. The moment their lips gently touched, he felt his heart leap. Slowly, he pulled her in deeper. His heart raced like never before.

He knew without a doubt she could handle the darkness and read him better than any other girl he ever dated. She was the girl who would stand there with him through anything. And most of all, she was the girl he always wanted. Thoughts of why he could not let her go anymore were so obvious. Her fighting spirit she showed at the club and the moment before Tay passed out at the hospital where she fought to make sure he survived among other things, made him realize how attractive she was to him. Plus, the way she walked without making a sound, as if she glided over the floor. Lastly, her beauty.

Tay remembered his dream. He realized he was beaming at the end for marrying her. He thought about why he didn't like her before because of her persistence and steadily showing up out of nowhere. But he knew now it was because she wanted to be there for him like he was for her. He couldn't think of anything else about her that he didn't like.

As they pulled away, tears were rolling down her face. She gripped his hand and shirt tightly, avoiding his eyes.

"Is it okay if I stay with you tonight?" she spoke softly. Tay finally found the girl he loved and knew he would deeply regret letting her go.

"As long as you like." With that, she fell onto him with her head on his chest, holding him tightly. He laid back.

"Please say this isn't a dream," she whispered, as if saying a prayer.

"No, this is as real as it gets," Tay whispered. She whimpered as Tay stroked her hair. Tay heard a door creak. Tim stood there with a grin on his face. Tay knew Tim had heard and saw everything, but at the moment he didn't care. Shortly afterward, Tay fell asleep.

Birds were chirping outside and the sun shone through the window onto Tay's face, pulling him from his slumber. He slowly opened his eyes and stretched. Judging by the way the sunlight streamed in, it was likely just before noon. After he stretched, he look to his side and saw Aria was still asleep with a beautiful smile on her face. He gently touched her face and leaned down to kiss her forehead before turning to get out of bed.

He gingerly placed weight on his feet and found he had the strength to move around now. He went to his dresser to grab some clothes and saw the book with the rings and key on it. He didn't remember anyone putting it there and then thought of Tim.

Tim must have put it there after Aria and I fell asleep. He glanced back at Aria before grabbing some clothes, getting changed and pocketed the rings. Once done, he walked downstairs to find Tim on the sofa, looking like he was asleep. As Tay tried to walk into the kitchen without making a sound, he stumbled and caught himself on the frame leading to the kitchen.

"Hey, bro," Tim said with a yawn. "I see that you are up. Had a good night?"

"Best sleep ever but how did you know it was me?" Tay said curiously.

"Mirrors, man." Tim pointed to the mirror on the wall facing the foyer.

"Yea, didn't see that." Tay observed the room. It was set up differently than before. "Why is everything rearranged in here?"

"Well, after the fight, the house was somewhat damaged. So, we hired some helpers to fix the place up. They even renovated a few places," Tim answered as he walked over to Tay.

"Oh, I see." Tay focused on Tim after he took in the room. "Bro, I have to say thanks for curing me. You always had a knack for being a doctor or scientist. You are truly amazing at it." Tay put a hand on Tim's shoulder. "You know, I have always wondered why you pushed for being like me and Dad when you had something so great in you."

"In all honesty—it was because I was jealous," Tim said.

"Jealous? Of what?" Tay asked as he began taking things out to cook.

"That sis and Mom looked at you two more than me. I thought that if I could surpass you then they would finally notice me."

"But you know they were looking at you whenever anyone of us was sick." Tay pointed out as he held up a bowl to Tim, who nodded and took the bowl. "You were always there to help us get better. Mom actually wanted you to teach her, but Dad thought that would hinder your growth, so he forbade her. Not to mention I caught sis watching you and then trying to copy you in her room with little success. She would even sneak in your room, take some of your notes, and perfect certain things."

"Really?" Tim stood up in disbelief. "I always wondered why some of my notes were misplaced."

"Yea. Everyone always looked at all of us shining in what we did best."

"But you got sis in the end." Tim's body quivered. "Man, it is still hard to believe that Aria is our real sister. Well, adopted sister. I'm still having trouble just trying to call her sis."

"I know what you mean. I personally can't seem to look at her as my sister. I mean, with the way things are going that would be weird."

"Yea, I get what you are saying. But still in the end, you found Aria and she is someone that can handle the world that we are a part of, whether we like it or not."

"Yea. And though I may have Aria, but you got Evelyn."

Tim looked at Tay, eyes wide. "Wh—what do you mean by that?"

"Dude, stop playing. I know you seen how she took care of you while you were treating me."

"I honestly thought it was Aria. She told me that she was my sister and even showed me the diary while you were unconscious," Tim answered. "So, I thought she was trying to show her sisterly side."

"What? For real?" Tay exclaimed as he stopped pouring cereal into his bowl.

"Yea. Dude, was I surprised when she told me. If it wasn't for the book, I still wouldn't have believed her."

"Tell me about it. At least you only had the book to validate her statement. I will have to tell you about how I found out about her being our sister," Tay said as he passed the cereal to Tim. "But back to my earlier statement. You have Evelyn."

"But isn't she into you still."

"No, we are just friends and besides, I think you being with her last night might have helped her see that she cares for you," Tay said.

"You are really sure about that?"

"Yea."

"So, you don't mind?"

"You're good. Besides, it isn't like we ever fully committed to dating. We only had one date where we found out a little about each other. You two have more in common and she seemed to thoroughly enjoy time with you when she spoke about it."

"I guess, I will just have to see."

"You do that." Tay took a bite of his cereal and looked back up at Tim. "But there are some things I need your opinion on."

"What's that?"

"How do you feel about me marrying Aria?"

"Bro," Tim said as he chewed his first bite. "Honestly, now that I know a bit more about Aria, I can honestly say you two have always been married to a degree to me. Even though y'all were apart for a few years, the best girl for you was and is Aria. I doubt you will ever be as happy with anyone else."

"Thanks, and one last thing. What is a normal life to you?"

Tim sat his bowl down and folded his arms. "Hmmm…That is difficult to answer. It could be what we consider average and bland, or it could be this life we are living now that is full of adventure. Yet we are prepared for it and live it daily due to it being our lifestyle. So, if I have to say then this is our true normal life, one of adventure and excitement and a lifestyle that we can live in comfortably, being true to who we are. Can't see us living any other way."

Tay nodded. "Thanks, Tim, that truly helped me see what it is I have been looking for over these years and why I wasn't satisfied sitting still."

Aria walked in, yawning and rubbing her eyes. "What are y'all talking about?" She was wearing a spaghetti strap tank top that showed her stomach and basketball shorts. Tay felt himself gawking at her and shook his head to stop his fantasy.

"Oh nothing." Tim chuckled, noticing Tay's reaction and got up to leave as he finished his cereal.

Tay caught his shoulder. "Please wait a minute," Tay said as he gently pushed Tim back in his seat then walked to Aria. He took her hands then got on one knee. Aria stared at him, her eyes ablaze with happiness and excitement. "Aria. Will you be there for me and allow me to be there for you?"

"Yes," she said excitedly.

"Will you guide me if I were to lose my way on this road called life and be patient if I was to lose myself in rage?"

"Yes." Tears were slowly forming in her eyes.

"I know I was mean to you at first but over the time we have been together, I feel like you are the missing piece in my life. And that isn't because we shared history as kids but after we reconnected. I always felt like you were my comfort and peace. So, I guess what I'm trying to say is..." Tay took a deep breath before letting it out. "Will you marry me?"

"Most definitely Yes! Yes!!!" Aria cried. Tay stood, took out his mother's engagement ring, and slid it on her finger. She jumped up and down happily before she hopped on Tay. She wrapped her arms and legs around him and kissed him deeply. She held him so tightly, as if saying she would never let him go anywhere. After a minute, she relaxed her grip and got down. Tay and Tim made eye contact.

"This is the start of our new family, and I want you to be a part of it," Tay said, holding out his hand.

"You make it seem like I will ever turn you down." Tim took his hand.

"No, but I just want you to be sure and for you to make the decision," Tay said, pulling him into a hug with both Tim and Aria. "But I want you both to know that I will never leave you and I will always be there to protect you."

"And we will be there for you, too," Aria said.

"And we will be there for one another as well," Tim added.

"No matter what the future holds, we will break through, for our bond is deeper than blood. This is our reality," Tay finished. They hugged and Tim peeled off, looking confusingly at Aria.

"So, sis," Tim said, as if he was trying to work the words out his mouth. "Sorry. It is still hard for me to try to call you that."

"That is okay." She looked at him, eyes gentle.

"So, what do you want to be called from now on?" Tim asked.

"Hmm. Good question. How about Aria Renee Blackwood? Well Blackwood-Davis now." She giggled, kissing Tay on the cheek. "But I'd like for you to call me Renee, everyone else calls me Aria."

"Renee I can definitely do," Tim said with a nod.

"Great. Now how about we begin living our new normal life with a lunch celebration," Tay said.

"That sounds like a plan to me," Tim said.

"I am so down for that," Aria agreed.

They all went to the living room with smiles as they discussed where they wanted to go. After much deliberation and some playful back and forth, they agreed on a cozy brunch spot across town. Tay had Tim call Evelyn to ask her to join them—she agreed to meet them there with little hesitation.

Once they were ready, the three walked out the door. As they settled in the car, Tay felt his heart swell with something deeper than happiness—he felt peace and the world was right for the first time in a long time.

And though the shadow of vengeance burned in the corner of his mind, he decided he would enjoy the moments he had with his family to the fullest.

Whatever came next, he'd face it with his new family. Together.

Back in Tay's room, the tablet on the dresser flickered to life.

"Ring accepted willingly." It read.

"Access to restricted room approved for: Aria Blackwood, Tagen Davis, and Timothy Davis. Temporary access granted to Evelyn Lewis. Door shielding removed."

No one would take notice of this until they came back home that evening.

****

At the Blackwood's estate, in the room where Tay and Aria found the diary, a section of the wall slid away to reveal a metal door. In the middle of that was a keyhole with a crest engraved above it.

A crest that matched the key found in the diary. To the side of the crest flashed a red button—then a voice echoed in the empty room on a loop.

Meanwhile...

****

Somewhere in Florida, outside a luxury beach house, sat a bald, stout man smoking a cigar. He was relaxing until his ring vibrated. He sat up and removed his shades as he looked at the ring. A big smile crept on his face.

"Finally, the Blackwood and Davis treasure vault is about to be opened." He took another pull of his cigar. "Good. Very good. It's time to erase the last remnant of their dynasty... and take my rightful place as ruler of the Dark Belt."

About the Author

Hi everyone. I am Tailon Dow.

First, thank you for reading my very first book. This journey was exciting, nerve-wracking, and very self-conscious for me — and honestly, I'm still nervous about whether you enjoyed it. I truly hope you did.

A little about me: I'm a husband and father before anything else. I've been married for 15 years and a father for 16 — yea, do the math, it adds up.

Besides that, I am a vet that has served for 12 years 10 months before getting out to pursue my career as a software developer. But I have been writing and imagining since I was 15 years old. I live through my characters and experience their world as if I'm watching them live. I love to get inspiration from daily life things like music, scenes from a movie, watching the sky, or people walking around.

So, beyond that I like anime, k-dramas, manga, kingdom hearts, taekwondo, and other things that would've certified me as a nerd between 1998–2008 — I proudly hold that badge.

Thank you for reading my first book and stepping into this world with me. I hope you'll walk with me into the next one as we get to see how Tim handles his new reality after everything that's happened. And if this story wasn't your personal vibe, I still have more stand-alone books on the way that might speak to you differently — because their stories are far from finished, and neither am I.

Lead by your heart, reason with your mind, and experience life for your soul.

— Tailon Dow